Somewhere
Different
Now

Somewhere
Different
Now

a novel
Donna Peizer

atmoaphere press

Contents

Part 3

Preface

My name is Annie Cahill, and the story I am about to tell began in the spring of 1949, roughly four years after the end of World War II. I was living with my family in Denver, Colorado, in the same house in the same middle-class neighborhood where I had lived since birth. I was several months short of my 13th birthday, but in terms of my awareness of what was going on in the larger world, I was still very much a child. To put it another way, I was oblivious to the ways in which cataclysmic events in the outer world were shaping my life experience, and would continue do so, whether I liked it or not.

At school, I was a shy kid. I spoke rarely, got good grades but made few friends. Having skipped a grade in elementary school didn't help my situation any. By eighth grade, my peers were moving ever more firmly into adolescence without me, and I became more of an outlier than ever.

Not so on the block, my block and others nearby. That was a different story altogether. I was not dogged by the habitual timidity that characterized me at school (and also at home, where intimidation was a fact of life). Out and about in the neighborhood, I felt expansive, competent, in control. Where this other persona came from, I do not know, but therein lived my joy. On the block, I was outgoing, friendly, and engaging. I talked to people, got to know them, and in recent years had developed a reputation as a Pied Piper of sorts. While moms tended to household chores and dads were off at work, I spent my spare time entertaining the neighborhood children. I'd gather a small gaggle of pint-sized humans of various ages, take them to the park, buy them penny candies, teach them to skate, ride bikes, invent games, whatever they wanted. In the wintertime, I'd pull sleds on icy streets, help them build snowmen, and teach them how to make snow angels. They loved it and I had a purpose, one that earned me considerable appreciation, as well as the occasional fifty-cent piece tossed my way.

Eventually, even folks like Mr. Pastore knew me by name. He was the man who worked in the butcher shop several blocks away where my mother occasionally sent me to buy pork chops for dinner. It thrilled me when people recognized me, invited me in, gave me warm chocolate brownies to eat and willingly sent their little ones off with me to play. I was happy and free, not knowing that none of this was going to last.

The neighborhood bubble I lived in had arisen in no small measure because folks were forced by circumstances to stay put during the war years. Not a single family moved in or out of our neighborhood in all the years we lived there. During the war, rubber, gasoline, sugar, and many other commodities were in short supply or simply not available at all. There were strict restrictions on nonessential automobile travel. I remember my mother riding shotgun in our old brown Pontiac, counting gasoline ration coupons while my father drove around looking for a station that had a supply of gasoline to sell. Finding none, we returned home with an empty tank and a For Sale sign in the window. After the car was gone, we walked, rode buses, and in an emergency, called a Yellow Cab. Everyone was in the same boat. Were people afraid? I don't remember. I was not afraid.

I don't mean to sound all Pollyannish or suggest that trouble did not visit me from time to time, because it did. I'm only saying that the environment created by the circumstances of that unique historical period was a perfect fit for me and allowed me to blossom in ways I did not experience at school or behind the closed doors of my often-chaotic family life.

When the long war finally ended and life began to return to "normal," people bought new cars as fast as they came off the assembly lines, and the population of the city exploded. Me? I took no particular notice of the changes taking place around me. Instead, I looked to Mary and Grace, two ancient souls, who, every summer

ii

evening, rocked in the same swing on the porch of the same house they had lived in their entire lives. My life, I presumed, was going to be something like that, although I rarely engaged in thoughts of the future at all.

Our neighborhood was dotted with vacant lots, the property of phantom owners who never appeared. As far as those of us who lived there were concerned, those lots belonged to anyone who had need and staked a claim. During the war, when the government urged folks to grow as much of their own food as possible by planting "victory gardens," the Eagletons, who lived in the house on the corner of our block, had done just that. On the lot directly behind their property, they raised rows of lush green spinach, green beans, climbing vines of sweet peas, gigantic pumpkins, squash, tomatoes and more, all surrounded by a border of orange and yellow marigolds, which Mr. Eagleton said kept the bugs away.

By the spring of 1949, the war had been over for a few years. But still, like many others who had grown accustomed to homegrown vegetables, the Eagletons continued to plant their garden every spring, not knowing, as none of us did, that 1949 would be different.

One day in early spring came the surprise that set in motion the chain of events that eventually disrupted my well-ordered life and took me to that peculiar place known as "the suburbs." We awoke that morning to the whines and groans of a diesel engine coming from one of the vacant lots. It was a clear, sunny day, but a chilly breeze blew off the snow-covered mountains to the west, raising gooseflesh on bare arms when we went outside to see what was going on. The whole neighborhood gathered in the Mahoney's backyard, where we had a clear view of a giant yellow bulldozer trundling over the uneven ground, belching clouds of foul-smelling black smoke. Waves of heat hovered over the bulldozer's engine compartment, and the huge tires were soon caked with mud.

"What's happening?" my mother wheezed as she came charging up the Mahoney's steep driveway, hugging herself to keep warm.

"Oh, Vivian, come see!" said Mrs. Mahoney, taking hold of my mother's elbow and pulling her into the gathering.

"The lot's been sold," said sour old Mr. Eagleton, scowling at the bulldozer as it lumbered about, scraping up the remains of his garden from the previous fall. "They're getting ready to build on it."

All eyes turned back to the bulldozer as if a brand-new house might magically appear before lunch.

None of the houses in our neighborhood were new. They were old brick bungalows in various muted colors, with wide concrete porches and terraced yards built in the 1920s and before. They had windows that rattled in the wind and coal-burning furnaces that squatted like fire-breathing dragons in damp basements. I would wager that none of us in the assembled company had ever laid eyes on a new house.

I soon grew bored and pulled a large leaf from a low-hanging branch of a nearby apple tree and held it between my thumbs the way Granddad taught me. I blew hard, and the vibration produced an ear-splitting whistle.

"Stop it, Annie! You scared me!" my mother yelped. "Come with me right now. I have things for you to do."

With that, she turned and headed back home. Charlie, my stupid nine-year-old brother, stuck his tongue out at me and made donkey ears with his hands. Everyone else was looking at me, too, so I dipped my head and smiled before walking away, pleased with the bit of mischief I had created.

School was out for Easter vacation. The bitter winter had finally ended, and the only thing on my mind was to run around and catch up with the neighbors, play some ball in the alley, strap on my roller skates and ride my bike. I was feeling the stirrings of the coming summer and eager to plan another backyard circus for the neighborhood kids, as I had done the year before.

But none of those things were on my mother's mind. I knew there would be a whole list of chores in store for me. Now that I was growing up, she saw it as her solemn duty to turn me into a proper lady and prospective wife and mother like herself, but I had yet to surrender to the expectations placed on girls whose ages had climbed into the double digits. Instead, I clung to the identity I had carefully crafted for myself in the neighborhood as the inveterate tomboy, outdoor adventurer, and neighborhood scout leader—or whatever it was I did.

The house was cold and dark inside, shaded as it was by the enormous apple tree in the backyard and the towering elms that lined the street out front. Two-year-old Willie, the younger of my two brothers, was fast asleep in his crib. I grabbed a sweater and went to the kitchen to clean up the clutter from breakfast. I gazed at the mess and fumed, wishing I was a boy like Charlie, who never had to stay in the house and do dishes, or any other chores for that matter.

"It's not fair!" I grumbled as I picked up the first dirty plate and began to scrape.

****

On Saturday morning, we could hear hammering coming from the construction site. "C'mon kids. Let's walk around the block to have a look," Dad said to Charlie and me.

When we got there, a man, a woman, and a young girl about my age were standing on the sidewalk watching the work in progress. The man was short and stout, with light-brown skin. He was dressed in a dingy white T-shirt and sagging dungarees slung low and belted beneath his considerable belly. He wore an old straw hat stained with sweat where it touched his head. His arms were folded over this chest, and his straight, jet-black hair fell softly over his forehead, tapering down over his left eyebrow.

The woman was shorter than he, thin, also with dark skin. Her shiny black hair was pulled back and tied with a red ribbon at the nape of her neck. She wore a three-tiered red skirt gathered at the waist and a white peasant blouse with short puffy sleeves. From shoulder to shoulder, the neckline in the front was embroidered with garlands of colorful flowers. I couldn't take my eyes off her blouse and wondered where I could get one like it, but I was feeling too shy to ask.

The young girl, who was barefoot, stood a distance away from the other two. Her hair was long and black like her mother's, and she wore a blue and green plaid dress that fell above her knees. It looked just like one of my school dresses, but mine was longer, which suggested to me that the girl had grown taller fairly recently.

"Morning," Dad said, nodding in the direction of the man. "What's going on?"

"We're getting ready to pour the foundation," the man replied.

"I'm Juan Ortiz, and this is my wife Rosa and my daughter Elena."

Mr. Ortiz spoke English with only a hint of an accent. His wife did not speak to us, but her dark eyes sparkled, and she smiled and nodded. The girl turned away and appeared to be studying the leaves on the lilac bushes near where she stood at the far edge of the lot.

"Stan Cahill," my father said, keeping his hands tucked deep in his pockets and ignoring Mr. Ortiz' offer to shake hands. "You must be the contractor then."

"No, we're the owners," Mr. Ortiz replied proudly.

"What?"

"We're the owners," Mr. Ortiz repeated, smiling broadly.

"Let's go," my father said sharply. Turning abruptly and shepherding us ahead of him, we marched back around the block.

"Dirty Mexicans," he muttered as we retreated.

His face looked red and puffy, and his lips were drawn back exposing his front teeth in an ugly grimace, a look I knew all too well. When that man got ahold of something, he was like a dog with a bone—licking it, chewing on it, but unlike a dog, never burying it. He could steam with anger for days over the smallest things. No telling what we were in for, and a feeling of dread dogged me as he rushed us toward home.

When we got there, Charlie and I took refuge in our room and closed the door. I sat on the window seat and covered my ears while Dad paced and fumed. Charlie stood nearby gazing out the window as he, too, waited for the storm to blow over. Worried, neither of us suggested a game or a book, and we lacked our usual enthusiasm for going outside.

By evening, the gale had intensified.

"You'll see," Dad seethed, standing close to our mother, who was in the kitchen preparing dinner. "A bunch of Mexicans will be living here before you know it, and the niggers will be right behind them!"

That's my dad, white-by-right Stanley, and by the next weekend he had decided we would move. He began poring over the financial pages of the newspaper as he smoked a Pall Mall cigarette and sipped his bourbon and ginger ale each evening before dinner. He was waiting for the perfect moment to sell stock he owned for enough money to make a down payment on a house.

Finally, one night, he leapt from his chair, and like a bowlegged cowboy, nearly tripped as he straddled the footstool in front of him. Sheets of newspaper went flying. Charlie and I were playing a card game on the floor. We put our hands over our mouths and laughed, turning away, making ourselves small.

"Okay, it's a go!" he told Mom.

The stock price had hit the target, and the next day, it was a done deal. Blueprints appeared, and the search for a place to build began.

In the meantime, the Mexican family moved into their new beige brick home around the corner. One day while Charlie and I were messing around in our backyard, Elena and two of her younger brothers came walking down the narrow alleyway. Charlie jumped up, hung over the low fence and shouted as loud as he could, "You dirty Mexicans!"

Alarmed, the Mexican kids ran away.

"Dirty Mexicans," Charlie screamed after them again.

"Shut up!" I shouted, but he simply looked at me with a crooked smirk on his face. He was proud of himself!

A few days passed, and once again, we saw the Mexican children coming down the alley, this time, from the other direction. "Keep still," I hissed, grabbing Charlie by the arm and squeezing.

"You keep still!" the little brat retorted, jerking away. He went to stand by the fence waiting for the trio to come closer. When they did, Elena whipped a large rock from behind her back and hurled it at him, scoring a direct hit on the left side of his forehead. Blood spurted, and Elena and company took off. Charlie began to scream, which brought Mom running from the house. A trip to the hospital followed, after which Dad went to threaten Elena's parents. Nothing came of it, though, no doubt because his getaway plan was already well underway.

The next year, not long after we moved to our new house in the suburbs, I read an article in the newspaper about the mass migration of white folks out of cities in a mad rush to get away from those with darker skins and foreign accents who were coming to seek jobs and a better life. "White flight," the newspaper called it. That said it all. We were white, and we had flown, our move having taken us to an unincorporated area west of Denver close to the mountains.

I dubbed the place Nowhere, Colorado.

Part 1

Part 1

Chapter 1
Annie

I am perched like some kind of clumsy raptor on the T-bar of one of my mother's new clothesline poles, the only structure available to climb in this muddy, treeless wasteland. Today, ten days after the move to the so-called "suburbs" west of town, I finally have a chance to take a closer look at my new surroundings, thanks to my assigned task for the day, which is to burn buckets of household waste, bags of newspapers, used cardboard boxes, and small pieces of wood and other debris, all collected and stacked near the ash pit at the back of the property.

The morning sun is shining, but a chilly wind vibrates the wires of the clothesline, making them emit a low hum. My bare legs, one of which is draped over the pole, take the full brunt of the breeze as I dangle from the cold steel, causing me to shift about uncomfortably. My thin cotton jacket, open down the front, does little to protect me from the wind, and with both of my hands wrapped around the clothesline pole, I am unable to reach for the zipper. *Should have thought of that before I shimmied up here,* I think regretfully. Still, despite the cold, I am determined to continue my inspection.

It's a bleak and dismal sight. The vast construction zone is a sea of mud and has been cleared almost as far as the eye can see. The uneven ground below me is pocked with gopher holes, mounds of clay, rocks, chunks of concrete, and other rubble from the recent construction. Our house is the first one on the block, and the dirt access road is rutted and unpaved, and there are no sidewalks. Our new home is made of brick, reddish-orange in color, with wood trim painted the color of green apples. To my eye, the color combination is so "off" it grates on my nerves worse than a herd of yowling cats.

There are two houses on the street behind ours. The nearest one is a relatively new-looking white frame structure, long and narrow, with high windows. To me, it looks more like a railroad boxcar than a home. The house next door to the boxcar is an old clapboard house with peeling white paint. Except for our house, these are the only other dwellings in sight. To the east, I can see all the way to the main drag many blocks away and beyond. There are no fences and not a tree or bush in sight.

Looking to the south, I spy an enormous fallen tree. It has been partially uprooted and lies on its side like an injured bull elephant. A deep trench has been dug around the exposed roots, and a thin column of smoke rises from the trench. The upper branches have not been cut away, and someone has looped a thick rope over one of them and attached an old tire to make a swing that goes out over the trench.

"Now we're talkin'," I murmur, wishing I could go check it out.

It is obvious the tree is in the process of being removed and won't be there for long. I envision the grinding bulldozers and men with chainsaws who will arrive any day to remove it, the last remaining tree anywhere in sight. The wind is making my right temple throb, so I lower myself to the ground.

In the short time we've lived here, I have seen nothing to make me want to stay. My youngest brother, Willie, now three years old, is so disoriented he runs smack into the walls of this new house as he dashes from room to room. He's used to another space, our old house, the only home he has ever known, and after just a few days, his little forehead is bruised black and blue.

It's like that for me, too, except my scrapes and bruises are more on the inside. I am desperately homesick for my old neighborhood. At night, I visit each house in my mind, tell myself the names of the people who live there, wonder how they're doing. Lived there, I should say, because we were not the only ones who left, nor were we the first, and reminding myself of that helps a little.

Most of all, I miss Pepper, my sweet black cocker spaniel. I have had Pepper since I was five years old, and now he's gone. The thought of him makes the tears I have been holding back for days spring to my eyes.

"Where are you?" I wail as the wind scours my face and blows tears into my ears.

My parents tell me he wandered off in the confusion of the move, but I secretly suspect my father took him away. What happened yesterday did nothing to make me change my mind, either.

Dad and I were taking a break from unpacking and organizing stuff. We were standing in the kitchen eating grilled cheese sandwiches. I said, very calmly so as not to rile him up, "Dad, things are shaping up around here, so how about we go back and look for Pepper this afternoon? He's probably waiting for us to come get him."

He turned red in the face, clenched his fists into angry balls and shouted at me, "Not again, Annie! How many times do I have to tell you? Pepper ran off. That's all there is to it, and I don't want to hear another word about that damn dog."

He tossed what was left of his sandwich on the kitchen counter and stormed off.

"Go put those boxes away under the stairs like I told you to," he ordered from somewhere deep in the house.

I stayed put. "Mom?"

My mother stood with her back to me, pouring formula through a funnel into baby bottles for Teresa, the latest addition to our family. When I spoke, her hand jerked and sent formula spilling down the sides of the bottle. Like I'd scared her or something.

"Go help your dad, Annie," she said.

"Urrrrr!" I growled.

I slammed the kitchen door behind me and stomped down the wooden stairs to the basement, my breath coming in hard, angry gasps.

Okay, I get it, I say to myself now as I stir the blaze in the red brick ash pit. *Pepper is gone, and I'm never going to see him again.*

Why? Because in my wildest imaginings, I can't see my father allowing me to bring Pepper anywhere near his new house. I picture the kinky matted fur under Pepper's belly; the ice balls that swing to and fro as he runs through the snow in wintertime; his paws caked with mud when the snow melts in the spring. Would he be welcome in this new kitchen with its gleaming red and white linoleum floor? Would his furry paws be allowed to touch down on the new light gray carpet in the living room? Not a chance. We used to keep him on the back porch at our old house, but there is nowhere like that for him here. Let's face it: All of those blueprints and drawings never included a place for my dog, or any dog for that matter.

Later, I walk out to the street in front of the house where cornfields meet the grass-covered foothills that roll from north to south along the base of the Rocky Mountains. A short distance off to the south, there is flat-topped mesa that seems to stand guard before the foothills and the mountainous peaks beyond. Thick stands of trees and shrubs crawl most of the way up the face of the mesa almost concealing it from view. The top of the mesa appears to be covered with tall grasses and dotted with short, stubby evergreens. The sandstone, what I can see of it, glows a bright salmon color in the morning sun, and despite the promise I made to myself to hate this place forever, the tomboy in me rises up with curiosity and the desire to explore.

Charlie comes outside and stands next to me. For a few moments, we forget to be enemies.

"Look at that," I say, pointing off to the northwest. "There's your new school over there." We stare at the one-story cream-colored building with a flat blue roof stranded in the middle of nowhere.

Charlie says nothing.

"But ... here's the thing." I let the words hang in the air as I look down at him and wiggle my eyebrows. "There is no road going over there, see?"

"How will I get there?"

"The swamp, I guess," I say, winking at him. "Take your chances with the snakes and crawdads, I suppose."

We both know the parents have already strictly forbidden him to go near the swamp. We look at each other and laugh at the absurdity.

"Will you go with me?"

I sigh. "No swamp crawling for me. I'll be going to the high school. Heaven only knows where that's at."

"Heaven only knows," he says, still gazing at his new school off in the distance.

"You're gonna be in fifth grade, right?"

"Yup."

"I skipped third grade. Did you know that?"

"No. How come?"

"They said I'm 'pre-co-shus,' so they moved me up a year. Now everybody in my class is older than me, so it ain't that great."

At that moment, the kitchen window opens and my mother calls out, "Annie Cahill, are you watching that ash pit?"

"I'm going back there right now," I say, and quickly head back where I belong.

****

That night, I undress and slide into my pajamas in the dark of my new bedroom. There are no curtains on the windows, and only the brightest stars are visible due to the dust that lingers in the atmosphere from today's breeze. Kneeling on my bed, I crank open the window and breathe in the delicious scent of pine that wafts down from the mountains. I consider turning on my radio, a gift from my parents for my birthday last year, but one of little use to me now. Three-month-old Teresa sleeps in her crib just a step or two from my bed, and the last thing I want is for her to wake up and bring my mother bristling with annoyance into the room. Reluctantly, I give up the idea of listening to the play-by-play of the baseball game, close the window and flop down on my back.

Teresa is giving her thumb a vigorous workout, and a faint smell of urine is coming from the pail of dirty diapers under the changing table. How in the world did I end up here with cranky parents, a baby living in *my* room, and to top it off, Pepper missing and no one willing to help me look for him? In my old neighborhood, I had my escapes mapped out, but here, there are none. So far, every day is nothing but endless chores, fights with Charlie, worry about Pepper, and homesickness.

For crying out loud, the *only* reason I got on board with this whole moving thing was because Dad promised I would have my own room. But that was early on in the house-building project, months before I overheard my mother telling Grandma that she was "expecting." I was excited and hoped for a baby sister to balance out my two brothers. My mother and I spent long afternoons discussing names, finally settling on Teresa. But I never once pictured the real baby Teresa, born a few weeks before we moved, ending up in *my* room. The day we moved in, I was completely blindsided.

"What's all this?" I sputtered when I staggered into the bedroom carrying a heavy box of my belongings. The room was painted light blue, the color *I* had chosen. But it was crowded with baby furniture, a crib, a changing table, a gigantic wicker rocking chair, and a new four-drawer highboy my mother was busy filling with stacks of receiving blankets, diapers, tiny white undershirts, and soft baby wash clothes and towels. There was barely enough room for my second-hand bed.

"Where's my room? Isn't this supposed to be it?"

"Of course," said my mother.

"This isn't how it was supposed to be! Dad said I would have my own room."

"Well, honey, that was before Teresa came along. You knew that."

"No, I didn't!" I insisted, taking in the scene. "Well, isn't this just cozy as heck!" I barked as I dropped the box in the closet and ran outside.

In truth, it's Teresa's room, not mine. I'm not allowed to come in here when she is sleeping. She takes two naps a day, and Mom puts her down for the night around seven o'clock. When it's my bedtime, I shuck off my clothes in the dark, and leave them in a heap on the closet floor. When the baby wakes up to be fed in the middle of the night, I can't possibly sleep through the diaper changing, the feeding, the rocking, and cooing. It keeps me awake for an hour or more, only to be repeated again around five or six in the morning.

Wide awake now, when I should be taking advantage of the quiet to catch some shuteye, I ponder my list of resentments and dread the sameness tomorrow will bring.

****

Dad eventually runs out of vacation time and has to go back to work. He drives off in the family car, a 1946 Ford two-door coupe shaped like a turtle but painted maroon. His departure leaves the rest of us stranded, unsettled, and wondering what to do with ourselves.

Boredom takes the place of the summertime activities that have carried Charlie and me along in previous years. He begins to pester me nonstop, and it wears me out. To make matters worse, one morning, promptly at eight o'clock, a string of dump trucks chugs up the hill and lines the road ready to haul off the only thing of any interest to me—the giant oak tree with the tire swing. Charlie and I stand nearby, watching as men wearing hard hats swarm like insects and prepare to finish butchering the old tree.

"Hey, mister. Can we swing one more time before you take the tree?" I call out to one of the men.

"Nah, 'fraid not. We gotta get this thing outta here this morning. They're comin' to fill the trench later today," the man shouts back, raising his voice over the noise of the idling truck engines. Prompted by our interest in the swing, he turns to one of the other men, and yells, "Get that tire offa there, will you Sam?"

Using footholds amongst the huge roots to mount the trunk of the tree, Sam crawls out on the branch to the tire swing. Lying flat on his belly, he slithers along until he reaches the rope. With one arm circling the large branch, he pulls a hunting knife from a pouch on his belt and cuts the rope cleanly with one stroke. The tire bounces as it hits the edge of the trench and tumbles in. The rope follows and coils like a snake in the bottom of the trench.

"Aww, did you have to do that?" complains the first man, peering into the ditch.

Sam scrambles back down the tree trunk. "I'll get it, boss," he says. He jumps in and heaves the tire and rope up over the edge, then climbs out himself, using the roots of the tree to gain purchase.

"You kids go on now," the boss says to the youthful audience gathered around the tree. "We got work to do here, and you might get hurt."

"Come on, Charlie," I say, but Charlie has other ideas.

"Hey," he calls to a boy standing on the other side of the trench. "Wanna see my cowboy boots?"

The boy comes closer to have a look, and in less than five

minutes, Charlie and his new pal are heading off in the direction of the swamp. I consider going after him, but the fumes and the constant construction noise, and now the whining of a bunch of chainsaws, are giving me a headache, so I head home instead. I'm tired and grouchy and dread facing the long list of chores my mother will have for me today. We're not used to being around each other day in and day out, and it's making both of us uneasy. Her answer is to keep me busy with one task after another until we're both worn out and have made it to the end of another day.

****

Sundays bring blessed relief. The various construction crews have a day off, and the absence of the constant racket is itself almost deafening. With the exception of Dad, who has been away at work all week, we listen anxiously for the construction equipment to come roaring to life. When it doesn't, our mood becomes one of celebration. Today, Mom makes a special breakfast of pancakes with butter and warm maple syrup along with a platter of crisp bacon and spicy sausage links.

"I'm gonna get out there and start leveling the front yard," announces Dad as he ties into his breakfast. "You can help me, Annie. I want to have the front yard ready to seed by fall."

A day baking in the sun raking and pulling weeds. I'd rather walk barefoot over a bed of hot coals, but instead I stare at my plate and groan, knowing there's no use arguing.

"Clean up these dishes and then come out front," he orders as he downs the last of his coffee.

After clearing the table, I stand at the kitchen sink washing the dishes and placing them in the rack to drain. My mother sits at the kitchen table with baby Teresa in her lap, spooning rice cereal into her mouth. Teresa grins like a toothless clown, and thick cereal bubbles course down her chin. I watch as my mother catches the mess with a quick swipe of the spoon and deftly packs it back into Teresa's mouth. Watching them makes me smile, and my dread of the rest of the day lifts a bit.

Through the window, I see Charlie running across the open field chasing the boy he met the other day. His friend's name is Larry, and he lives in the old frame house on the street behind us. Charlie is wearing his favorite outfit, a black shirt with a string tie, black pants covered by faux leather chaps, black cowboy boots with fancy embroidery and a tall black cowboy hat—his Hopalong Cassidy outfit. He's holding one hand over each holster to keep the pair of silver cap guns from bouncing out as he runs, and I laugh because he's such a dope.

I have yet to lay eyes on a single person my age, not surprising, since there are only three houses in the vast construction area where we now live. Feeling sorry for myself and a little bit mad at Charlie, I press down on a half-gallon glass milk bottle and hold it under the soapy water until it fills. I lift it and shake it vigorously. I lose my grip and it slips from my soapy hands and clatters into the empty sink on the other side of the divide.

"What was that?" Mom squeals. Before I can answer, Teresa begins to howl.

With horror, I see what I have done. Although the milk bottle is lying unbroken in the bottom of the sink, it has left a small black divot in the white porcelain at the edge of the sink. Trembling, not daring to say a word, I quickly finish the dishes and drape the floppy wet dishcloth over the disaster to hide it from view. I have broken my father's new house! Nothing could be worse, and I know it's only a matter of time before my transgression is discovered. My mind goes blank, and without thinking, I run out the backdoor and cower behind the ash pit, my breath coming in ragged gasps.

Sure enough, less than ten minutes later, my father is at the backdoor. "Anne Marie, get in here, now!" he screams.

I stand up, and with great effort, force my trembling legs to carry me forward.

"Get in here!" he shouts when I reach the backdoor. The door into the kitchen is closed. "Downstairs *now*," he commands.

I obey, placing both hands on the stairwell walls to steady myself.

"Take down your pants!" he orders.

I am still wearing my thin summer pajamas.

"No, please," I beg, but even as I speak, I lower my pajama bottoms, too afraid to do anything to hide my nakedness.

I watch as he goes to the wood box and selects a two-foot length of 2x4. "Come over here!" he roars, as he grabs a wooden crate and upends it.

I begin to cry. "I'm sorry, Dad. I didn't mean to ..." but he cuts me off.

"Come over here right now!" he shouts.

He is sitting on the crate, and his eyes blaze with rage. "You need to learn to be more careful!"

When I don't immediately comply, he grabs my arm and pulls me across his lap. The first blow falls. I try to squirm away, but he holds me fast with one hand and hits with the other, cursing. Finally, I can contain myself no longer and begin to scream. With no warning, I lose control and pee on him. Pee runs down his pants leg and onto the floor. He abruptly stops hitting me and tosses the 2x4 into the corner.

"Go clean yourself up," he bellows.

He storms out, leaving me in a puddle of urine on the dirty floor.

"Go to church! Take the kids!" I hear him yell at my mother as he bursts through the kitchen door, stomps through the house, and slams the bedroom door behind him.

Only then do I get up, very slowly pull my pajama bottoms back on and follow him upstairs.

My mother is still at the kitchen table with Teresa. She must have heard; we were right below where she is sitting.

I stand at the far end of the room waiting, for what I am not exactly sure. Maybe I need a word of comfort or sympathy, or maybe I need her to come right out and tell me whose side she's on. But what I get instead is nothing. She refuses to look at me, pulls Teresa closer, murmurs to her softly and turns away.

I stand there a moment longer weeping quietly, feeling as fragile as glass and no more visible than a wisp of smoke.

Until ... all at once, I am on fire. My gut tightens, and I seethe with rage. My head grows hot, and I can feel my face turn red. My pulse, rapid and strong, beats in my neck, my temples, my ears, and the palms of my hands.

"I hate you!" I mutter as I elbow my way through the swinging door into the living room and head for the shower.

****

Hot water cascades over my trembling body, and choking sobs nearly take my breath away. I'm just about to turn off the water and step out when Vivian (no longer Mom to me) has the nerve, without knocking, to open the bathroom door and walk in.

What is wrong with these people?

"Shut the door!" I shout. "Get out of here!"

"Calm down, Annie. I just came to tell you to hurry up and get dressed. We're going to church."

"Now?" I sputter. "Are you kidding me?"

"I'm not kidding. Hurry up."

Unbelievable. I heard what her atheist frickin' husband said, of course, but is she really going to do it? Haul us off to church after the morning we've had? I wipe the sweat off the bathroom mirror and study my puffy red face, my swollen, bloodshot eyes. I look affright.

But what choice do I have? I'm not about to hang around the house with Stanley (no longer Dad to me), so I do as I'm told and get dressed, then curl up in a ball on the living room sofa and wait.

Chapter 2
Vivian

"What? Go to church? He can't be serious," I mutter. I'm trembling, and Teresa begins to fuss.

Annie opens the kitchen door and stands at the far end looking at me. Glaring at me is more like it. I can feel her eyes, but I simply can't look up. Instead, I pull Teresa close and pretend to reposition her so that my body turns toward the window, away from Annie. Shame lodges in my chest, and my breath catches painfully in my throat. I feel a moment of panic, afraid that I may never be able to release breath again. When Annie finally moves on, I breathe out through pursed lips, but find no relief.

A beehive of disjointed thoughts swarm in my head as I try to name what I just heard coming from the basement directly below me. "No. He did not .... Yes. He did. Did what?" argues the chorus of buzzing voices.

"You don't know what happened down there. But wait ..."

I feel frozen in place, and even Teresa seems anxious, pulling at her wispy baby hair with one tiny fist as she sucks and swallows greedily.

The clock on the wall at the other end of the room is ticking. Still, I don't move, even when the baby begins to suck air from her empty bottle.

Annie is dressed and sitting on the living room sofa staring out the window when I hurry to the baby's room to put her down for a nap. I go to my room and flip impatiently through the dresses in my

16

closet, looking for something to wear, confusion threatening to overwhelm me. Stanley, the professed atheist has now, in the midst of this morning's chaos, ordered me to take the children and go to church. What in the world is going on? Stanley never sets foot in a church and would just as soon I didn't, either. Every so often, when I decide to take the kids to Sunday school because I think it's my duty as a parent, he does his best to talk me out of it and usually succeeds. So, what is it? Is it rage or regret or both driving him now? I'll never know, because we won't speak of it. It's not our way.

I run my tongue over my teeth, trying to dispel the bitter taste in my mouth, which I suspect is the taste of violence that still lingers like a poltergeist just below the surface of the day. I long to rewind the clock and start this day over. Impossible, of course, and so I slip my navy-blue dress over my head and prepare to soldier on.

"Charlie, put on your good pants and white shirt, and hurry," I call out as I breeze into the boys' room, tugging at the seams of my nylon stockings.

"Okay," Charlie says meekly, for once not arguing with me. Through the bedroom window, I see Stanley in the yard, attacking the copious overgrowth of weeds with a scythe he swings ferociously from side to side.

"Willie, you stay here with Daddy and Teresa."

Willie is sitting on the bedroom floor with his legs folded under him. He looks up at me, his forehead creased with worry.

"It's okay now, Willie," I say, but he's not so sure. Usually on Sundays, he is delighted to trail around after his father as he goes about his weekend chores. But today, he jumps up and tackles me around the knees like he's hanging on for dear life.

"Okay. Let's get you dressed," I sigh.

I have taken him to Sunday school only once, and he was miserable. Yet here he is all but begging me not to leave him behind, so I stand him on his bed, and quickly dress him in his new overalls and a clean blue-and-yellow striped T-shirt; not exactly church clothes, but they'll have to do.

By the time the four of us are in the car, there is no chance we will make it all the way into town in time for the eleven o'clock service. I writhe with discomfort when I think of walking into the sanctuary in the middle of the service. People will turn their heads and watch as I search for a place to sit, and I wonder how I can possibly tolerate that kind of scrutiny in the midst of this nightmare of a day.

At the end of the wide gravel driveway, I stop and it occurs to me that we could go anywhere for a couple of hours to give Stanley time to cool off. That's what this is all about, isn't it? But in my muddled state of mind, I have no idea if disobeying Stanley is an act of betrayal or a choice I have the right to make.

"I need a cigarette," I tell my children while I am considering this question. Having slipped the gears into neutral and set the emergency brake, I push in the dashboard lighter with one hand while I dig around in my purse with the other. In the front seat next to me, the boys are unusually still and watch silently as I touch the glowing lighter to the tip of the cigarette, inhale deeply and blow out a cloud of bluish smoke. It's a chilly morning, so I only open the tiny triangular wing window near the dashboard. I glance furtively at Annie in the rear-view mirror, waiting for the complaint that always comes. "Roll your window down! You're giving me a headache!" But today, nothing. Annie sits curled in the corner of the back seat dabbing at her eyes and nose with a fistful of wadded-up Kleenex, oblivious to the cigarette smoke that's filling the car.

As expected, we arrive at the church more than half an hour late. There is no point taking the children to their respective Sunday school classes. I suspect that Willie will put up a fight anyway, so I take a deep breath and brace myself. With Willie hanging on one hip and Charlie holding my free hand, I pull open the polished wooden door and walk into the sanctuary. Annie trails behind.

I am forced to walk the entire length of the long aisle to the very front row in order to find sufficient space for all of us to sit down together, only to discover that Annie is no longer with us. While my eyes dart here and there looking for her, Willie stands up on the wooden pew and stamps his feet, grinning with pleasure at the sound he's making. Humiliation crawls up my spine, and I have no choice but to grab Willie and sit down or traipse back up the aisle and search each row for Annie. The choir is singing, but Reverend Lesher, who is seated in an oversized chair on the burgundy carpeted dias, has turned his attention to us, further adding to my discomfort.

When the pastor rises to give his sermon, his deep voice echos from the high-arched ceiling of the old stone church. He is a compelling speaker, but today, I barely hear a word. What good is this to me now? What prayer could I possibly utter that would undo today? Instead, I busy myself entertaining Willie and Charlie by drawing silly pictures in the small notebook I carry in my black leather purse.

When the service ends, Reverend Lesher pronounces the benediction, and everyone follows him out. When the three of us reach the back of the church, Annie steps out of one of the back rows and folds in behind.

I skirt around the reception line and almost make it out the front door when Reverend Lesher calls out to me.

"Mrs. Cahill, do you have a moment? May I have a word, please?"

We all stop short.

"Certainly, Reverend," I say, nodding and giving him a tight-lipped smile.

"Just give me a minute, and I'll meet you over there," he says, pointing to the far corner of the vestibule, which is nearly empty of parishioners now.

"What now?" I sputter under my breath.

My scalp tingles as beads of perspiration break out underneath my gray felt hat. I put Willie down, and with my white-gloved hand, begin to fuss with the boys' hair. I glance at Annie. She's a wreck, and I suspect Reverend Lesher may have noticed. A wave of anxiety ripples through me.

"Hello, young man," Reverend Lesher says to Charlie a few moments later.

Charlie stares at the tall man but doesn't answer.

"Is everything all right, Mrs. Cahill?" Reverend Lesher asks.

"Oh yes, Reverend. Why do you ask?"

I give myself an internal head smack. I need to bite my tongue, keep this short and not be issuing any invitations.

"I was watching when you came in today. Your daughter, she doesn't look ... Well, she doesn't look herself today, and I was just wondering if everything is all right with you folks."

"We're fine, Reverend," I assure him. "But thank you for

asking."

"Annie?" he queries, bending back, trying to get a look at her.

She's standing with her back to the rest of us, studying some pamphlets in a rack underneath the round stained-glass window that graces the lobby of the church.

"I'm okay," she mumbles. "I was upset, but I'm okay now."

"Well, if there's anything I can do, Mrs. Cahill ...."

"I don't think so, Reverend. We're fine," I say again as I hurry the three kids toward the outer door and the sunny day beyond.

"Well, I guess that's that," mutters Annie as she clatters down the stairs and heads for the car. Before long, she's a full city block ahead of the rest of us.

Willie refuses to walk, forcing me to carry him. I'm not used to walking several long blocks in high heels carrying a 30-pound child. I'm desperate for a smoke. My hat is skewed to one side, and my armpits sting with sweat.

"What's the matter, Mom?" Charlie asks, tugging on my sleeve.

"Nothing, Charlie. I'm just anxious to get home is all."

Charlie looks up at me, still worried, but says no more and skips along beside me until we finally reach the car.

****

Somehow, we make it through the rest of the day. I allow Annie to stay in her room all afternoon because I have no idea what to say to her. At dinnertime, I open her bedroom door without knocking, intending to go to her. But when I see her lying on her back staring at the ceiling, my hand freezes on the doorknob, and I am incapable of covering the distance between the open door and the bed a few feet away.

"Come set the table for dinner," is all I can manage to say.

The words sound harsh, and the tone of my voice makes me wince. But Annie gets up, slips on her shoes, and follows me into the kitchen.

An uneasy silence prevails as we eat. The boys are still on shaky ground around their father, and Annie does not speak or raise her eyes from the food on her plate, which she barely touches.

"May I be excused?" she asks at last.

"Yes, go on," Stanley barks.

Later, after I finish Teresa's bedtime feeding, I stand next to her crib, patting her gently on the back to put her to sleep. In the quiet room, the deliberations of the jurors in my head pick up where they left off earlier in the day, louder now, suggesting cover-ups and confrontations, making excuses and accusations, crafting denials and guilty pleas, life sentences and dismissals for lack of evidence. The baby falls asleep somewhere in the middle of the trial, and although my back is aching, it's a while yet before I can bear to tear myself away from her comforting presence.

Finally, I straighten up, pull myself together, and proclaim the verdict of the court, the outcome with which I must live: "I will endure, and Annie must learn to endure as well. In fact, it is in her own best interest to do so," I pronounce firmly. I push aside all doubt, pinch the flesh on my arm hard and blink to clear the sheen of any remaining confusion from my eyes. I put a smile on my face and join Stanley in the living room, expecting that everything will now go back to normal.

Chapter 3
Annie

Teresa is sound asleep by the time I finish washing and drying the dinner dishes, so I close myself in the hall closet with my new flashlight, intending to read a stack of comic books until bedtime. Stanley and Vivian—no longer Mom and Dad, I remind myself—are sitting in the living room, and I can hear their conversation clearly.

"Look at this, Vivian," Stanley says, rattling the newspaper he's reading. "They've called another nigger up to the major leagues. Willie Mays, this fella from the Minneapolis farm club. It says here he's an outfielder gonna play for the New York Giants."

"Is he any good?" asks Vivian.

"Hummph," I scoff. I know she could care less, the phony.

"Well, I guess he must be. But why can't they find enough white guys? That's what I want to know."

"Ummm, well, uhhh ..." she trails off.

Ahh, yes. More of what they call racism. It runs deep in the veins of my Scots-Irish forebears. It's kikes this, cheating Jews that, crooked Spics and slanty-eyed Japs, ignorant niggers, dirty Mexicans—and on and on and on. Just one more reason I'm convinced I don't belong in this tribe. I mean, really, what am I doing trapped with these people?

Disgusted, I leave the closet and slip into my room, silently closing the door behind me, though it is not yet eight o'clock. I have just fallen into a light sleep when Willie begins to scream, and I sit up, my heart pounding.

22

"I don't want to!" he yells over and over again. "No! No! No!"

I can hear water running in the bathroom. Willie's bath, but Willie is having none of it. Instead, he is throwing a full-blown fit, a first for the usually good-natured little guy. I hear the parents sweet talk and then threaten him, all to no avail.

I can't help laughing, and it feels wonderful.

"Stop it now!" shouts Stanley.

But Willie screams louder and kicks harder on the wood floor of the hallway outside the bathroom. Apparently, he has no intention of backing down.

"Willie, it's okay," Vivian soothes, but he ignores her, too.

I hope he is enjoying the commotion he's causing, because I definitely am.

In subdued tones, the parents discuss what to do, and in the end, they give in. There will be no bath. Willie has won the battle, his first in our household where the prevailing attitude is "you'd better not go there, or else."

"Good for you, Willie," I whisper in the dark, throwing my arms in the air.

The gurgle of the water draining from the tub sets off another gale of laughter, which I smother with my pillow so I don't wake Teresa. When the house is quiet again, I wonder what it would be like to fight back like that. It's certainly something I've never done.

"I'm a coward! Willie has more courage than I do," I chastise myself, getting up to stare out the window. "I should have run today. Stayed away long enough to ... to whatever." I breathe in the night air and imagine how it would have felt, where I could have gone and for how long. It seems obvious now—but this morning, to put up even that much resistance never once crossed my mind.

I sleep fitfully, my body tender when I roll over on certain spots, my feelings even more bruised than that. Just before dawn, I fall into a deep sleep and have a dream more vivid than any I have ever had in my life.

In the dream, I am standing alone on top of a low hill under a blazing sun. Before me is vast emptiness, nothing but barren rolling hills, brown and windswept. A hot wind scours the land, which seems to pulsate in the heat. No creature, no other human being, not even so much as a plant exists as far as the eye can see.

"Help! Help! Is anyone there?" I cry.

When there's no answer, I sit, pull my knees up to my chest, close my eyes and lay my head down. Panic rises and threatens to swallow me. The heat is so thick I'm nearly unable to breathe.

All at once, a shadow creeps over me, and instantly, my burning skin cools. Where is it coming from? The sun is still directly overhead, and the sky is a clear blue with no clouds in sight, yet here I am in the center of an eerie shadow from nowhere. Alarmed, I jump to my feet. A single point of light is coming toward me from the horizon. As it moves closer, I can see multi-colored beams of light radiating in all directions from a pulsating brilliant-white center. As it approaches, I am delighted to discover that when I make certain movements, the colors of the beams change from gold to rose to violet to blue and more.

I am so fascinated by my seeming ability to induce these color changes I fail to notice that my feet are slowly sinking into the sandy earth. When I realize what's happening, I begin to struggle and groan, trying to pull myself free, but it's no use. The more I fight, the deeper I go, until I'm stuck in sand above my knees and can't move at all. Still, the elusive shadow hovers over me like an umbrella. The light is very close now, and instinctively, I bend over and wrap my arms around my head to shield myself from what, in my dream state, I decide must be an asteroid.

"Oh, my! Oh, my! Well, what do you know, here I am," says a melodious voice.

I am so startled, I open my eyes and try to scramble away, but discover that I can't.

"Get away from me!" I shout as I throw my body this way and that.

"Quiet down, child. Quiet down," the shadow-light soothes, becoming rose colored at its center. "My goodness! Such a fuss. I've come to help. Didn't I hear you call for help a moment ago?"

"Are you God?"

The light jumps and vibrates, changes to violet. Is it *laughing* at me?

"Oh, my dear child, no. Nothing of the sort. My name is Sophia, and I am a guardian angel. *Your* guardian angel, to be precise."

"Bullshit! My dad says there's no such thing as angels."

"As you wish, my dear," says the light merrily. "It's Annie this time around, am I right?"

I don't answer. What does she mean, 'this time around?'

"I can assure you, Annie, I have been with you over eons of time. You have just forgotten. As well you should, my young friend, because that's how it works."

"Double bullshit! What are you talking about? I'm only 14 years old, and I haven't forgotten anything."

The light dims slightly, and ... oh, my God! I'm terrified she's going to leave me. "Wait! Wait! Sophia? Don't go. I'm sorry. I shouldn't have said 'bullshit,' and I shouldn't have said I'm 14. I'm not 14 yet."

"Who cares? Say whatever you like."

The light wiggles and turns a happy gold color.

"Okay, then." I say after thinking this over for a minute. "If you really are my guardian angel, get me out of here. I don't know where I am. It's blistering hot. I can't move, and I'm dying of thirst."

As soon as I say these words, an earthenware jug nearly the same color as the sand with bright orange and turquoise triangles and other designs painted on it appears on the ground next to me. The jug is heavy, but when I hoist it up, I hear water sloshing around inside.

I drink and I drink until an ocean of water pours out of my mouth, down my chin, onto the ground, and melts the sand around my legs. I stare at my feet, delighted to find myself planted back on solid ground. Before I can get my bearings and run away, a gigantic forest springs up around me. The tops of the trees bend in toward one another like they are having a conversation up in the sky. They sway this way and that and smell wonderful. I feel safe now.

Ahhh, I say to myself. *I get it. The shadow came from those trees,* and for a moment, everything seems normal again. I have figured it out. All is well. Until ... that fricking light with all of its piercing rays comes dancing into the center of the clearing where I am lying very peacefully on a large, flat rock gazing at the treetops.

"Sophia?"

"Yes, Annie, my precious," intones the voice with such profound gentleness that it draws me to my feet, and I reach out my two hands to touch it. I want to be enveloped by it. I want to live in it forever.

"Listen to me, and listen well," the light commands gently, floating up over my head and out of reach.

I stop in my tracks and listen. I wonder if Sophia has hypnotized me. But I don't care.

"What is it?" I say eagerly, drained of any desire to be anywhere else but here, listening, as I have been commanded to do.

"Your broken heart is an open door," she says.

I don't want to hear any more. I put my hands over my ears, but it does no good, because the sound of her voice just moves inside my own head. "You must discover this for yourself," it continues, "but you don't have much time. You must do it before the portal you have been given closes."

"Portal?" I ask, confused, taking my hands from my ears. "You mean like Alice in *Through the Looking-Glass*?"

"Exactly like that, my dear," the voice sings to me.

The light slowly fades away, and the last thing I hear is this: "I am Sophia, and I have spoken."

"Wait! Wait! Can I ask you ...?"

But she's already gone. My eyes fly open, and I fall out of bed and land hard on my sore bottom.

****

A moment later, I sit up and rub my eyes. Still lost in the dream, my mind a fog, I stretch out on the floor on my back and replay the dream like a movie. When it slips away, as dreams do, the memory of the day before slithers in instead. I grumble irritably, climb back into bed and squeeze my eyes shut, feeling defeated before the day has even begun. Suddenly, the soles of my feet begin to tingle. It's like the soft tickling of bubbles in my mouth when I take a big gulp of Coca-Cola, and the sensation forces me to move whether I want to or not.

I jump up, stand at the window, and roll my feet around on the floor. The sky to the east is glowing with the coming dawn. A vision of that mesa off to the south arises in my mind's eye, the one place I've been wanting to explore.

"Okay, then, Sophia, whoever you are," I announce. "I know exactly what door I intend to open: the one that will get me the hell out of here!"

Of course, I'm not supposed to say bad words like 'hell' or 'damn' or 'bullshit,' but that was *before*. This is *after,* and all bets are off as far as I'm concerned.

It's early. Everyone is still asleep, even Teresa. I creep into the kitchen and pull the door closed behind me ready to make my getaway. I am stopped in my tracks once again by the black divot that glares at me from the sea of white porcelain, an evil eye, condemning me for what I have done.

Stop it! I scold myself, dragging my gaze away from the catastrophe. *You are getting the hell out of here, remember?*

And with that, I get to work. I take out four slices of Rainbo bread, pillow-soft and white as snow, smelling of yeast and ovens. I make two peanut butter and grape jelly sandwiches and wrap them in waxed paper. I retrieve the black lunch bucket I used to carry to school on snowy days. It's so ugly, it humiliated me then, but now it's just what I need to hold my sandwiches, an orange, and a thermos of cold milk.

Carrying the lunch box and wearing my light jacket, I wheel my bicycle out to the end of the driveway and consider my options. Am I really going to do this? Break the rules, leave without permission? Maybe I'll run away, do what I should have done yesterday.

At any moment, I expect to hear Vivian calling me back, but all I hear is the morning song of the meadowlarks down among the cattails in the swamp. It's so peaceful, I almost talk myself into abandoning whatever it is I think I'm doing.

"Go on inside. Have some breakfast, do the dishes and forget yesterday ever happened," I tell myself. "It's over now. Don't make a bad situation worse."

But then I remember Willie, and a stubborn "NO!" erupts like a volcano from somewhere deep inside. "NO!" I shout again, and with that, I jump on my bike and take off.

"New rules, damn it!" I yell.

Once I'm on my way, I feel exhilarated and free. I imagine Pepper running beside me, his long black ears flapping with the rhythm of his four-legged gait. But missing him doesn't help me now, so I focus on the bumpy road and the rhythm of the pedals moving me forward.

The low mesa rides the face of the foothills and rises up cleanly against the clear blue sky. After a few false starts, I find a road that appears to head in the right direction. I am sweating now, and the breeze feels cool as it caresses my skin and blows hair into my eyes. A white frame house surrounded by a white picket fence comes into view, the only evidence of human habitation I have seen since I rode off. The well-kept dwelling is shaded by giant cottonwoods, their leaves shimmering in the early morning breeze. Out back is a shed, a red barn, and a windmill. A few goats meander about in a nearby pasture, and chickens cluck and peck at the ground, their red wattles swaying.

A quarter-mile or so past the white house, I round another bend. The road peters out and becomes nothing more than a one-lane path that hugs the base of the mesa and then abruptly ends. I hide my bicycle in some dense brush and head off on foot, goose-stepping through tall grasses and prickly underbrush.

"Ouch! Ouch!" I fume as the sharp grasses slap my bare legs and thorns poke through the holes in my sandals.

I don't see any way up to the mesa, and I'm about to retrace my steps when my eye catches sight of spears of light glinting off of something partially hidden in the underbrush. Reminded of my dream, I bushwhack over to have a closer look and find an old galvanized washtub full of sand and silt, disintegrating with age. Not Sophia, as I had half hoped. But there is something odd about the intensity of the light that radiates from the exposed edges of the old tub, and I stumble around, turning this way and that trying to follow the beams with my eyes.

One particular ray illuminates what appears to be the bottom of a rocky trail, difficult to see otherwise, which ascends the north side of the mesa. Particles of mica embedded in the rocks sparkle like crystals in the too-bright sunlight, and the whole scene shimmers a little with an otherworldly quality that makes me shudder. I take another look around and tell myself all is well; there is nothing to be afraid of.

"It's just that stupid dream," I mutter as I head off to explore the trail.

As I suspected, it's not really a trail, but more like a steep rocky creek bed that carries rainwater down from somewhere above. It's what my granddad would call 'a wash.' I scramble up the steep grade, and soon both knees and the palms of my hands are scraped, and the strap of one of my sandals is stretched and threatening to break. Eventually, though, the wash narrows and begins to level out, leading, not to the top of the mesa as I expected, but to a flat ledge some distance below. The surface is less rocky here and wide enough for me to pass without fear of tumbling down the steep incline off to one side. I did not see the ledge when I rode toward the mesa a few minutes ago, because the trees and other vegetation clinging to the steep downhill slope conceal it from view. Jagged rocky outcroppings project out from the top of the mesa, and from what I can tell, hide the ledge from view from above as well.

Following the gentle curve of the graveled shelf, I am taken by surprise when a lean-to comes into view, constructed at a place where the ledge widens. It is fashioned of rough, weathered boards, their outer surfaces covered with peeling bark. They stand on solid ground at the bottom and come to rest beneath the rocky outcropping at the top. Rocks have been placed at the base of each of the planks to stabilize them.

"Fantastic!" I whisper, but caution makes me squeeze into a nearby crevice to scope it out before I go any closer.

Keeping my eyes peeled, I wolf down both peanut butter sandwiches and the entire thermos of milk, shivering as the sweat cools on my back and arms. After half an hour, having detected no movement in or around the lean-to, I decide it's time to make my move.

I approach cautiously and slip in behind the boards that form the lean-to, where I am amazed to find a small cave that extends back ten feet or so. About six feet in, the height of the cave tapers and I can no longer stand upright. It's cool inside, and the only light filters in through the spaces between the planks. It smells damp, and when I run my hands along the walls on one side, I touch soft, furry moss.

"Nobody home!" I say with delight. In my wildest dreams, I could not have imagined such a find. I am so excited I let out a yelp, then immediately clamp my hand over my mouth and peer out each side of the plank wall. Fortunately, no one is coming from either direction.

Continuing my exploration of the cave, I nearly trip over a rusted tin cup lying on its side. Inside the cup, of all things, is a dried-up crab leg, or maybe it's a lobster claw—how would I know? On hands and knees, I feel along a narrow shelf in the very back of the cave and come across an old cigarette lighter. I sit back on my heels and spin the tiny wheel with my thumb, but nothing happens. A blanket stuffed in one corner falls to pieces when I pick it up. Other than that, and some dried animal scat, the place appears to have been abandoned by its previous occupant. I begin to dance and shout with joy.

"This will be *my* place now. *My* room. *Mine* and no one else's!"

With spirits soaring, I head for home full of ideas and bursting with gratitude for this amazing stroke of good fortune. With this morning's dream still fresh, I wonder: Does this have anything to do with the "portal" Sophia was instructing me to find? All I know is that those weird rainbow-colored beams of light shining from a half-buried, beat-up old washtub seem to have led me to the perfect place for me to be right now. Am I making this up, or am I not as alone as I thought I was?

****

Since I have been put in charge of organizing storage under the basement stairwell, it is easy to find what I want: a canvas cot, a sleeping bag, a tarp, a jack knife, a small shovel, a camp stool, and a couple of old army canteens we used to take fishing. I have dubbed the lean-to "Annie's Place," and I am preparing to move in.

Every few days, I snatch an empty glass milk bottle from the wooden box that sits outside the backdoor, fill it with water, and carry it up to the mesa. Ironically, these bottles are exactly like the one that got me in so much trouble. Making off with the bottles leaves us short of milk, because the milkman only replaces the number of empties he finds in the box. But no one suspects me, and I make no confession when I hear Vivian fussing at the milkman and blaming the shortages on him.

A couple of weeks have gone by since Stanley's meltdown. Vivian is still guarded around me, and I do nothing to let her off the hook. Instead, we have come to an agreement, although we never speak of it. It boils down to this: "I won't take you to task for failing miserably as my mother, and you, Vivian, will cut me loose."

It's not like she gets nothing out of the deal. Without complaint, I spend mornings doing dishes, making beds, and ironing napkins, pillowcases, and Stanley's white monogrammed handkerchiefs. I entertain Willie, feed and change Teresa and do whatever else Vivian asks of me. I become her willing handmaiden until the little kids have had their lunch and go down for naps. And then I leave.

"Where are you going?" Vivian asks almost every day as I bang out through the screen door.

"Oh, I'm just taking a picnic lunch," I declare vaguely.

I understand why she does this. She's either pretending to have authority over me she no longer has, or she is feeling too guilty to exercise it. Either way, I don't care.

Today, when I arrive at Annie's Place, I sigh with happiness and revel in the solitude and the warmth of early summer under a crystalline blue sky. At home, I gobble my food as fast as I can and get the hell out of the kitchen before Stanley has any reason to notice me. But here, I eat slowly, savoring each bite of my tuna sandwich and each sip of the cold milk I have brought to enjoy. While I eat, I sit with my back to the wall of the ledge and gaze out over the flatlands. The hawks cut lazy circles, sometimes nearly at eye level, and the sun-warmed trees release the pungent fragrance of flowing sap. Smaller birds flit about the branches, filling the day with joyful sounds as they feed on pine nuts and insects, sometimes swooping so close I can hear the hum and feel the motion of their beating wings.

After lunch, I slip inside my room and lie down on the cot to read. Before long, the heat of the afternoon and the peace of being alone lull me into a deep, untroubled sleep.

I never oversleep, though. Vivian can count on me to reappear each afternoon before Stanley arrives home from work. On this we are united: It is better if we are all in our proper places at the end of the day when the household braces itself for his homecoming and shrinks in around his presence.

Chapter 4
Eva

I am sitting alone in my kitchen, having a bite of lunch and reflecting on all of the changes I have endured these past three years. This white frame house where I have lived my entire adult life, an old shed, and a barn on five acres of land are all that's left of the 125 acres Maury and I once owned and farmed. After the war, the developers descended on us like vultures, tried every trick in the book, picked at every bone. We held out for as long as we could, but the time came when Maury could no longer work, and the medical bills were piling up, so we were forced to let the land go.

It was a terrible time for us, heartbreaking to watch nearly everything we had built sold off. Maury, God rest his soul, lived long enough to see us through all the legal wrangling, and I am grateful for that. Frankly, that was as bad or worse than the suffering we endured because of his illness and our son's disappearance. But what I know for sure is that wherever Maury is now, wherever my son may be, they are counting on me to stay right here.

"What's that?" I say to Rocky, who has let out a sharp bark. I get up to take a look out the window. It's that young girl riding by again on her two-toned blue and white bike with the large basket mounted on the handlebars. The loads she carries make it difficult for her to take the rise that starts just past my house, and sometimes she's forced to dismount and walk. I go outside to the back porch to get a better look.

"Where do you suppose she goes, Rocky?"

Mine is the only place out this way, and the road ends just yonder. There is something about the way the girl leans forward with such single-minded focus that makes me stop and watch every time I see her go by.

"Must live in one of those new houses being built on what used to be our land. Didn't know anyone had moved in there yet, but where else could she be from way out here?"

After the girl disappears from sight, I go outside to feed the goats and chickens and do a few other chores. I need to move a bunch of heavy wooden pallets out of the way so I can enlarge the garden, and I ponder how best to accomplish this. Jobs like this used to be done by hired hands, but no more. Finally, I decide to break the pallets down right where they are, and then cut and stack the wood for use in the fireplace next winter.

****

A few days later, I'm headed to the shed to get a hammer and crowbar from Maury's toolbox. I don't notice the girl at first, but when I come out, there she is, standing with her arms dangling over the fence, watching me. Her bicycle, basket loaded to the hilt as usual, is propped on its kickstand on the side of the road and looks like it might tip over any second. Her light brown hair, slightly longer than shoulder length, shines in the sun. She is wearing gray cotton shorts, a faded red cotton jacket over a white T-shirt, and glasses with plaid frames. She has on scuffed brown oxfords with heavy soles and white socks.

"You need any help?" she calls out.

I look off into the distance, considering this for a moment.

"Well yes, I reckon I could use some help. Come around to the front, and I'll let you in. Why don't you bring your bike along, get it out of the road."

I meet her by the front gate, grab Rocky by the collar, and invite her in.

"I'm Eva."

"Annie," the girl says, with a timid smile.

"Well, Annie, it's nice to meet you, and thank you for offering to help. I have a job to do that I think is going to be a little more than I bargained for."

I can't help taking a peek to see what she has in her basket. The basket is lined with a small canvas tarp, neatly folded. On top of the tarp, there's a tall black lunch box with a rounded top and a silver handle, the kind Maury used to carry with him into the fields. There are also two glass milk bottles filled with water and covered by makeshift caps, several comic books, a small flashlight, and a pearl-handled pocketknife.

"Can I pet your dog?" she asks as we walk around toward the back of the house.

"Of course. His name is Rocky, and he is very friendly, as you can see."

I release the collar of my ten-year-old black and white border collie, and Annie kneels down and scratches him behind his ears, murmuring softly. Rocky licks her face, and she laughs with childish glee.

"I used to have a dog," she tells me. "His name was Pepper. He ran away."

"Oh! I'm sorry to hear that, Annie."

"Yeah," she sighs. "I really miss him." She rises, and something else catches her eye. "Those are goats, right?"

"Yes, they are. I keep them for milk and to keep the weeds down around the place."

"What are their names?"

"That brown and white one, that's Mollie. The lighter colored one I call Bridget. Pete is the one that's grazing next to Mollie, and that old black one over there with the white spots and the horns, that's Zeke."

"Can I pet them?"

"You certainly can. They're curious creatures, so if you just hang around a while, one of them is likely to come over and give you a gentle shove. That means they're ready to make friends."

Annie looks around some more, taking in the windmill, the old barn, the chicken coop, the garden with the sweet peas already starting to climb the wire fence, and the grove of cottonwoods that line the creek that flows down from the south side of the mesa.

"Nice," she pronounces.

"If you ever need a place to fill your bottles, feel free to use that hose on the watering trough over there."

"Oh! Thanks." she says. "Thanks very much."

She asks me a few more questions about the animals and the garden, and then we turn our attention to the task at hand.

"If you could hold these pallets on end while I pry the slats off, it would be a tremendous help and so much easier on my back!" I chuckle.

Together, we turn one of the pallets onto its end, and I show Annie how to steady it. She is strong and instinctively brings her stomach and thigh muscles into play to resist the force when I begin to loosen the nails in the crosspieces. The work goes quickly, and soon the pieces lay scattered about like broad, flat toothpicks.

"Let's quit now," I suggest. "I'll take the rest of the nails out another time. Come on in and have a snack."

Annie follows me up the three stairs to the small wooden porch and through the screen door into the kitchen. Rocky is lying in a shallow hole he has dug for himself out by the shed and doesn't stir.

"Wow! Sweet," Annie murmurs as she walks around my sun-filled kitchen. She studies the notes I have taped to the refrigerator and gently touches the brightly colored ceramics that decorate the walls.

"I have some lemonade, or I can make iced tea," I offer.

"Lemonade, please."

"You can wash there at the sink if you'd like, Annie."

When she is finished, I pour two frosty glasses of lemonade and spill Oreos out onto a small plate.

"Please sit down and help yourself," I say, gesturing to the breakfast nook with its padded bench seats and windows on three sides. This was my husband's special gift to me for our twenty-fifth wedding anniversary, and it's my favorite place in the house.

Annie slides in and takes a large gulp of her lemonade as she reaches for a cookie. "Good!" she sighs with such whimsy that for an instant I'm reminded of my son at that age, and tears collect in the back of my throat.

"So, Annie, how old are you?"

"Almost 14," she says shyly.

"Where do you live?"

"New house. Over there," she gestures vaguely.

"I'm curious. I've seen you pass by before. Do you mind if I ask where you go?"

"Uhhh ... nowhere, really."

She shrinks back. Clearly, this is not a topic open for discussion, and so I shift to more neutral ground.

"Do you have brothers and sisters?"

"Two brothers, Charlie and Willie, and one sister. She's a baby, and her name is Teresa. I'm the oldest."

We sit quietly for a few minutes, finishing our snack. I can't help but wonder what her story is, what has caused the sadness I detect. The way she lowers her eyes when I attempt to make eye contact. The faint bluish smudges beneath her lower lids that suggest sleeplessness.

"I'd better be going," she sighs finally, looking at the clock on the wall. "Thank you for the lemonade and cookies, Mrs ..."

"You can call me Eva."

"My parents don't allow me to call grownups by their first names."

"Okay, then. Call me Mrs. Borsheim, or Mrs. B for short, if you'd like."

I walk with her around to the front of the house and hold open the gate while she wheels her bicycle through.

"Thank you, Mrs. Borsheim. I really like your dog," she shouts as she rounds the corner.

What a precious child, I think as I watch her disappear.

"Well, Rocky, I hope we'll be seeing more of her this summer, don't you?"

Chapter 5
Annie

On the weekends, Stanley is the jailer, and Charlie and I are the chain gang, minus the striped pajamas. We work in the front yard picking up chunks of construction debris and large rocks and piling them in a corner of the driveway while Stanley digs and rakes. There are no child-sized gloves and no place to buy any here in the boondocks, and by the end of the weekend, our hands are scrapped and bruised, our faces, arms, and necks are sunburned to a crisp.

"From now on, I want you kids to spend an hour a day pulling weeds in the backyard," Stanley announces at dinner on Sunday evening. "Vivian, you make sure they do it."

Charlie and I stop chewing and look at one another. Vivian shifts her eyes and swallows hard. Other than Stanley, no one is pleased with this new development.

The chore turns out to be pure torture. Charlie and I bake in the hot sun, pull a weed or two, and then one of us starts a fight. We're frustrated and desperate for any escape from the task at hand, so it doesn't take much to light the fire.

"Cut it out, Charlie," I shout one day as he starts pelting me with dirt clods and rocks. "You're going to break my glasses, stupid."

"Four eyes!" he shouts back.

That does it. The chase is on. Around and around the yard we go, and just when Charlie is within my grasp, I stumble and fall. Charlie keeps going.

"I'll get you, you brat!" I scream.

I sit up, intending to resume the chase, but blood is spurting from a long gash below my right kneecap. I have fallen on a hoe that was turned blade up. Right now, I don't feel anything, but I know for sure it's going to start to hurt like the dickens very soon.

"Charlie, get Mom!" I scream.

He takes one look at the blood pouring down my leg and runs to the house.

Vivian comes dashing out, Teresa glued to her right hip.

"Oh, my God!" she cries, and urges me into the house.

Once I am seated in the kitchen with my leg up, Vivian wraps a towel around it to stop the bleeding, then picks up the phone. First, she calls Stanley and then Dr. Barker, our pediatrician. Charlie sits in a corner looking pale despite his sunburned face.

"The doctor will meet you and Dad at the hospital," she reports.

"I don't want to go," I whine, leaving out the part where I especially don't want to go with *him*.

"That cut needs stitches," Vivian says in a no-nonsense tone of voice. "Dad will take you."

It takes Stanley over half an hour to get home. He unwraps the towel and looks at the nasty three-cornered tear. The bleeding has slowed, and a flap of flesh dangles loosely from the wound, exposing tendon and muscle beneath.

"Get in the car, Annie," he says, scowling at me, not happy his day has been interrupted.

I limp out to the driveway and scoot into the front seat, carefully lifting my now throbbing right leg in last. He slides into the driver's seat, lights a Pall Mall and inhales deeply. He turns to me and blows out the smoke.

"I could kill you for this," he says.

I look away and don't say anything. We drive off, and before long, I am chewing my thumbnail, not even realizing I'm doing it.

Stanley slams on the brakes and slaps my hand away from my mouth. "Get your fingers out of your mouth!" he yells for at least the millionth time in my life. I lock my hands between my knees where they cannot misbehave again. This increases the throbbing in my injured leg, but I decide it's best to leave them there anyway.

Dr. Barker, a friendly guy who has known me most of my life, sews up the wound and applies a splint to keep me from bending my knee. For the next two weeks, I walk around as stiff-legged as the Tin Man, doing as many of my usual chores as possible. Charlie and I do not return to the weeding, and to our great relief, Stanley seems to forget about it.

****

Two weeks later, Dr. Barker removes the stitches, but just when I am ready to try riding my bike again, Willie comes down with the chicken pox. I am the only one he seems to want around during his ordeal, and so I abandon my plans to return to Annie's Place and stay home with him instead. In what now seems like somebody else's life, I had plenty of practice dealing with irritable kids, and besides that, Willie's my favorite.

He's covered with swollen, red bumps that ooze a nasty, thin, yellowish liquid. His sores itch like crazy, and he is feverish and miserable. His eyelids and lips are puffy, and he has pox inside his ears that itch so furiously, he screams and stamps his feet with discomfort and frustration.

"Don't scratch, Willie!" I tell him again and again, but it does no good. He goes at the sores constantly.

One morning, as I am trying to pull a clean cotton t-shirt over his head, he makes things worse by pushing me away and rolling around on the floor until he bangs his head against the leg of his bed and raises a nice goose egg on his forehead.

When he stops crying, I gather him close and say, "Never mind the shirt. Let's try a bath, okay?"

Frankly, he is a handful, and Vivian seems happy to busy herself elsewhere and let me take care of him.

While he sits in a cool oatmeal bath, I sing his favorite songs and squeeze the thickened liquid over his back and shoulders. Afterwards, I pat him dry, and dab a bit of carbolated Vaseline on each of the pox. There are so many of them that before I finish, he runs out of patience and begins to fuss and pull away.

"Willie, if you let me finish putting the medicine on, I'll get you an orange soda," I offer, glancing at Vivian, who has come to check on things. She does not approve, but orange soda is his favorite, and it will settle him down, so she nods and says it's okay.

Once he is tucked into bed with a sheet draped loosely over him, I bring him the orange soda and a piece of buttered toast to go with it. While he's eating, I go to the hall closet and riffle through the comic books, calling out the titles.

"Don-od Duck!" he shouts at last. I climb into bed with him and read until he falls asleep.

So go the days until Willie's fever breaks and he return to his normal ball-of-fire little self, freeing me to pick up my life where I left off before my injury. I hope Vivian hasn't forgotten our deal. Guess I'll find out.

Later in the week, Stanley goes out of town on business, and we have dinner earlier than usual. I jump up, clear the table, and start washing the dishes as soon as Charlie and Willie wander off and Vivian takes Teresa to have her bath. By the time I finish, it's not yet six o'clock. The sun won't set for another couple of hours, which gives me plenty of time.

"I'm going for a bike ride," I holler as I head for the garage.

"Be careful of your leg!" Vivian calls after me.

I head straight for the mesa and discover that my right knee is stiff, and my leg is quite weak. The climb up the wash is much more difficult than I had anticipated, and I am forced to stop to rest several times. It's a beautiful evening, so I don't mind taking time to bask in the coolness and breathe in the scents of sage and wild clover released by the heat of the day. At last, I reach the ledge that leads to Annie's Place—*my* place, I think with excitement.

Everything looks the same, so I take a few more moments to gaze at the shadows cast by the mountains as the sun continues its westward journey. I have never been up here at this time of day before, and it's magical. The rocky cliff, which looks golden in the bright light of the noonday sun, has now taken on a pinkish glow, which merges with red and fades to purple in the shadows. A breeze trickles down from the mountains, and I stretch out my arms and close my eyes, tasting the fragrance of pine, fir, and cedar. I am thrilled to be returning to my secret place where everything is quiet and simple and all mine.

As the lean-to comes into view, I notice immediately that something is amiss. Two of the quart bottles of water I left in the back of the cave the last time I was here are now empty and lying on the ground outside the lean-to.

"What the hell?" I mutter.

I hold my breath and squeeze into the same crevice where I hid that first day. It's edging toward sunset, and I don't have all day, so before long, I leave my place of refuge, tiptoe toward the cave and peer inside. Before my eyes adjust to the darkness, a bloodcurdling scream comes from inside and sends me scuttling back as fast as I can go.

"Crap!" I shout, terrified. "What was that?"

I flatten my back against the rocky wall. My heart is racing, and my legs are shaking. Once I am able to slow my breathing, I have a silent conversation with myself about what to do next. "Should I run?" (Not a bad idea.) "Should I hide?" (Too late for that.) "Well, then, what?" I whisper, but, of course, no answer comes.

When I grow calmer, I creep back down the wash to look for a weapon. I select a two-foot length of broken tree branch, testing its weight and heft before starting back up the wash, where I withdraw once again into the crevice. I watch but detect no further movement around the lean-to.

"Time's up," I whisper, looking anxiously at the deepening shadows.

Shivering slightly, I step out of hiding and take up a position a few feet from the lean-to, legs wide apart, makeshift club at my side. In my mind's eye, I study myself in an imaginary mirror to see whether I look as threatening as I intend. I do not, so I up my game.

I growl in my throat, sling the tree branch over my shoulder like a baseball bat, and cry out in a shaky voice, "This is *my* place, damn it! Whatever you are, whoever you are, I am in charge here, so git along now and leave this place!"

No response. It takes every bit of courage I can muster not to turn tail and run, but I manage to hold steady and wait. I am just about to start ranting again when I behold a dark face with two bright eyes looking straight at me from low to the ground near the front of the cave. Scared to death, I pull back and make tracks for my hiding place. Feeling safer there, I peer around the edge of the crevice for another look, but the face, if, indeed, there had been one, is gone.

"Come out of there! Let me see you!" I shout from my position of relative safety. This time my voice shakes even more, but what can I do?

No answer. No movement. It's a standoff, like in the Saturday afternoon cowboy movies at the theater near our old house. Someone has to shoot first to get things going, so now, I guess it's gonna be me. Firing off bullets of angry words has gotten me nowhere, and besides, my arms and hands are hurting from gripping the heavy rough tree branch, so I put it down.

"Look," I say quietly, relaxing my shoulders and discarding the aggressive tone along with my club. "You're in my place. I don't know what you're doing here, but just come on out. That's my water you're drinking and my cot you're sleeping on. I just want to see who's in my place, is all."

Still no answer, but somehow, I sense a softening.

"C'mon. Please come out. I'm not gonna hurt you."

At last she reveals herself. She's a skinny waif of a girl about my age but taller, dressed in bright plaid cotton pedal pushers, a dirty lime-green T-shirt and dusty bare feet. Her skin is dark, and wild corkscrews of hair stick out all over her head.

We stand for a long moment staring at each other. It's hard to tell which of us is more surprised. I have never been this close to a person who looks like this before, and all kinds of thoughts tumble through my head as I gawk at her with disbelief.

She looks terrified.

What is she doing way out here anyway? She's a Negro, isn't she? Lord knows there are none of those out here. For heaven's sake, that was the whole point of moving here, wasn't it? Shaking my head at the irony, I picture how upset Stanley would be if he were to discover that this Negro—and others?—have already invaded what he has assured us over and over again is whites-only territory where we will be safe from such unwanted intruders.

The girl seems to pose no threat, so I take my eyes off of her long enough to kick my weapon off of the ledge. I hold out my hands, palms up, and take a step or two toward her. The girl shrinks back and watches me warily.

"See. I'm not gonna to hurt you," I say again.

Without taking her eyes off of me, she emerges fully and positions herself with her back against the rocky wall, arms folded over her chest, frowning.

Gazing out over the landscape below so as not to threaten her, I say, "Can we talk?"

I sit down on the edge of the ledge, pull my knees up to my chin, wrap my arms around them and wait. Before long, the barefooted ragamuffin hobbles over the rocky ground and sits down a little ways away, which is fine with me, because she smells terrible.

I peer at the long-legged girl. "You're ... you're a Negro, right?"

"What's it to you?" she replies.

First impression? She sounds a little snotty, if you ask me.

"Well, it's just that I've never been this close to one before."

"I don't bite, if that be what you's worried 'bout," she snorts.

"Well, no, I wasn't worried about that. But I was wondering why your hair is sticking straight up like that."

"That jus' the way it grow, and I ain't got no comb or nothin' to fix it with."

"Okay. That makes sense."

"You white. You don't know nothin' 'bout that."

I'm not clear on exactly what she is referring to, but I don't ask.

"So," I say finally, "my name's Ty."

I'm tired of being Annie the Wimp, so on the spot, I make up a new name for myself. I think it sounds tough, and I feel proud when I say it.

She says nothing

"So what's your name?" I ask.

She looks away and doesn't answer.

"How old are you?"

Again, no answer.

After a long silence, I open my mouth and start to talk. I mean to make something up, like I did with the new name I've just given myself, but instead, all of the painful happenings of the last few months come spewing out of me. I tell this stranger all about having to move, how I accidentally damaged Stanley's new house and got a beating for it, and if that isn't enough, how unfair it is that I have to share my bedroom with a baby. I tell her about losing Pepper, how we packed up a whole houseful of our belongings but left him behind.

I am powerless to stop the torrent of words. The girl watches me the entire time, solemn and unsmiling, but I can tell she's listening. Even if she weren't, I don't think I could stop talking.

"I almost ran away," I say at last. "But then I found this place up here, and it was like maybe I have a guardian angel who wanted me to have my own room after all. Can you believe it? I came here nearly every day until I hurt myself and my little brother got the chickenpox, oh, almost three weeks ago now." Just to prove to her that what I am saying is true, I stand up and point to the fresh scar on my leg that now looks like an angry red zipper.

"I brought all this stuff up here," I say, gesturing back to the cave, "and it was not easy, I can tell you that!"

I go on and on, and all the while there's a voice inside my head demanding to know what the hell I think I'm doing. Why am I talking to this stranger like this, telling her all of the embarrassing stuff that's happened to me? The answer, when it comes, is simple. I want her to leave, the sooner the better. Once she understands that this place is mine and what it means to me, I'm sure that's exactly what she'll do, and I will never see her again.

When I finally shut up, empty as a cistern in a drought, the girl scoots a bit closer, fixes me with piercing black eyes, and says in a low voice, "My name's Clydeen. I turned 14 last October, and I have nowhere else to go."

"Oh, my God," I say, drawing back and studying her closely. "You're serious."

She looks away, and I can almost taste the shame and sadness that roll off of her, feelings I am all too familiar with myself these days.

"Okay then. Wow! That is *not* what I expected."

"Well, it ain't what I 'spected neither," she shoots back.

"Okay. Okay. I get it."

I blow out a long breath. "Clydeen is it?"

"Yas."

"Stand up and let me show you something." We stand together, and I point. "See that white house down there?"

"Where?"

"Over to your right. You might have to lean that way a little bit."

"Oh, yas. I sees it."

"That's where a lady named Mrs. Borsheim—Mrs. B—lives. She

lets me play with her dog, and she lets me get water from her hose. So if you bring me those empty bottles and find the lids for me, I'll fill them and bring them back tomorrow."

The girl limps off, leaving me to ponder this new twist of fate. What am I going to do? Tell her she can't stay here when I know how much I need this place for my own reasons? I know it's probably not the same, but still ....

Clydeen returns with the bottles and makeshift caps. I feel awkward all of a sudden, like leaving her is wrong, but it's getting dark, and I have to go. I want to give her something before I leave, and so I reach into the pocket of my shorts and pull out a handful of lint-covered raisins and offer them to her. She extends her hand, and I drop them in, careful not to touch her. She pops the whole mess into her mouth and sighs, a soft sound of gratitude.

"Sorry!" I call as I hurry away in the gathering dusk. "I'll be back tomorrow with food," and off I go.

Chapter 6
Clydeen

Tonight this white girl showed up here, say she gonna bring me food. Ha! More'n likely, she jus' be bringin' trouble. Them cans a food I had in my suitcase only last me a couple of days, and they be long gone now. I'm so scared and hongry I can't think no mo' what to do. Should I leave this place now while I can still git away? If I do, where's I gonna go? Should I stay here awhile? Maybe git me some food to eat tomorrow? What if she don't come back, or worse, what if she come back with peoples wanna drag me outta here and put me in one of them places?

"Daddy, Daddy. Please come git me. Please! Please!" I cry, tears streaming down my face. If he was here, this wouldn't be happenin'. But I know he ain't never comin' for me. Wherever he at, I reckon he ain't nothin' but a ghost now, and I'm scared a ghosts, even if one a them be my daddy.

After what seems like hours, I git up from the cot and go outside, where it's almos' as light as day under a full moon ridin' high in the sky 'long with 'bout a million stars. I feel like prayin', 'cause the man in the moon looks like the face a Jesus to me.

Sometimes my mama, she git real angry at Jesus, 'specially since what happened to Daddy, and she ain't shy 'bout lettin' Him know, neither. She say He took Daddy from us, and she mad as hell 'bout it. Far as I can tell, Jesus don't seem to mind her goin' off like that, and since it's the rage and the fear risin' up in me right now that's keepin' me from fallin' asleep, I decides to do some a that Mama

46

prayin' myself.

Pretty soon I starts really gittin' into it, stompin' up and down that narrow shelf a moonlit ground, takin' the Lord to task jus' like I seen Mama do. I rant like a crazy person, throwin' my arms in the air, bruisin' my feet all up and axin' Jesus to please, please, please speak to me.

"Jesus!" I call out. "Is that you up there?" I shout, starin' at the moon, imaginin' the Lord lookin' down on me from that glowin' ball a golden light.

I'm so worked up, I forgit all 'bout hidin' in the cave and bein' quiet so nobody find me.

"Ain't you caused this po' colored girl e'nuff trouble? Huh? Huh? What you 'spect me to do now?" I cry out, holding the palms of my hands out in front of me so they's bathed in moonlight.

I don't know how many times I have heard Mama say stuff like that when she mad at Jesus. But when them words come outta my own mouf, it jus' makes my chest hurt with missin' her, and a course that makes me madder.

I wait, breathin' hard, cryin'. Don't hear nothin'. No answer a'tall.

"Answer me! I need an answer tonight. What you want me to do, now you brung me to this place? Should I stay, or should I go? Where my mama at? She comin' for me, or she locked up someplace? What 'bout that white girl? She one a yours or not?"

I yell and scream at the face in that ol' moon till I can't hardly catch my breath, but the only thing I hear b'sides my own voice is the wind playin' in the trees. I go 'round and 'round like this till the moon start to fade, and then I give up, git down on my hands and knees and touch my forehead to the ground.

"There it is," I murmur.

It's a sound like our ol' icebox a-hummin'. I've heard it before when I put my head to the ground like this. I axed Mama 'bout it one time, but she say she never heard nothin' like that. I definitely hear it, though, and as the earth hums its way into me, the vibration soothes me.

I stay like that for as long as I can, with the rocks cuttin' into my skin and all. Finally, tired to the bone and quiet now, I get to my feet and give that face in the moon my parting shot.

"If that's all you got for me, it ain't enough."

I go back inside the cave and curl up on the cot like a baby, so tired I can't help but fall asleep.

The next thing I know, the sun is out and she back.

Chapter 7
Annie

While Vivian is busy downstairs doing the laundry, I hurry to the kitchen and make as many peanut butter and jelly sandwiches as my lunch bucket will hold. I make them two at a time, wrap them in waxed paper, grab two bananas and some cookies. The amount of food I am stealing makes my spine tingle with dread. I don't understand why I am taking this risk. For what? For some strange dark-skinned girl who showed up out of nowhere and took over *my* place? If Vivian catches me, she will no doubt put an end to my precious freedom, and then where will I be?

Finally, the whine of the wringers on the washing machine stops. Vivian comes upstairs carrying a basket of flattened wet clothes and heads for the clothesline out back. When she comes back in, I'm itching to be on my way. At the last minute, right in front of her, I grab an unopened family-size bag of potato chips. I can't believe I did something so brazen. Am I testing her to see how far I can go, daring her to lower the boom on me? My breath catches in my throat, but she looks away and to my great surprise says not one word when I walk out the door with chips in hand.

"She is definitely still feeling guilty," I mutter as I ride off. "Good!" I shout into the wind, relieved to see that our unspoken agreement is intact.

After stopping to fill the water bottles at Mrs. B's, I reach Annie's Place around one o'clock. I find the Negro girl in the cave lying on *my* cot with her eyes closed. For some reason, I feel like I should ask

49

her permission before I go inside.

"Clydeen, it's me, Ty," I call out softly. "Do you remember me?"

"Course I remember you. What you think, girl? C'mon in," she says.

When I come close, I can see she is trembling slightly.

"Are you cold?"

"Nah. Jus' tired and hongry." She stares at the lunch box and the bag of potato chips I'm carrying tucked under one arm, which, after the trip up the wash, is probably mostly crumbs.

"I brought food," I tell her, stating the obvious.

I lay the tarp on the ground, open the lunch box, set out the sandwiches, open the bag of crumbled potato chips, and take a seat. Clydeen joins me and reaches for the food, but then pulls back and looks at me. Now she's the one that needs permission.

"It's okay, Clydeen. Take as much as you want. It's for you."

She dives in like a starving dog. So as not to embarrass her, I busy myself digging around in the lunchbox for the bottle opener and pop the top on a Coca-Cola and hand it to her.

"Sorry it's not cold."

"Don't care," she says as she takes a long pull.

We eat in silence, glancing at each other now and then, each of us sizing up the other as best we can.

It's hot in the lean-to, and frankly, it's even more apparent today that Clydeen needs a bath. I make a mental note to bring some soap and towels and a basin so she can wash up. When we have eaten our fill and I have packed up what's left and stowed it in the back of the cave for her to eat later, I suggest we go down the wash a ways where it's cool and shady and there's more of a breeze.

"No! Somebody might see me," she protests. She looks scared, and her eyes, as dark as coffee beans, grow wide.

"So what if they do see you?"

Instead of answering my question, she flops down on the cot and pulls the sleeping bag up around her ears. *My* cot. *My* sleeping bag. Damn it! How am I gonna get my room back? That stupid Sophia! If this is how it's gonna be, then I've been giving her way too much credit. Portal, my eye! I should have known better.

"So ... have you done something wrong?" I ask after a while. "Is that why you're here and don't want anybody to see you?"

She jumps up. "Hell, no, I ain't done nothin' wrong. You think jus' 'cause I'm colored I musta done sumpthin' wrong? Tha's what all you white people seem to think."

She glares at me with her head thrust forward and her hands on her hips, and I take a step back. All it took was a good meal and some water, and she's ready to rumble.

"Well, my father—I mean Stanley—says ..." I begin.

"Oh, that's good. That's *real* good. I didn't axe what yo' daddy think. I axe you what *you* think."

"How old are you anyway?" I ask. I think she told me 14 last night, but I was so hyper I'm not sure I'm remembering correctly.

"Ain't none a yo' bidniss," she says today. "Now answer my question."

I shake my head and a little laugh escapes me. This is one feisty girl right here.

"What's so funny?"

"What's funny is that no one in my world ever asks me what I think. So I need a minute to think about what I think."

"Hummpf," she says and goes to sit down on the cot.

I turn my back for a couple of minutes, and then I say, "Well, I guess the answer to your question is, I don't know. I don't really know anything about Negros. Didn't I tell you last night I never met one before?"

"Well, you met one now," she sputters, and with that, she gets up and steps outside.

I follow her, and we stand next to each other with our backs against the sun-warmed sandstone wall.

Finally, I say, "Okay. If you haven't done anything wrong, then what are you doing here, and how did you get here?"

"Tha's two questions," she says.

She's at least three inches taller than I am, and the top of my head tingles as she looks down on me.

"Oh, shit," she sighs. "You ain't gonna give up, is you?"

Our eyes meet, and I see sadness and perhaps fear. I decide not to push.

"Never mind for now. It's getting too hot here, so please let's go down where the trees are. I know a place a little ways down where no one will see us."

She flaps her hand uncertainly, but when I start down the wash, she follows.

Clydeen has on the crappiest pair of shoes I have ever seen. They look like battered old ballet slippers, with soles so thin she might as well be barefoot. For that reason, I step carefully and proceed slowly as I lead her down the wash close to where I went to select my weapon just a few hours ago. It seems like years ago now.

When I see the place I am looking for, I point, but do not speak. Clydeen nods her approval, and soon we are seated on a bed of pine needles behind a large boulder where we are invisible to anyone who might start up the wash. To the best of my knowledge, no one ever does, but what do I know? Somebody built that lean-to, and both of us somehow found our way up there, didn't we?

Clydeen looks around this way and that. It takes a while, but eventually, she's satisfied that we are, indeed, safe. She smiles at me and seems to relax. We sit next to each other, our upper arms and shoulders almost touching, picking at the pine needles and watching the ants as they haul their bits and pieces over one obstacle after another. It is a beautiful spot, cool and quiet, and Mother Earth seems to welcome our presence.

"So I still want to know, Clydeen. How in the world did you get up here anyway?"

She bends her knees, wraps her arms around them and stares off into the distance. I can almost hear the wheels turning. *Should I tell the truth? How much should I say? Does it matter? Is she jus' gonna call the police anyway so's she can be rid of me?*

I clear my throat to remind her I'm still waiting.

At last, she makes up her mind and throws me a crumb. "Ol' washtub. Like my mama's. It sparkles, and I seen it."

Well isn't that just swell! I knew I should have scooped the dirt out of that thing and gotten rid of it. On the other hand, it's comforting to know that I'm not the only one who ... who what? Had a weird encounter with a washtub? That's just plain stupid. It's some kind of optical illusion, is all.

"So what about before that?" I ask, turning back to our conversation.

"I come on a bus."

"What bus? There's no bus around here."

"Well, I come on one, and then I started in to walkin'."

I doubt this. The nearest bus line has got to be miles away.

"The driver put me off. I must a gone to sleep, and next thing I know, that man poke me. 'End of the line,' he say. 'You gotta get off now or else pay another fare to go back.' I ain't got no money to give him, and I got nowhere to go back to nohow, so I git down off. It was dark, and all I seen is a few white people. I was lookin' for some food, but I never saw no place, and I weren't about to steal from no white store anyhow, so I jus' kep' walkin.' I'm from Texas, and I ain't never been 'round no mountains. B'sides that, I thought it might be safer over here, so I decided to have a closer look.

"Yeah? So then what happened?"

"Well, I spent the night in a field b'side the road—two nights, actually. Tall grass. Cold. I did have a jacket with me, but it weren't enough. Mornin's real early, I started walkin' agin, and the next afternoon, that's when I ended up up there." She points with her index finger, moving it up and down a few times. "At that cave or whatever you call it."

"But where'd you come from when you got on the bus?"

"Now, why you gotta go axin' me that? Ain't that my bidniss?"

"I'm asking because you're in my place, and I want to know."

"Okay then. I come from colored town."

I know what she means. Downtown by the railroad station where the shabby people live. Negros mostly. Bums, Stanley calls them, even his own uncle, who's a drunk and hangs around down there when he's in town.

"So what about your people? Your mom? Your dad? Aren't they looking for you? Worrying about you, wondering where you are?"

She shakes her head and gazes off into the trees.

This time, I'm undone by her sadness, and like an idiot, I stammer on in such a cheery voice it makes me cringe. "Okay. Bus. I get it. So tell me how long you've been here."

"Three, four days is all. When I found that cave with yo' stuff and all, and the water and a place to lie down, this here is the God's honest truth, Ty. I weren't never so happy to git someplace in all a my born days! I was so thirsty I could a drank a gallon."

"You did," I laugh. "Drink a gallon."

A smile breaks out on her face.

"So what is that place anyway? You say it be yo' place. Did you build it, or what?"

"That lean-to? Are you kidding me? No, I didn't build it. It was already there, and I started going up there to get away from my annoying family. I say it's my place 'cause of what I told you last night about wanting my own room. I did have this dream, though. Well ... the dream's not important. I found my way same as you— that old broken-up washtub. Sunbeams coming off what's left of it that seemed to land right at the bottom of the wash and light it up like it was the Yellow Brick Road or something. I figured it was some trick of my imagination, but I don't think I would have seen it otherwise."

"It looked like that to me, too, Ty, and it was really eerie, because I didn't git here until nearly sunset. So where was the light comin' from at that time a day? I noticed how strange it was, but I was too tired to be axin' hard questions."

"This sounds ridiculous, but if the light that reflects off that old washtub is what calls people's attention to the way up here, then maybe we outta get rid of it so it doesn't invite any unwelcome visitors. What do you think?"

"Don't want no mo' company. Can't hurt none."

We sit silently for a while, and then the question I've been dreading all afternoon finally comes. She wants to know if she can stay until she "figures some things out."

I hesitate, because I don't know what I'm getting myself into, but what am I gonna do? Keep my so-called room all to myself and tell her she can't stay? Be the one to send her off in those lousy shoes carrying that broken-down suitcase I saw stashed in the back of the cave?

"Oh, for chrissake! Stay if you want, Clydeen. But at least tell me why you have nowhere else to go."

She looks at me, distrust blooming from deep within her dark eyes. She ignores my question, and instead, she says, "I 'preciates the food. What I brung with me is all gone now."

"I will bring you food, Clydeen."

I try to smile reassuringly, but at the same time, I am petrified by the idea of stealing more food from my family's kitchen. And for how long? Vivian's one thing, but if Stanley finds out, which seems inevitable, I will be in the worst trouble of my life. Ten times worse when he finds out I'm doing it to feed a colored girl who's living in a cave out here where he says Negros aren't allowed. He'll throw a fit. I have to admit, though, there's a part of me that wants to be the cause of him blowing his top. Like knowing the stove is hot, but wanting to touch it anyway. But what tips the scales is not Vivian or Stanley, but my loneliness, my need for a friend my own age, because out here, there's nobody that fills the bill.

"Screw them," I mutter. "Especially Stanley."

"What?"

"Nothing. Uhhh ... what do you like to do, Clydeen?" I ask my new friend. "Do you like to read?"

"Ain't had all my schoolin' recently, but yas, I do like to read some," she grins, lowering her head and looking away.

I consider this. In my world, I'm expected to go to school every day unless I have a fever of 103 or the snow is five-feet deep.

"What do you mean, you haven't had all your schooling?"

"Oh ..." She hesitates and busies herself picking at a mosquito bite on her arm. "You know. I maybe haven't been goin' to school much as I shoulda these last couple a years or so. Stuff to do, things like that."

No, I don't know, but now I have another question that's been bugging me. "So that's why you talk funny, right? Because you haven't been going to school?"

She tosses her head and laughs. "Oh, my Lord. What do you mean, I talk funny? You think you got a monopoly on how to talk?"

"I didn't mean anything by it, Clydeen. I'm just asking."

"Believe me, I've had my share of schooling in the King's English," she says, crisply enunciating every word. "I can talk exactly like you if I want to. But my people have their own way of talking, and that is what I prefer, Miss Ty, because I don't want to sound 'white' like you. Any more questions?"

"Uhhh ... no. That's all."

I'm blushing, and it takes me a minute to collect myself.

"Burrrr. It's getting chilly here in the shade. Let's go back up, shall we?"

I get up and stick my hand out offering to pull Clydeen to her feet, but she ignores me.

When we get back to the lean-to, I take a deck of cards out of my pocket. "Do you know how to play 500 rummy?"

"The only card game I know is five-card draw, but you could teach me some rummy."

"Five-card draw is good. We can play rummy another time."

Focusing on the cards lightens things up between us and I start thinking what it would be like if we really could be friends. But maybe she won't even be here tomorrow. She scares me a little, too. But despite that, being with her this afternoon has made me feel less depressed and more like myself than I have in ages.

When it's time for me to go home, I fill the canteens and take two empty glass milk bottles with me. I leave the lunchbox packed with leftovers, and make a mental note to dig up another cot and sleeping bag.

Clydeen watches while I gather my stuff.

"Can't you stay a little longer, Ty?" she asks.

For some reason, this surprises me, and I turn to her.

"Are you afraid up here by yourself, Clydeen?"

"A little at night, maybe. I do hear a lot a rustlin' 'round when it's dark. I ... I think they might be ghosts around here, so I pray to Jesus to make 'em go away."

"Pray to Jesus? It's critters, Clydeen, not ghosts," I assure her. "There's no such thing as ghosts."

"You sho' 'bout that?"

"Pretty sure, yeah."

"Well, maybe you's right. We used to keep our windows wide open at night on account a the heat in Texas, and I would hear noises outside. My mama, she tol' me the same thing. Critters. So I reckon I'll git used to it by and by."

Which begs the question: Where is this mama of hers, and why in the heck is Clydeen alone and so far from home? I still don't have a clue. Not really.

I wait for her to go on, but she doesn't, so I tell her about being in Wyoming at my grandparents' cabin at night, hoping she'll reciprocate with a story of her own.

"When we were up there in the mountains, Clydeen, I'd hear those 'rustling around' sounds at night just like you're talking about, but it was just critters. Except for this one time when my granddad snuck outside and started scratching the window screens and moaning." I laugh thinking about it. "My brother and I, we thought for sure it was a ghost, and it liked to scared us to death. We should have known, though. It was just Granddad. He loved to play tricks on us like that. When he came back inside, he just about laughed himself sick. Do you know anyone who does stuff like that?"

"Can't rightly say as I do," says Clydeen.

Memories of times like those with Grandma and Granddad are precious to me now. I'm sure Clydeen has sweet memories of her own. Will she ever tell me about them?

"So what critters you got 'round here?" she says, bringing me back to our conversation.

"Well, I haven't lived here very long, but I'd say raccoons, weasels, mice, rats, chipmunks, squirrels, probably some deer, but not down here on this ledge I'd guess. But hey, I know what you need."

"What?"

"You need a bigger flashlight so you can check out what's going on at night. I'll bet that puny little one of mine doesn't do you a bit of good, am I right?"

"Too dark."

"Okay. I'll see what I can find."

I feel like hugging her, but I don't. Instead I offer her my deck of cards and tell her I can't stay.

"But I promise I'll come back tomorrow, Clydeen. I'll bring some more comic books, and maybe I'll bring another cot and sleeping bag, if that's okay with you."

"Course it is. Place for both of us to rest."

"Good. I'll see you tomorrow."

At the bottom of the wash, before I walk into the tall grasses where I have hidden my bicycle, I turn to wave. I'm disappointed to see that Clydeen has already disappeared from view.

Chapter 8
Clydeen

I been here over three weeks now. Some days, Ty can't come, and when she ain't gonna be here, I sleep much as I can. When I git up, I eat, watch the trees, the birds, the chipmunks and squirrels, play with the beetles and ants that crawl around everywhere. I read the comic books Ty brung and wait for her to come back. Wait for my mama, too. Try not to think too much 'bout what could be comin' next for me.

Most days, Ty stay with me all afternoon till she have to go 'cause a her daddy. She bring me food and water, and other stuff, too, like a toothbrush, soap and a towel, toilet paper and a shovel to bury stuff that need buryin'. She brung a couple a orange crates, too, and we set one of 'em up as a "wash station." Don't know why she do all a that for me, but thank you Jesus, 'cause I don't know what would a become of me without her. Guess I'd be gone from here now and prob'ly ended up in one of them bad places agin, or maybe in jail, who knows?

She mostly quit axin' me so many questions 'bout my bidniss, so I don't have to worry no mo' what to say. When she git here, we have an easy time together, eatin' our lunch and playin' all the games we like.

Then yesta'day, out of the blue, she say to me, "Clydeen, I think we need a new name for this place."

"What you talkin' 'bout, Ty? New name? What we callin' it now?"

She goes all red in the face like maybe she chokin' on sumpthin'. So course I gave it a push.

"C'mon now. Tell me."

"Uhhh ... never mind. It doesn't matter. Maybe I'll tell you later. We just need one we decide on together, don't you think?"

"Ty, you one crazy white girl. I don't know nothin' 'bout no namin', 'but I do have a question."

"Shoot."

"If we gives this place a name together, does that mean it's okay for me to stay here some mo'?" I axed her, pullin' a silly grin.

But she don't grin back.

"You don't need my permission to stay here, Clydeen, and you don't need my permission to go, either. Just so we're clear."

"Course. I know that."

But no, I really did not know that till she say it jus' now.

"Anyway, as long as we are hanging out up here together, I thought it would be fun to choose our own secret name. Don't get me wrong. It doesn't mean I wouldn't like to know why you want to stay up here by yourself week after week. It doesn't mean I've stopped wondering what you're hiding from, or when I might come up here and find you gone, either."

"Who said I was hidin'? I tol' you. I need to figure some stuff out. Is that so hard to understand?"

"What things? Where is your family, Clydeen? Did you run away all the way up here from Texas?"

"No, I did not run away from Texas. Now will you let me be so's we can git back to this namin' business?"

She sighs, purses her lips and rubs her eyes, looks me over, gives up.

"Okay," she say. "Let's just move on."

After we got that settled between us, we spent a long time callin' out ideas. We thought up 'bout a hun'ert names, but none of 'em stuck. When we's worn out and fresh out of ideas, we opened a couple bottles of Coca Cola and sat on the ledge in the sun watching the hawks circlin' above the treetops.

"I know!" I whisper-shouted, leanin' over close to her. "Let's call it our Nest."

"That's brilliant, Clydeen!" she say. "It's perfect!"

Boy oh boy, that fo' sho the first time in my sorry life *anybody* call me brilliant. I looked at her to see if she makin' fun, but she jus' kep' on talkin'.

"Yes! I like it! Our place is high up like a bird's nest. We have our cots and our sleeping bags in the cave, like feathers lining a nest, right? We have the lean-to that shelters the cave, like the branches of the trees shelter the nests of birds. And I'm like the mama bird bringing you food and water!"

"Guess that make me the baby bird, then," I chirped.

"Cheep, cheep. Cheepcheepcheep!" Annie screeched, and we 'jus 'bout to pee our pants we's laughin' so hard.

When we settle down she say, "Seriously, Clydeen, it really does feel like a nest up here, doesn't it?"

"Ahhhh, yas, it do."

I got a good feelin' in my innards, 'cause she not makin' fun a me a'tall, and she not axin' me no mo' questions, neither. Tha's how I like it.

"So from now on, whenever we talk about this place, we will call it the Nest," she say in that bossy voice she gits sometimes. We sat there lookin' at each other like we 'bout the smartest couple a almos' grown young'uns in existence.

Then all a sudden, she sucked in a big gulp a air, jumped up, and say, "I gotta go."

She took off slidin' down the wash, shoutin' back at me, "My real name's Annie, and this place used to be called 'Annie's Place.' But I don't want to call it that anymore. Bye, Clydeen!"

Lord Jesus, I jus' stood at the top of the wash and laughed my head off. So why you 'spose she tol' me her name Ty? I swear, that white girl, she a'ways up to sumpthin'.

Chapter 9
Clydeen

When Annie git here today, don't you know it, I'm waitin' for her, all sassy like, hands on my hips, twitchin' this way and that real smooth like a movie star.

"Well, hellooo, Miss Annnnie," I say as she clambers onto the ledge.

She laughs, say she shoulda tol' me a long time ago Ty not her real name.

"So why you tell me yo' name Ty, Annnnie?" I tease some mo'.

"Oh, I don't know," she say, breathin' hard from the climb up the wash.

When she catch her breath, she say, "Okay. Here it is. That first night when I found you here, I was scared, but I was mad, too. I guess you know that."

"Weren't no secret."

"Anyway, I was trying to be somebody tough, tough enough to chase you outta here. That was my plan. That name, Ty? It just popped out of me. Ty. It seemed like a name a bully might have. One who could make you do what I wanted. It seems stupid now, and I'm sorry."

"Jus' so's you know, I didn't really git that you's tryin' to be a bully."

"Well, good," she laughs. "Because when I came back the next day, you were still here, and I'm glad. Anyway, everything's different now. I don't feel like being Ty anymore, but I'd lied to you

61

for so long, I didn't know how get out of it. Besides, being friends with you is way better than pretending to have a stupid room up here by myself, Clydeen. It was way past time to stop the lie and tell you my real name. It didn't go quite as planned, though. I almost chickened out."

Wait. Did she say we's friends now? Lord have mercy! I thought we's jus' playin' around? But friends? Tha's diff'rent. What would my mama and daddy say 'bout me bein' friends with some white girl? They'd say, be careful. She ain't doin' all a this for you for nothin'. At some point, that white girl prob'ly gonna to pull the rug out and leave you high and dry, or worse.

While I'm busy thinkin' on that, Annie, she still talkin'.

"Shoot, right now, you're my only friend, Clydeen, except for Mrs. B. But that's different."

"Uh-huh, a'ight. Let me git this straight. You come up here, bring me stuff, stay with me on account a you ain't got no other friends?"

"Well, sort of, but not exactly."

"So lemme axe you what yo' mama and daddy say if they knowed you's bein' friends with a girl like me?"

"Holy cow, Clydeen!"

"C'mon. Tell me. What would they say?"

All a sudden, the laughin'-teasin'-fun part of a few minutes ago has gone right outta me. Truth is I feel mean. A little afraid, too.

"Damn it, Clydeen. Stop. I don't want to talk about this."

"Oh, okay. So now we bumped up against sumpthin' *you* don't wanna talk about. I bet they'd be mad, wouldn't they? You've a'ready tol' me as much. They wouldn't want they little white girl rubbin' up against some no-count colored, ain't that right? Would they say 'colored' or sumpthin' worse?"

She jus' sits there siftin' rocks through her hand, lookin' like she ready to cry, and it takes her a long time b'fo she answers me.

"Okay," she say, clearin' her throat and blowin' her breath out. "You're right. They wouldn't like it. Are you happy now?"

I ain't the least bit happy. Fact is, I'm so unhappy, I don't know how to stop my mouf a'runnin', so I jus' keep on drivin' the train off the rails.

"Well, my mama and daddy wouldn't be thrilled neither. So

what you think 'bout that, huh?"

Her eyebrows shoot up like she really is surprised to hear this. Who she think she is anyhow? But luckily, b'fo things really get outta hand, Annie, she gits up and starts walkin' back toward the lean-to.

"You think I can't take care a myself, is that it? I don't need you! I been takin' care a myself my whole life jus' fine!" I shout after her.

"Oh, shut up, Clydeen! You want some water?" she axes me as she ducks inside the cave.

"Yas! I'll take some water!" I yell, full a rage, my mouth dry and nasty tastin'.

After a while she come back with a bottle a water, and we both take long drinks, one after the other, lettin' the water dribble down our chins and soak the fronts a our shirts. Coolin' us off in more ways than one. She sits beside me for a long time b'fo she start in to talkin' agin. Her words come out soft and slow at first, then faster as she makes her way into what she wanna say.

"I don't know about any of this, Clydeen—you, me, white, colored, what other people think. I try not to think about it. If nobody ever finds out, then everything's okay, isn't it? I just like being with you. I want to know more about you, what's happened to you in your life, who your people are, where they are. Sometimes, you mention your mama. But I wonder if you really have a mother because you don't tell me squat about her—or about yourself, for that matter."

"I tol' you ..."

"C'mon! You think I don't know there's more to it than that? That you just happened to come way out here on a bus and your two feet? Don't you think I know we are both here because we've got trouble, and you don't trust me enough to tell me what your trouble is? Right now, though, I can only hope we get through it before the wrong people find us up here, because if they do, I have an awful feeling we're both gonna be very sorry, and then the trouble might really be all about what color you are and what color I am."

"You could be right 'bout that," I agree.

She studies me for a long time, and then she says, "I gotta tell you, Clydeen, I don't come up here just to bring you stuff. I've never met anyone like you. I'm fascinated by you, and I have never laughed so much in my life as I do when I'm here with you. I love listening to you talk, and I'm sorry I said you talk funny that one day. Every day when I wake up, I can't wait to see you. Days I can't make it up here, you're all I think about. I wonder if you're okay, if you slept at night, what you're doing, and whether you miss me as much as I miss you. Sometimes I pretend you're my sister. No, that's not quite right. I wish we were sisters."

"Sisters, huh? Well, if that don't beat all."

She smiles at me and takes a deep breath.

"But I have to tell you, Clydeen, for a skinny bean pole of a girl, you sure do eat a lot!"

This last bit jus' cracks me up. I can't help it. I starts laughin' and cryin' at the same time, ashamed a bein' so ornery. My anger melts away, and I thank Jesus for finally shuttin' my mouf, and givin' me not another cross word to say. Instead, I crawl over to where Annie sittin' and we hug each other for a long time, which is sumpthin' we ain't done b'fo.

"Don't think I don't 'preciate what you do for me, Annie," I say drawing back. "Cause I do. I jus' don't want you to think ..."

"Oh, please, Clydeen. Do you think I don't have skin in this game?"

"Well now there you go talkin' some colored folks' talk. Where you hear 'bout skin in the game?"

"Oh, I don't know. Probably my grandad. He came up from the South," she says, wavin' a hand in front of her face dismissively.

"But here's what I want to tell you, Clydeen. After my father—Stanley—beat the crap out of me, I felt hurt and humiliated, yes. But also betrayed and filled with hatred. Since then, though, I've come to the conclusion that I was a coward for letting it happen to me in the first place. I've asked myself about a hundred times why the hell I didn't run."

"Why didn't you?"

"It's simple. I didn't think I could. In fact, I didn't think of it at all. I've always been such a good little girl, trying to obey the rules and do what everybody tells me. It didn't occur to me that I could protect myself by moving my feet and taking off for a while. I think things would have come out differently if I had. I know you would've done it," she says, pounding her fist on the ground.

"Yas. I done me some runnin' in my time," I admit with a giggle.

"While I was struggling with all of that and hating myself even more than I hated Stanley, you came along. You needed some help, but so did I. You being here? It was the push that lifted me out of the depression I was in. I needed a thing to do, something *I chose for myself* and kept to myself, but one that also terrified me so I would have to learn to be brave.

"So now look at me!" she say, jumpin' to her feet. "In just a few short weeks, I have become the chief thief and bottle washer. The queen of rule breakers. It would have made my former self shudder with dread, not that I don't still shudder a little. But now there's no telling what heights of mischief-making I'm going to achieve."

I bust out laughin'. Annie, she laughin', too, and falls down next to me.

"Even if Stanley finds out what I'm doing, finds out about you, and wants to kill me for it, that doesn't stop me. Because now I care more about you and what I want and what you need than I do about what he might do to make me pay for it. You're here, Clydeen. I'm glad, and I'm so much happier being me now. It's like I can breathe better, and if Stanley ever threatens me like that again, I'm gonna be ready. So there you have it. That's my skin in this game."

A fat old blue jay catches my eye, squawkin' at us from a nearby tree, lookin' for a handout. I point to it and look at Annie.

"Beautiful, huh?" says my friend, Annie.

"Yas." I say, my voice soft and quiet now, my hand touching her knee.

"So what do *you* want, Clydeen?" she say to me, real quiet like.

I think about it for a while b'fo I decides what to say. They's lots I want, but only two things I want to tell her.

"I want my mama to find me and take me home, even though I don't exactly know where home is right now. That be the main thing. Second thing is I want to stop thinkin' that 'cause you's white, the day gonna come you gonna do sumpthin' crazy like call somebody, maybe never come back—I don't know what. Today when you say we's friends, all those scary feelin's closed in on me, and tha's what made me so touchy."

"Because I'm white."

"Well, yeah. You tellin' me what you think yo' daddy do to you if he find out about you being 'round me? What you think be the reason for that? It's all about hatred. Hatred of peoples like me. It's hard to take, Annie."

"But that's him. *I* don't hate you, Clydeen. I love you!"

"You a kid, Annie. You think you can stand up to that hate?" she scoffs. "Plus you might a hated me jus' a little when you found me up here at your place that night, right?"

"No! Yes. Maybe. I don't know, Clydeen. But I know I don't hate you now."

"But wouldn't you start hatin' me agin if yo' daddy come walkin' up that wash over there someday?"

"Absolutely not!"

But I sees her shiver a little, so I knows the truth a things still ain't easy for her.

"So do you hate *me*?" she axe me now, laying a hand on her chest.

"Well, I might hate you some for what you got that I ain't."

Again, she give me that surprised look.

"Like parents who can take care a you, a nice home to go to, a soft bed, plenty to eat, good shoes. What you think you done to deserve all a that 'cept be born white?"

"Is that my fault?" she shouts.

"No. It ain't your fault, but maybe it wouldn't hurt you white peoples none to level the playin' field a little bit."

"How?"

"Well, that be a bigger question than I got the answer to. I don't know. Give us our 40 acres and mule, for starters, maybe?"

"I don't know what you're talking about."

"I know. Never mind."

"I don't think of you as colored, though. I just think of you as a person, as my friend."

"Well I am colored, and it has everything to do with me bein' here and us bein' together right now. Maybe one day we'll talk about all a that. But for now, you axe me what I want? Well, here's one more thing. If we's gonna be friends, I want you to see me exactly as I am, and I don't want you tellin' me you don't see my colored skin. I don't buy it, and I wouldn't want it, neither."

"Fair enough," Annie sighs, pulling me to my feet and leaning in to give me a hug.

The rest of the afternoon rolls on. We do the same things we usually do, but it be diff'rent now. Like sumpthin's been called out and settled b'tween Annie and me, at least for now.

Chapter 10
Annie

My work is never done, and this evening I'm sitting at the kitchen table with my Big Chief tablet and a pencil making a list of items I will need to talk Vivian into buying on Saturday when we go grocery shopping. I cup my hand over the top of the page to shield it from Charlie's prying eyes. He's sitting on the other side of the table drawing a picture of a sailboat. He's shading it carefully, making the shadows fall just right. I watch his hand move confidently over the page, and I must confess, he's pretty good. I'm a little jealous. The clock on the wall says it's nearly five-thirty. Stanley will be home any minute, so I hurry to finish.

A few moments later, car wheels crunch on the gravel driveway. The garage door rattles up and then down. Stanley strolls in trailing the smell of stale cigarette smoke and Old Spice. Vivian is standing at the sink peeling potatoes. He presses himself against her from behind and cups her right breast, jiggling it up and down. Disgusting! She keeps her eyes on the potato and the paring knife and says nothing.

"Break out the ice cubes, Beanie," he calls as he heads for the bedroom to change clothes.

Beanie. That's my nickname, but he is the only one who calls me that, and only when he's in a good mood and wants me to do stuff for him. His arrival is my cue to abandon whatever I'm doing and get down to the business of serving him. He needs a drink, so I hop to and spill two trays of ice cubes into the freezer bin.

He hurries back into the kitchen, rubbing his hands together in anticipation. He mixes two highballs—bourbon and ginger ale—one for himself and a lighter one for Vivian—and then goes to the living room to sit in his easy chair until dinner. He lights a Pall Mall, draws the smoke into his lungs, and calls out, "Beanie, go bring in the newspaper."

I bring it in from the front porch and hand it to him. He sits back and opens the paper, which no one else is allowed to touch until he has read and discarded it.

Vivian remains in the kitchen preparing dinner while she sips her cocktail and smokes her own cigarette. She looks sad, or maybe tired, and speaks little except to direct me to open a can of peas and set the table. When all is ready, she sends me off to gather the troops. Stanley fixes himself another highball, the second of several he will drink between now and whenever he decides to call it a night.

There is no blessing of the meal at our crowded table. We get right down to the business of passing around bowls of mashed potatoes, gray-looking canned peas, and chicken fried steak, which Vivian has tenderized with a hammer and some sort of chemical she uses.

Charlie and I grab slices of white bread from a plate in the center of the table, stuff them into our mouths, and take gulps of milk that leave mustaches on our upper lips. While I am passing a bowl of peas across the table to my brothers, the heavy bowl tips and spills a small amount of liquid on Willie. It's hot. He screams.

"Goddamn it, Annie. What is the matter with you?" Stanley growls. He snatches me out of my chair, grabs his wooden paddle out of the drawer, yanks me across his lap and begins to pound on me. My baby sister, who is sitting nearby in her highchair, begins to wail.

My butt stings with each whack, but I don't cry. In fact, I almost feel like laughing. It's as if my body is an empty shell, and the essence of me has taken a walk. I will soon be 14 years old, and in my opinion, way beyond the age when hitting me is going to do any good. Still, I'm sure the humiliation factor is worth the effort as far as Stanley is concerned.

Just as Stanley finishes with me, Willie comes bouncing back into the kitchen, unhurt, according to Vivian, who has helped him into pajama bottoms. We resume our places like flustered brood hens returning to their nests after the fox has gone. I sit down, but I no longer want to eat.

"Eat your dinner!" Stanley barks at me.

Like a robot, I pick up my fork, spear a single pea and put it in my mouth. I look at him, daring him to challenge me.

He scowls, then looks away and resumes his usual dinnertime monologue—reciting the miseries of his day at work.

"I should tell that goddamn bastard to go to hell!" he tells Vivian, as he shovels up a forkful of mashed potatoes. "Damn it, I'm in line for that promotion, and he's trying to make it look like ..." On and on he goes, as he does every night.

Vivian seems to listen, but remains silent, eyes downcast, slowly consuming her meal.

I tune him out and stare at the plate of food in front of me. The rule for the children in our house is this: We are to clean our plates of every morsel. If we do not, the remaining food, will be served to us again at the next meal, cold after having spent the intervening hours in the refrigerator. Dreading the thought of cold greasy meat for breakfast, my fork hangs suspended, perched on the diving board of my forefinger while I try to decide whether or not to plunge it into the mashed potatoes.

While my fork awaits my decision, I think of Clydeen alone up on the mesa. Clydeen, and her fascination with my "real life" and the house I live in, what I have that she "ain't got," as she says. Sometimes these days, we venture away from the safety of our Nest and climb to the top of the mesa, careful not to expose ourselves for very long. From one particular spot, this reddish brick house—the one I'm in right now—can be seen standing out like a sore thumb against the rest of the nearly naked construction zone. One day, I pointed it out to her. What a mistake that was! Now, every few days, she insists on returning to gaze down on what she calls "the Palace Cahill."

"You daddy rich?" she asked me today, as usual.

"No, Clydeen," I mumbled.

She drives me crazy with her questions, the same ones over and over again.

"Oh, c'mon now. You daddy got to be rich, you live in a house like that," she accused, looking over her shoulder and glaring at me.

"We're not rich, Clydeen. My parents saved up for years to buy that house."

"But you not po' neither, is you?"

"No, I suppose we're not poor."

Being with Clydeen, I have figured out by now that I do, by virtue of my birth, enjoy a level of privilege that Clydeen does not, and it pains me. It's embarrassing, too. I'm not proud of my station, and today, I launched into a feeble attempt to convince her that there's more to the story than meets the eye.

I stab another pea and eat it.

"Look, Clydeen," I told her. "I have enough food, a warm winter coat and shoes that fit. I go to school regularly and I live in a new house. But that doesn't mean I have a perfect life."

"Uhh-huh," she said, rolling her eyes.

"Vivian makes my school clothes from scratch or else she alters ugly hand-me-downs that smell funny, because she says department store clothes are too expensive. You think that's what rich folks do?"

"Don't know," she said, not looking at me.

"Well, I just want what other girls have. Isn't it the same for you?"

"Don't know," she said again.

"You know what living with Stanley is like. On top of everything else, I'm supposed to get an allowance of fifty cents a week, but when I ask him to give it to me, nine times out of ten, he says he doesn't have it, and he'll give it to me tomorrow. Tomorrow never comes, and that means I hardly ever have any money of my own."

"Uhh-huh. Too bad."

"Seriously, Clydeen. There are things about my 'real life' that are not that great."

She turned her dark eyes on me then, and the look she gave me said she didn't believe a word of it. My shabby attempts to draw comparisons made me feel petty and self-conscious, so I stopped and said no more.

But what about right now? What would she make of the chaotic scenario at tonight's family dinner table?

I take a tiny bite of meat, dip it in catsup, put it in my mouth and immediately begin to choke. I run to the sink, bend over and cough violently to dislodge the meat that's gone down the wrong pipe. Finally, I spit it out, and run out the backdoor. Cold chicken fried steak and peas for breakfast? Bring it on. I jump on my bike and head to Mrs. B's. I want—no, I need—to be sitting in her quiet kitchen, listening to the refrigerator hum while we drink glasses of sweet iced tea and watch the sun go down.

When I arrive at the white house, Mrs. B isn't there. No Rocky, either. Where can they be? While I'm waiting, I fill the water bottles I left in the grass this afternoon, and walk out to the pasture, where Zeke and Pete are butting heads and chasing around like a couple of frisky puppies.

Finally, I sit down on the back stairway, too tired and disheartened to start for home just yet. There is a gnawing pain in my stomach. I double over and rock back and forth, hoping the motion will make it better. One time at school, I saw picture of a tapeworm. It was thin and white and very long, and these days, I'm sure there must be one of those inside of me, gobbling me up bit by bit.

Chapter 11
Eva

It's late when I get back from town, and I find Annie sitting on the back stoop waiting for me. Rocky begins to bark with excitement, and I roll down the window and call out.

"Hello, Annie! What are you doing here, child?"

"I was just filling those bottles I brought by earlier. Where were you, Mrs. B?"

"Come on in. I'll tell you."

"I have to go soon," she says, looking anxiously down the road.

"Can you come in for a quick glass of iced tea before you go? I'm thirsty, and I need to feed Rocky."

We settle ourselves in the breakfast nook. Annie sighs deeply, and we sip our tea in silence for a few moments.

"So where'd you go, Mrs. B?" she asks me again, and this time the question sounds almost like an accusation.

I peer at her for a long moment. "What's wrong, Annie?"

Her cheeks burn under my gaze. She turns her tea around and around on the tabletop, playing with the wet ring formed by the sweating glass. She squirms, and I fully expect her to jump up and leave, because I usually avoid asking direct questions that I suspect will make her uncomfortable. Instead of bolting, though, she looks out the window for a long while. The muscles in her jaw work as she clenches and unclenches her teeth.

Finally, she raises her eyes and says, "My dad, you know. He flies off the handle sometimes." She turns both palms skyward and attempts to smile, as if to say, "Whatta ya gonna do?"

"Are you hurt, Annie?"

"Not really. I spilled something and he blew his stack. Punished me. Just needed to get away from him, so I came here looking for you."

"I'm sorry I wasn't here. I had to go into town to see a lawyer about something, and it took longer than I expected. I'm glad you waited."

"Me, too," she says, turning toward the window, and I can see she's close tears.

"You say he punished you. What does that mean?"

She shrugs.

"You can tell me, Annie."

"He has this wooden paddle thing he keeps in a drawer in the kitchen, and when we do something bad, he paddles us with it. Twenty swats."

She shrugs again and averts her eyes.

"Has he ever done more than that?"

"Well, there was this one time ... my dad ..."

She shakes herself, almost like a dog shaking off water.

"My dad ..." she tries again, looking away.

"What is it, Annie?"

She begins to cry. Like water held too long behind a dam, the story comes spilling out with the tears. About a Sunday morning shortly after her family moved into their new house when she accidentally damaged something. Her father's rage, and the harsh punishment that followed. The shame of being dragged off to church still traumatized by the beating she had received. Her words come in fits and starts, sobs and sniffles.

When I can stand it no longer, I jump up and take her in my arms and hold her close. When at last she coughs and pulls away, I pull a clean, white handkerchief from my pocket and hand it to her. There's no going back now, not for me and not for her. I hand her a glass of water, which she finishes in three gulps, and then another, as if she has never been so thirsty in her life.

"I have to go," she says, but she doesn't move.

"Annie," I begin, holding her by both shoulders. "If anyone hurts you like that again, will you come to me right away, please? Will you promise me that?"

She sighs. "My father will kill me if he finds out I told you any of this, Mrs. B."

"But you did tell me, Annie, and that changes things. Do you know what that makes me?"

"What?"

"Your guardian angel. I am now your guardian angel, and my assignment is to look after your well-being. Do you understand?"

"Yeah, I guess."

"So let's agree. I am your guardian angel, and if you need anything, including protection, that will be my job from here on out. Everyone's supposed to have a guardian angel, you know, maybe even more than one."

"So I've been told," she says, a slight smile playing over her lips.

"Well now, I've just appointed myself to be yours."

I reach out and tousle her hair playfully to lighten the mood.

"There's one catch, though."

"Yeah? What's that?" A small frown mars the smooth skin between her eyes. "I hope it doesn't have anything to do with ..."

"With what?"

"Never mind. What's the catch?"

"I need your permission. Without that, no can do."

"Okaaay," she says slowly, a giggle bubbling up.

"So here's the deal. If you are hurt or in danger or even just sad or upset about something, I'll be right here ready to listen. In exchange, I promise never to betray your confidences, unless it becomes absolutely necessary for your safety. Agreed?"

"You're not kidding, are you?" she says, grinning from ear to ear now.

"I am most definitely not kidding, Annie. So what do you say? Do you accept?"

"Okay, then. Mrs. B, guardian angel. Should I call you Mrs. Angel from now on?"

The skin around my eyes tightens as I, too, begin to laugh.

"Well, you can do whatever you want, but Mrs. B is fine with me. Or you can call me Eva."

"I'll stick with Mrs. B."

"Oh, I forgot to tell you one other very important thing. You can fire me anytime you wish. That power is in your hands, not mine."

"Power," she muses.

And with that, she is up and out the door, hops on her bike and disappears into the fading light.

Chapter 12
Annie

When I get home a half hour later, the dinner dishes are waiting for me, but for once, I don't mind. It gives me time to replay my talk with Mrs. B and worry about whether it was wrong to talk to her the way I did. I'm pretty sure it was. Until I met Clydeen, I never told anyone those sorts of things. I remember the time I told some lady from Stanley's work that he had lost a hundred dollars playing poker, and he was so mad, he tore up the circus tickets he'd bought that day and threw them in the trash. I got the message. But isn't this my story to tell? Don't I have the right? I have no idea.

When I am finished in the kitchen, I go straight to bed to avoid revealing any guilty looks that might be lurking on my face. Teresa is already asleep, lying on her back, breathing softly. In the soft twilight from the curtainless windows, I root around in my closet looking through the few books I own, four of them about Cherrie Ames, a girl who grows up and lives an exciting life as a nurse. I've read these books many times, but not in the last couple of years. I pick up the first in the series, *Cherrie Ames, Student Nurse*, duck under the covers with my flashlight and start reading from the beginning.

Before long, Stanley begins snoring so loudly the walls are shaking, and I regret not having gotten to sleep before his engine cranked up. How does Vivian stand it, I wonder, grinding my teeth with irritation.

I haven't been sleeping well lately. Now that Teresa is a little

77

older, when she awakens during the night, Vivian is hesitant to get up to feed her. So tonight it becomes a contest between Stanley's snoring and Teresa's fussing. Just to shut one of them up, I pick Teresa up and take her into my bed with me. Most nights, she snuggles close, sighs contentedly, pops her thumb in her mouth, and promptly falls back to sleep. But for me, it's not so easy. I squirm around trying to get her hot little body off me. It's impossible for me to keep reading now.

While I struggle to get comfortable, the best idea ever strikes me! Tomorrow I will take the first volume of Cherrie Ames up to the Nest for us to read together. It will be so much fun! Maybe I'm too old to be reading the Cherrie Ames books now, but I feel like doing it anyway. After all, they were my favorites for a really long time, and I want to share the stories with Clydeen. In my mind's eye, I imagine how she'll laugh when we get to the part where Cherrie accidentally finds herself wheeling a dead body around the hospital corridors, not knowing what to do with it. Thankfully, my fantasies distract me from the snorts and whistles coming from the next room, and I soon drift off to sleep.

****

Today, I make my getaway around one o'clock, taking with me the book, a roll of toilet paper, sandwiches, apples, cookies, and a thermos of cold milk I manage to filch while Vivian is busy putting the little ones down for their naps. I stop to say hello to Mrs. B's, pick up the water bottles, then make my way to the Nest where Clydeen is anxiously awaiting my arrival.

After lunch and a couple of hands of rummy, I open my bag and pull out *Cherrie Ames*. "Ta-da!" I sing out, showing her the cover of the book with a close-up of a red-cheeked young woman with dark curly hair gazing off into a distant sky.

Cherrie is dressed in her student nurse's uniform, a blue and white striped short-sleeved dress covered by a starched white pinafore. Her dark curly hair is haloed by a crisp white cap with a narrow black band.

"What's that?" asks Clydeen.

"It's only my favorite book of all time, Clydeen. This is about a girl named Cherrie Ames and her adventures as a student nurse. That's what I'm going to do some day—go to nursing school and become a nurse just like Cherrie. Anyway, I thought maybe we could read it together, 'cause I think you're gonna love it."

"Okay," she says without much enthusiasm.

"So what do you want to be when you grow up, Clydeen?"

"I wanna play music."

"Really? Is that a real job?"

"Don't know, but that be what I want. I used to have my daddy's fiddle. Learned to play it some. But I lef' it someplace, and now I don't have it no mo'."

"There's an old fiddle down in our basement, Clydeen. Stanley used to play it, or at least he says he did. I'm gonna get it for you."

"For real?" she asks perking up again.

"Sure, why not. He'll never miss it."

"Well, that be right nice a you, Miss Annie," she says, grinning from ear to ear. "I be lookin' forward to that."

"You look tired, Clydeen. Why don't you lie down on the cot and I'll read to you."

"Okay," she agrees.

I take a seat nearby with my back against the sidewall near the front of the cave where there's enough light. I pull my knees up, prop Cherrie Ames against them and begin.

Clydeen tolerates the first few pages with sleepy-eyed amusement until I get to the part where Cherrie is taking a last long look around her room at home before going away to nursing school.

At the window, crisp white ruffled curtains were gracefully looped back with red ribbon. Her little dressing table wore white dotted swiss skirts and saucy red bows. The oval hooked rug was one her great-grandmother had made. Her bookshelf held the books she had carried to school and now was leaving behind.

"Is that what your room look like?" Clydeen bursts out.

"Clydeen," I say, annoyed by the interruption just as I am getting into the story, "this here's my room. The Nest. Up here, with you. At home, I live in a baby's room. Most of the time, I'm not even allowed in there. So no, it's not what my room looks like."

"Well, what kind of curtains you got?"

"No curtains yet."

"What about a dressing table. What's that?"

"I don't have one, but Vivian does. It's a thing with drawers and a big mirror. It has a bench. She sits on the bench so she can look in the mirror while she combs her hair and puts on her lipstick."

"Oh," she says, apparently satisfied.

I continue. Cherrie gets to the railroad station and is about to board the train that will take her into her new life. Her father shows up to say goodbye, and Cherrie says, "'Thought you were so busy with your real estate you wouldn't have time for me!'"

"What's real estate?" Clydeen breaks in again.

"Property. You know, land, houses and such. Like down below where they're building those houses, that's real estate."

"Is that like your daddy?"

"A little, I suppose, but mine works for the telephone company downtown. He does dress up in a suit and tie like that when he goes to work," I say holding up the book so she can see the picture of Cherrie's dad.

"Ummm," she muses. "This a story 'bout some rich white girl, ain't it."

"What? No!"

Honestly, this has never crossed my mind before, and suddenly I wonder: Would someone like Clydeen be welcome at Cherrie's nursing school, or would she be rejected because of her dark skin, or maybe just because she's poor? I don't say anything about this to Clydeen, though. Instead, I keep reading, and soon I get to the part where Cherrie describes her new room at school.

It was a darling room, small, but complete and attractive, and all hers. A maple day bed with a luxuriously good mattress, a chest of drawers with a mirror, and a desk, also in maple, were arranged against the pale green walls. Couch cover and matching curtains were of gay chintz. Two chairs looked inviting—

"What's chintz?"

"It's a kind of cloth, I think." I show her the picture of the flowery print fabric draped over the furniture in Cherrie's new room.

"Damn! They give that white girl all a that just for goin' to they fancy school? I be goin' there if I could get a nice room like that. Me'n my mama, we ain't never had nothin' good as that."

I try unsuccessfully to wipe the look of surprise off my face, and again, I don't know what to say, so I just go on reading. The third time I come to a passage referring to Cherrie's rosy cheeks, a loud guffaw emanates from inside the sleeping bag which is now fully covering Clydeen from the top of her head to the tip of her toes.

"What?" I say irritably.

"This your fav'rit book?"

"Well, I guess it was. Maybe not so much now, 'cause I'm older."

She snickers.

"Just listen, Clydeen. We haven't gotten to the good parts yet."

"Oh, I can just imagine," she hoots.

"This isn't gonna work for you, is it?" I sigh, closing the book.

"Prob'ly not."

"Okay, okay. I'll tell you what. I am gonna ask Mrs. B if there's a library around here. If I can find someone to take me, I'll see if the librarian can find something more to your liking. What do you say to that?"

She pops out of the sleeping bag, sits on the edge of the cot, and says, "That would be jus' fine with me. Bound to be better'n this crap."

I'm shocked by her reaction and maybe a little insulted, but when I look at her, I can't help it. She can't, either. We both burst out laughing.

Part 2

Part 2

Chapter 13
Eva

It's only nine o'clock in the morning, but the temperature is already creeping toward 90 degrees. Out near the barn, Zeke is giving me a bit of a run for my money, and I am so intent on trying to corner him, it startles me when Rocky gives a welcoming bark as Annie rides up. I straighten up and squint into the bright morning sun where I see Annie leaning over the fence, giving Rocky a scratch behind the ears.

"Oh, Annie, child. Come on in."

She wheels her bike around to the front and enters the yard through the gate. Rocky runs around to the side of the house to meet her. She stoops to give him more pets, and he licks her face, his tail wagging and his rear end wiggling with excitement.

"Is that a violin case you have there, my girl?" I ask, taking in the contents of her basket.

"Uhhh ... yeah."

"Do you play the violin?"

Well, no, not yet, but I might start," she says, turning away and walking rapidly to the backyard.

"Well, good for you," I say laughing, and then I let the matter drop. "So what's going on today, Annie? You're early."

"Well, let's see. My mother took the kids downtown to the doctor for checkups and some kind of booster shots. She left me home so I could bring the milk in after the milkman came because it's so hot today. He came, I put the milk away, and so here I am, getting an early start."

"You couldn't have come at a better time, my dear. Maybe you could give me a hand. Zeke seems to have gotten tangled up in some barbed wire and cut his leg all up. The old grouch won't let me get close enough to take care of it,"

"Sure thing. What do you want me to do?"

"Let's corner him first, and once we get ahold of him, I want you to straddle him like a horse. When you feel balanced, just grab his horns and hold him steady. He might buck a little, but just hang on. That will give me a chance to clean those cuts and put some ointment on them."

Once Zeke is restrained, he quiets, and I am able to take care of his wounds without further difficulty. When we release him, he heads for the pasture, charging and bucking to let us know exactly how unhappy we've made him. Annie and I look at one another, shake our heads and laugh. Once Zeke settles down and starts to graze, we go indoors to cool off.

"I made a lemon sponge cake last night. How does that sound?"

"Oh, my grandma makes that. I love it!"

Sipping cold glasses of lemonade, we make our way to the living room. I take my usual place in the old rocker, while Annie, as she has many times before, wanders around, studying my collection of small bronze statues from various religious traditions and examining the photographs displayed on the broad brick fireplace mantle.

"I've been meaning to ask you, Mrs. B—who's this?" she asks, pointing to a small black and white photograph of a smiling teenage boy with sparkling eyes set in a silver heart-shaped frame.

"That's my son."

"Your son? You have a son?" she asks with surprise.

I laugh. "Why, yes, I do. Is that so hard to believe?"

"Well no, I guess not, but you've never said anything about him."

"Probably not," I sigh.

"What's his name?"

"Oh, my. His name is Jesse Ulysses Borsheim. I named him Jesse, which means 'gift,' because the mister and I had given up hope of ever having a child when he came along. His dad gave him his middle name. Jesse never stuck, and we ended up calling him Ulie—

short for Ulysses."

I gaze off into the middle distance for a moment, remembering. "He was named after General Ulysses S. Grant."

"Who's that?"

I look down, arrange my face and smooth away the grief before I go on. "Oh, Annie, I wish you could have met my Maury. He would have loved your inquisitive mind and your bright spirit."

"Uh-huh," she says uncertainly.

"Maury was an enigma."

"A what?"

"A puzzlement, I guess you could say. If you were to meet him by day, you would have met a farmer in faded overalls and boots covered with mud, a simple man who loved working the land. But by night, he was a scholar, an immigrant who wanted to learn everything he could about this country and its history. He was particularly fascinated by slavery and the history of the Civil War. Ulysses S. Grant, Ulie's namesake, was the general who led the Union troops to victory. Later, he was elected president of the United States—the eighteenth, if I'm not mistaken."

"Oh, yeah! That's where I've heard that name before. In fifth grade, we had to memorize the names of the presidents in order.

"So how old is Ulie?" she asks me, studying the photograph.

"That picture was taken when he was about your age. But he's in his twenties now."

"Where does he live?"

"Ah, well. That's just it. I'm not sure where he is, sweetheart. He disappeared during the war."

Annie stares at me, not at all satisfied with my answer, so I go on.

"Our Ulie turned out to be an intense, artistic boy, a dreamer. Very different from his father and me. Where he got all of that, I have no idea," I chuckle softly.

My heart squeezes as I think of my precious free-spirited boy. I pause and put my hand on my chest to steady myself for a moment before I continue.

"Anyway, when he was only 16, he got it into his head that he wanted to go abroad to study art. He never had gotten along very well in school. From day one, he didn't fit in, and he didn't see any reason to try, either. By the time he was in his teens, instead of studying and making friends with kids his own age, he spent his time alone, drawing and sculpting. Painting huge colorful murals. Camping out by himself. Not much help to his dad and me, that's for sure!" I laugh.

"There was never any question about his talent, though. It was obvious he had a gift. See that sculpture over there by the fireplace? He made that with the help of his dad, who showed him how to use chisels and taught him to weld."

Annie turns and studies the wood and metal figure of a prancing deer that sits on one side of the fireplace. "That's Ulie's? He made that?"

"Yes. I have more out in the barn, but that deer is my favorite. It keeps me in touch with him somehow. He made it when he was just 13 years old, if I remember right."

"My age. So did he go abroad?"

"Yes, he certainly did."

"And then what happened?"

I gaze out the window on the south side of the house. The sun blazes, and waves of heat shimmer in the stillness of the day. It's so hot even the birds have gone silent. Annie is looking at me with raised eyebrows, her lips slightly parted, expecting me to go on, but I'm wondering whether I really want to have this conversation.

"Okay," I say, leaning forward in the rocker, taking some deep breaths before I speak. "When Ulie wanted to go abroad to school, I didn't want to let him go. I thought he was too young, but the mister said at the rate Ulie was going, he was never going to be a proper farmer anyway. We used to laugh about it sometimes, cry about it other times. He said trying to keep Ulie here was just going to make him unhappy—or worse. Maury had been a bit of a wild boy himself. He stowed away on a tramp steamer and made his way from Norway to the United States when he was 16 years old, so he saw the whole thing from a very different point of view than I did. He thought we should give Ulie our support and let him go if that's what he wanted.

"'It's not always the worst thing to get what you want,' Maury told me.

"I couldn't argue with that. Eventually, the two of them

convinced me that my fears were exaggerated and Ulie would be fine. After all, he would only be away for two years.

"He wanted to go to France, but we settled on England for two reasons. Hitler's rise to power in Germany was disconcerting, and Ulie didn't speak a word of French. We were fortunate enough to find a private arts academy outside of London where we could afford to send Ulie if we were careful, and our crops were good. The idea that Great Britain would declare war on Germany before Ulie returned home was unthinkable.

"Ulie was so excited. He said it was exactly the kind of place he needed to develop his talents, and so we let him go. Biggest mistake of our lives, Annie."

"You mean because of the war? I barely remember anything about it."

"Not surprising, my dear. You're too young. It was a war between Germany and its allies, Italy and Russia, on one side, and a number of western European countries on the other. At least, that's how it started out when Hitler began rolling his tanks across Europe, conquering country after country. The United States was slow to get involved, but after years of fighting and millions of deaths overseas, we finally woke up and realized that if England were to fall into German hands, America would likely be next."

"So what about Ulie?"

"Well, he did well in England. For a while there, I thought his father had been right. He wrote long letters full of news about his school, his friends, and his teachers. Most of his letters included funny drawings depicting something that had happened in the dining hall or out on the soccer field. He couldn't have been happier. But when Hitler set his sights on Great Britain, after capturing a number of other European nations, including France, everything changed."

I go to the bookshelf and pull down an atlas, opening it to a map of Europe and the British Isles. I point to where Ulie was living.

"Here, you see, France is just a short distance across this body of water called the English Channel. England was in grave danger, and the country turned all of its resources to fighting a war against an enemy intent on destroying it.

"Ulie's school closed sometime during 1940. We're not sure

exactly when. We tried desperately to locate our son to tell him we had wired money for him to come home. We sent telegram after telegram but neither the telegrams nor the money were ever picked up. Eventually, two months after the air attacks on London began, we received one short wire."

I go to my desk, open the top drawer and hand Annie the thin, yellowed sheet of paper dated November 5, 1940.

"'School closed STOP. Going to France to help out STOP. Love you both, Ulie STOP,'" Annie reads aloud, then hands the telegram back.

"So how did he get across the English Channel?" she asks, pointing to the map in the atlas.

"We don't know. But a few weeks later, a letter arrived from Paris. He tried to reassure us, but we had been following the situation carefully and knew that wherever he was, he was in the belly of the beast, so to speak. We were frantic with worry, and to this day, we have not heard another word. His father died not knowing what happened to him."

"Wow," breathes Annie softly. "That is so sad."

"I still don't know if he's dead or alive. I don't know if he was arrested or simply went into hiding. He may have gotten involved with the people in France who were resisting the German occupation. Ulie was a free spirit, and it would be just like him to do something crazy like that. I do know that many people are still being held in what they call displaced persons camps in Europe. That's where people who don't have proper identification papers are waiting to get sorted out so they can go home. I pray to God he's alive in one of those camps. Maury felt terrible about having been so offhanded about letting him go, but I didn't blame him then, and I don't blame him now. It was the war. Nothing more."

After a long pause, when the only sound is the clock ticking on the mantle, Annie comes and kneels by my chair. She takes my hand in her smaller ones, and when she looks up, tears glisten on her long dark lashes.

"I knew there was a war, Mrs. B, but it didn't seem real. To me, it was just something to be mad about when my Saturday morning radio programs were cancelled on account of men making loud speeches. Or those boring newsreels at the Saturday afternoon movies before Superman started. Who cared? I would just walk out to the lobby to buy myself some Necco wafers or something. Oh ... and all the fun my friend and I had playing with the things her brother gave us after he came home from the war—helmets and ammo belts and stuff. I never thought about how lucky he was to be alive and back home in one piece. I'm a dope, I guess."

"No, Annie. Not at all. You were very young, much too young to understand what was happening, and I'm sure your parents wanted to keep it that way."

"So how will you find him?"

"By not giving up, for one thing. I write to congressmen, the governor, the Red Cross, talk to lawyers, anyone I can think of who might be able to help. I even wrote to the president. So far, nothing has turned up one way or the other. My worst fear is that the Germans got hold of him and threw him in one of their concentration camps in Poland or somewhere."

"What's that?" she asks me, sitting cross-legged on the floor in front of my rocking chair.

"What's what?"

"You said concentration camps. What's that?"

"You're a child, my darling. You don't need to be thinking about things like that," realizing too late I never should have mentioned it.

"Tell me. I want to know. I'm not a baby! I'm starting high school this year," she insists.

How can I explain the horror of the camps to this innocent child? Is it my place to expose her to something so dreadful? I think it's time to wind up this conversation and go make some lunch instead. But she's sitting up very straight, her brown eyes wide, watching me, waiting for me to explain.

"Really, Annie. I don't know if this is something I should be talking to you about."

"Mrs. B, c'mon. Please. Just tell me. You're the only adult I know that doesn't talk to me like I'm some stupid kid. That's why I like to come over here so much. So tell me. I *want* to know the rest of it— the rest of what you think might have happened to Ulie."

"Oh, Annie, alright. But this is going to be hard to hear."

"I'm ready, Mrs. B. Just tell me."

So I do. I tell her about Nazi Germany, about the camps, the millions of people gassed, starved and worked to death, sparing as many of the more shocking details as possible. I try to explain the unexplainable, but sugarcoating only takes me so far, and before long, I am sitting on the floor with her, and we are crying in one another's arms, our hearts having burst open with grief. I grieve for my lost son, yes. But I also grieve for the warriors wounded and killed, the civilians whose lives were destroyed, the Jews, some of them relatives of my husband possibly, and others, many of whom were betrayed by their own countrymen and subsequently perished in the camps. I'm terrified my own eccentric boy might have become one of them.

When we recover, we sit silently for a long time. The clock continues its insistent tick-tock.

At last, Annie rises and says, "I'd better go, Mrs. B. I need to take that water."

We go outside, and I help her tuck two bottles of water into her bike basket.

"Wait just a minute, Annie."

I run back into the house and retrieve a brown bag with a few cans of tuna and vegetables and place it on top of everything else. I don't know what she's doing with all of the stuff she carries day in and day out, but her intense earnestness reminds me of Ulie and moves me to want to help with whatever it is she's up to.

Her eyes sparkle as she takes a look at the contents of the bag.

"Thank you so much, Mrs. B!" she says and pulls me in for a hug.

I take comfort in spite of myself, ashamed of the loneliness that makes it so welcome.

"Can you manage?" I ask, eyeing the basket, which is now so full she must clutch the violin case in one hand while she steers the bike.

"I'll manage," she says, and pedals off, the load making her a little wobbly at first.

I stand in the road and watch until she turns the corner and disappears from view. Back in the house, I plan to spend the rest of the day writing letters to more agencies that might be able to help me find my son. For a long time, I stare at the blank sheets of paper on my desk and worry about the conversation with Annie. I hope I have not overstepped and placed a burden on a young soul not yet prepared to handle it.

"Forgive me if I have," I sigh as I turn my attention to the task at hand.

Chapter 14
Clydeen

I'm feeling a little sad and lonely today. I think 'bout my mama, wonder how she doin', if she gonna come find me soon. I think 'bout my cousins back in Texas. Them boys used to drive me crazy, but now I miss 'em. They'd love it here. My girl cousins? Maybe not so much. I think 'bout Auntie Henrietta, a lady at our church who worked all year to make Easter hats for all the women outta every scrap she could git her hands on. I think about my friend Deja. We's born on the same day. And a course I think 'bout Daddy. Will I see him agin when I gits to heaven one day? I sure hope so, 'cause I miss him sumpthin' awful.

Annie, she ain't comin' today. Tha's why I got all this time on my hands. Time to fret and remember and wish. She brought me her daddy's fiddle, though, and I spend an hour tryin' to remember how to play. Ain't much use though. The strings is old and brittle, and pretty soon, they's only one lef' that ain't broke.

I decides to wander down behind the big rock where Annie and me likes to sit in the shade, but bein' in our spot ain't no good without her there, so I roam farther out into the trees. After a time, I come to a big ol' fallen log and sit down on it for a minute to rest. That's when I hear some critter makin' a squeakin' sound. I go to one end of the log where it be hollowed out some and peer in. I can still hear the squeak, but it ain't comin' from in there.

Hmmm. Mus' be the other end.

Sho 'nuff, when I looks into the other end of the log they's a tiny

94

critter sittin' there in the hollowed-out space jus' a' squeakin' and a shakin'. I'm afraid he'll bite me if I reach for him. But he seems so upset, I take off my shirt, cover my hand and shove it into the log so I can stroke his little back. He quiets down, but he still tremblin'. After a time, I take ahold a him and pull him outta the log. A baby squirrel, and he fits right in the palm of my hand. His fur messed up, but otherwise, he seems okay. I take him with me and head back to our Nest, where I have some sunflower seeds and water, too. I talk to him real soft so's I don't scare him.

He don't eat at first. He jus' sit there lookin' at me, still shakin' in his boots. I go 'bout my bidniss and pay him no mind, and pretty soon, he picks up one a them sunflower seeds. He sits back on his haunches and twiches his little black nose, holdin' the sunflower seed real careful between his two front paws. He cracks that seed, eats it, then goes for another, and another. He's so cute, I can't take my eyes off a him. When he done eatin' his fill, I offer him a drink from one a the milk bottle caps, and he drinks a little water, too.

When I pick him up, his furry little body is warm, and it feels real good to hold him close. He sits on my lap for a while, and then crawls up between the two shirts I have on and hangs there.

"Now what I s'posed to do?" I laugh.

After a while, I pull him out and set him on this rickety orange crate we got and look at him eye to eye.

"So what's your name, little fella?"

He stares at me, his tiny jaws workin' and his nose twitchin'.

"Hmmm. Gary you say? Yo' name Gary? Okay, then, that's what I'mma call you, but right now, I got some chores to do."

He hangs around with me for the rest of the day, and he don't never try to bite me, neither. That night, I use a towel to make him a bed on the floor of the cave right next to my cot. Course I don't 'spect him to be there in the mornin', but when I wake up early to check, sho 'nuff, he still there, and I'm right glad to see him, too.

"Annie gonna love you!" I tell him.

I pick him up and settle him on my chest, and the comfort a his little body on mine feels so good, it puts us both right back to sleep.

Chapter 15
Vivian

It's Sunday evening, and Annie and I are busy fixing a light supper. Stanley and the boys are out back, and Teresa has fallen asleep on the living room floor. I'm enjoying a rare moment of calm in the house when out of the blue, Annie asks me if I've ever heard of the Nazis.

"Well, yes, Annie, I have, but where did you ...?"

"I read about it," she says, shrugging her shoulders. "In some old newspapers downstairs when we were unpacking."

I sit down at the table with my highball and an ashtray. Annie sits down too. I take a drag off my cigarette and squint at her as smoke drifts toward the ceiling.

"So, Mom? I want to know what you think. About what the Nazis did. About all of the people who were starved and gassed, the children murdered for no reason. Did you know about that?"

Did I know? When did I know? I can't really recall. Instead of trying to come up with something, I sit back, take a sip of my drink and gaze at this daughter of mine, who now wants answers to such probing questions. This is not the kind of thing we talk about in this household.

"Well, for one thing, I think you're too young to be thinking about stuff like that," I say, but she ignores me and goes right on asking me questions.

"Why didn't America do something?"

"America did do something, Annie. We went to war and won,"

I declare, puffing up a bit as I deliver the good news. "And now it's over. End of story, nothing for you to worry about."

"Really," she muses, as if she has a different opinion. "Did Dad fight in the war?"

"No, he didn't."

"Why not?"

"Because he works for the telephone company, and telephone and telegraph communications were essential to the war effort, so he got to stay here at home."

I get up from the table, stir the green beans, crack some eggs into a bowl, and check to see if the potatoes are done.

"That's enough about that, Annie. There are no more Nazis, and we need to get dinner ready now. Go find your brothers and tell them to wash their hands, will you please?"

"That's it?" she says, giving me a disappointed look.

"Yes. That's all I can tell you, and it's time for supper."

A short time later, we're gathered around the dinner table. I keep my eye on Annie, watch as she cuts her cheese omelet into tiny triangles and lines them up around the edge of her plate. She has shoved her buttered potatoes into the middle of the circle and mixes in the green beans. She moves the food around but does not eat. She looks like her mind is a million miles away.

In that moment, I realize how much Annie has changed in just these past few weeks. Maybe I should have kept the conversation going. But I don't understand why she wants to talk about something so awful when everyone's trying to forget the war and get on with having a nice life.

She sighs and crams a few of the triangles into her mouth, then resumes moving the food around on her plate.

"I'm not very hungry tonight," she says a moment later. "May I please be excused?"

Stanley and I look at each other.

"You're excused, but you know the rule," he says.

"Again?"

"You can clean your plate now or tomorrow morning. Your choice."

"I choose tomorrow," she says as she tosses her napkin on the table and walks out the door.

Chapter 16
Annie

I've done it again, and it's times like these when I really miss Pepper. He would've taken care of this cold breakfast situation for me in a flash! But he's not here, and I'm left to choke it down on my own.

When I finish, I go looking for Vivian.

"Mom, I have an appointment with Mrs. B this morning. She's gonna teach me to milk the goats. I'm supposed to be there around 8:30, so I need to go early today."

I say this in an offhanded way, trying to convey the message that this is no big deal.

But she's paying closer attention than usual, and she trails after me as I walk away.

"Annie, wait," she says.

I stop, turn around. "What?"

"Why?" she asks, showing me the palms of her hands.

"Why what?"

"Why is she teaching you to milk her goats?"

"So I can take care of them when she needs to be away for some reason. She's going to pay me a dollar for each milking and three dollars a day if I take care of Rocky and the chickens, too."

"Well ..." she says skeptically.

"Mom, I need to go early this one time," I proclaim breezily, "but I'll be back this afternoon by the time Teresa gets up from her nap, okay? Whatever you need me to do, I'll take care of it then."

I smile and nod, looking Vivian straight in the eye, my lying

98

ways second nature to me now.

In my own defense, though, what I have said is not entirely untrue. Mrs. B *is* going to teach me, just not today. What I am really trying to do is wheedle some extra time with Clydeen so I can talk to her about my birthday next week. I have a fantastic idea. I'm not sure she'll go for it, but I'm determined to talk her into it no matter how long it takes.

Vivian pulls a red pack of Pall Malls from her apron pocket, lights one, and stares out the window at the clouds of gray-brown dust kicked up by the bulldozers crawling like insects around the construction zone. Her shoulders droop, and she looks sad.

Turning to me, she says, "Okay, Annie. I guess I don't really need you this morning, so go on."

"Thanks, Mom!" I say, shamelessly sucking up like she's just handed me a hundred bucks.

When Vivian goes to check on Charlie, who is taking a bath after wading in mud up to his knees—already this morning!—I pour a thermos of milk for Clydeen and get ready to head out.

Something to drink is all I need from the kitchen today. My secret life weighs on me, and the fear of someone getting in my way is always in the back of my mind. I try to be smart about what I'm doing. When Vivian started to complain about running out of bread before the Rainbo deliveryman comes on Wednesdays, I stopped making so many sandwiches. Instead, I have built up a stash of canned goods in my hiding place in the basement, and that, plus Mrs. B's contributions, is enough to keep my nerves calm and Clydeen well fed.

"Clydeen? Clydeen?" I call out a half hour later, breathing hard as I reach the top of the steep slope. I drop the load I'm carrying and find her sound asleep, wrapped in her sleeping bag.

"C'mon lazybones. Get up!" I shout.

"Holy crap! What you tryin' to do, scare me to death?"

She jumps up, pulling the sleeping bag along with her. She's holding something.

"What you doin' here so early anyway? You're scaring Gary!"

"Who?"

"Gary! Right here. This little guy," she says, holding him out to me cupped in both hands.

"He's shaking."

"Well, yeah. Course he is, with you makin' all a that racket!"

"Where'd you get him?"

"Found him in a hollow log down there in the woods a ways from the big rock."

"So his name is Gary? Strange name for a squirrel. How'd you come up with that?"

"He tol' me what it was," she says, looking off in the distance. The corners of her mouth quiver a little; she's trying hard to keep from laughing.

"You liar! Can I pet him?"

"Well, I don't know. Let me axe him."

She raises Gary up to eye level, and asks him if I can pet him, then she moves him around to one ear and pretends to listen to his answer. I stand there watching with my hands on my hips, my shoulders shaking with laughter. Clydeen likes nothing better than to put on a show like this.

"Okay," she says after a minute or so. "He say it be okay for you to pet him."

"Does he bite?"

"Ain't bit me yet, so I guess not."

I reach out carefully and stroke Gary down his back with two fingers "Soft. Whatcha gonna do with him?"

"I don't know. Keep him, I guess. Course he be free to go, but he don't seem to want to."

"What does he eat?"

"C'mon, I'll show you."

She goes to the lunch bucket and pulls out the sunflower seeds and scatters a few on the ground. Gary's not a bit shy. He starts eating them right away, and I sit and watch him while Clydeen goes to get him some water.

"How cute is that, Clydeen?"

"Ain't it?"

After Gary eats, Clydeen picks him up, and he works his way up under her shirt.

She shrugs. "He like to ride around like this," she tells me. "Course now I have to wear two shirts so he don't scratch me."

She pulls up the outside shirt to show me how the baby squirrel clings to her like she's a tree trunk.

"Wow! I think that little guy's in love with you."

"Yas," she laughs, stretching out the neck of her shirt to peer down at the baby squirrel. "But what you doin' here so early, Annie? Not that I ain't glad to see you ..."

"Oh. I almost forgot in all the excitement of meeting Gary. I want to talk to you about my birthday next week."

"Yo' birthday."

"Yeah, my birthday. I'm finally gonna be 14 like you, and I have a plan."

"Okay. But first, what you brung me to eat? I'm starvin'."

"I brought tuna fish and baked beans, some carrots, milk, and that jug of water over there. How's that sound?"

"Sound good to me. Here, you hold Gary while I go tend to my bidniss, and then while I'm eatin' you can tell me all 'bout yo' big plan."

When she returns, I get the can opener and a spoon and hand them to her. We settle ourselves side-by-side making a table out of the orange crate, the same one Stanley sat on the day he took me to the basement.

"So what's goin' on, Miss Annie," she asks, her words muffled by the cracker topped with tuna fish she just stuffed into her mouth.

"Okay. Here's it is," I say, clearing my throat.

I'm finding it hard to spit the words out. What if she says no? I pause and look down at my hands. I'm so nervous my ten fingers flutter like hummingbirds. I grab one hand with the other and stick both of them between my thighs.

"Please don't say no. Just hear me out, okay?"

"A'ight."

"I'm having a birthday party, and I want you to come."

"What you talkin' 'bout?"

"It's gonna be at Mrs. B's house, Clydeen. It will be fine. I want you to meet her. We'll have cake, cold lemonade—a celebration. C'mon, please?"

"Are you insane, girl?" she shouts, jumping up and nearly pitching the can of beans onto the ground. Poor Gary! She almost dumps him on the ground along with the beans.

"Calm down! You said you'd hear me out."

"Well, I didn't know you's gonna say sumpthin' so crazy! How can I explain this to you? A girl with skin the color a mine don't jus' go here, go there without thinkin' what might happen. I 'specially ain't goin' to no white lady house, with or without you! What you think she gonna do, you drag some colored girl to her doorstep? If you think she gonna invite me in, sit me down in her fancy house and give me some cake, yo' outta yo' mind!" she yells.

"That's exactly what I think!"

"More'n likely she call the po-lice,"she snorts. "What's it gonna take for you to understand this? You scared a how yo' daddy gonna react if he sees me? Well, what about when the shoe's on the other foot? How scary you think sumpthin' like that be for me? Huh?"

"But, Clydeen, not everybody is like Stanley. Mrs. B's ..."

"How do you know? You axed her? You tol' her 'bout me?"

"No! I haven't told her anything about you."

"So I'mma be the birthday surprise, huh? Underage Negro girl showin' up jus' like that on yo' say-so? Great. Tha's jus' great. Girl, you really got yo' head up yo' ass on this one."

"Clydeen. Think for a minute. Wouldn't you like to have a hot bath, wash your hair? You could do that at Mrs. B's. I know her, and I know she would welcome you, 'cause that's the kind of person she is."

"Says you. You don't know shit, Annie, so stop talkin' nonsense. I ain't goin'!"

I'm so mad, I get right in her face.

"What about your nonsense, Clydeen? Here's something I've been wondering about. How in the world do you expect you and your mother to find each other? If you even have a mother, that is, or is that something you made up instead of telling me the truth about what's really going on?"

We lean in, square off, eyes flashing. Gary is sitting on the ground quivering, looking from one of us to the other, like he wishes he were big enough to push us apart.

"You hush!" screams Clydeen. "Course I have a mother!"

"Well, then, why aren't you with her? Where is she? I'm not stupid, you know. You didn't wind up way out here because you decided to take a bus ride one day. So tell me the rest of the story. Where is your mother? Why are you hiding up here? 'Cause I don't understand, and you owe me an explanation!"

"The hell I do! I don't owe you nothin', white girl."

She storms off and starts down the wash.

"Clydeen, wait! Wait! Where are you going?"

"I'm tryin' to git away from you! Ouch!" she cries as the rocks penetrate her thin, worn-out shoes.

"Come on back. Please. You left Gary."

No response.

"Okay then, I'm outta here!" I yell.

I gather up my stuff and follow her down the wash. I know where she is, but I don't go there. Instead, I go all the way down, hop on my bike and pedal home as hard and fast as I can. Tears are streaming down my face all the way home, blurring my vision and blowing into my ears.

Chapter 17
Clydeen

It's the worst argument we's ever had, and I don't 'spect she'll be comin' back. I lay up in my sleepin' bag all night cryin', prayin' to Jesus and tryin' to sort out what happened this afternoon. We jus' don't understand each other, the worlds we come from, is all. I'm sorry for some a the things I said to her. Even sorrier I'll prob'ly never see her again so's I can apologize.

"Please, Jesus," I pray into the darkness, raisin' both arms toward the heavens. "I don't know another livin' soul in this here North, 'cept Annie, and I ain't ready to leave her yet, unless Mama come for me. But I 'specially don't wanna go like this, with or without Mama, after what happened b'tween me'n Annie today!"

I hope Jesus listenin', 'cause I axe him to give me a sign, show me what I'm s'posed to do next. That be a big axe, and I know from experience I can't expect a answer right away. He got to think on it awhile.

In the meantime, my thoughts wander back to the good times me'n Annie been havin' together all summer and how much I'mma miss her if she don't come back. *Maybe she layin' up in her bed right now thinkin' 'bout me the same way I am 'bout her. Or maybe she's jus' done with me and I'll never see her agin. Guess I'll know soon enough.*

If she do come back, though, I'mma apologize, cut her some slack. It ain't her fault she don't know nothin' 'bout how it is for me, b'cause—she right about this—I ain't tol' her nothin'. I don't know

104

what a person like her gonna think if I tell her a story like mine, and I don't want her judgin' me. It be tiresome tryin' to explain how threatening white peoples are to colored folks, but maybe I do owe it to Annie to try.

Besides, don't I a'ready feel judged? 'Cause she makes assumptions 'bout me that ain't necessarily true. Can't blame her for that, though. When peoples don't know, they fill in the blanks. I reckon they's a difference b'tween ignorance and judgment. Finally, I settle on it. If she come back, I'mma talk to her, see what happens.

Next thing I know, the sun is high in the sky, and I hear them water bottles clankin' together. I jump outta the bed and stumble out in my bare feet to see if tha's her comin'. It is!

"Annie," I say, burstin' into tears. "I thought you'd never come back after I got so mad."

"Oh, c'mon, Clydeen. You weren't the only one to lose it yesterday. You think I'd never come back, just because we had a fight?"

"Uhhh ... I thought maybe, yas."

"I hardly slept all night thinking about you. I'm sorry, and I won't push you like that again."

She sets down the water bottles and pulls me close, wiping my tears away with her thumbs.

"So we good now?"

"We're good, Clydeen. Get your shoes on. I'll get our lunch."

"Okay. And then I got some things I wanna tell you."

****

And so at last I begin.

"My mama, she called Beth Hollifield. Her real name Bethany, but everybody call her Beth. My daddy, he was James Hollifield. My mama call me Baby, and she tol' me the story of my birth 'bout a million times. How she lift me up naked to the full moon and whispered my name to me, not Baby, mind you, but my real name, Clydeen. Is it a true story or jus' her imaginins? I don't know, but I like the story anyhow. It makes me feel like there was a time she loved me best.

"That was my beginnin'. We's livin' in Texas back then, and it took a while for things to go sour. My daddy was a sharecropper, and my mama, she helped out in the fields and in the kitchen where the peoples who own the land live. When havest time come 'round, they both work hard in the fields to bring in e'nuff cotton to make some money. We got by, too, till my daddy got hisself killed."

"Your father got killed, Clydeen? How?"

"Some white men murdered him."

"Why?"

I laugh bitterly.

"What, you think they need a reason? But I don't wanna go into it right now."

"Okay," she say, lookin' confused and upset.

"I'll tell you about it one day. Right now, I want to give you the answer to your question: how I come to be here."

She nods, and I continue with my story.

"Anyway, after Daddy gone, Mama jus' folded up on herself, started talkin' nonsense, starin' out the window or sittin' on the porch drinkin' and cussin' 'stead a goin' to work. The folks at the Redeemer Baptist Church tried to help us, but Mama, she'd run 'em off. Finally, they gave up, jus' lef' us alone. Same with my daddy's people, his brothers, my aunts, and cousins. Once my daddy was gone, Mama didn't want nothin' to do with any of them, neither. Like it was their fault Daddy gone, which it weren't.

"So by the time we lef' to come up here, I was lookin' after Mama and had lost touch with near everybody close to me. I didn't have no brothers and sisters, but I had a bunch a cousins I been raised with. They didn't come 'round no mo', and neither did my uncles, Noah and Ike or my aunties, Corrine and Grace. Not to mention all a those other 'uncles and aunties' from the church, who knew me my whole life. Missin' all a them pains me so much, sometimes it actually hurts me right in here," I say, tapping a spot b'low my ribs with my fist. "They all drifted away 'cause a Mama actin' so mean to anybody wantin' to help us out. So it ain't jus' Mama I'm missin'. It's all the folks back home, too."

"That's a lot of hurt, Clydeen."

I clear my throat and take a breath. It is a lot a hurt, and I'mma 'bout to cry, so I axe Annie to get me a drink a water. If my uncles knew what was happenin' to me now, would they come git me? I'll tell you one thing. If I could blink my eyes and fly back there right now, I'd do it in heartbeat, even if I had to go without Mama. But maybe not. How many of them people are still there? How many have been evicted and sent packin' by now? This thought had not occurred to me b'fo, but now that it has, it makes me feel even more lost.

"Thanks, Annie," I say when she hand me the water. I drink, wait a few beats, and then I go on.

"Finally, me and Mama got to the point we's near starvin' to death. I begged Mama to let folks give us some help, but she say she couldn't stand them people no mo', and we'd best be goin'. The owner of the property was buyin' these new machines for pickin' cotton, and sharecroppers was bein' evicted left and right anyhow.

"Once she got the idea a leavin' in her head, Mama perked up and managed to git it together, say we's goin' to stay with Uncle Oren for a while. We hitched ourselves a ride in the back of pickup with some other colored folks going to San Antonio, another ride to Albuquerque, and then we took a bus from there till finally, we landed on my Uncle Oren's doorstep in Denver. By that time, we's so wore out and hongry, we fell asleep on his front porch waitin' for him to show up. Course he didn't know we's comin'. I didn't find that out till later.

"Oren is my daddy's youngest brother. I'd never met him b'fo, but Mama was countin' on him bein' willin' to take us in. He did for a time, but it weren't long b'fo he took up with some floozie over on 18th Street and say we gotta go. He give us one month's rent, and that was that. Next thing we know, he jus' gone, and we couldn't find him no mo'.

"So Mama and me, we ended up livin' in this cheap hotel room downtown. Mama, she pretty good for a time, takin' in ironin' during the day, workin' at a bar at night. I even started in goin' to school, tryin' to catch up. We's scrapin' by, but then she started slippin', and things got tough agin. She went back to bein' like she was in Texas, and I had to stop goin' to school to keep a eye on her during the day and make sure we both got sumpthin' to eat. I'd go out once in a while, git us what food I could, steal her a pack of cigarettes, and bring her a beer or two.

"At that time, she was still goin' to her job at the bar mos' nights. Then one night, she didn't come home from work. Next mornin', I set out to find her. I took myself down to the bar and waited around outside. Pretty soon, some old colored man come rollin' up the street and started bangin' on the door.

"'Not open yet!' I yelled to git him to stop makin' all that racket.

"'Well after last night, no wonder!' he say, grinin' so's I could see his ugly yellow teeth and smell his nasty breath.

"So I axed him what happen last night.

"'Oh, kid, you don't wanna know,' he say, flappin' his hand at me.

"But I could see he's dyin' to tell me, so I egged him on a little. 'Well, you might as well go on and tell me while you standin' here waitin',' I say to him like it ain't nothin' to me.

"'Okay then,' he say. 'Lemme lay it out for ya. You happen to know that 'ho work here? Jasmine her name?' He lean in real close like he tellin' me a secret or sumpthin.

"'Yeah, I think I seen her around,' I say, all casual like. 'What about her?'

"I don't let on the person he talkin' 'bout be Mama. She use that name Jasmine at the bar, say it make her fancier.

"'Well, she and Pete got into a big argument 'bout how much tips she git for the night. This 'bout 1:30 in the mornin', right around closin' time, and she ...' (He be laughin' so hard by then he can hardly catch his breath, slappin' his knee through his filthy pants) ... 'she jus' went off. She done grabbed a kitchen knife from behind the bar and took off after him. Yes, she do! A couple of us, we tried grabbin' her, but she jus' goin' wild, swingin' that knife around every which way so's we couldn't git nowheres near her.

"'By the time the po-lice got here, she like foamin' at the mouth or sumpthin', real strange, cussin' and screamin'. The po-lice took her down and drug her off, and that be the end of it. But she be off her rocker, I can tell you that. I been knowin' that for a long time!'

"Right then another rummie come wanderin' down the street, and he started puttin' his two cents worth in. 'Yeah, she crazy a'ight,' he say, slappin' the first guy on the back. 'She put on quite a show last night didn't she, my brother?'

"Those two assholes kep' carryin' on, havin' theyselves a good ol' time, snickerin' and slappin' at each other like my po' mama goin' off the deep end be 'bout the mos' entertainin' thing happen to them all year.

"Bout that time, Pete, the owner, he finally showed up. He a fine colored man with a gold front tooth wearin' a snazzy lookin' hat with a red band.

"'What you doin' comin' 'round here,' he axed me, lookin' me up and down.

"'Lookin' for my mama. She didn't come home las' night. Where she at?'

"'Don't know,' he say. 'Po-lice got her.'

"'How do I find her?' I axed him.

"'Don't know that neither,' he say. 'But I'll tell you one thing. She won't be workin' here no mo'.'

"I thought 'bout that, and then I axed him, do he owe her any money?

"'C'mon in, kid,' he say. 'In all of the excitement, I couldn't give her her tips.'

"*I'll bet*, I thought to myself, as I followed him into the bar.

"It stunk sumpthin' awful in there—like whiskey, old cigarette smoke, piss, and sweat. Underneath that, it smelled like pure filth so bad I had to pinch my nose. How my mama stand workin' in that place, I don't know. No wonder she had a fit.

"So Pete, he went to the cash register, pulled out a ten-dollar bill and handed it to me. It was way more'n she'd been bringin' home in tips lately. I jus' stared at it, 'fraid to reach out and take it.

"'Go on. Take it, kid,' he say. 'You's gonna need it.'

"He let me out the backdoor so those lowlifes couldn't take my ten off a me, and I ran fast back to the hotel. I locked the door to our room and put the ten on the windowsill wheres I could see it day and night. I didn't go back to school. I jus' stayed in waitin' for mama. I be careful about how much I eat, 'cause I don't know how long it gonna be b'fo she come back."

Annie sittin' real quiet, listenin', not sayin' nothin', and so after a time, I go on.

"Well ... what happened was, she jus' never showed up. It ain't like I didn't see it comin'. All the pacin', around, the chain smokin', not sleepin', mumblin' to herself, starin' off at nothin'. I noticed the tips fallin' off, and I figured she be shootin' her mouf off at work, gettin' folks all riled up like she do when she gits like that.

"So one day—I lost track a time by then—the electricity cut off, and this itty-bitty ice box we had stopped its rattlin' and started leakin' all over the place. They's a few hot dogs, a half a head of lettuce, a bottle of catsup and a beer in there. Soon's I could, I finished off all the hot dogs raw with some of the catsup so they wouldn't spoil and saved the lettuce and beer. I found some cereal and a few cans a beans in the closet, too.

"Next day, somebody come 'round bangin' on the door, and I jumped 'bout a foot. I grabbed the ten off the windowsill and stuffed it in my pocket, and then I stood stock still till whoever it was give up and went away. I didn't know who it was, but it couldn't be mama, 'cause she have a key.

"I thought I was saved a couple days later when I heard a key rattlin' in the lock. 'She finally back!' I shouted.

"I snatched the ten from the windowsill jus' in case and ran to the door. But it weren't Mama. It was that big ol' white man, the landlord. I almos' fall down to my knees he scared me so bad.

"He jammed his way right on in, wantin' to know where mama at, say she late with the rent agin. I jus' 'bout started to cry 'cause I was missin' her so much by then and still didn't know where she's at. But I didn't cry, and I didn't tell him nothin' neither.

"'The rent is due, young lady, so you better tell her when she gets home,' he say in this mean growly voice.

"He tried the light switch. Nothin' happened.

"'What's goin' on here anyway,' he axed me, lookin' around, starin' at the leaky refrigerator and the lettuce leaves scattered on the bed.

"'My mama, she be back real soon,' was all I could think of to say.

"'When? When will she be back? Today? Tomorrow? When?' His eyes was starin' at me so hard I had to back up a little bit.

"'Soon. Real soon,' I tol' him agin.

"He give me a disgusted look, then he slammed the door and left.

"I couldn't help it, Annie. I cried after that till I fell asleep.

"Well, course that weren't the end of it. That man, he come back, let hisself in with his key agin. When he saw Mama still not there, he say, 'Honey, I'm gonna have to call the county, have them find you a place.'

"He ain't so mean talkin' that time, so I stepped right up and axed him, 'You mean a orphanage or sumpthin' like that?'

"'Don't know for sure,' he say, 'but you can't stay here. You stay put, and I'll give them a call. They'll take good care of you, alright?'

"So what was I gonna do, Annie? I had to go. I was in a place like that down in Texas once when I was 'bout eight years old, and I promised myself I ain't never goin' back agin."

"What do you mean, Clydeen? You were in an orphanage? Why?"

I figure I might as well go ahead on and tell her the whole thing so she understand everything I been through. So I pull Gary to me and keep on talkin'.

"Okay, Annie. This here what happened in Texas. I hurt myself at school one day, and they couldn't find Mama or Daddy. They axed me was I on my own mos' of the time, and I tol' 'em yes. With Mama and Daddy working so much, and Daddy goin' into town mos' nights, I was on my own quite a lot. Tha's jus' how things was, but they didn't like it. Guess it was against the rules, me lookin' after my own self, even though they's always a aunty or a cousin or somebody's old granny close by 'round there where we lived. Guess I shoulda told them that, but I didn't know.

"Anyway, the peoples at the school patched me up, and a while later, a white lady come git me. She's wearin' white gloves, and I thought she was takin' me home. But no. She put me in her car, say I got to stay in a place for children with no families. She call it a orphanage. I tol' her I got family. But she say she can't find my family, so I got to stay in the orphanage for a while till she do.

"It took Mama and Daddy a few days to clear things up and git me outta there, but the days I spent in that place was the worst of my life. This up here? This here Nest you and me got? This like heaven compared to a place like that, Annie."

"So what happened in the orphanage, Clydeen?"

"Well, bigger kids, teenagers mostly, took my food, spit in my face, called me names. Boys, girls, didn't matter. No one took up for me, and the grownups? They jus' turned they backs. I thought I might git killed in that place.

"Mos' night, I laid on my cot shiverin' and cryin', prayin', not sleepin' much. Then one night, I did fall asleep, and I wet bed. Some of those mean girls slep' in the same big room as me wrapped me in the wet sheets and shoved me in a closet, say I too smelly. The white lady that come the next morning, the housemother they called her, was so mad when she found out what I done, she locked the door to the closet and lef' me in there all mornin' long. Teach me a lesson, she say.

"When she let me out, she told me to take the sheets to the laundry room and wash them in this big tub filled with soapy water. It was so hot it jus' 'bout took my skin clean off, but I did what she said. When I tried to lift the wet sheets to move them to another tub for rinsin', I spilled water all over the floor. She took a switch from someplace and started hittin' my ankles. It stung, and I started jumpin' around like a jack rabbit tryin' to git away from them blows. But she kep' right on hittin' me the whole time I was tryin' to clean up the mess. Finally, I started to cry. She tossed me in the tub of soapy water, and tol' me, 'Now clean yourself up, you filthy little nigger.'"

"Wow, Clydeen. That's terrible!"

"The next day, my folks showed up to get me out. They made me go back to school, but I was real careful after that. No foolin' around, no playin', no doin' nothin' might land me back in that hellhole.

"So when that landlord tol' me what was comin', what was I s'posed to do, Annie? I took the can opener and what was lef' of the canned food, packed up whatever else I could carry, and got the hell outta there. I went to the bus stop by the railroad station and got on the first bus that come along. You know the rest. Are you happy now? Is that what you been wantin' to know?"

Annie nods and draws me close. I let her, even though it's almos' too much for me right now. When I back away, she pulls me to my feet, grabs my hand, and without sayin' a word, starts headin' to our secret place behind the boulder. I scoop up Gary and settle him on my shoulder. His furry tail tickles my face as he twitches it back and forth to balance hisself as we walk down the uneven rocky slope.

It's shady now, and for the longest time, ain't no words pass b'tween us. Usually, Annie be talkin' nonstop, an endless gush a words, but now? Nothin'. Not a single word, so we jus' sit together, shoulder to shoulder, Annie's hand on my outstretched leg. Out of the corner of my eye, I see tears glistenin' on her cheeks. I don't dare look at her full on, though, or I won't be able to swallow the sobs clawin' at the back of my own throat.

"Okay," she croaks after a long while. "So no bath and no cake then."

I burst out laughin' and the heaviness b'tween us drifts away.

"Oh, for God's sake, Clydeen! Get up here," she say, springin' up and offerin' her hand. "We've been sitting around way too long."

I leap to my feet, and we start dancin' on the soft ground, jumpin' up and down, holdin' onto each other with both hands. My heart is burstin', and I'm laughin' and cryin' at the same time. When we run out of breath, we fall back down and lean into each other, gaspin' for air.

I am so glad she came back!

Chapter 18
Annie

I lay awake for a long time last night thinking about Clydeen, not knowing where to begin to sort through the strands of her story, but grateful we seem to have survived such a terrible argument and come out on the other side.

After finally hearing some of what Clydeen has experienced in her life, I marvel that the two of us, so different in every conceivable way, have found each other in this big world. And now here we are in a situation that is not only full of challenges, but also, because of our seclusion, unusually intimate. I feel closer to Clydeen than I have to any other person in my life so far, and I don't really know what that means. What I do know is how important it is, for me at least, to find a path to understanding that will keep us from breaking each other's hearts in the end. It's entirely up to us to figure it out, which is pretty scary, but also kind of exciting.

I go back in my mind and try to unwind the infinity of chance happenings that had to occur to set all of this in motion, but it's way too vast for me to unravel. I sense there is mystery at its core. What else could it be? It's too random to be anything else. Does that mean I can relax a little where Clydeen's predicament is concerned and let the mystery unfold? Maybe, but I probably won't. I don't trust it enough.

In the morning, lack of sleep has left me exhausted, but I knuckle down and slog through every chore Vivian gives me. By one o'clock, Clydeen, Gary, and I are settled around the orange crate ready for a bite of lunch.

"Annie, I need you to understand something," says Clydeen, not smiling, her brow furrowed.

"What?"

"I only tol' you all a that yesta'day so's you'd know why ..."

"I know, Clydeen, and I'm sorry."

"I ain't askin' for no pity," she says sharply. "That ain't the point."

"Not pity, Clydeen."

"Oh. What then?"

"I'm apologizing for using my birthday to try to get you to do something I knew you wouldn't want to do. It was wrong. It was less about my birthday than me thinking you need some help, and Mrs. B might be a person who could do it. But it's not my place. That's what I'm trying to say."

"You's right 'bout one thing, Annie, when you said I never told you nothin'—'bout me, I mean. That part ain't your fault. Dang it all, Annie, don't you know a birthday party, a hot bath—all a that sound like the best thing in the world to me right now. I wish I *could* do it. But I can't take a chance some white lady go gittin' all up in my bidniss. All she gotta do is pick up her telephone, and I'd be done for. They'd be comin' to git me, and boom, I'd be back in some orphanage with no mama and no daddy to come for me this time. Maybe they keep me there forever."

I'm tempted to argue, tell Clydeen that's not going to happen because Mrs. B isn't like that, but then I remember something really creepy that happened when I was in third grade.

There were kids in my old neighborhood who lived in an orphanage and went to my school. They always seemed pretty much like the rest of us, except for this one time.

It was a cold winter day, and the bell had just rung for recess. Kids were spilling into the hall, pulling on boots and winter coats, getting ready to go outside to play when this lady came storming out of the principal's office, dragging one of the orphanage girls by the arm. I didn't know the girl. She was older than me, but the woman looked fierce and so angry! In my memory, she seems gigantic, like one of those humongous balloons you see in parades. She wore a black coat that flared out behind her as she dragged the girl toward the exit. The girl was screaming and crying as the woman yanked her out the door and down the steps. That was the last I ever saw of that girl. No wonder Clydeen is wary.

"Okay, then. So what are we going to do?" I ask her, awakening from my reverie.

"What, 'bout yo' birthday?"

"No, silly. About getting you a bath."

"I guess it ain't gonna happen," she shrugs. "It ain't the worst thing. But it would be nice if you could bring me some lotion for these ashy knees and elbows."

With that, she's ready to let the matter drop, but I'm not.

"Lotion. Sure. But I have another idea."

"Jus' so long it don't involve me goin' down outta here to nobody's house."

"What if I start bringing extra water every day and we collect it until we have enough for you to have some kind of a bath?"

"You mean take my clothes off an' all?" she says, drawing back and laying a hand on her chest.

Gary has come back and is perched on my lap.

"I won't look, I promise. And Gary, he's already seen it all, the way he crawls up under your shirt all the time."

She laughs, and then turns serious again.

"That'd be a lot of work, Annie. It ain't easy haulin' those bottles up here. Maybe we jus' let it go, a'ight?"

"I don't think so, Clydeen. It's worth a try. It might take a week or so, but while we're getting it ready, the water can sit in the sun and warm up. Make it real nice for you."

After a lot of discussion, she finally agrees.

"I can come down and help you carry, can't I?"

"I appreciate it, Clydeen, but it's not a good idea, not with those worthless shoes you've got. I'll try to find something better, then we'll see."

Chapter 19
Annie

After hearing Clydeen's story, all the enthusiasm for my birthday leaves me, and I make no plans at all. Vivian bakes a cake. I eat some, take some to Clydeen and Mrs. B, and that's about it. I feel distant and withdrawn, and in the end, I decide that turning 14 is really nothing special.

And then, much to my surprise, on Saturday morning a few days after my birthday, Vivian comes into the kitchen while I'm cleaning up after breakfast, and says, "Hey, Annie, how about we go downtown and celebrate your birthday by having lunch at Woolworths."

"When?"

"Today."

I want to refuse, but my mouth waters when I picture those absolutely fabulous greasy hamburgers with even greasier onion rings and French fries. I remember the smell of old fryer fat and raw onions, the pungent bitterness of dill pickles and the creamy sweet coleslaw. It's all too much to pass up.

"Okay," I tell her. "Why not?"

It's a cloudy day, cooler than it's been for the past couple of weeks. We drive off in the Ford around ten o'clock, leaving Stanley to mind the home front for a change.

I know that window shopping will be the order of the day. We won't be buying much of anything, but I hope I can at least talk Vivian into buying me a tube of Tangee, the barely colored lipstick

117

substitute considered appropriate for girls my age. It won't cost much, but it will make me feel a lot more confident when I have to face the wolf pack of strange new girls at school in a few weeks, all of them a year older than me.

We walk around for a while, but the rush and confusion of the crowd of people and the noise of all of the cars, trucks, and buses makes me jumpy, and I want to get inside someplace. Looking around, I spy something interesting across the street.

"Let's go over there and have a look, Mom," I say, pointing.

"What is it?" she asks.

"I think it's a television. See? In that window over there. I want to go look at it."

"Okay. I've never actually seen one," she says.

"Neither have I."

We go to the corner, wait for the light to change, and make our way back a half a block to the store. Sure enough, there's a sign that says the thing in the window is a television set. It's about the size of a small refrigerator, but the screen itself is tiny. The outline of a speaker is visible in the lower part of the cabinet, which is covered with dark brown fabric with shiny gold threads running through it. There's some kind of antenna on top of the shiny walnut cabinet and a sign that reads "Rabbit Ears included."

Vivian and I stand in front of the window and stare, fascinated by this new contraption we've heard so much about. The noise around us seems to fade, and I forget all about getting inside.

The store proprietor sees us peering in the window. He smiles at us, mounts the platform where the set is sitting and turns it on. After some delay, vague figures like those in black and white photographs can be seen moving around on the screen, but there are flecks of white light flickering over the screen, too, so we can't really make out the picture very well. The man fiddles with the dials, which makes the picture flop up and down and then side to side. He fools around with the antenna, and finally, the picture stops flopping and the snowstorm clears up, but now the people on the screen look elongated as if they are reflections in the fun house mirror at the amusement park. He makes more adjustments, glancing our way occasionally and smiling nervously. All in all, it takes him a good half hour to get it working properly.

Finally, Vivian sighs and says, "Well, I sure wouldn't pay hundreds of dollars for that!"

"Yeah. It's a lot of trouble, isn't it?"

"Sure is. I wouldn't give a plug nickel for it."

That settled, we walk a few blocks to Woolworths and sit at the counter. Vivian orders a bacon, lettuce, and tomato sandwich, and I order a cheeseburger and both fries and onion rings, which we share. Oh, and tall, frosty chocolate malts, the kind that come in big metal cans with cold glasses you can fill more than once.

The lunch puts Vivian in a good mood, and she purchases the Tangee for me without batting an eye. "For your birthday," she says.

This is one of the few days I have ever spent alone with Vivian since Charlie was born, ten years ago now, and although I hate to admit it, it's fun.

Later, after dinner, I'm missing Clydeen, and I decide to make a quick trip up to the Nest to see her. Stanley is well into his third or fourth highball so I'm hoping he won't notice when I sneak out before he can give me the third degree. I want to tell Clydeen about the day, and I also want to make sure she has enough food to last until Monday.

"Well, lookee here, if it ain't Miss Annie," she drawls as I reach the top of the wash. "What you doin' up here this time of evenin', girl?"

"I missed you, Clydeen. And, guess what? Vivian took me into town today, and we saw a television set. Have you ever seen one?"

"Can't say as I have. I heard of it, though. It be like movies, right?"

"Supposed to be, I guess. We saw one in a store window."

"So what's it like?"

"Well, it costs a lot. And you have to fiddle with it every few minutes to get the picture to show right. Half the time, it looks like a snowstorm, and the other half, the picture flops around so much it feels like your eyeballs are spinning."

"Sounds worthless to me."

"I know, right? It wasn't anything like I expected. Stanley wants to buy one, but personally, I think it's a waste of money, and if I was him, I'd can that idea. So what you been doin'?" I ask her, changing the subject.

119

"Lemme show you."

She hands Gary to me and runs into the cave. She pops out a minute later with the pocketknife my granddad gave me in one hand, and a tiny wood carving in the other. She sets it up on a flat rock nearby.

"What you think it is, Annie?" she asks, looking at me hopefully.

"A bear?"

"Tha's right! A baby bear."

"That's pretty good, Clydeen. Is that the first time you've made a carving like that?"

"Yas. First time. It give me sumpthin' fun to do," she says, scooping up Gary.

I feel lighter tonight, my mood lifted by the day's adventure and the easy comfort of being with Clydeen, her laughter bubbling all the way up from her toes and rolling out of her like music.

"I hate to go, Clydeen, but it's getting late, and the sun is going down. I'll get here as early as I can on Monday, okay?"

"See you, Annie," my friend says, touching my arm as I go.

She watches until I reach the bottom. In the dim light, I turn and wave, and she waves back.

We'll miss each other tomorrow, but with Stanley around, it's best if I stick close to home and not give him a reason to point his radar in my direction.

Chapter 20
Annie

After more than a week of preparation, tomorrow is bath day for Clydeen. Numerous containers of water are lined up in the sun along the ledge like toy soldiers standing at attention. A new bar of soap and Vivian's good sewing scissors are wrapped in towels and stowed at the back of the cave.

We need just one more thing—clean clothes. My own clothes are too small for Clydeen and too few to share anyway. This morning, I tiptoed into my parents' bedroom and stood in front of their closet to see what it might have to offer. I pictured Clydeen dressed in one of Vivian's faded cotton housedresses or my father's worn serge trousers and shirts with long sleeves. Hopeless. Once again, I decide my only course of action is to turn to Mrs. B for help. Isn't that what a guardian angel is supposed to be for?

Her truck is gone when I arrive at the white frame house. I head out to the watering trough and fill more bottles. Just as I finish, Rocky comes running around the corner with Mrs. B close behind. I stoop down and give the pup a good long scratch behind his ears, then go to help Mrs. B unload bags of groceries from her truck.

"You're early today, Annie," she says, smiling at me.

"I am, yeah."

We go inside and draw glasses of cold water from the tap at the kitchen sink. I shift nervously from foot to foot, no longer feeling so cocky. Do I dare ask such a thing of this kind woman whose son is missing? If I had any other options, I would never ...

"Ummm ... Mrs. B?" I begin. "I want to ask you something, and it's gonna seem really strange."

"Okay. What is it, Annie?"

My mouth is dry as dirt, and I can feel my Adam's apple bobbing up and down as I try to shake loose the words that are stuck in my throat.

"Uhhh ... Mrs. B ... do you have any old clothes that might fit someone a little taller than me?"

"Well, yes, I think so. Who might they be for, if you don't mind my asking?"

I have no tall tale at the ready, and I'm sick of lying, so I offer a tiny sliver of truth. "I'd rather not say. Is that okay?" I murmur anxiously, staring at my dusty shoes.

I am teetering, and if she asks me again, I'm afraid I'll tumble right off the edge of the cliff and spill everything.

"You don't have to say, Annie. But tell me this. Are you in any danger, or will you be if I give you what you are asking for? I am your guardian angel, remember?"

"Oh, no. Don't worry, Mrs. B. There's no danger. It's nothing like that," I say with a giggle, hoping she won't press me further.

"Please understand, my reticent young friend, I have to ask."

"I know. I just can't say right now."

"Okay, sweetheart. Come on, then. Let's see what we can find."

I suddenly feel like crying. Overwhelmed once again by this woman's unfailing generosity, I have to stop in the hallway for a moment to get a handle on my emotions.

"Annie!" she cries with alarm when she notices I'm no longer with her.

She has turned to find me standing with my eyes closed and my forehead against the wall.

"Are you all right, child?"

"Fine. I'm fine. I just felt a little dizzy for a minute."

"Would you like to lie down for a bit?"

Wouldn't I love too! I have been working so hard all week it would feel wonderful to rest in Mrs. B's cool, quiet house for the rest of the morning. But Clydeen is waiting for me, and we have much to do today.

"I'm fine now," I tell her, smiling.

"Come on in here, then."

We go into one of the bedrooms—I'm guessing it's Ulie's room.

I look around and gasp. I've never seen anything like it. On one wall is a mural depicting a dense forest with imaginary creatures draped over trees and unicorns traipsing about the forest floor. Intersecting rainbows of brilliant colors cascade over another wall, and the third shows a field of corn growing under a brilliant blue sky with puffy white clouds floating by. But the fourth wall, except for the door to the closet, is covered by small pen-and-ink drawings of explosions. Cars exploding, buildings exploding, giant firecrackers exploding. Severed limbs flying in all directions. Is that supposed to be a joke? The contrast with the rest of the room is so stark, I don't know what to make of it.

"Ulie did all of this?" I ask, awestruck.

"Oh, yes. Many times over," she laughs. "That boy loved bright colors, absolutely loved them, but he was also preoccupied with blowing things up, as you can see. I never could figure it out, but his father said ... Oh I don't remember what he said anymore, Annie. That's just how he was."

The hairs on my arms stand at attention as I sense the presence of the boy who once occupied this room. Surely Mrs. B feels it, too, but she gives no sign.

While I continue to stare, Mrs. B digs a couple pairs of jeans and some T-shirts out of a dresser drawer. She goes to the closet and grabs two long-sleeved work shirts.

"Will these do?" she asks.

I unfold them and hold them up. "Uhhh ... perfect," I stammer. "Do you mind if I cut off the jeans and make shorts out of them?"

"No, Annie. I don't mind at all."

"You wouldn't happen to have some shoes, would you?"

"Over there. Take whatever you like," she says, gesturing toward the closet at the far end of the room. "There are socks in that top dresser drawer and there may be a belt in there, too. Help yourself."

I go to the closet and pick up a pair of brown oxfords with thick soles and take several pairs of socks and a belt from the dresser.

"These things ... they belong to Ulie, don't they, Mrs. B."

"They were his things, Annie, but they probably wouldn't fit him now. You can have them."

There is sadness in her eyes as she carefully loads a paper bag with the folded garments and lays the shoes and socks on top.

I feel like I should apologize. If she only knew how desperately a lost girl needs these things, would it help? But since I've been muzzled by that very same girl, I say no more and race for the door.

Chapter 21
Annie

"Well, I guess they's better'n what I got now," Clydeen sighs, looking at the new wardrobe I have laid out for her inspection. "Leastwise my feets be better off with them shoes and socks."

"So shall we get started?"

"A'ight then. Hope I don't freeze to death gittin' all necked out here! If I don't chicken out, that is," she says, smiling wickedly.

"Are you kidding me? You'll be in Dutch with me for the rest of your life if you back out now, after all I've done to haul this water up here for you!"

"Jus' playin' witchya, Miss Annie. Jus' playin'," she says, popping me gently on the upper arm. "So let's git on with it 'fo I change my mind for real."

"Oh, boy! You gonna be like this all day?"

"Prob'ly. Yas."

"Where shall we start?"

"I say hair first."

"Good idea."

There's no use trying to comb out Clydeen's kinky, unruly hair, which has now grown quite long. She has no comb in that cardboard suitcase of hers, and I certainly don't own one that will work. We have come to the conclusion that a haircut is the only option.

I upend the flimsy orange crate and move it into the shade. Clydeen perches on it. Gary scampers into the bottom of the crate and retreats to the far corner like he wants no part of what we are about to do. I unwrap the scissors, and Clydeen turns and stares at them.

"You sho' you knows what you doin?"

"Yeah, of course I do. I've cut the hair offa dozens of Negros before you. Did I forget to tell you that?"

"Liar!"

She turns away and sits up tall. I drape the towel over her shoulders and give her a little squeeze. She reaches up, her arms crossed, and pats my hands.

"Jus' so you know, I'd never let you do this if my hair hadn't got in such a matted mess."

"Duly noted. So shall I do it or not?"

She sighs. "Yas. Go on then. Cut it off. But you gonna hafta cut it short enough so's I don't need no comb or oil or nothin'."

"I'll try."

Her hair is dry and brittle and feels something like steel wool, very different from the texture of my own white-girl hair. Right away I realize I should have brought hair clips to hold Clydeen's thick matted hair on top while I start cutting at the bottom. But it's too late now, and when I carefully try to separate out the first hank of hair, she yelps.

"Ouch! You pullin' it."

"Sorry, sorry, sorry, Clydeen!" I stamp my feet in frustration. "I'll try again."

When at last I have a hunk of hair separated out and I'm holding it in one hand, I begin to cut. The scissors protest, and I have to divide the piece into even smaller chunks and go at it again.

"Well, will you look at that," I say with surprise as I show Clydeen the hank of hair I have finally succeeded in separating from her head.

"A'ight, a'ight, I don't need to see none a that," she laughs.

I drop the hair into a paper bag and get down to business. It takes well over an hour to shear her thick head of hair, and when I'm finished, all that's left are tight little corkscrews clinging to her dirt-encrusted scalp.

"Oh, my God, Clydeen," I whisper. "You look so different!"

She looks older, her nearly bald head round and elegant atop her long, graceful neck. Her long black eyelashes make her dark eyes stand out, and the skin of her coffee-colored face seems to glow in the softness of the warm afternoon sun.

"You look like an Egyptian princess. All you need is one of those gold collars around your neck," I tease.

"Stop foolin' with me! And don't go talkin' to me 'bout no collar," she protests.

"Haven't you seen pictures of beautiful Egyptian women with gold collars?"

"No, I ain't. But I sho' 'nuff seen pictures of slaves with iron collars draggin' heavy chains."

We stare at each other. What do I say to that? I really stepped into it this time. Insulted her when all I was trying to do was give her a compliment, tell her how beautiful she is. I cough, clear my throat and buy myself some time to erase the image she has evoked.

"Sorry, Clydeen. I didn't mean to ..."

"Jus' forgit it. I know you didn't mean nothin' by it. Jus' sayin'..."

"Okay, I hear you, but tomorrow I *am* gonna bring a mirror so you can see what I see."

A black sheep shorn of its wool, she studies me out of the corners of her eyes as she runs her hands over her new do.

"Bet my own mama not recognize me now," she says wistfully.

"Course she would, Clydeen. A mama bear always recognizes her own cub."

"So now I'm a cub, not a baby bird anymore?" she snorts.

"Take your pick, my friend. C'mon. Let's wash you off."

There are two four-gallon buckets filled with water and more bottles lined up and waiting. Is it enough for a bath? We'll soon find out.

"Bring them things inside," says Clydeen, gesturing to the two full buckets.

"Okay, but if I do, you're gonna get the ground all wet in there, and it'll take forever to dry out. Do you want that?"

"Well, maybe not. It be warmer out here in the sun anyway. You just go on now and leave me be. I can take care a this myself."

"Okay."

I set the bar of soap and the towel on the orange crate and take Gary with me around the bend in the ledge, but next thing I know, she's calling me back.

"Annie! I needs some help!"

I find her standing in one of the buckets of water, now filthy with the dust and grime she has washed off, her head soapy. Her arms are wrapped around her chest, and she's shivering.

"Pour that other bucket over me and DON'T LOOK," she says urgently.

I put Gary on the ground and cover him with the box we use to confine him. I grab a coffee can to use as a scoop and try not to look as I rinse her off, but there's no way to avoid it. Her brown skin is smooth and shiny, darker in some places than others. She has hair in places I don't, and she's very thin. I pour one, two, and then three buckets of water over her before all of the soap's off and the water gone.

"Now hand me that towel and go!" she orders.

I go down to the boulder, leaving Gary where he is. Eventually, she appears dressed in a pair of jeans belted at the waist and a dark green T-shirt that actually fit her quite well. She sets Gary down on a nearby log and then holds out both arms and twirls around to give me the full picture.

"What you think?"

"Like you said, better'n what you been wearing."

"I never had no shoes like these, but mines all tore up. So I like 'em. They feel okay, Annie. Thank you."

"You're welcome." I pull her down beside me. "Ummm ... you smell good!"

"At least for now," she laughs. "It do feel good, though. Glad I didn't chicken out."

A gray squirrel darts by, and we watch as she disappears into a hole at the base of a nearby tree. Gary has taken refuge under Clydeen's new shirt and doesn't see it.

"What she be doin' you think?" Clydeen asks.

"Making a nest, storing food for winter, I guess. See how her cheeks are bulging when she goes underground?"

We sit very quietly and watch for a while as she comes and goes. She ignores us until suddenly on one of her return trips, she stops a few feet away, sits up on her haunches and studies us for a moment.

"Hello, mama," I say softly. "Hope you aren't looking for Gary."

She twitches her nose, then scurries off. The next time she goes by, she stops just outside the burrow she's made for herself and chatters, scolding us.

"I guess we're disturbing her, Clydeen. Let's take Gary and go up, okay?"

"I loved seein' that," Clydeen says, looking back as we make our way to the wash. "But I hope that ain't Gary's mama, 'cause I'd miss the little critter if he was to go off now."

"So would I. He's part of our family," I laugh.

We are both tired from the rigmarole of the haircut and bath, so we go into the cave and lie down on our cots.

Clydeen props herself up on one elbow facing me, with Gary tucked in close to her chest. "So where you git these things, Annie?"

"What? The clothes?"

"Yas. Where you git 'em from?"

"Mrs. B gave them to me." I hold my hands up in a gesture of surrender. "Now before you jump on me, no I did not tell her who they were for."

"Okay. Thanks," she says sheepishly. "So these clothes—they's boy clothes, ain't they?"

"Yes. They belonged to her son, Ulie."

"Her son? She got a son? You ain't never tol' me that b'fo," she says, sitting up.

"I know. He's missing."

"What you mean, he missing? He run away or sumpthin'?"

"Not exactly. But that's how I knew she might have some clothes."

"So what'd she say 'bout her son?"

"Uhhh ...." I hesitate, not knowing where to start. "So have you ever heard of the Nazis, Clydeen?

"Maybe, yeah. Well, I think so. What about 'em?"

"I didn't really know what the Nazis were until the other day when Mrs. B told me all about the Second World War and how her son disappeared on account of it. You want me to tell you what she told me?"

"Course I do. I'm wearin' the boy's clothes, ain't I?"

"It's a long story."

"I got time," she says, lying back.

So I tell her everything, and she listens without interrupting me even once.

"Lord, Jesus!" she says when I finally wind down. "All a that killin' and carryin' on."

"Yeah. And now we gotta worry about the atom bomb, too. Mrs. B told me that the United States was also in a war with Japan at the same time Hitler was trying to take over the world from Europe. She told me that when the United States dropped the atomic bomb on the Japanese islands to end that war, it changed everything for all time."

"What you mean?"

"Well, she said that for the first time in history, human beings have the power to destroy the whole planet, including ourselves. She said our generation is the first to grow up with that reality. As far as we know, future generations will never again live in a world where that is not true."

"Wow! I never thought about that. Like forever?"

"Forever. I knew those bombs were special for some reason, but I had no idea it was that bad. Do you think people realize how dangerous our world is now?"

"Don't think mos' a them give it much thought, would be my guess. Mos' peoples jus' tryin' to git by."

"Yeah. I guess so. Okay, Clydeen here's another question for you. Do you think our Nest will protect us if the Russians decide to drop one of those bombs around here someplace?"

I'm teasing, but I'm also curious to hear what she will say.

"Well, I bet it be a lot better'n duck and cover!" she laughs.

Duck and cover, the drills carried out in every school these days. When a siren begins to wail, everyone "ducks" under their desks and "covers" by wrapping their arms around the backs of their heads.

"I think you're right about that, Clydeen! People are digging bomb shelters in their backyards left and right, lining them with concrete. So what's a flimsy school desk supposed to do? It's stupid."

"Is yo' daddy diggin' a bomb shelter, Annie?"

"Not yet. Maybe he should, though."

I think about the threat of atom bombs dropping from the sky, killing thousands, millions, or maybe all of life. It's terrifying, and all of this "duck and cover" business at school? Every time that ear-splitting air-raid siren cranks up and we dive under our desks, it reawakens my fear and makes me wonder if it's just a matter of time until we wipe ourselves off the face of the earth no matter what we do. Mrs. B is right. From now on, it's something we will always be thinking about, generation after generation.

"So yo' friend, Miz B," says Clydeen, breaking into my thoughts of doom and gloom. "She be a mama lookin' for her boy."

"That's right. She even wrote to the president asking him to help her find Ulie."

"Uhh-huh. Makes me wonder what my mama be doin' to find me."

"Oh, Clydeen, I didn't mean ..."

"No, no. It's a'ight. It jus' made me think. Is my mama tryin' to find out where I gone off to? You think she gonna find me one a these days, Annie?"

For the first time, there's a note of doubt in her voice, a crack in the wall of certainty she seems to have that someday, out of the blue, her mama will show up to claim her.

"I don't know, Clydeen. Way out here? I just don't know. We might have to think about ways for you to start looking for her."

"What? How's that gonna work?"

"Honestly? I hate to bring this up again, but I still think I could ask Mrs. B about it. Because she knows who to write to and stuff."

"No!" she shouts jumping up. "No! You can't do that, Annie! I tol' you!"

Here we go again.

"Settle down, Clydeen! I'm not gonna do anything without your say-so. It's just an idea."

She sighs and sits back down. "I'm gonna wait awhile. See if she come."

"Okay, then. Whatever you say. Hope we don't get caught out before then, is all."

She lies down and rolls over on her back. Her eyes are open, staring at the roof of the cave. Gary climbs onto her chest.

"I can't think 'bout that. Not right now," she says, stroking the little fellow gently. "I'm gonna wait and see."

In my heart of hearts, I know this is not a workable plan. Not a soul has come near this place in all the weeks we've been here together. How likely is it that if anyone ever does come, it will be Clydeen's mother? There's not one chance in a million of that happening, but right now, we still have time. The truth is I'm far from ready to let her go anyway, and so I say nothing more about it.

Chapter 22
Annie

I have developed an insatiable curiosity about the Second World War, which is really strange, because I have never had the slightest interest in anything "historical." In eighth grade, when we had to take a class in Colorado history, I spent the whole semester ignoring the teacher, doodling in my notebook, and staring out the window while begging the bell to ring.

But now? I'm alive with curiosity about what happened during the Second World War. Mrs. B, who used to be a teacher, has become my private tutor and guide. She has boxes full of newspaper clippings and magazine articles that she has collected over the years. She provides me with a steady stream of information and keeps me from going off the deep end by talking with me about everything I read. With her help, I am in the process of putting together a timeline of the major events that occurred before, during, and after the war, including the trials of Nazi war criminals that began in November 1945. Just think of it: Those trials ended less than four years ago, when I was ten. On my fourth birthday, July 16, 1940, I learned that Hitler issued the first orders for his armies to prepare for the invasion of Great Britain where Ulie was living at the time.

Whatever I'm learning, I describe in detail to Clydeen. In fact, I never shut up about it.

One day, as usual, I'm giving her the old blah, blah, blah about the Nazi persecution of the Jews and my amazement that so many people in country after country seemed willing to go along with the deportation of their fellow citizens, many of them their close friends and neighbors. Clydeen is lying on her cot with her arm over her eyes, listening. Every so often, she murmurs a reply just so I know she hasn't fallen asleep yet.

All of a sudden, she sits up, and says, "You hush now, Annie, and lemme axe you sumpthin'. You ever hear of slavery? Violence against colored folks, stuff like that?"

I stop my pacing and stare at her.

"What do you mean, Clydeen? Of course I've heard of slavery. We learned all about it in school, about Abraham Lincoln and how he freed the slaves. What does that have to do with anything?"

"Well, here's sumpthin' for you to think on. The Nazis ain't the only bad peoples in the world. Ain't no colored child like me anywhere in this here country whose kin weren't brought over from Africa in chains so's they could be the pro'pity a some white man. Bought and sold, bought and sold agin, for they whole lives. Pro'pity, Annie. Jus' like a horse or a dog, or a bale a hay. Right here in this country. You think the slaves had it any better'n those folks you talkin' about? Huh? And it lasted hun'erts a years longer'n what you talkin' 'bout, too!"

"Geez, Clydeen. I never thought ..."

"Right. You and your kind never thought. That be my point, Annie. Abraham Lincoln, he be a good man and all, but that weren't the end of it. Not by a long shot. White people may like to think that, but lemme tell you, that ain't how it went."

"Ok-ay," I say uncertainly, wondering what she's getting at.

"Like I tol' you, my daddy was a sharecropper in Texas, work the same fields as his daddy and his grandaddy b'fo him. His great-grandaddy was a slave, owned by a man name of Hollifield, and the plantation be called Hollifield Manor back then. Today, it called by the name a Hollifield Family Farms."

"Wait a minute. Hollifield is your last name. Do your people own Hollifield Family Farms?"

She rolls onto her back, kicks her feet up in the air, and laughs. "Hell no, we don't own no Hollifield nothin'. What they teach you in that school of yours anyhow? Hollifield be a slave name. Slaves not allowed to have they own names. If they have any las' name a'tall, it be on account a they been given the las' name of they owners, so my family, we end up goin' by the name a Hollifield passed down from my great-great-grandaddy.

"So anyhow, accordin' to my daddy, each colored family s'posed to git 40 acres a land and a mule to git 'em started off bein' free after slavery ended. But my daddy's people? They never got none a that, and neither did mos' other colored folks. Lots a them jus' ended up stayin' right where they's at, workin' the same fields for the same white man as always, hopin' to eke out a few bucks for theyselves and they families come harvest time. Know what my daddy used to say?"

"What?"

"He say, 'Lookee here, daughter. Ain't that much changed. 'Bout the only thing diff'rent now is I be free to go to town and tie one on.' And then he'd laugh his great big laugh, the one that made his chest rumble when he hug me."

A muffled sound comes from the other cot. Is Clydeen crying 'cause she misses her daddy? I don't ask. I just wait.

"My daddy?" she says, sniffling and clearing her throat. "Him bein' free to tie one on? That be exactly how he go and git hisself killed. He come out of the bar one night 'three sheets to the wind,' like he used to say. Some white boys out joy ridin' and drunk outta they minds offered him a ride home, say they goin' out his way. So he hopped in the back a they pickup. His buddy Virgil saw him, we found out later. But 'stead a bringin' him home, them white boys took him down by the river, tied him to a tree, and treated theyselves to a little target practice. I didn't see him after that, but mama tol' me he be shot up sumpthin' awful. Not much a him lef' to bury, but we buried what we could."

"So that's what happened to your dad? That's horrible. But the people who did that to him got arrested and put in jail, right? Those white men who took him?"

She scoffs at this. "You kiddin' me? You think anybody care 'bout some po' field nigger gettin' shot up? They ain't even pretend they lookin' for who done it. Hell, they a'ready knowed who done it. You wanna talk 'bout injustice? Well, I seen some fine injustices where I come from. And like I tol' you b'fo—my mama? It drove her plum outta her mind. She a little crazy after that, walkin' around cussin' and spittin' like those white boys be standin' right in front a her, which lucky for her they weren't.

"Anyhow, we couldn't get our cotton in, me and Mama without Daddy, she bein' in the shape she in and all, and so one day, like I tol' you b'fo, we jus' picked up and lef'. Lef' mos' everything behind, not that we had much worth takin'.'"

"Oh my God, Clydeen, maybe it's a good thing you left. Sounds like it was really dangerous down there in Texas where you were living."

"Honey, it be dangerous for my peoples, no matter where they's at," she says. "Some places worse'n others, is all.

"Some things better up here, though. In Texas, I had to go to a school jus' for coloreds. Our books, our desks, everything was hand-me-downs from the white schools. By the time we got 'em, they's pretty much nothin' lef' of 'em, they's so old and beat up. If a colored person dared take a drink a water from a fountain say it jus' for white people? Lord have mercy, you'd a thought it was the end a the world. That right there was enough to git the tar beat outta you or your black ass hung from the nearest tree."

"Really?"

"You better b'lieve it. What, you think I'm foolin'? I know it, 'cause I seen it."

I think back to the times I have wanted to ask Mrs. B for her help and been rebuffed by Clydeen. Now I see there are good reasons for her to feel endangered. After all, she hasn't been here that long, and I'm sure the tales about my family's prejudices haven't helped matters any.

"So what about your mama's folks?" I ask her after a while.

"I ain't never met Mama's people. My mama and daddy met when he was in the Army home on leave. He be stayin' with a buddy a his in Jackson, Mississippi where my mama come from. When he come back to git Mama after he got out of the service, her daddy try to run him off. But Mama? She tol' her folks she a'ready married him, and after that, they didn't want nothin' more to do with her. After Daddy died, turned out they wasn't really married, and them white peoples say Mama got no claim to anything a Daddy's. So we got nothin'. It would a been jus' a matter of time till we'd a had to leave anyhow on account a them new cotton-pickin' machines the land owners was buyin'."

136

"So what was wrong with your daddy that your mama wasn't supposed to marry him?"

"She tol' me her parents thought she married b'neath her. They wanted her to marry this high yella man sell insurance to other Negro folks in her town. But Mama say that man be one mean son of a bitch, and she don't want no part a him. So she run off with my daddy, and he took her back to his old homeplace in Texas."

"What does that mean—what you just said—high yella?"

"Oh. That what we call light-skinned black folks. Skin a few shades lighter'n mine, I guess. Skin that looks yellowish."

"Is it a mean thing to say?"

"Ummm ... depends. Some folks, they be proud of they light skin, think they better'n dark folks, so they might like it. Other folks? It be almost like you callin' 'em white or sumpthin', and to them, it be an insult."

I take a big deep breath.

"Oh, my God, Clydeen," I say slapping my forehead and throwing myself back onto my pillow. "There's a whole world out there I know nothing about. This is supposed to be summer vacation, but I'm learning more this summer than I ever do in school. You and Mrs. B are telling me about things I never would have heard of if I hadn't met the two of you."

"What makes you so sho' you wanna know 'bout all this stuff, Miss Annie, white girl livin' in the suburbs? Maybe you better off not knowin'."

"No, I'm not," I say, ignoring her sarcasm. "I'm older now. I want to know what's going on. C'mon, don't you think it's better that way, Clydeen?"

She scoffs. "Oh, I don't know nothin' 'bout that. It all be hard if you axe me."

Chapter 23
Clydeen

A couple days later, we be sittin' down behind the boulder in the shade playin' Chinese checkers and feedin' Gary peanuts. His tail fluffier now 'cause he growin', but he don't seem interested in climbin' trees jus' yet. Me and Annie's real glad 'bout that, 'cause we love havin' him around, 'specially me, and we don't want him to run off and git lost.

When we finish the game we's playin', Annie say, "C'mon, Clydeen. Let's go back up. I have something I want us to do."

We make our way back up to the Nest, Gary ridin' on my shoulder and chatterin' in my ear. Annie poke around in that black bag a hers and pulls out a short piece a red candle, a glass candle holder, and a paper plate. She sets the paper plate on top a the orange crate, puts the candle in the holder, and sets it on top a the plate.

"What you up to now, Miss Annie?" I axe her.

"I want to light a candle for all of the people killed in the war: the soldiers, the people bombed, the people put in concentration camps, all of them. And for your people, too, Clydeen, the ones who were slaves right here in America. What do you say?"

"Well, maybe," I say uncertainly. "What good you think candle lightin' gonna do?"

"I don't know. Maybe no good at all, but we have to do something, some kind of remembering, don't you think? What else can a couple of kids like us do?"

138

"You got me there."

"Okay, then."

She hands me a book of matches and nods at the candle. It takes a couple a tries. The candle flickers at first, but then settles down nice and steady. We sit nearby for a few minutes, holding our breath, waitin' for the afternoon breeze to blow it out. But that little flame jus' hangs on.

"Okay, Annie. So what we gonna do now?"

"Heck if I know. Do you know any prayers? Maybe we ought to say a prayer."

"This was your idea. Don't you know any prayers?"

"The only one I can think of is this one: 'Now I lay me down to sleep. I pray the Lord my soul to keep ....'"

"Nah. Stop. I don't like that one. Baby in a cradle fallin' outta the tree and all? What the heck is that?"

"Okay. Your turn then. You're the one who went to church every Sunday of your entire life, aren't you?" she say, grinnin' at me.

"Oh, honey, you bet I did. Wednesdays and Fridays, too. Picnics, ice cream socials, fundraisers, youth choir, all of it. Right up till we lef', even though Mama quit the church by then. I was still goin', though, so's I could axe 'em to pray for me and Mama."

"So tell me some prayers you learned."

"Prayin' in our church is less about rememberin' certain prayers and mo' 'bout talkin' to God and talkin' to Jesus—in the moment, like. We lift up our voices and let God know what's goin' on. We read the scriptures. We do a lot a singin', too, which is jus' another way a prayin' and praisin' God."

"Oh, okay. I didn't know that. I haven't been to church very often in my life, but what you're describing doesn't sound much like ..." she trails off. "But you still pray, Clydeen, even without your church, don't you?"

"Course I do. I talk to Jesus jus' like I'm talkin' to you right now. Axe Him to look out for me and my people. Axe Him to look out for you, too, Annie."

"Hmmm," she say, thinkin' it over. "My granddad prays. When we're at his house, he says a blessing at mealtime. It always makes me uncomfortable, because Stanley sits there with his eyes open and a smirk on his face, and I feel like I'm supposed to choose sides or something."

"Well, I ain't never uncomfortable with somebody prayin'. My mama? Oh, Lord. If you's sick or sumpthin'? She could pray the very heart a Jesus into you for your healin'. After Daddy died, though, she's so mad at Jesus, she stopped all a that. She didn't mind lettin' Jesus know exactly how she's feelin', though," I say laughing a little. "Truth is sometimes when I needs to let off a little steam, I pray like that myself. If I feel guilty 'bout it later, I blame it on Mama. I tell Jesus she's the one taught me to do it."

"Oh, for crying out loud, Clydeen. That's ridiculous. But I want to hear it."

"Hear what?"

"How your Mama prays to blow off steam. Teach me how to do that."

"Nah, I don't think so," I tell her, all of a sudden feelin' protective of Mama.

"Why not?"

"It might be disrespectin' to her, is all."

"Ok-ay," she say slowly, lookin' at me with a puzzled expression on her face. She disappointed and don't understand what I'm gittin' at, but this time, I don't try to explain. We's quiet for a while, but then Annie git all excited and jump to her feet.

"I just remembered! When I was younger, and we lived in our old neighborhood, I had a friend, Mary Margaret. She lived next door. We used to play all kinds of things, but our favorite was school, and she used to teach me what she called 'katty kism.' Something like that."

"Katty what?"

"Katty kism. Mary Margaret was Catholic. In her school, they had a class called 'katty kism' where they learned all about God and Jesus and stuff. So when we played school, she would be the nun— the teacher—and I would be the student, and she would teach me things she learned in her 'katty kism' class. She had a real school desk and a trunk full of more dress-up clothes than you could ever imagine, Clydeen. She would put on a long black dress and tie a black scarf over her head to make herself look like a nun."

"What's a nun?"

"Haven't you ever seen those women who wear long black dresses with black and white veils over their heads? They wear big crosses around their waists, too. Mary Margaret didn't have one of those, though."

"I ain't never seen nothin' like that, no."

"Well, anyway, I learned this prayer from Mary Margaret. She said the words are in Latin, but it's not hard, 'cause it's just four words. Kyrie Eleison, which means Lord have mercy, and Christie Eleison, which means Christ have mercy. We used to say it real slow, sing-songy like, and I would get this tingly feeling all over. I'd forgotten all about it, but I think it might be one of those prayers that works, you know? So shall we start with that? You want to try it?"

"Sho', why not."

The candle is still burnin' steady and strong. She takes my hand and closes her eyes. She starts in to singin' *Kyrie Eleison, Christie Eleison*, slow like a chant, and after a couple rounds, I join in. While I'm singin', the words, *Lord have mercy, Lord have mercy, Lord have mercy*, repeat in my mind. These are familiar words, and all at once, I feel myself touchin' down on one a my fav'rit Negro spirtuals. The connection thrills me, and my heart busts wide open, drenching me with joy as I move back, back into the past, times I have loved singing to God.

I feel my cousins, Desiree and Ebony, take their places on either side of me in the choir. I shut my eyes tight and strain to keep everything out but this feelin' a bein' home singin' this song, *my* people's song. Unaware I have made the switch, I'm singin' it now, and a sparklin' violet light begins to dance behind my eyes.

Let us break bread together on our knees
Let us break bread together on our knees
As I fall on my knees with my face to risin' sun
O Lord have mercy on me.

I sing three verses b'fo I realize I'm singin' by myself. I pop my eyes open to see what's goin' on, and Annie, she jus' standin' there starin' at me.

"What? What's the matter?" I axe her, wipin' tears away.

141

"Nothing's the matter. Dang girl! You can sing. Sing some more. Please."

So I do, church music and old spirituals from slave times jus' a flowin' through me like an unstoppable stream. I teach some to Annie, and we sing 'em together.

After that, every couple days, Annie scrounge up a old candle or two, and we sing. Before long, we makin' up our own prayer songs, prayin' for the slaves and people lost in the war like we say we's gonna do. But we also start namin' all a those we love and some we don't. We call out my mama, my daddy, Miz B, Ulie, Annie's daddy, too, even though she don't like him one bit, and my Uncle Oren who lef' us high and dry. We pray for all a the folks back home who's likely been evicted by now. We bring blessin's down on all a them peoples. We pray for it to rain, and we pray for it not to rain. We pray for my mama to come, and we pray for her not to come too soon. We pray that trouble don't find us, and if it do, we pray we knows what to do.

Chapter 24
Vivian

Saturday mornings have become a nightmare. For the last several weeks, Annie has insisted on coming with me to do our weekly grocery shopping. I don't know what's gotten into that girl, but we do nothing but argue over what to get, and today is no exception. Annie has her arms laden with all sorts of things I have no intention of buying—a tall package of cheese slices, a gigantic jar of peanut butter, cans of beans, tuna fish, pineapple, and who knows what else. A loaf of bread, too, even though the breadman delivers midweek, and we have no need of that at all. As a result, we are standing at one end of the canned goods aisle, arguing like a couple of angry jaybirds fighting over a hunk of suet.

"Don't you dare drop that stuff in my cart! Put it back, right now. All of it," I tell her, my voice rising to a pitch unfit for a public place. I look around to see if anyone has noticed, but thank God it's early yet, and the store is nearly empty.

So what does my daughter do? She just looks at me and makes no move to obey. At this point, I am literally draped over the cart to keep her from dropping her load, and from this awkward angle, I see a short, slender woman with gray hair approaching from the other end of the aisle.

"Damn it, Annie," I hiss. "Now look what you've done. Here comes the manager."

"That's not the manager, Mom," she laughs. "It's Mrs. Borsheim, the lady I told you about. The one who lives in the white

143

house over on T-road. She's probably coming to say hello."

At that point, taking advantage of my distraction, Annie drops all of the items she's holding into the basket. I peer into the cart after them as they rattle around and get lost among my own selections, and for a moment I forget all about Mrs. Borsheim.

"Hello," she says with a warm smile when she reaches us. "I don't mean to interrupt, but I wanted to say good morning to you, Annie, and introduce myself to your mother, I presume?"

"Well, yes, this *is* my mother, Mrs. B. We were just ..."

"Yes, I can see that," the woman chuckles, giving my daughter a hug.

When, after a few uncomfortable seconds, Annie makes no attempt to make the formal introduction, the woman extends her hand, and says, "I'm Eva Borsheim. Please call me Eva."

"Hello," I say, still flustered by being caught in the midst of a heated argument with a 14-year-old.

The woman is dressed in a clean pair of denim overalls over a white T-shirt. The scuffed toes of leather boots peak out from beneath the cuffs of her pants. Her graying hair is cut short and combed back behind her ears. She wears no makeup or jewelry, except for a large round timepiece on her left wrist.

"I apologize," I say, recovering myself. "I'm Vivian. Annie and I were just discussing why she thinks we need all this stuff." I sigh and wave my hand over the grocery cart. "I have to watch the budget, but I can't seem to explain that to her."

Mrs. Borsheim and I both glance at Annie, who is clinging to the side of the cart, looking smug and triumphant.

The woman shakes her head, gives another merry chuckle, and then says, "I'm very happy we ran into each other today. As you probably know, Annie visits me quite often. She's a wonderful girl, and I do so enjoy her company."

I glance at Annie with surprise. I'm caught off guard by this stranger's enthusiastic endorsement of my daughter, and for a moment or two, I can't think of what to say next.

"I swear, I don't know where this girl is most of the time these days," I tell the woman, picking up the thread of the conversation again. "With three younger kids at home running in all directions, sometimes I feel like I'm losing track of all of them."

"I hope you don't worry about this one too much," she says, smiling at Annie. "Your girl seems to have things well in hand. By the way, would it be all right if I take her to the county library this afternoon? I'm going, and I would be happy for her to come along."

Annie looks down and shuffles her feet.

"Mom, I really want to go," she pleads. "Can I?"

"Well, I suppose ..." but then I hesitate. "Actually, Annie, you'll need to check with your dad. He may have other plans for you this afternoon."

She rolls her eyes, throws her head back, and huffs with frustration.

"You can call me later, Annie," Eva says. "I was planning to leave around one o'clock, but I can go any time before three or so."

"Thank you for thinking of her, Eva. I don't have a car, except on the weekends, and then there's so much to do ..." I trail off.

"I understand completely. The responsibility of raising a family of four children is enormous, especially with two so young."

Again, I'm surprised and a little taken aback that she seems to know so much about us.

"Well, anyway," I say, waving my hand in front of my face as if to erase the unease I feel. "We'll see if we can work it out so Annie can go with you this afternoon."

Eva says her goodbyes. Once her back is turned, I begin plucking the unwanted items from my grocery cart and handing them to Annie to put back.

"Mom! Please," she whines. "Everything?"

"You may pick out two things, Annie, and no more. I'm sick and tired of this three-ring circus at the grocery store every weekend. There will be no library for you if you say one more word or try to sneak anything else into this cart before we check out, do you hear me?"

She takes the items and stalks off. I allow myself a self-satisfied smile. Leverage. It's what I lack these days, but having Eva's invitation to use as a threat is just what I needed to win the battle, at least for this week.

Chapter 25
Annie

On the way home from the grocery store, I huddle in the back seat, dreading the conversation I will now have to have with Stanley when I get home.

Why can't Vivian, just once in her life, make a friggin' decision on her own? I grumble to myself, biting the nail of my little finger down to the quick. It hurts.

I have been through this a million times. I will ask Stanley if I can go to the library with Mrs. B. He'll give me the third degree and come up with a dozen reasons why I shouldn't be allowed to go. We will argue. Once he runs out of steam, he might refuse my request outright without giving me a reason. If he says yes, he will do so reluctantly, just to let me know that what I am asking is a matter of great inconvenience to him, and I should know better. At that point, I will be left feeling angry, frustrated, and guilty. The pleasure of getting my way will be so watered down I might not care to go anymore. Either way, he will have won this ridiculous game one more time.

While I put the groceries away, I mentally run through the arguments I will make to persuade Stanley to release me for a couple of hours. This time, I vow it will be different. I promise myself I will not come away feeling bad, as if I have committed some grave wrong merely by asking permission to go to the stupid library.

When I go looking for him, I find him poking around in the backyard, drinking a beer.

"Dad, Mrs. Borsheim is going to the library this afternoon, and she said I could come along. Is it okay if I go?"

"You haven't finished your chores."

"I have, yes. I helped mom with the shopping. The groceries are all put away, and I cleaned up my room first thing this morning. I think that's it."

That's nowhere near "it," but he doesn't know anything about all of the other chores I've done so far today, and there's no point going into it. That's not what this is about.

"What about the stuff in the basement?"

He's talking about stuff that's still accumulating from our recent move as we continue to get things organized.

"I didn't know you wanted me to work on that today, but I promise I'll get right on it as soon as I get back. I can work on it tomorrow, too."

"You're supposed to finish your chores first, then get special privileges, not the other way around."

His eyes shift, and he takes a loud gulp from his can of Pabst Blue Ribbon.

"Who is this Mrs. Borsheim anyway? Sounds like a kike name to me."

I am so sick of hearing him say this every single time I mention Mrs. B by name.

"I told you before, Dad. I don't know anything about that. She's a friend, that's all. She's the lady who lives out on T-road where I ride my bike."

"Where's T-road?"

I start to explain, but he cuts me off.

"Never mind. Is she a kike, or not?"

"I don't know. All I know is that she and her husband were farmers, and all of the land around here used to belong to them. Her husband died. She lives by herself, and sometimes I stop by and visit. We ran into her at the grocery store this morning, and I introduced her to Mom."

Not quite true, but close enough.

"Well, I don't think it's necessary for you to go all the way across town with some stranger when we have books right here at home. There's a boxful in the basement. Why don't you pick one of those to read?"

My parents are not big readers, and believe me, after this move, I know every inch of what's in the basement. As far as books go, there's a biography of Supreme Court Justice Oliver Wendell Holmes and a few trashy novels Stanley has picked up for entertainment when he travels. I have other things on my mind.

"I'd like to pick out my own books," I tell him now. "Remember how I used to go to the library when we lived in our old house?"

"You did?" he asks, eyeing me curiously.

Is it possible he never knew this about me?

"Yes. I used to walk there almost every week unless the weather was bad. This is no different, except here, the library is a lot farther away, and I need a ride."

He considers this for a moment, and while I am waiting for his next move, a brilliant idea pops into my head.

"Maybe you'd rather drive me to the library yourself, Dad. What do you say?"

"No," he snorts. "Hell, no. I want to take a nap."

"Well, then, can I go with Mrs. Borsheim? I promise I'll be home in plenty of time to start on the stuff downstairs and help Mom with dinner."

Sweat is pouring down the back of my neck, and I am squirming with frustration, but I take a breath and try to quiet the hammering in my chest.

Instead of giving me an answer, he simply gets up and stalks off, tossing back another swig of beer as he goes.

Is it yes or is it no? I don't wait to pursue it further. I grab the money I've saved from my occasional allowance and run out the door, hoping Mrs. B hasn't left without me. Luckily she is still waiting, though it's now half past one.

"Sorry!" I cry out as I wheel my bike through the gate. "I didn't think my dad was going to let me go!"

Has he let me go? If not, I'll hear about it later, and there will be consequences. I am torn between my desire to go to the library and the very real possibility I could be grounded for it, leaving Clydeen stranded up on the mesa without food or water, unless Vivian ... but I don't know how far she's willing to go. Fear prickles my skin, and the hairs on my forearms rise. He never actually said no, did he? Maybe he did, and maybe when his back was turned, I didn't hear him. The whole discussion is now a blur, and my mind races with confusion as I climb into the passenger seat of Mrs. B's gray Chevy truck. She shifts into gear, and off we go.

My hands are icy cold, even though the day is warm. My breath comes in shallow bursts. Much to my dismay, I am stuck once again with that familiar feeling of wrongdoing that can spoil even the most ordinary of pleasures. I sigh with disappointment and try not to cry.

"For the life of me, I don't understand why everything has to be so difficult!" I exclaim.

"What's that, Annie?" asks Mrs. B, her eyes fastened on the road.

"Nothing," I mutter as I glare out the passenger side window.

My battered spirit recovers a bit when we reach the library. It's a small place, just two rooms, but the smell! How I love the smell of all those books. Ink and old paper, glue and dust. Do all libraries smell this way? Mrs. B signs me up for a library card, and then she wanders off to browse in the new arrivals section.

I go to the desk and ask the librarian to help me find a book on slavery. I want to learn more about the Second World War, too, but that can wait. Slavery is what interests Clydeen, so I'm going with that.

The librarian, Miss Clark, leads me to the children's section and we sit down at a low table. She tells me in an excited whisper that someone recently donated a bag of books, and in the bag was a very old and unusual book about slavery that might be exactly what I am looking for. "It's called *Incidents in the Life of a Slave Girl*, and it was published in 1861 during the Civil War, two years before the Emancipation Proclamation. Do you know about the Emancipation Proclamation?"

"Yeah, I think so. Isn't that when Abraham Lincoln freed the slaves?"

"Yes, but somehow, this woman named Harriet Ann Jacobs, writing under an assumed name, Linda Brent, managed to write an account of her life as a slave at a time when it was illegal for slaves to learn to read and write. Friends in the North published it for her, and it must have been dangerous not only for the author, but also for those involved in its publication. And now, a copy of that very book has made its way here, to our tiny library! It's astonishing, don't you think?"

I nod and smile, even though I don't quite get what all the excitement is about.

"Like I said," she continues, "in those days, it was illegal to teach slaves to read or write. Slaves who managed to learn and were discovered were subjected to severe beatings and other terrible punishments, ones that could result in death."

"Why?"

"Because reading and writing open doors to new ideas and information."

"Open doors," I muse.

"Yes. The slaveholders were afraid that even if a small portion of the enslaved population were to become literate, anti-slavery notions would take root, and the slaves, who outnumbered their owners, would rise up against them."

I think about this and wonder if Clydeen knows about all of this.

"Well, let me get the book for you," Miss Clark offers. "It has a new binding, courtesy of the county, but it is still very fragile. You will need to take especially good care of it. Will you give me your word on that?"

"Oh, yes. Absolutely, Miss Clark."

"All right then. Meet me up at the desk when you're ready, and I'll check you out."

When I get to the desk, Miss Clark offers me another book: *The Adventures of Huckleberry Finn.*

"Have you read this one, Annie?"

"No, I haven't."

"Well, this is a book that deals with slavery from another point of view. It was written by Mark Twain and takes place around 1840 before the Civil War. Some say it was the first great American novel, and many of today's critics claim the book is anti-slavery. I don't necessarily agree with that, but you can decide for yourself. Shall I check that one out for you, too?"

"Yes, please," I say, appreciating this helpful librarian who has done me the favor of talking to me like I have half a brain. "I'll take both."

Back in Mrs. B's truck, I ask her if there's a music store nearby.

"Well, yes," she says, "just down the street, as a matter of fact. Do you want to stop there?"

"If it's not too much trouble."

"No trouble at all, Annie."

The music store is small and cramped. A young man sits behind the counter, plucking a ukulele.

"Excuse me," I say timidly. "Do you have any violin strings?"

"What kind?"

"I don't know. Ones that don't cost too much, I guess."

He reaches below the glass-topped counter and pulls out a square package. "These are your best buy. Four for $1.79, plus tax."

I place the change from my pocket on the counter and count it out. I'm five cents short. I stare at my meager savings with dismay.

"Well, guess I'm out of luck. Maybe another time."

I turn to walk away and almost slam into Mrs. B, who has been standing behind me, watching.

"Never mind, Annie. I have it right here."

"Oh, no, Mrs. B. My parents—"

"It's alright, Annie. You can pay me back next time you have a spare nickel."

"Well, okay. Thank you, Mrs. B," I say as she steps up and hands the man five cents.

I can't wait to take the new strings to Clydeen. She's down to only one unbroken string and has given up trying to play the thing, so this will be a wonderful surprise for her.

As we are about to drive off, Mrs. B glances at the cover of the book that is topmost on my lap. "Huckleberry Finn, huh?"

"Yes, ma'am," I answer.

"I have a copy of that one at home. I didn't know you were interested in reading it, or I would have loaned it to you myself."

That gives me an idea. If we have two copies of Huckleberry Finn, Clydeen and I can read it at the same time.

"Maybe I could borrow your copy, too?" I ask, realizing too late that I have just put my foot in my mouth.

"Why?" she asks, looking at me curiously.

"Well, uhhh ..." I sputter.

I feel myself start to sweat under my arms.

"Never mind," she says good-naturedly as we swing into her driveway. "Of course you can borrow it, Annie."

She's used to my evasive tactics by now, and it no longer surprises her when I avoid answering her questions. Why she doesn't push me for answers, I have no idea, but I am grateful that she does not.

"I'll go get the book for you right now," she says, heading for the house. "Do you want to come in?"

"No thanks, Mrs. B. I have to go now."

As soon as she returns and hands me the book, I offer my thanks and pedal off.

At home, I tiptoe through the living room so as not to awaken the snoring hulk lying on the sofa. But he senses my presence anyway and sits up so abruptly, I jump.

"Where have you been?" he demands, digging into his eyes with both fists.

"I went to the library." I show him the books I have borrowed, but he's not interested.

"Did I say you could go?"

"Not exactly, but you didn't say I couldn't, either. You didn't say anything."

He glares at me, and I glare back. This is my first act of overt disobedience since I dropped the milk bottle in his new kitchen sink weeks ago.

"You stay away from that kike, do you understand me?"

Vivian has come in from the kitchen, drying her hands on one of the white towels she makes from flour sacks.

"Stanley, I don't think ..." she begins.

He turns and shushes her.

I am standing stock still, waiting for him to pronounce my punishment. My feet are glued to the floor, and my heart pounds, but I lift my chin and look him right in the eye anyway. We glare at each other for a long moment, and I'm astonished by what I see in his eyes. His fury actually looks more like fear. He blinks, breaks eye contact, puts on his shoes, and marches outside, slamming the door behind him.

Chapter 26
Annie

It's Monday at last, and I'm free! When I get to the bottom of the wash, I whistle so Clydeen knows I'm coming up. She's there to greet me as I reach the ledge.

"Glad you back, Annie!"

I drop what I am carrying and hug her tight. "Me, too, Clydeen. What's going on up here?"

"I was thinkin' about my aunts and uncles in Texas. Wonderin' where would they go if they git evicted on account a them new cotton-pickin' machines."

"So what do you think?"

"I'm pretty sure they wouldn't come here," she sighs.

"Why not?"

"'Cause they a'ways talk 'bout Chicago. Tha's the place in the North they be wantin' to go. That's not anywhere near here, is it?"

"No."

"So I'm still on my own then," she sighs. "Hey. What's wrong, Annie? You look like somebody turned you upside down and shook you out."

"It's nothing. Allergies," I say as I suppress the tears that have unexpectedly sprung to my eyes because I am so glad to see her.

I fake a sneeze, and that prompts a bunch of real ones.

"See?" I say when my head clears. "Allergies. Let's eat."

We sit in the sun feeding peanuts to Gary while we eat. I don't want to burden Clydeen with my weekend drama. I'm more careful

153

about what I tell her these days. As much as I'd like to describe my outing with Mrs. B and complain about Stanley, Clydeen, who has just spent two days by herself, doesn't need to hear this stuff from me.

Instead, I pull the violin strings from my bag and hand them to her.

"Oh, Annie! Thank you," she says. "I hope I remember how to put them on, but I reckon I can figure it out."

"I reckon you can, too. Don't ask me. I don't have a clue. "

I notice that she doesn't ask me where I got them, which confirms my suspicion that it's hard for her to hear about the simple privileges I enjoy that she does not. Privileges I don't even think about, such as going to the grocery store or going into a music store and buying a small gift for a friend.

"You want to see what else I brought?" I say when we've cleaned up and settled ourselves in our usual place down by the boulder where it's shady.

"Course I do," she says.

I open my bag and hand one of the books to her for her inspection.

"So what's this here? *Incidents in the Life of a Slave Girl.* Hmmm," she muses. "This for real? You think I wanna read 'bout slavery, huh?"

"I thought you might, and so do I. I asked the librarian to help me find a book, and this is what she gave me. It was written by woman who was a slave in the 1800s. Miss Clark, the librarian, told me it's incredible that such a rare book exists. It was forbidden for slaves to learn to read and write. Did you know that?"

"Yas, I knowed that. That be why my daddy, he a'ways want me in school. He say learnin' be my right and my responsibility. But you's sayin' this here slave girl, she learned to read anyhow?"

"Yeah. It's the true story of her life, Clydeen. Her real name was Harriet Jacobs, but she calls herself Linda Brent in the book to hide her true identity."

"Did you read it a'ready?" she asks as she opens the cover to the front plate and begins turning the pages.

"Just a little over the weekend."

When she closes the book, I reach for it.

"Not so fast Miss Annie," she says, holding the book with both hands and jerking it back over her shoulder. "I'mma read it, hear?"

"Okay, Clydeen," I snicker, surprised by her passion. "Sorry."

"So I can keep it, right?" she asks, hugging it to her chest.

"I promised Miss Clark I would take really good care of it, is all. The cover is new, but see how the pages are thin and yellowed at the edges?"

"Yas. So I be real careful," she says, holding the book between her two hands the way I have seen people hold Bibles. She rubs the covers of the book, back and front, as if trying to absorb its contents through her hands.

"I have to take it back to the library in three weeks, but until then ..."

"So what's that other book you got there?"

"*The Adventures of Huckleberry Finn*. Have you ever read it? It was written after the Civil War by a white guy name of Mark Twain, but the story takes place about the same time as the one in the *Slave Girl* book."

She takes the book and begins paging through it.

"Look like this dude say 'nigger' on every page. No wonder I ain't heard of it."

"He does?" I say, moving in to take a look.

"Colored folks like me, we don't like that word."

"I don't like it either, Clydeen. I had an experience with that word when I was really young that stuck with me. Can I tell you about it?"

"A'ight. Go ahead."

"Knowing my family, I doubt it was the first time I heard somebody say 'nigger,' but this one time when I was only four years old, I overheard a conversation. Even though I didn't completely understand what was going on, it apparently upset me enough to leave a lasting impression on me, because I still remember it today."

"Okay. So what happened?"

"Well, Vivian was in the hospital for a really long time before Charlie was born, and then after he was born, he had to stay in the hospital for another few months. I stayed with my grandparents in Cheyenne all that time while Stanley worked and Vivian, I guess, stayed at the hospital.

"Finally, my parents came for a visit. I remember standing in the hallway in my grandparents' house, and I overheard a conversation between my grandparents and my mother. They didn't know I was listening. It was just the three of them, Vivian and her parents, my Grandma and Granddad Mack. I don't know where Stanley was.

"Anyway, they were talking about Charlie, and Grandma asked Vivian what they were feeding him in the hospital.

"'They're feeding him breast milk,' she said.

"At my age, I didn't know for sure what that was, but I think I got the gist of it anyway.

"'Where do they get the breast milk?' Grandma wanted to know.

"Before Vivian could answer, Granddad piped up, and asked, 'Is it nigger milk?'

"He sounded angry. I had never heard him speak that way before, and it made me go very quiet and stay in my hiding place in the hallway.

"'Because if it's nigger milk, you don't know what that might do to him. You'd better check on that as soon as you get back,' Granddad warned her.

"I peeked around the doorframe. Vivian was sitting in a rocking chair at the far end of the room. She was slumped forward with her elbows on her knees, looking down at the floor.

"'Oh, I don't know, Dad,' she said. 'I think it's alright. I don't think they would give him anything that would hurt him.'

"'I don't like the idea of my grandson being fed nigger milk,' Granddad insisted.

"They talked about it some more, and then Vivian and Grandma went into the kitchen to make dinner or something. That's it. That's what I heard."

"Wow," she says, frowning. "Yo' granddaddy think milk from a colored mama be poison or sumpthin'?"

"Sure sounds like it, doesn't it?"

I feel ashamed, and I wish Clydeen weren't staring at me the way she is.

We sit silently for a while, watching a swarm of velvety green and blue dragonflies zip this way and that under the trees. It so hot today, our drinking water is as warm as bath water, but we pass the bottle back and forth between us and gulp it down anyway.

I sigh deeply before I pick up the thread again.

"Like I said, that conversation has stuck with me my whole life. I won't lie to you, Clydeen. Certain people in my family say that word every chance they get, but ... not me."

"Well, thank you, Jesus, for that!" she says, pulling me to my feet and charging up the wash with me trailing behind.

"Wait a minute, Clydeen." I say when we get back up to the Nest. "I want to ask you something, okay?"

"Yas, okay," she says, bending down to give Gary some pinon nuts we found in the woods.

"I want to know, as a colored person, what does that word actually mean?"

"Well, it ain't nothing good, that's fo' sho. My daddy say it be a word from slave times still used today to insult colored people. Course you knowed that part a'ready. But it be more'n jus' an ordinary insult. It means we not as good as other human bein's. Maybe we not even human at all. We lazy, stupid, worthless, dirty, can't manage without somebody, white folks that is, tellin' us what we outta be doin', but then not lettin' us do it. Oh, and we prob'ly gonna steal all a' yo' stuff, too. It means all kinds a bad stuff like that and mo'. When somebody call you that, it make you shrivel up inside. Make you wanna fight, too."

"So maybe you don't want to read *Huckleberry Finn*."

"Maybe, maybe not. We'll see."

"Okay, then. Mrs. B gave me another copy, so I'm going to start reading it while you're reading the one written by the slave girl."

"Okay then Miss Annie, why don't you g'won home now and let me get started on this readin'?" she says grinning at me, standing on the ledge in her heavy boy shoes with her legs spread apart like she's ready to take on the world.

"Whatever you say, my friend," I chuckle.

She seems to have forgotten all about being lonely.

"You have enough batteries?"

"I still got two extra."

"Good. I'll see you tomorrow. There's plenty of food, thanks to Mrs. B."

"I appreciates it, what you done, Annie."

"I know. It may rain tonight, so stay warm and dry, okay?"

"Sure thing. You don't have to worry 'bout me none."

But of course, I do. Worry. All the time.

Chapter 27
Annie

A few days later, just as I am about to leave the house with *Huckleberry Finn* tucked under one arm, Vivian says, "You know, Annie, school is starting in a little over three weeks. We should think about getting you a few things."

"What? No, Mom. School doesn't start until September, after Labor Day."

"Sorry, kid. It starts earlier out here."

"Holy cow!"

Figures. Only in Nowhere, Colorado, would somebody come up with a stupid idea like that.

"I thought you'd be happy to go back to school and make some new friends," Vivian says.

No, not really. Not anymore. But I don't tell her that.

"Hmmm. I suppose I'll have to drive Dad to work one day next week so I can take you to register, too" she says with a sigh.

"Yeah. I know. I'm such an inconvenience," I shoot back.

"Oh, Annie. I didn't mean it like that."

"Right," I say under my breath and head out the backdoor.

Once I'm on my bike, the reality of what she has just told me sinks in. I knew this was coming. But so soon? Once school starts, there's no way I'll be able to provide for Clydeen. I haven't been paying much attention, but the days are shorter now. Some of the leaves on the cottonwoods that grow along the creek behind Mrs. B's place are already showing tinges of yellow, and up at the Nest, flocks of squawking geese fly overhead nearly every day.

When we sing our prayers today, my own prayer for Clydeen to be reunited with her mother is more fervent than ever, although deep down, I still have no faith it will happen without the help of someone of the human persuasion. Unfortunately, Clydeen has yet to come to that conclusion, and ever since the day of her first bath and haircut, I've been all too willing to go along with her and pretend our summer together will end only on the day her mama comes panting up the wash to take her away, which in all honesty, I dread. I don't want her to go, but what's the alternative?

I remain quiet for a long time after our prayers and songs today. I *must* talk to Clydeen about leaving the mesa, and I *must* do it soon, but I don't know what to say or how to say it. She'll probably yell at me again, put her hands over her ears and run away. A calm discussion is the last thing I expect.

While I am pondering this, Clydeen goes to the cave and brings out Stanley's violin case. She goes to the bucket and washes her hands, then takes the instrument very gently from the case. She holds the violin with her left hand and steadies it between her chin and shoulder. She stands poised for a moment before lowering the bow and beginning to work it over the strings. While I am sitting there listening and combing my fingers through Gary's tail, an idea begins to form, a way I might be able to talk to Clydeen that won't be so hard for her to hear.

"That was beautiful, Clydeen," I say as she lays the violin lovingly back into its case a few minutes later.

"Ain't nothin'," she says, smiling shyly in spite of herself. "Been practicin', is all."

"Did your daddy teach you to play that song?"

"Nah. I jus' made it up, tryin' to git the feel of it agin, now I have all four strings. And for that, I got you to thank, Miss Annie," she says, patting me on the top of my head as she goes by on her way to put the violin away.

"I took piano lessons. I couldn't do it," I say when she returns.

"Tha's 'cause you's a grasshopper. Jumpin' here, jumpin' there, never still long enough. That'd be my guess."

"Yeah, you're probably right," I laugh. "Anyway, I want to tell you something, okay?"

"Okay. What is it?"

"Well ... I was talking to Mrs. B the other day, and I asked her about Ulie. If she thinks he's going to come back after such a long time. Maybe I shouldn't have asked, but I really wanted to know."

"What'd she say?"

"She didn't say yes or no. Instead, she showed me a deck of cards, special ones, she said. Each card had a picture on it, and a name and a number, too. She showed me how she lays them out and then she asks a question about finding Ulie. She knows how to study them. She says reading the cards gives her the insight she needs to decide what to do next."

"'So what do the cards say 'bout Ulie? Did she tell you?'"

"She said right now, they are telling her there are more avenues open for her to try. Something like that anyway."

"Like what avenues? What you mean?"

"Oh, like maybe going to Washington D.C. to talk to people in person. Writing more letters to the German and French governments, but this time having them translated before she sends them. Contacting the relief organization at the United Nations again to ask if they have any news. I don't know how it works exactly, but she says those cards keep her spirits up and help her figure out the next steps to take."

She scoffs. "Mus' not work very well, 'cause she ain't found Ulie yet, has she?"

She doesn't look at me as she says this. She's busy arranging small stones in a ring on the ground next to where she's sitting. Spiraling, as she calls it, is something she does to keep herself calm.

"I know we have talked about this before, Clydeen. But we have to figure out a way to start searching for your mother, don't you think?"

"*I* ain't been talkin' 'bout it. *You* been talkin' 'bout it. I told you what I'm gonna do," she says, adding another ring to the spiral she's making.

She's referring, as usual, to her mostly firm conviction that her mama will find her up here one day. The more often she repeats this, the more firmly she seems to cling to it. It's kept us both from talking about other possibilities. I don't pretend to know what those might be, but it's starting to feel like one of these days, we could be faced with something devastating we won't see coming.

"Look, Clydeen. Vivian told me today that school is starting sooner than I thought, and I won't be able to come up here and bring you what you need anymore. Besides that, winter's coming. What if your mama doesn't come? How would she possibly know where to look for you anyway? She's probably worried sick about you, just like Mrs. B is about Ulie."

Clydeen sighs, looking off over the edge of the outcropping. She rubs the stones together so hard in her clenched fist they make a grinding noise.

"Shoot, Annie! There you go, tryin' to ruin everything!" she shouts and throws the handful of rocks as hard as she can off the ledge.

"I'm not trying to ruin anything, Clydeen! I love our place up here. I love talking to you, the books we're reading together, singing and praying, watching Gary, the games we play, and most of all, the stuff we talk to each other about. But I love *you* more than any of that, Clydeen," I choke out, sobbing now. "I'm not bringing this up to upset you. I'm bringing it up because I care about what might happen to you, and I'm scared."

She hisses at me, but says nothing. She knows where I'm going with this.

"Wouldn't a good friend stop being so selfish and start helping you find your mama, instead of pretending all of this up here is some kind of magical forever, when it's not?" I croak.

"You ain't in charge a me," she mumbles into her raised knees.

"Well, for some reason I feel like maybe I am. You need to be with your mama, and you need to go back to school. We need to start trying to make that happen," I say, convinced I'm right, and it really is on me.

She looks at me skeptically, then she gets up and stalks off. But she doesn't yell at me this time.

I promised Clydeen in the past I would not push her, but now, I've probably gone overboard again despite my best intentions. A few minutes later, though, she returns, takes Gary from me and puts him on her shoulder.

"Okay," she says. "What you wanna do?"

I'm so surprised, it takes me a minute to collect my thoughts.

"I was thinking I could ask Mrs. B for one of her card readings." I sniffle. "See if those cards have anything to tell *us* about *our* situation."

"My situation, you mean. Seems to me I'm the only one you think got a 'situation,' ain't that right?"

"Whatever, Clydeen. Do we have to argue about that right now?"

"So you mean to tell her 'bout 'our situation,' as you call it."

"No! I promised I wouldn't."

"Well then, seems like we got ourselves a problem."

"Wait a second, Clydeen. Maybe she can do a reading without me saying anything about you, and if she can't, I'll let it go."

Her face is all screwed up as she thinks about this.

"I knowed some colored womens back home who be diviners. Tell fortunes, read the cards, tea leaves, palms of yo' hand, bones, stuff like that. Is Miz B one a them?"

"I don't know, Clydeen. All I know is what she showed me. Tarot cards, the box said."

"Hmmm. Okay, then. But please, I'm beggin' you, don't tell that white lady nothin' 'bout me."

"Understood."

"Meantime, I'm gonna be prayin' on it, more'n I have been. Maybe Jesus give me a clue 'bout my mama and where she at, 'cause the truth is," she says, swallowing hard, "I *am* startin' to wonder why she ain't come yet."

Okay! Yes! I'm flooded with relief. Really, nothing has changed, but this one small step seems huge. When I stand up and straighten my spine, I feel taller, as if a load has been lifted off my shoulders. Clydeen hugs me and wipes away the tears that are running down my cheeks again.

"Gonna be okay, Annie," she calls out a few minutes later as I head down the wash.

"Yes. It's gonna be okay," I answer.

I don't mean to be in a panic, but if there's ever a time for that to be true, it's now.

Chapter 28
Annie

When I get to Mrs. B's this afternoon to ask about a reading, I'm surprised to see a strange car parked out front. I hesitate before interrupting, wondering if I should talk to her later. But I'm afraid I'll miss her, and this will just take a minute anyway, so I go around to the back and tap gently on the door.

"Annie! Come in. There's someone here I'd like you to meet."

I step into the kitchen, and sitting at the table is a tall, buxom Negro woman. Her kinky black hair is pulled up into a knot on the top of her head, held in place by a colorful wrap. She has a scarf of deep purple around her shoulders, and a heavy gold bracelet on one wrist. She gives me an open, friendly smile as I approach the breakfast nook, where it appears she had Mrs. B have been having lunch and are now lingering over cups of coffee.

I'm speechless to find a Negro sitting in Mrs. B's kitchen. But why should I be so surprised? Stanley's bullshit about the rules, I suppose. Still, the tape that plays in my mind jumps to the idea that this person with dark skin shouldn't be here. I have to mentally crawl through my resident Stanley-isms to eventually grab hold of that fact that indeed, she has as much right here as I do, maybe more. In the meantime, I suddenly become conscious of my mouth gaping open, and I snap my jaw closed with an audible click of my teeth.

Mrs. B cocks her head to one side and looks at me funny. She doesn't get what this is all about, of course.

"Annie," she says finally. "This is my good friend Imani Jackson. Imani, this is Annie Cahill. She lives over yonder where those new houses are going in."

"Hello, young lady," says the woman, extending her hand to me.

"Uhhh ... hello, Mrs. Jackson," I say, taking her warm hand in mine.

"Imani and I were in a study group together for many years, before Imani and her family moved away."

"That's so," she says, turning and smiling at Eva. "Oooo, how I miss those days! I've just moved back to the area, and today, for the first time, I'm able to pay this lovely lady a visit."

"Naturally, I had to take advantage of her considerable skills in reading the Tarot cards this morning," Eva tells me. "We did readings for each other like in the old days and now —lunch, as you can see."

I'm brimming with questions, but I feel shy around this stranger, so I stand there awkwardly, not sure what to do next.

"Sit down, Annie. I'll get you a glass of lemonade."

"No thank you, Mrs. B. I can't stay. I just stopped by to ask you something."

"Shoot."

"I wanted to ask you if you would give *me* one of those readings."

My eyes shift to Mrs. Jackson, and she nods approvingly.

"Of course, Annie. I could do it later this week or early next week."

We make the necessary arrangements, and I say my goodbyes and head to the Nest. When I arrive, Clydeen comes out of the cave, calling to me and waving her copy of *Huckleberry Finn*. She's got that squirrel clinging to the front of her chest again, but she moves around like he isn't even there. He's nearly twice the size he was when she found him, and his tail hangs way down past the bottom of her shirt now. Clydeen's hair is growing out, too, and the sun shining through it as she strides toward me makes it sparkle like a halo.

"Good afternoon, friend," I wheeze as I take the last few steps before reaching the ledge.

"Ain't you done readin' this yet, Annie?" she asks without so much as a "hello."

"Almost finished," I pant. "You?"

"Yup. All done. Can we start talkin' 'bout it now?"

"Give me a minute, okay?"

"Sumpthin' wrong with you?"

"Yeah. I can't breathe. Take these bottles of water and let me sit a minute."

When Clydeen comes back from putting the water away, I suggest we wait until tomorrow to talk about *Huckleberry Finn* so I can finish reading it.

She seems disappointed, but she agrees.

"So you brung some food?" she asks.

"Sure. Don't I always?" I say, grinning at her as I open my black bag and show her what's inside.

"Oranges! And those cookies I like! Shoot! My mouf be waterin' a'ready. What sandwiches is that?"

"Spam with mustard, and some apples and a can of beans for you to have later on with the rest of the leftovers."

"Yum!"

"So let's eat."

The sun has crept behind the top of the mesa far enough to make a nice ribbon of shade on the ledge. Clydeen settles Gary on the orange crate, our makeshift altar, which I've covered with an old pink baby blanket dotted with tiny bunny rabbits. Candle remnants of many colors, rocks that sparkle with sheets of mica, feathers from a variety of birds, sprigs of greenery, even a piece of what appears to be petrified wood adorn the altar, as do several of Clydeen's critter carvings.

We pull our campstools up close so we can feed Gary tiny bits of our lunch. The little guy knows the drill. He's already sitting back on his haunches, twitching his little black nose in anticipation of the goodies to come.

"I have something to tell you, Clydeen."

"What?"

"I just came from Mrs. B's house. A colored lady was visiting her. Her name is Mrs. Imani Jackson."

"You kiddin' me. What? She cleanin' Miz B's house or sumpthin'?"

"No, no, no, Clydeen. They're old friends. Mrs. Jackson's one of those Tarot card readers, too."

"Oooooo, ain't that a surprise. But right now, I'm starvin', and this food looks so good!"

I'm hungry, too, and we eat in silence for several minutes, gazing off into the trees, listening to the birds, and breathing in the warm, sweet air of the summer afternoon. The cicadas have arrived and sing their song every few minutes.

"Okay. Here's sumpthin'," Clydeen pipes up, breaking the silence. "But first you gotta swear to me. Are you absolutely sure this Miz Jackson ain't no housekeeper?"

"One hundred percent, Clydeen. She's Mrs. B's friend."

"Okay, then. Since we ain't gonna discuss *Huckleberry Finn* today, I might like to go down there and take a closer look at Miz B's place. Outside. Not knock on her door or nothin'. Jus' have a look. See what it feels like 'round there. You think it be safe to do that?"

"I think it would be fine, Clydeen. Mrs. Jackson was getting ready to leave, and Mrs. B said she was going shopping this afternoon, so don't I expect anybody will be around. That road I come up, the one you can't see from up here? It's a dead end, barely a road at all, and I have never seen anyone there. We can walk down that road to the corner. You can get a pretty good look at Mrs. B's place from there. If you want to go closer, we can walk out into the field across the road from her house."

"Okay, then. Let's do that today."

I try not to show how excited I am. Another step in the right direction, one I didn't even see coming.

We finish our lunch and secure Gary under the box we use to contain him. I throw a handful of peanuts inside to keep him busy while we're gone. I'm sure he could get out if he wanted to, but so far, when we come back, he's always right where we left him.

"Whoa! I don't know how you do this every day, Annie," Clydeen says in a stage whisper as we start down the wash, going further than our place behind the boulder this time. "This be tricky bidniss gittin' down outta here."

"Stay close, Clydeen. I've had a lot of practice, and I have a certain way of doing it that keeps me from falling on my ass."

She follows my footsteps and avoids the most treacherous spots of loose rock. We both make it to the bottom in one piece, and for the first time, I get to show her my Schwinn and where I hide it every day.

"Wow! That be a right nice bike you got there, Annie."

"Yeah. It's the best present I ever got. Look here." I press the button that blows the horn, and then I turn on the headlight that's mounted under the basket.

She laughs. "I ain't never seen no bicycle with a horn b'fo."

"Neither have I," I laugh. "I think mine might be the only one."

I'm proud of my bike, and it makes me happy, but a little embarrassed, too, to be showing it to Clydeen.

When we get out to the dirt road, which is really only a path, Clydeen stops. She looks panicked.

"It's okay, Clydeen. Nobody around, see?"

She grabs my hand and turns, looks this way and that. When she is satisfied we are alone, she nods, and we go on.

I point out how protected the Nest is from down here. The road hugs the base of the mesa so tightly that the ledge itself is invisible, made more so by the trees and boulders that dot the upslope.

"Huh," she says, surprised. "I can't see our place a'tall."

"Right! That's what makes it such a great place for us to be. I often think whoever built it must have picked that exact spot on purpose. Of course, ours is the only cave I know of, so maybe it's just a coincidence."

As we approach the corner where the road turns left and goes past Mrs. B's house, Clydeen stops again and stares.

"That be it, huh?"

"Yup. That's it."

"What's that?" she says, pointing.

"That's the barn."

"What's that over there where them trees are?"

"There's a creek that runs along there. Mrs. B and I walk down there sometimes. It's cool there on hot days, but the mosquitos will eat you alive!"

"That her backdoor right there?" she asks, pointing to the small stoop at the back of the house.

"Yes. The front door is around the other side."

The window shades are down, and Mrs. B's truck is gone.

"Do you want to go a little closer?"

"Yas. Okay," she says, picking up my hand again.

Instead of walking down the road, I lead her into the field, and we walk parallel to Mrs. B's property. I show Clydeen the garden. Tell her the names of the goats grazing in the pasture. Point to the water trough where I get our water.

"Very peaceful, ain't it."

"Yes, it is."

I could have said more. Told her again how much I trust Mrs. B, but I don't. Let today's revelation of Mrs. B's friendship with Imani Jackson speak for itself. I'm pretty sure if it weren't for that, we would not be standing where we are right now.

We gaze at the house, the barn, the goats, and the chickens for quite a long time, when suddenly, a cloud of dust appears off to the east. It's moving toward us on the road leading to Mrs. B's property.

"Get down, Clydeen," I whisper. "A car is coming."

We flatten ourselves to the ground amongst the tall, prickly grasses. Mrs. B pulls into her driveway less than a hundred yards from where we're hiding. Rocky hits the ground and begins to bark, sensing our presence no doubt.

"That dog ..." murmurs Clydeen.

"Shhhh. It'll be okay. That's Rocky."

Mrs. B begins to unload boxes of groceries and other items from the bed of the truck. Rocky is staring right at us now, wagging his tail, and Mrs. B pauses and looks in our direction. I cross my fingers, hoping Rocky doesn't come charging over to say hello. Clydeen and I instinctively lower our heads and shut our eyes, as if that's going to keep the border collie from flushing us out. After a couple of minutes, I take a peek and see Mrs. B shake her head, hoist the box she is carrying and head for the house. Rocky dashes to the door ahead of her and waits. I breathe a sigh of relief; he's forgotten all about us.

"It's okay now, Clydeen," I whisper.

Clydeen raises her head, and her eyes follow Mrs. B as she walks up the steps and sets down the box so she can open the door. Mrs. B is a small woman with short gray hair. It is tucked neatly into the broad-brimmed straw hat she wears whenever she's outside. She holds her head high, and there is a spring in her step when she walks. She is wearing a pair of blue jeans and a short-sleeved plaid shirt, clothes she prefers for gardening, fence mending, and other chores. Her work gloves and some tools are lying on the porch railing.

I gaze at her with longing. Watching her now, I realize how much I miss her. I've stayed away for a while, because the urge to talk to her about Clydeen has become too strong, and I don't trust myself not to spill the beans, as it were. I groan inwardly as I think about the day very soon when she's going to read the cards for me and what it will take for me to keep track of all my secrets.

"So that's Miz B," Clydeen says softly, calling me back from my musings.

"Yes. That's Miz B."

"Okay then. We can go back now."

We hurry, low to the ground until we are out of sight of Mrs. B's house.

When we get back to our Nest, Clydeen says, "Well, she don't look so bad."

"What did you expect? A wolf in sheep's clothing," I laugh.

"No ... course not."

Once again, I'm tempted to jump in and say too much, but I hold my tongue. It's getting late anyway. Stanley will be home soon, and I need to leave.

"What about the book?"

"Tomorrow, Clydeen. I'll finish it tonight."

"Okay. And thanks for takin' me down there, showin' me what I needed to see."

"You're welcome, my friend."

She gives me a hug, and we cling to each other for a long moment, gathering courage under the cloud of uncertainty the future is threatening to bring into our lives

Chapter 29
Annie

We've both finished reading *The Adventures of Huckleberry Finn*, and now we're settling in to talk about it—maybe. We're not getting off to a very good start. Clydeen is moody and her eyes are dark and hooded, so who knows what will happen?

"This book be full a nigger this, nigger that," she says testily, standing over me, shaking her copy of the book at me, which I can't help noticing is loaded with pine needle markers.

"I know. I read it. But I also read in our encyclopedias that the story takes place around 1840 before the Civil War, even though the book wasn't written until after the Civil War."

"So?"

"So that was a time when people didn't think there was anything wrong with saying that word, especially in the South, so I'm wondering ..."

"I tol' you this b'fo, girl. Don't you git it? It's an insult. A'ways has been and a'ways will be, and when I sees it on every damn page ...!"

"Okay, okay, I hear you," I say, astonished by her fervor. "But Linda Brent used that word in *Incidents in the Life of a Slave Girl*, and you didn't say a thing about it."

"It ain't the same, Annie. In *Slave Girl*, she only say it a few times and only when she quotin' what some white person say, like Dr. Flint. She never say it 'bout herself or any other colored. But in *Huckleberry Finn*, for cryin' out loud, Huck don't call Jim nothin' but

171

nigger!"

"That's because Mark Twain was white and Huck is white. In *Slave Girl*, Linda Brent is colored, Clydeen. You wouldn't expect her to use that word in the same way, would you?" I say, the pitch of my voice rising. "All I'm saying is that's just the way they talked back then."

"No. That ain't it, Annie. It's to remind us constantly that Jim is diff'rent. He's an 'other.' Whites is human beings, but colored folks, they's others—sumpthin' else and definitely inferior. Remember what Linda Brent say 'bout white people and they opinion a they slaves?"

"Not exactly. What?"

She picks up *Incidents in the Life of a Slave Girl*, which she has brought with her to our place behind the boulder. "Right here," she says, pulling a pine needle marker from its place in the book. "This on page 16. 'These God-breathing machines' [she mean the slaves] are no more, in the sight of their masters than the cotton they plant, or the horses they tend.' So when the white peoples in this book, includin' Huckleberry Finn, call Jim a 'nigger' over and over agin, it's to make sure we don't forgit Jim's station in life, inferior, and maybe not quite human, either."

"Why are you taking it so personally?"

"'Cause it is personal! People still use that word today to shame colored folks, put them in they place so they don't git too uppity, and go thinkin' they might have some rights or be equal to white folks," she says, groaning with impatience. "Remember when I was in that orphanage? How I tol' you it felt?"

"Yeah, I remember," I say, lowering my eyes. I also remember telling her about "nigger milk," how ashamed I felt. So why am I arguing with her about this?

"You think I care 'bout any a what yo' en-cy-clo-pedia say?"

"No, I can see that you don't, and I get the point you're making. I'm sorry."

Clydeen's is so upset, her face has gone dark, and we haven't even opened the book yet. We had no disagreements about *Incidents in the Life of a Slave Girl* when we discussed it last week. There was no argument to be made that the lives of the slaves, and Linda Brent's life in particular, were not pure hell. But today's discussion is taking off in an entirely different direction. The atmosphere between us is already crackling with contention—my fault—and I'm a little worried about what we might be wading into if we don't cool it down a bit.

"Okay, let's not say that word," I offer. "Is there something we can instead?"

"No. We's gonna say it. We's gonna say nigger. There ain't no other word for it. If we's gonna talk 'bout this book, we's gonna hafta say it."

This surprises me, but I agree

"Please sit down now, Clydeen," I say, reaching up to take her hand.

She whacks my hand away and plops down next to me. The heat of her anger radiates off of her body. I smother a yawn and wait to see if she has anything more to say.

She does.

"I thought you tol' me this be a book *against* slavery," she exclaims, not looking at me.

"Well, that's what Miss Clark said," I reply with an authority I don't actually feel.

The truth is, now, almost three weeks later, I don't clearly remember what Miss Clark said. Still, I cling to my position and don't reveal my uncertainty to Clydeen.

She snorts and throws a rock.

"So you think it be anti-slavery jus' 'cause some white lady say so?"

"Well, no. Not exactly. Do you say it's not, just because of that word you hate?"

"That be one thing. But I got more to say 'bout these fools, so les' git on with it."

"Good idea. Shall I start us off?"

"Go ahead."

"So Huck and Jim are both on the run. Agreed?"

"Agreed."

"Huck has faked his own death to escape from his mean father, and Jim, a slave, has run away from Miss Watson, his owner, because he overheard her say she's gonna sell him. Huck's been hiding on Jackson Island, and he's gotten pretty lonesome all by himself, so he's delighted when he discovers Jim's hiding there, too. He's so happy to have Jim's company that he promises Jim he won't turn him in for being a runaway. Okay so far?"

"'Ceptin' for one thing," she says, plucking a pine needle marker from between the pages of the book. "Right here on page 32, Huck say he only makin' that promise 'cause they ain't in 'sivilization', where he say *'people would call me a low-down Abolitionist and despise me for keeping mum.'*"

"You're saying Jim can only trust Huck to keep his promise because they're away from their town?"

"Yas. What Huck called 'sivilization.' But if they was to go back, then what do you 'spose Huck would do?"

"Turn Jim in?"

"Seem to me he say as much."

"Huh ... maybe so. You've really thought about this, haven't you Clydeen?"

"Well, like I tol' you b'fo, what else I got to do?"

"Well then, I guess it was lucky for Jim they didn't go back. Instead, they caught a raft and started traveling down the Mississippi River. The way I understand it, there was some kind of shelter on the raft where Jim could hide. They called it the wigwam."

"Agreed," she says, smiling at me. "They 'sposed to be headin' for the Ohio river where they planned to sell the raft and get on a steamship going north to the free states where Jim gonna claim his freedom. So far, sounds like things goin' great, 'ceptin' the mean tricks Huck plays on Jim."

"Huck's not mean, Clydeen. That's just how he is. If you'd read *The Adventures of Tom Sawyer,* you'd understand that."

"Well then, I'm glad I'm ignorant a that. 'Cause what I seen was Huck playin' with Jim in some mean and dangerous ways, like the time he put a snake in Jim's bed and Jim got bit on the foot and nearly died, and that was b'fo they ever got off Jackson Island!"

"But once they're out on the river together, Huck started to respect Jim more, didn't he?"

"Did he now," says Clydeen, placing a hand on her chest and drawing back.

"Well, yes. Like right here," I say after a few minutes of searching through the markers in my book. "Page 59. Remember this part?"

Clydeen looks over my shoulder and reads for a bit before I go on.

"Huck talked Jim into boarding a wrecked steamboat. While they were on board, their raft got loose and floated away. Turned out there were some bad guys on board the steamboat, and Huck and Jim barely escaped. Later on, after they retrieved the raft and everything settled down, Huck raved on and on about what a wonderful adventure they'd had. But not Jim. He told Huck he didn't want any more adventures.

[Jim] said that when [he found the raft] gone he nearly died, because he judged it was all up with him anyway it could be fixed; for if he didn't get saved he would get drownded; and if he did get saved, whoever saved him would send him back home so as to get the reward, and then Miss Watson would sell him South, sure. Well, he was right; he was most always right; he had an uncommon level head for a nigger.

See there, Clydeen? Huck understood that the risks were much greater for Jim as a runaway slave than they were for him, and he praised Jim for his common sense."

Clydeen scoffs. "You gonna hafta to do better'n that, Annie. Huck did give Jim a credit, yas, but in the next breath, he jus' *had* to add the insult. He say Jim level headed *for a nigger*. Like Jim's in some other class a critter and not jus' another human bein' like Huck hisself."

She spits on the ground, pounds her thigh with her fist.

"For a niiiggger," she says again, drawing out the word like she's never gonna let go of it. "He might jus' as well a said Jim had the uncommon good sense of a cow or a pig," she hisses, jus' like Linda Brent say.

"Aren't you being a little ..."

"... a little what?"

"... a little too touchy, maybe?"

"Hell no, I ain't. Otherwise I never would a kep' on readin' this book. I would a had you bring me some matches and built a fire outta it. But since I did read it, here's the next thing I got to say. If what you say be true, 'bout Huck respectin' Jim and all a that, you'd think it would a stopped him from playin' his next mean trick on Jim."

"Where?"

"Right here," she says, dropping a pine needle from amongst the pages and showing me page 104 of the book. "This was after they got separated on the river at night in the fog. Remember? Huck was in a canoe and got lost somewhere behind Jim, who was on the raft. They was so far apart, they couldn't hear each other, and it was so foggy, they couldn't see each other's lights, neither.

"Next morning, Huck finally caught up to the raft and found Jim sleepin'. When Jim woke up and saw Huck, he couldn't b'lieve his eyes.

Goodness gracious, is dat you, Huck? En you ain' dead—you ain' drownded—you's back agin? It's too good for true, honey, it's too good for true. Lemme look at you chile, lemme feel o' you. No, you ain' dead! you's back agin, 'live en soun', jis de same ole Huck—de same ole Huck, thanks to goodness!

Jim was so glad Huck didn't drown, he was b'side hisself with happiness, callin' Huck 'honey', and all like he do. But Huck, all he saw was a chance to trick Jim. He started actin' like Jim crazy, tellin' him they never was separated, that he'd been right with Jim the whole time, and the long, scary night lost in the fog never happened."

"I remember now. He kept on and on until he convinced Jim he'd dreamt the whole thing, right?"

"Yas. And then when Huck finally got tired a his stupid game, he showed Jim a broken oar and some other trash on the raft. He axed Jim, '[What] does these things stand for?' Jim looked around for a minute, and then he figured it out," she says. "Flip on over to page 106, Annie, and I'mma read it to you.

What do dey stan' for? I'me gwyne to tell you. When I got all wore out wid work, en wid de callin' for you, en went to sleep, my heart wuz mos' broke bekase you wuz los', en I didn' k'yer no' mo' what become er me en de raf'. En when I wake up en fine you back agin, all safe en soun', de tears come, en I could a got down on my knees en kiss yo' foot, I'm so thankful. En all you wuz thinkin' 'bout wuz how you could make a fool uv ole Jim wid a lie. Dat truck dah is trash; en trash is what people is dat puts dirt on de head er dey fren's en makes 'em ashamed.

So lemme axe you, Annie. Is there anything 'bout that scene be respectin' a Jim? Huck makin' Jim disbelieve his own self? Hurtin' his feelin's jus' for the fun of it?" she sneers.

"Wait a minute, Clydeen. That's not fair. You have to look at the next part, too."

"Damn it, Annie!" she yells. "You best show me when the anti-slavery bidniss come up, 'cause I might be too stupid to reco'nize it!"

"Just listen for a minute, Clydeen," I shout back, grabbing the book from her and running my finger down the same page until I get to the part I want to read to her.

[Jim] got up slow and walked to the wigwam, and went in there without saying anything but that. But that was enough. It made me feel so mean I could almost kissed his foot to get him to take it back. It was fifteen minutes before I could work myself up to go and humble myself to a nigger; but I done it, and I warn't ever sorry for it afterwards, neither. I didn't do him no more mean tricks, and I wouldn't done that one if I'd a knowed it would make him feel that way.

"See there, Clydeen? Huck was sorry he hurt Jim's feelings. That attitude is nothing like what Linda Brent said in that sentence you read before. Huck did see Jim as a person with feelings like anybody else. In fact, he was so ashamed he went to apologize to Jim."

"Oh, c'mon, Annie. He did go and apologize, or at least the book say he did, but not b'fo he go on and on 'bout how humiliatin' it was for him to do it. Where does Huck git off thinkin' a *boy* like him be so superior to Jim, a *grown man*, that to apologize is so b'neath him, he can hardly bring hisself to do it? Another thing, too: If the two a them had been back in the town they come from, or in any slave town, I bet you a hun'ert bucks Jim wouldn't a dared call Huck 'trash' and show his feelin's the way he done. I wager he'd a been riskin' his life to talk like that."

"Well, if that's true, maybe on a raft in the middle of the river was the only place Huck would even consider owing Jim an apology, let alone give him one."

But I'm talking to myself. Clydeen has scrambled to her feet and taken off running.

"Listen to me, Clydeen! Where you going?"

She runs to a tree with a low-hanging branch and jumps up and grabs it. She swings out wide, her long, skinny legs splayed out like a frog.

"Ouch! That hurt!" she says, dropping to the ground, holding up her two hands, which are skinned and scraped from the rough tree bark.

"Well, that wasn't so smart."

"Shut up, Annie!"

"Well, what do you call it?"

"I calls it painful!" she laughs, shaking her hands and racing back to the boulder.

We are both out of breath, so I fetch a bottle of water, hand it to Clydeen and then take a long drink myself.

She pours some into the foil bottle cap and offers it to Gary.

"So where we at?"

"Well, I was about to mention in that same scene, Huck promised himself he wouldn't play any more mean tricks on Jim. And he never did, either."

"Oh, God! Are you outta yo' mind, girl?" she says, getting up and glaring at me, her tone one of disgust. "Didn't he forgit all about that promise the minute they's back in 'sivilization' and Tom Sawyer showed up?"

It's hard to argue with what she's saying, so this time, I don't try.

"Lemme put it to you straight, Annie. To me as a Negro *person*, which I am, this book boil down to two white boys and a few other fools humiliatin' a colored man who only want one thing—his freedom. And to make it worse, nobody really care that much 'bout helpin' him git there neither, includin' Huckleberry Finn."

Wow! I pass Gary off to Clydeen and walk away. There's a lot more to this book than I realized. I'm forced to admit that there *was* a lot of mistreatment and sadness in store for Jim that Twain tried to cloak in satirizing supposedly harmless "adventures."

When I go back, I sit down next to Clydeen, touch my arm to hers and stare at them, one light tan, the other a rich brown. Fine dark hairs on my arm, none on hers. I can't help wondering if I should go home, stop this conversation right now. But if I do, she'll think I don't want to hear what she has to say.

Finally, I decide we're too deep into it to stop now, and so I press on. "I did think Huck was the hero of this book, Clydeen. I thought he was a boy with a good heart dedicated to being free himself and understanding that Jim deserved the same. What you've been saying, though, is beginning to shake my faith a little. Still, I can show you one place in the story where Huck is definitely on Jim's side against the forces of slavery."

"Okay," she says dubiously. "Show me what you got."

I pick up my book and look for the place marker.

"Right here. The time Huck used his cleverness and trickery to protect Jim from a couple of slave hunters. Remember?"

"Go ahead."

"Well, they were getting close to Cairo, Illinois, where they were supposed to end their journey and head up the Ohio River to the free states. But Cairo was such a small village, Huck wasn't sure they would see it at night, so he told Jim he was going to take the canoe ashore to ask about their location. Soon after he pushed off in the canoe, two men with guns came alongside and told Huck they were looking for five runaway slaves. They wanted to search the raft where Jim was hiding. But Huck completely bamboozled them and saved Jim from being captured.

"This part starts on page 112. When the slave hunters told Huck they were going to board the raft, here's what Huck said:

> *'I wish you would, because it's pap that's there, and maybe you'd help me tow the raft ashore where the light is. He's sick— and so is mam and Mary Ann. Pap'll be mighty much obleeged to you, I can tell you. Everybody goes away when I want them to help me tow the raft ashore, and I can't do it by myself.'*
>
> *'Well, that's infernal mean. Odd, too. Say, boy, what's the*

matter with your father?'

'It's the—a—the—well, it ain't anything much.'

One says: 'Boy, that's a lie. What IS the matter with your pap? Answer up square now, and it'll be the better for you.'

'I will, sir, I will, honest—but don't leave us, please. It's the—the —Gentlemen, if you'll only pull ahead, and let me heave you the headline, you won't have to come a-near the raft—please do.'

'Set her back, John, set her back!' says one. They backed water. 'Keep away, boy.... Confound it, I just expect the wind has blowed it to us. Your pap's got the small-pox, and you know it precious well.'

"See?" I say, laughing. "What a great passage! Huck uses his trickery to save Jim from being captured, Clydeen."

"That part was good, a'ight. But the fact is, my friend, you ignored what happened just *b'fo* the slave traders showed up. Look back on pages 110 and 111. Like you say, Huck told Jim he afraid they might miss Cairo, so he gonna go ashore to find out where they's at. But Jim was tastin' freedom, and all he could do was rave 'bout what he gonna do with it. Huck was horrified.

Jim said it made him all over trembly and feverish to be so close to freedom.... He was saying how the first thing he would do when he got to a free State he would go to saving up money and never spend a single cent, and when he got enough he would buy his wife, which was owned on a farm close to where Miss Watson lived; and then they would both work to buy the two children, and if their master wouldn't sell them, they'd get an Ab'litionist to go and steal them. It most froze me to hear such talk. He wouldn't ever dared to talk such talk in his life before. Just see what a difference it made in him the minute he judged he was about free.

"So when Huck shoved off in the canoe, Annie, it weren't to find Cairo. He goin' ashore to turn Jim in, and all the while Huck was rowin' away from the raft, Jim be heapin' praise on him for bein' his true friend.

Pooty soon I'll be a-shout'n' for joy, en I'll say, it's all on accounts o' Huck; I'm a free man, en I couldn't ever ben free ef it hadn' ben for Huck; Huck done it. Jim won't ever forgit you, Huck; you's de bes' fren' Jim's ever had; en you's de ONLY fren' ole Jim's got now.' I was paddling off, all in a sweat to tell on him; but when he says this, it seemed to kind of take the tuck all out of me. I went along slow then, and I warn't right down certain whether I was glad I started or whether I warn't. When I was fifty yards off, Jim says: 'Dah you goes, de ole true Huck; de on'y white genlman dat ever kep' his promise to ole Jim." Well, I just felt sick. But I says, I GOT to do it—I can't get OUT of it.

"But then the slave hunters came along, Clydeen. Huck could have betrayed Jim right then and there, but he couldn't bring himself to do it, despite his conscience nagging at him."

"Maybe so, but we'll never know if Huck would a let Jim go free. He'd sure lost his enthusiasm for it, and by the time he got to shore, he found out they a'ready passed by Cairo anyhow. Lucky for Huck and his conscience. Too bad for Jim, 'cause he missed his one chance for freedom, and he was plum outta luck, Annie. At that point, Huck didn't need to turn him in or let him go free, 'cause that raft was headed straight for New Orleans where the slave market was at, and there weren't no more free states along the way. To me, that be the saddest part a this whole book, even sadder 'n the chapters at the end. All a Jim's excitement 'cause he 'bout to be a free man wantin' to buy back his family one day—gone."

"Hmmm. So do you think Mark Twain wrote it that way to avoid saying it would be a good thing, a heroic thing, for a white Southerner like Huck to help a slave get to freedom?"

"Looks that way, don't it," she sighs. "If it had happened that way, that would a said anti-slavery to me. But it would a been a completely different story, too."

"If you look at it from Jim's point of view, Miss Watson was the real hero, even though she was such a small part of the story. She's the one who freed Jim, even though she did it in one of the only socially acceptable ways such things could be done, and that was in her will."

"I think that Twain guy be all twisted up 'bout this slavery bidniss. I don't know what he be tryin' to git at. In the beginnin', Huck was so glad to have Jim with him, he promised never to turn him in. Still, he played all kinds a mean tricks on him. But after a time on the river together, maybe Huck did recognize that Jim had some human qualities like hisself, as you say. And true, he did protect Jim from the slave hunters, even though he'd already decided he's gonna turn Jim in hisself. He didn't do it, but that's only 'cause by then they passed Cairo, and he knew that was Jim's last jumpin' off place b'fo the slave markets in New Orleans. Jus' a lot a fence walkin', you axe me, nobody in this book fallin' off on the side of abolition, either."

I'm not quite ready to concede the point, but right now, I can't come up with anything favorable to the anti-slavery side of the argument, so I keep my mouth shut.

"Another time Mark Twain let Huckleberry Finn off the hook was when he let Jim's fate fall into the hands a those two scoundrels, the King and the Duke. The King is the one who ended up betrayin' Jim and sellin' him for forty dollars to them peoples name a Phelps, who turned out to be Tom Sawyer's aunt and uncle. The Phelps' locked Jim in a shed so they could look for his owner and collect the reward."

"True. But remember, Huck did hang around hoping to help Jim escape."

"You still tryin' to make out like Huck some hero? That part you talkin' 'bout now? I myself actually hoped I was finally gittin' to the anti-slavery part, 'cause I sho ain't seein' it so far, and the book almos' over. But then Tom Sawyer showed up and say he gonna help Huck free Jim. Instead a jus' doin' it like Huck planned b'fo Tom got there, them two boys turned it into one a they silly games and put Jim through all kinds a sufferin' jus' for the fun of it. In the end, they almos' got Jim killed, and they own selves right along with him.

"Those last few chapters was so painful to read, I thought I was never gonna git to the end. It turned out Tom Sawyer knew all along Jim had been freed. All that unnecessary hell them boys put Jim through was jus' another one a they 'adventures.' Why'd they do that? 'Cause they's back in 'sivilization', a 'sivilization' that gave them permission. If Jim had been killed, there would a been no comeuppance, neither. Jus' like there was no comeuppance when my daddy was killed. Nobody cared!"

She's shouting now, beating her fists against the boulder.

I grab her hands to stop her from hurting herself.

"Stop! Stop, Clydeen." I gather her in my arms. "Nobody should ever have go through what was done to your father, what it put your whole family through, Clydeen!"

"Damn right! And I'm hell a angry about it, too!" she yells into my shoulder.

She doesn't cry, but her body trembles in my arms.

"Of course you are, as well you should be, Clydeen," I soothe. I am *so sorry* that happened."

After a time, her body stills. She pulls back, picks up her book, gets to her feet and stands right in front of me. Waving the *Huckleberry Finn* in my face, she speaks in a voice cold with rage.

"Huckleberry Finn was jus' some white racisit Southern boy had no real interest a'tall in helpin' Jim get to freedom. Fact is in his heart a hearts, he was against it. This book is as racist as they come, Annie, and from where I sit, ain't no other way to look at it! It hurt me to see Jim treated that a-way by them two white boys, and it hurt me even more when Jim lost all hope of escapin' the slave market. Weren't no humor in it for me! No sir! It jus' made me so mad I wanted to smack them two ridiculous boys upside they heads. Them two swindlers who sold Jim, too!

"Then at the end, Jim finds out he's free, and in about one sentence, he jus' walks off and outta the picture. What the hell endin' is that for Jim? He served his purpose? Everybody done abusin' him now, and so he can jus' fade away?"

"I hear you, Clydeen. It was bad."

"Bad ain't the half of it!"

She sits down next to me, and I tell her to breathe. She quiets herself, but it's a long while before I dare to break the silence.

"I want to ask you something, Clydeen," I say eventually.

"Yeah, what?"

"One of our books at school showed pictures of Negros standing around cabins grinning and playing music, looking all happy and showing their white teeth like life was treating them just fine. These were supposed to be pictures of slave life. That was a lie, wasn't it?"

"Well, course it was, Annie. You know that by now."

"Yes." I say, averting my eyes, lapsing into silence again.

"Whew!" says Clydeen at last. "I think I've had more than enough for today. I'm hongry. Let's go eat those cookies b'fo you have to go."

She picks up Gary with one hand, tucks her books under the same arm, and grabs my hand as we head up the wash.

We sit in the shade of the cloudy afternoon. There's thunder and lightning off to the east, and I will need to leave soon. The package of cookies lies open on the ground, and Gary scarfs up the small pieces we break off for him.

"Okay, so what about us?" I blurt out, spraying cookie crumbs all over both of our laps. I think I'm finally grasping something I hadn't seen before.

"What about us?" she says, raising her eyebrows as she absentmindedly combs through Gary's tail with her fingers.

"Are we like Huck and Jim? Is it only because we are up here alone, away from *our* civilization that we can find a way to be friends like we are?"

She looks at me, unruffled, and says, "Well, ain't there at least some truth to that, Annie?"

Damn! It hurts to hear that. I turn away and let my mind wander over the happenings of the past few weeks. If I hadn't been so desperately lonely when I found Clydeen here, maybe I would have ratted her out without giving it a second thought. And what about right now? Am I doing what's best for her, or have I been more interested in having an 'adventure' like Huck and Tom? Here's the really hard question: Would I be so scared of my folks finding out about the two of us up here if she were white? Maybe it wouldn't worry me at all the way it does now.

I stare at her, and she nods, almost like she's read my mind.

"Jus' like my daddy say—not so diff'rent," she whispers.

I put my arm around her shoulders and pull her close—this most amazing of friends, the one who has reawakened love in *my* heart, the very same love I was so determined to bury forever just a few short weeks ago. So where do we go from here, I wonder.

"I have to go," I say a few minutes later. "Can I take this book with me, Clydeen?" I ask, holding up *Incidents in the Life of a Slave*

Girl.

"Sure. You gonna read it agin?"

"No. Nothing like that. I have a feeling I've missed something important. I want to see if I can figure it out before the books have to go back to the library."

Raindrops begin to fall. I scramble to my feet, gather my stuff and head down before the wash goes slick.

"It gonna be a'ight, Annie," Clydeen calls after me as she so often does when she wants to reassure me.

"We'll see," I shout over the thunder that has moved in with the coming storm.

Jacobs, Harriet A. (Harriet Ann), 1813-1897; Child, Mrs. (Lydia Maria), 1802-1880, ed. *Incidents in the life of a slave girl.* (Kindle edition) Boston: Published for the Author.

Twain, Mark. *The Adventures of Huckleberry Finn.* Amazon Classics, Kindle Edition.

Chapter 30
Annie

I'm exhausted when I get home. The discussion of *Huckleberry Finn* has left me as limp as a wet dishrag, and I can barely keep my eyes open long enough to eat dinner. It's only 7:30 when I finish washing and drying the dishes, but I'm so tired, I head straight to my room. I groan with pleasure as I drop my weary body onto the bed, being careful not to disturb Teresa.

About midnight, though, I wake up, charged with energy, my mind churning. Grabbing the two books, *Huckleberry Finn* and *Incidents in the Life of a Slave Girl*, my Big Chief tablet and a pencil, I tiptoe into the kitchen and quietly close the door behind me before turning on the light. I lay everything out on the kitchen table and stare at it. I sit. And then I sit some more. I yawn. I scratch my mosquito bites. I hunch over the books and examine the covers. I don't know what I'm looking for or how to find it.

The sliding door into the kitchen opens. It's Vivian, her hair wild, eyes blurry. "What are you doing, Annie? Are you alright?"

"I'm fine. I went to bed too early, and now I can't sleep."

"Oh," she says.

She goes to the sink, draws a glass of water from the tap, then leaves me to it.

What is it I am trying to understand about these two books? I ask myself for what seems like the millionth time.

I sweep my hair off the back of my sweaty neck and flip through pages. No answer comes.

Is it something about the mistreatment Jim and Linda Brent endured?

I reread certain passages in both books looking for hints. In my opinion, the mistreatment of slaves described in *Slave Girl* is far worse than that portrayed in *Huckleberry Finn*, but so what? It's all bad. I still have the feeling there's something important hiding in plain sight, but I haven't found it yet.

I take a deep breath, drink a glass of water, tap my pencil, and try to think. What about the characters themselves—Jim in *Huckleberry Finn*, Linda Brent in *Incidents in the Life of a Slave Girl*? It's easy to overlook their essential nature, because the horrific descriptions of what they are going through tend to overshadow everything else about them.

Maybe I should look more closely at Jim and Linda and who they are as human beings.

With that thought in mind, I read passages from one book, and then the other. It's not long before I begin to find what I have been searching for. I continue reading and making notes until I'm so sleepy I have no choice but to drag myself back to bed.

I'm excited, but what will Clydeen think? Maybe she'll think this is a whole lot of nothing.

****

I sleep later than usual, making up for the two or three hours I spent in the kitchen last night. Stanley has already left for work. I find Teresa sitting in her highchair in the kitchen, babbling away. No sign of Vivian. Willie and Charlie are down on their hands and knees in the dust in the front yard. Charlie is trying to teach Willie how to play marbles, but Willie's too young. He can't flick the marble into the ring, so he sets it on the ground and gives it a shove. Charlie must be really hard up for something to do, because he is being way more patient than usual.

I pour Cheerios onto the tray of Teresa's highchair and make a bowl with milk for myself.

"Where's Vivian?" I ask her.

She looks at me as she drops one of the Cheerios into her mouth. She knows I don't really expect an answer from her.

Vivian walks in.

"Oh, Annie. You're finally up. I have a whole pile of mending to do this morning, so I'm putting you in charge of the other kids."

Up in smoke goes any chance I may have had of leaving this joint before lunchtime. I don't mind, though. I spend as much time as I can hunched over my Big Chief tablet, writing, erasing, writing some more. Between short bursts of writing, I chase Willie around, which he loves. After that, I lie on the floor with Teresa, entertaining her with a sequence of toys while she lies on her tummy and coos, blowing spit bubbles from between her baby lips.

Finally, it's time to go. Everything I'm taking is packed and waiting in my bike basket. There's still enough water up at the Nest, so there will be no stops today.

"Hey, Annie," Clydeen calls out, smiling down at me as I make my way up the wash.

"Whatcha doin'?"

"Waitin' for you, is all. Man, was I tired las' night. I jus' woke up a little while ago."

"I was up half the night, but at least I think I have something to show for it."

I pull the two books and my tablet out of my bag and lay them on the altar while we eat lunch.

"Okay, Miss Annie. What you got?" Clydeen asks as we pack up the leftovers.

"Something was nagging at me, and I couldn't figure out what it was."

"Okay. What?"

"Last night, I started focusing on the similarities and differences in the enslaved characters as human beings, and not just on what was happening *to* them. First, I asked this question: What is it both Jim and Linda Brent want?"

"That's easy. Freedom."

"Right. But their beliefs about themselves and how they view the world and themselves in it color the way they go about getting this thing called freedom."

"Okay. How's that?"

"Jim puts his trust in a ne'er-do-well *white boy*, Huckleberry Finn, and expects Huck to get him to the free states. He looks up to

Huck (and other white people) as if they are the adults and he is a child, even when those white people actually are children."

"Like Huck and Tom, you mean."

"Yeah. Jim barely ever protests the treatment he gets, and when he does, it doesn't take much for some white person to talk him into going along with it. He never gets angry or fed up, and he does not see it as his place to take any initiative on his own behalf, even when he has the opportunity."

"I wondered 'bout that myself. When we talked about some a them scenes yesta'day, I was like, 'Why is this colored man a'ways pourin' love, love, love and more love on Huck? Why does Jim love Huck so much?'"

"Jim loves Huck because Huck is white. Maybe he thinks that's what white people want from him, and in Mark Twain's world, maybe they do—did. In any event, Jim assumes all white people have the intelligence, understanding, and judgment that he believes he does not have. Granted, Jim seems to be a person with a kind and loving nature, but I think he is also a true believer in the absolute superiority of white people. Their white skin alone makes them worthy of his love and admiration. Deferring to white people, no matter how bizarre the circumstances, is always the right thing—actually, the only thing for Jim to do."

"And it ain't like Huck be lovin' Jim back, neither. Huck be playin' tricks on him, plannin' to turn him in, and exposin' him to all sorts a bad characters."

"Right. And when Tom Sawyer enters the picture and enlists Huck in his elaborate plans to free Jim, their 'play' only serves to endanger Jim and subject him to a great deal of unnecessary torment. Again, Jim protests very little, and ultimately he gives in to every foolish misery Tom and Huck devise for him."

"But ain't Jim jus' tryin' to survive, Annie? Ain't it jus' his way?"

"Sure it is. I'm not judging it. I'm just noticing it, for comparison purposes, Clydeen. I think maybe we have to cut Jim some slack, too, because he is a fictional character, while Linda Brent is not."

"Ooooo, I think I sees where you's goin' with this. Real smart, Annie. You usin' Jim to light up Linda Brent, ain't you?" she says, picking up *Incidents in the Life of a Slave Girl* and waving it at me. "So let's see. We's sayin' Jim loves them white people, thinks he's so inferior that they's right 'bout everything. He depends on them in every way, 'cause he feel like he's got nothin'."

"Pre-cisely."

I smile at her. I love these talks we've been having. Talking this way about books we've read is a new experience for both of us, and Clydeen is the perfect partner for the journey. I'm captivated by her quick mind, but even more by her willingness to jump on board with me and ride the train all the way into the station, like we're doing now.

"Okay," I say then. "Let's go back to comparing Jim and Linda Brent, who both want the same thing—freedom. She gets it, but I'm not sure Jim ever does."

"Why not?"

"Because Jim is so tied to the likes of Huckleberry Finn, who, as clever as he is, is nothing more than a destitute orphaned child who can't be expected, for many reasons, to help Jim at all. But from Jim's perspective, simply because he is white, Huck has the answers and all of the powers Jim feels he lacks. So he relies one hundred percent on Huck to get him to the free states, which Huck fails to do. In fact, when Huck is confronted with the actuality of Jim going free, it goes against everything he's been taught by his 'sivilization,' and he feels duty-bound to turn him in.

"Later, when Jim learns that Mrs. Watson has freed him in her will, he walks away with nothing, not even an iota of appreciation from the white people he has served and revered his entire life. Worse than that, he's at great risk, because—"

"—b'cause he *still in slave territory*; he not in a free state."

"Right."

"So what you think gonna happen to him?"

"Ha! I don't think freedom's going be in Jim's future for long. He'll probably end up enslaved by the first white person comes along with a trick up his sleeve and grabs him up."

"Uhh-huh. Prob'ly so," says Clydeen glumly. "But I'm guessin' the point you's fixin' to make is that Linda Brent ain't like Jim?"

"That's what I was about to say, yes. Is it so obvious to you that it's not the big deal I'm making it out to be?"

"Don't worry about that. I like where this is goin'."

"Okay then, when I started to think about who Linda Brent is as a person, as a human being, I realized she shares none of Jim's qualities."

Clydeen gets to her feet, excited now.

"You's right, Annie. Linda Brent had *no* love for white peoples. From a early age, she knowed exactly who they was and what they likely to do. No way she gonna trust any of 'em."

"Then when her master, Dr. Flint, started chasing after her when she was just 14—our age, Clydeen!—she knew exactly what he wanted, and she was having none of it."

"She promised herself she ain't never gonna be that man's whore."

"And she never was, either," I shout, pumping my arms in the air. "It was all because she knew she couldn't rely on anyone but herself to protect her. She saw that so clearly, no threat, no punishment, no nothing could break her will and force her to submit the way so many other slave women had to do when push came to shove."

"It was all b'cause she had been taught by her grandmother to respect herself, Annie. It was b'cause she didn't think she was inferior to nobody. And it was b'cause she was determined to be free, and if she couldn't do that, she was gonna make sumpthin' of herself anyway, even if it was jus' to live a righteous life as best she could under the circumstances."

"Yup. That's it exactly it, Clydeen."

I pick up the book and find one of my place markers from last night.

"Here's Linda having a conversation with her master, Dr. Flint. This one passage says everything about who she is. Dr. Flint says to her: 'Do you know that I have a right to do as I like with you,—that I can kill you, if I please?' And she comes right back with this: 'You have tried to kill me, and I wish you had, but you have no right to do as you like with me.'

"She was 16 years old then, but she'd a'ready come into her own and taken control a her own life, even though it meant fightin' tooth and nail every single day. When her first escape attempt failed, a course she didn't dare show herself on the plantation. Tha's how she ended up spendin' *seven years* in that tiny crawl space, hidin' from Dr. Flint."

Clydeen has her arms wrapped around herself, rocking back and forth as she recalls the horror of what Linda went through.

"For me, that was the most awful part a that book, Annie. I jus' couldn't imagine anyone survivin' that misery, 'specially for such a long period of time."

"I know it, Clydeen. She was crippled after that, remember? But still she managed to get to the North and out of Dr. Flint's clutches. She got herself a job, reunited with her children and her brother, and wrote this book."

"That weren't the end a Dr. Flint, though. He was so determined she'd never escape him, he kep' goin' North searchin' for her. He spent all a his money tryin' to chase her down, and when he died, his daughter didn't git a penny!"

Clydeen slaps her thighs and laughs so hard, tears run down her face.

"That nasty white dude jus' couldn't stand the idea that he'd been bested by a Negro slave girl he supposedly owned body and soul. It really is some story!"

"Linda dealt with every obstacle imaginable, every loss, every tragedy, but she never developed a mentality like Jim's. Jim's true self was hidden, except for those few moments when he thought he was going to go free at the mouth of the Ohio River. Otherwise, he never belonged to himself. Linda's true self was never hidden, and she never belonged to anyone but herself. I think that's where the lesson lies, Clydeen. That's what I was trying so hard to grasp."

"That Linda. She was sumpthin', a'ight."

"I'm so glad we read these two books together. I have to say if I had read *Slave Girl* without reading *Huckleberry Finn*, too, I don't think I'd appreciate Linda and her strength of character the way I do now. It makes me wonder if freedom is as much a state of mind as anything else."

"Hmmm," Clydeen muses. "Wow, ain't that sumpthin' to think about. From now on, I'mma take a page outta Linda Brent's book, 'cause I sure don't wanna be no Jim. Nothin' personal."

"Well put, Clydeen. Me neither!"

Part 3

Part 3

Chapter 31
Clydeen

When I first got here, nights with thunder and lightnin' and no moon like tonight was so scary, I'd jus' hunker down in my sleepin' bag and shiver mos' a the night. But then Annie brung me that big ol' flashlight and hung it on a root comin' through the roof a the cave so's I'd have light. Since then, I been fixin' a tarp over the lean-to boards at night to keep anyone from seein' the light when I have it on.

A few days later, she brung me a baseball bat made a wood and tol' me to put it under the cot jus' in case. She say it belong to Charlie, but he quit baseball, so he ain't never gonna miss it. Lucky for me, they ain't been a single soul 'cept Annie come up the wash in all the weeks I been here, and that baseball bat is right where we put it the day she brung it.

'Cause a the rain, I climb into my sleepin' bag early and turn out the light. Gary curls up beside me, and his soft breathin' be a comfort to me. I lie back listenin' to the rain and start thinkin' 'bout *Huckleberry Finn* and all me'n Annie been talkin' 'bout these past few days. After we's all done today, she tol' me she thinks I must be pre-co-shus, whatever that is, but it seemed to make her happy.

All at once, I hear sumpthin' that make the hair on the back a my neck stand up. I feel around for Gary and find him sittin' on his haunches on the edge of the cot like he be listenin', too.

"Gary, git back in here," I whisper. "It prob'ly jus' a' animal passin' by. Maybe a coon or sumpthin' wantin' to git in outta the rain."

Annie was right when she said the sounds I hear at night ain't ghosts. Jus' like she said, they's critters prowl around here at night, lots of 'em—I don't know the names a mos' a them, but I did learn they's nothin' to be afraid of long's I don't leave no food layin' around. But this here sound? It ain't like that.

I listen real hard but all I hears is the soft patter of rain, so I pull Gary in next to me and drop off to sleep for a while. Next thing I know, my eyes fly open, and my whole body jumps. The rocks outside the cave are crunchin' and rattlin' like somebody steppin' on 'em.

"Annie? That you?" I say in a loud whisper.

No answer. Nothin'. Can't be Annie nohow. When she sneak out and come back at night, she whistles so's I knows it's her and don't git scared. But she'd never come up here in the rain.

I sit up on the edge of the cot, terrified, my body tense with listenin'. Minutes tick by and nothin' more happens. Careful not to make a sound, I feel around for Gary and put him under the box, and then pull the baseball bat up beside me. My skin prickles. A chill runs through me, and goosebumps come up on my arms. My whole body knows sumpthin's comin'.

A giant black bird swoops into the cave. The monster is so big it makes the inside of the cave go pitch dark on account a the shadow of its massive wings loomin' over me. I jump to my feet, grab the bat and lunge, swingin' blind, my heart poundin' in my ears.

"Ahhh!" screams the monster as the bat connects.

It weren't a solid hit, so I move in closer, screamin' at the top of my lungs. "Git outta here, you hear me! You git on outta here!"

"Ow! Stop! Stop," cries the bird, flapping its wings like crazy. "Crap, will you please cut it out?"

I freeze right where I am, maybe three feet from the creature, the bat over my shoulder ready to swing again. My muscles tremble, and I'm weak with fear. I growl like a dog, and the two of us prance in a slow circle, peerin' at each other in the dark, waitin' to see what the other one gonna do next.

"Please! I'm not going to hurt you. You're scaring me," yells the bird, not daring to stop the dance.

"Uh-huh," I reply, drawin' it out long and low hoping I sound dangerous while I try to figure out what to do next.

Well, says I to myself, *ain't no monster. White man by the sound of it. Could be jus' as bad.*

I tighten my grip on the bat and hold it out in front me like a sword, swingin' it from side to side while I retreat behind my cot. As if that flimsy thing gonna protect me!

"What are you doing here?" he axe me.

He sounds a little whiny.

"What am *I* doin' here? What are *you* doing here?" I shout.

"This is *my* place," he say.

"Oh, yeah? Well this here *my* place now, and you best be movin' along b'fo I take yo' head clean off!"

He thinks this over for a minute or two, and then he say, "Do you have a light in here by chance?"

"Who wants to know?" I bark and move a little further back where I have to bend over a little 'cause the ceilin' so low here.

"My name is Ulysses. People call me Ulie."

"Ulie? Did you say Ulie?"

"Yes, Ulie. Why? Do I know you?"

"No, but I know who you are. Yas, I do. I have a light. Let me turn it on." I lower the bat and turn on the flashlight.

Standing there is a tall young man, white by the looks a him under a righteous coat a dirt. His hair is all matted and twisted, and a scruffy beard covers mos' a his face. His eyes are dark pools in the dim light. I can't make out the color, but they's worry in them eyes. He be way too skinny, hongry lookin', like he ain't had sufficient to eat for a while. He wearin' a T-shirt way too big for him, filthy and torn. His pants are ripped at both knees, and they hang so loose, he holdin' 'em up with a piece a rope strung through the belt loops and tied 'round his waist. His boots be worse 'n my old shoes was, and he's got 'em held together with some tape. Over his clothes, he be wearin' sumphin' like a poncho or maybe a raincoat. When he raise and lower his arms, that thing spread out like giant bat wings.

He smell bad, too. Oh, boy, do he ever, and the longer we stand there inside the cave, the worse it git. I know that smell; I smelled it on myself b'fo Annie started bringin' me the washin' stuff.

"I thought you's some bird monster, waving 'round that thing you got on the way you done."

"Well, I'm not, as you can see. Wow," he say, takin' a look around at my stuff, the metal lunch box, the water bottles I keep on the back ledge of the cave, the books, games, and cards, my violin, the hanging flashlight, and the two cots, one for Annie and one for me. And of course, the baseball bat.

"Are you living here?"

"What's it look like?"

"Uhhh ... do you think you could you put that bat away?"

"You gonna hurt me if I do?"

"Hell, no, I'm not gonna hurt you! Are you gonna hurt me?"

"Not unless I have to. What you after?"

"Nothing. Like I said, this is my place."

"Ain't yo' place right now, though, is it?"

"I built it when I was a kid," he say, pattin' his chest with one hand, all proud a hisself. "It was my studio. So to speak," he laughs like this a joke. "I'm an artist. Well, I used to be an artist. Long time ago now."

"Well, Mister Ulie, artist or not, this be the second time somebody tol' me this place belong to them, and I'm still here. Whatcha think a that?"

I smirk at him as I lower the bat.

"Oh, really," he replies, all sarcastic like. "But it looks like two of you are living here. So who would the other occupant of this fine piece of real estate be?"

"Her name Annie."

"So which one of you do I talk to about making a reservation at this fine establishment, you or this Annie person?"

I don't answer, 'cause I don't know what the hell he talkin' 'bout.

"Okay, so where is this Annie now? Is she about to clobber me, too?"

"She home, sleepin', I reckon."

"Where is home?"

"Come outside. I'll show you."

The rain has stopped now, so I slip on my big shoes, laces untied, and clomp outside. I take a few deep breaths a fresh air and pull down the tarp, shake it out and put it away so the smell can clear out the cave.

"Annie? She live down there." I point vaguely in the direction of the Cahill Palace down below. "When I come, she say this place hers, jus' like you sayin' now. But here I am, still here, as you can see."

Ulie scratches his head and stares, like he confused or sumpthin'.

"Well, what do you know? Wow! A lot has changed since I been gone. My folks own that land. Or at least they did when I left. Shit, did they sell it to a developer or something?"

"Don't know. You gonna hafta axe Annie when she come back."

Ulie sits down on the ledge and begins rockin' back and forth with his head in his hands.

"Oh boy, oh boy, oh boy," he mutters to hisself. "What a mess! How long have I been gone, anyway?"

"Now how's I s'posed answer a question like that? Don't you know?"

He don't answer me, jus' continues to rock. After a few minutes, his head pops up, like he jus' thought a sumpthin'. He looks me up and down, and then he say, "I can't see you very well in the dark, but those clothes you got on sure do look familiar. Any chance you're wearing my clothes?"

I look down at the pants and shirt I'm wearin', the shoes, socks.

"I reckon so. Annie brung 'em to me."

I hold up one foot, show him the heavy brown boy shoes I'm wearin'.

"These yours?"

"Well, shoot. Could be."

"My other ones all tore up, like those," I say, nodding at his feet.

"Uhhh ... do you think maybe I could have some of that water you got in there?"

"Sure. I'll get you some."

I go back inside the cave and open the metal lunch box. They's a cheese sandwich and a couple apples left, so I take the sandwich and one a the bottles a water and hand 'em to him.

He takes long gulps of water.

"Oh! That really hits the spot," he say, handing the empty bottle back to me "You sure you can spare this?"

"Ain't it a little late to be worryin' 'bout that?"

"I suppose it is," he laughs.

He start in eatin' the sandwich like he afraid it might bite him first.

"Where'd you get this anyway?" he axe, his mouth so full I can barely understand him.

"The food and water? Annie brung it. She brings me stuff. I reckon I couldn't stay up here without her."

"I guess not. How old is this Annie?"

"She 14 now. She goin' to high school," I say proudly, as if it's my accomplishment.

"And how old are you?"

"'Bout the same."

I don't want any more questions, so I turn the tables and axe him, "How old are you?"

"Well, there ain't that much left of my twenties, near as I can tell," he say with a sigh, his shoulders droopin' like they be some powerful sadness or regret in him. "Sit down, will you please? You're making me nervous."

I sit down on the ledge, and we gaze out over the land below.

"You haven't told me your name," Ulie say after a while.

"You tell me what you doin' here first," says I, "then I'll decide whether to tell you my name or not."

"Do you know my mom and dad?" he axe me, 'stead a answerin' my question.

"No, but Annie do."

And then it hits me. Lord have mercy, the boy has no idea his daddy passed.

He studies me for a while, and then he heaves another big sigh.

"Okay. I'll go first, but let me ask you just one more thing before I do. You have on my clothes and you say you know about me, but I don't know you, so ...?"

"So what?"

"How come?"

I hesitate, wonderin' if I should tell him or make sumpthin' up. 'Cause really, I don't know this white boy from Adam. I jus' think I do. It gittin' light now, and he be lookin' at me with such befuddlement, I'm startin' to feel sorry for him, so I decides to go ahead and tell him.

"Okay, here it is. I know about you, your name and all, from Annie. She tol' me you went to another country to go to school and got lost. I know 'bout the war and concentration camps and all kinds a crazy stuff in them other places, and I know yo' mama been lookin' for you for a long time. That's what I know. Now, could you tell me sumpthin'? Why don't you jus' go on home to yo' mama so she don't have to worry over you no mo'?"

I watch him and wait. His long hair is so dirty and tangled it barely moves in the soft breeze comin' up b'fo morinin'.

"I can't go home yet. Something's not right, and I'm not sure what it is. I need to stay up here for a while," he say, lookin' at me, waitin' for what he sayin' to sink in.

I remember the first night Annie come up here, and I tol' her almos' the exact same thing.

"I took off from a work detail at a camp I was in after the war. I left with nothing but the clothes on my back, literally. No identity papers of any kind. Certainly no money," he snorts. "I'm not exactly sure how I got back here, and that's the strange part. I think I might be in trouble."

"What trouble we's talkin' 'bout?"

"No idea. I think maybe I lost some time somehow, because I don't remember much of anything except this thing," he says, pinching a piece of the poncho thing he's got on. "I remember getting this from a bloke who stowed away on a train in a boxcar I was riding. I don't know exactly when that was. It was freezing cold in there, though, and I guess he felt sorry for me. He tried talking to me, but I couldn't understand him. He spoke Polish or Russian or something. He was sitting at one end of the car, and I was sitting at the other end, shivering like my bones were gonna break. He took off this heavy rain poncho thing, folded it up, and threw it across the car. Got me through the night, got me here, I guess. That's why I'm kind of attached to it," he say, crossin' his arms and rubbin' 'em up and down on the dark green rubbery material like it be his security blanket.

"Well, you like to scared me to death, flappin' that thing around like you done."

"Only because you scared me first!"

I laugh, and Ulie give me a little punch on the arm.

"So c'mon. What's your name?"

"Are you gonna try to make me leave now you back, or do I hafta ...?"

"Hafta what? Kill me with that baseball bat? Look, long as you don't clock me with that thing, I don't mind sharing. Do you?"

I think that over for a bit. *Do I? Do I have a choice?*

"Hmmm. Well, I'm not crazy 'bout white 'blokes,' as you call 'em, but if you not dangerous ..."

He laughs. "No, I'm not the dangerous bloke type, white or otherwise, I promise. But what about you?"

"Depends. What you think 'bout Negros? You one a them racists?"

"Oh, hell no. Do we have to go there? Listen to me. Things are a lot different in other countries than they are here in the good old U.S. of A. When I was in Europe, I knew lots of colored guys, and I owe my life to some of them. Although I have to confess, I can't say as I ever knew any skinny teenage Negro *girls*. So you got me there."

I can't help it. I'm startin' to warm up to this white boy. Maybe he okay after all.

"Look, I'm sorry if I scared you. It never occurred to me I might come back here and find a new tenant in my space. Especially not someone like you. I'll bet there's an interesting story there, am I right?"

He peers at me from under his eyebrows, waitin' for me to tell him sumpthin', but I go back to axin' him questions instead.

"What's a tenant?"

He shakes his head and laughs.

"Somebody who's renting a place owned by another person. That would be you, in this case, but something tells me I'm not gonna be collecting much rent."

I bust out laughin'.

"You right about that, Mister Ulie! You crazy if you think I got any money. But c'mon now. What's the rest of the story? Why you hidin' out when yo' mama live right down there?" I axe, pointing toward Mrs. B's house, which we can now see faintly outlined in the dim light b'fo dawn.

"Like I told you before, I think I might be in some kind of trouble. All I'm trying to do is clear my head and get my bearings, not get arrested, and not get my folks in any trouble, either. I need to know what's what and if anybody's after me before I show up on their doorstep."

"Okay. I git that. That be pretty much what I'm tryin' to do, too."

"Explain. And while you're at it, tell me your name. Otherwise, I'm gonna have to call you Cleopatra. Because that's who you look like to me, especially in the dark. Cleopatra, Queen of the Nile," he say, makin' a big sweep with one a his wings and laughin' softly.

"And I'm gonna have to call you Scary Bird Monster."

We quiet for a while, and I think over what I want to tell this stranger. I remind myself that I don't 'xactly *know* Ulie. I jus' know *of* him. I'm too weary to talk anyhow.

"I'm so tired, Ulie. Aren't you?"

"Exhausted."

"Let's get some sleep, okay? That other cot in the cave? That b'long to Annie, but you can lie down there."

"Swell!" he say scrambling to his feet. "Just put that bat away, will you? And by the way, you don't have any other dangerous weapons around here, do you?"

Laughter bubbles up in me agin.

"No, I ain't got nothin, and I ain't no axe murderer, neither. Are you?"

"Hmmmm. I believe I can absolutely guarantee you that I have never taken an axe to anyone," Ulie say, tipping his head to one side and grinnin'.

He opens his wings.

"See? Look for yourself. I have no weapons of any kind."

"C'mon, then," I choke out, still giggling. I sound like one a them silly flirty girls I hate.

We walk into the cave together, and I lift Gary's box and pick him up. "This here Gary," I say. "He my watchdog, but he be sleepin' on the job when you come 'round tonight."

Ulie laughs and gives the baby squirrel a stroke on the top of his head.

"Hi, there, Gary. Nice to meet you. Sure glad you were sleepin' on the job, or I'd have been a goner for sure!"

It's lighter now, and Ulie takes a closer look around the inside of the cave.

"Right there," I tell him, pointing to Annie's cot.

"Uhhh ... no, I don't think so. A grown man like me doesn't belong in here with a teenage girl. You keep this for your space. I know another place—if I can just borrow the cot and sleeping bag?"

"Sure. Take 'em."

I'm relieved by his consideration. Don't know what I was thinkin' invitin' him in here where he don't b'long.

Chapter 32
Clydeen

"What's that!" Ulie hisses.

He's standing outside the cave on the side away from the wash, what we call the rear entrance.

I sit up and rub my eyes. "Wha's the matter?"

"I hear something!"

"Jus' calm down there, Mister Ulie. Good Lord, what time is it?"

I look at the clock I keep on the shelf at the back a the cave and see that it's past noon a'ready.

"What you hear is prob'ly Annie comin'. Nothin' to be afraid of."

"Can you get rid of her? How do I know this Annie person won't rat me out if she finds me here?" he whispers.

"What's wrong with you, boy? You shakin' like a leaf, and you's sweatin' like you jus' run five miles. You havin' a panic attack or sumpthin'?

"Something like that, yeah."

He seemed fine last night, but now he tremblin' all over and actin' like a crazy person.

"Can you please get rid of her? I'm not ready."

"C'mon in here and settle yourself down. I'll take care of it, a'ight?"

He steps in and goes to sit hunched over on the ledge at the back of the cave where it's dark.

"So mum's the word for now?"

"Wha's that mean—'mum's the word'?"

205

"It means 'don't tell.'"

"I'm jus' playin' witchya. I got it the first time," I say, lacin' up my shoes.

I go outside to meet Annie and go part way down the wash to help. She brung three bottles of water, and her black bag is stuffed full. I'm really glad to see her, but I don't rightly know how to act with Ulie hidin' hisself in the cave. So I play it cool and try to act like nothin' be any diff'rent than it was yesta'day.

"Hey, Clydeen. I thought I heard you talkin' to someone just now, or was it my imagination?"

"Not your imagination," I tells her. "Jus' talkin' to myself—pretty much. You know. Talkin' to Gary, too."

Since that usually be what I do when I'm by myself, I ain't lied to my friend jus' yet.

"You're all alone up here. Why wouldn't you talk to yourself? I would," she says, laughing. "So where is Gary?"

Gary still in the cave. How I gonna keep Annie from goin' in there? Lucky me! B'fo I can answer, Gary come runnin' out and climbs up my pants leg and ducks under my shirt.

"There he is!" Annie say, pulling him out and holding him up to her face nose to nose. "I brought you a treat, Gary. Sunflower seeds in the shells and some pieces of apple. Just for you, little fella."

She hands Gary back to me.

"You seem a little off. Is anything wrong?"

"No. Why?"

"'Cause you have this odd look on your face. Like this," she say wrinklin' her forehead and pullin' down the corners of her mouth to make a upside down smile. "See? Not like you, Clydeen."

"It jus' the sun. It be so bright ...."

"Okay, okay. Don't tell me. Save it for another time. I have to go anyway, but I didn't want you to run low on food and water. Mrs. B gave me most of the food I brought today. She buys stuff on sale."

"Thank you, Jesus!" I murmur, 'cause Ulie managed to polish off every bit a leftovers I had, which weren't much.

"What?" she says.

"Never mind. You havin' yo' readin' with Miz B today?"

"Yes. That's why I can't stay."

With that, she turn around and start walkin' toward the cave.

"Wait! Wait!" I shout. "Where you goin?"

"To get the empty water bottles," she say, givin' me a puzzled look.

"Uhhh ... lemme git 'em for you."

She shrugs and waits while I get the bottles.

"Go on now," I tell her, and then realize I may have made another mistake.

I haven't shown the slightest interest in the food she's brought. Usually, I'd be all over it by now, and of course, she notices.

"Are you sure you're okay, Clydeen?" she axes me again, moving in close and putting her hand on my forehead. "Maybe you're running a little fever?"

"Nah, I ain't got no fever, and I ain't sick, neither," I say, pushin' her hand away. "I'm jus' tired and I wanna go take a nap b'fo I eat."

She don't believe a word of it, I can tell. Thank God she got things to attend to, or I'd be in big trouble, tryin' to hide that white boy in there. But as it is she got to go and hurries back down the wash.

"Thank you, Annie. I be seein' you tomorrow, right?" I call out after her.

She turns and studies me for a minute, and then she smiles and says yes, she will be back tomorrow.

"Ulie better pull hisself together, that's all I can say," I mumble as I walk back toward the cave.

As soon as Annie's gone, Ulie comes out.

"The pee place gonna be over yonder," I tell him, pointing through the lean-to to the other side, where there's a short trail (if you can call it that) goin' down a short distance off the ledge.

"Oh. Okay, Cleopatra. Uhhh ... I was just wondering. Did Annie bring anything?"

I roll my eyes and laugh.

"Yes, Ulie. She brung water, and they's food in that bag over there."

"Can I look?"

At least he polite about it.

"Sure, go ahead."

Pretty soon we's enjoyin' a breakfast a Spam and crackers, with apples and oranges for desert and a couple a bottles a Coke to drink.

The Cokes are still cold, which is a treat. There's also a half a loaf a bread, a jar of peanut butter, cucumber slices, canned beans, bananas, and a thermos of milk to share later on. Gary sits nearby while we eat, cracking open the sunflower seeds I laid out for him, happy as a baby squirrel can be.

"So, Ulie, what we gonna tell Annie when she comes back? She heard me talkin' to you this morning. You gonna have to hide somewheres else if you ain't ready to make her acquaintance. I ain't gonna out and out lie to her, 'cause that ain't how we do, me'n Annie."

"Okay. When will she be back?"

"Tomorrow. You heard her."

He's lyin' on the ground, propped up on one elbow, thinkin' it over. "She's white, isn't she? Talks white."

"Course she is."

"Okay, Cleopatra. Tomorrow you say? That's long enough for me to find out what in God's name you and some white girl are doing hanging out up here—or is it hiding out? Tell me the story so I can make up my mind about whether this Annie person is a threat to me or not."

"Well, first off, I like that name. Cleopatra. You can jus' go ahead and call me that. But b'fo I tell you anything 'bout me, why don't you tell me 'bout that bidniss a little while ago."

"It's nothing much," he shrugs. "I have these nightmares, and sometimes I get up and start walking around when I'm not really awake. I think I'm someplace else, and I probably sound a little crazy. I think I'm a little shell-shocked, if you want the truth, even though I was never a proper soldier."

"Shell-shocked, you say."

"Yeah. That's what they call it when soldiers come back from the war not quite right in the head because of what happened to them over there. I think that might be why I feel so strange and out of touch, like I don't know what I'm doing half the time."

"What did you do 'over there' as you say?"

He stares at the sky for a long while b'fo he answers me.

"You know, Cleopatra, when I was a kid, I used to pretend to blow stuff up all the time. Used to draw pictures of big explosions, body parts flying this way and that. A regular baby Picasso, I was, if you've ever seen any of his paintings."

"No, I haven't."

"Maybe someday you will. But over there? That was my job. Blowing things up. Yup. That's what I did."

"Like what things?"

"Oh, bridges, trains, Nazi supply depots, shit like that. Found out what it's *really* like when things blow up," he snorts bitterly. "And now, I dream about it like I'm still in it. It's so real, I get scared, and it makes me act a little crazy sometimes."

"Uh-huh. So what else do you do when you git to actin' crazy?"

"I'm not sure, but if you just leave me be and don't get too close to me, I'll be fine. I'm just trying to figure what's happening and where I'm at."

"Okay, then. That's how it'll be."

I reach out my hand. He takes it and we shake on it. In daylight, I can see his eyes clearly now. They's blue, and yas, they be a world a confusion and trouble in them eyes.

"Your turn, Cleopatra. What am I to make of a brown-skinned teenager living up here in my old hideout?"

My face git real hot under his gaze, and I feel myself grinnin' at him, even though I don't want to. They's something so soft and welcoming in them eyes, they like magnets.

"Well, there ain't much to it, really," I say, lookin' away, tryin' to keep my cool.

I mus' be goin' soft in the head or sumpthin', 'cause I end up tellin' this stranger, this white boy I don't know from a hole in the ground, all 'bout my home in Texas and what happened to my daddy. I tell him 'bout comin' North and losin' track a Mama. I go on and on for over an hour tellin' him all there is to tell. I tell him 'bout the bus, and after two days, findin' that old washtub down at the bottom of the wash.

"Oh, yeah. I remember that thing," says Ulie. "The way it sparkled. Something really odd about it, right?"

"Yeah. Me and Annie got rid of it, 'cause we think that washtub be what showed us the way, and we didn't want nobody else findin' it. The day I come, I had on these really tore-up shoes. I don't know why I thought it would be a good idea to follow that light and climb up here over all those sharp loose rocks, but I did it. One thing was

I figured nobody else gonna be dumb e'nuff to do it and maybe I'd be safe for a while. I was jus' lookin' for a place to rest, you know? When I got up here and saw this place, I couldn't believe it! There was water and a cot with a sleeping bag. I was so tired by then, it was better'n findin' a pot a gold.

"After I got some rest, I realized I was lost, pure and simple. No way I could find my way back to town; I'd come too far. I had nowhere to go back to anyway, so I stayed put while I was tryin' to figure out what to do next. Then a few days later, Annie come. It was in the evenin'. Scared the bejesus outta me. Thought she was gonna whack me with this piece of tree branch she's wavin' around."

"Sounds like you with that baseball bat. Pretty goddamn intimidating."

"Well, yeah, but I was jus' tryin' to protect myself."

"No. I get it," says Ulie, his eyes smilin' at me. "So then what happened? How'd you two gals get to be friends?"

Gals? That's a new one. I set Gary on the orange crate and try to unravel for Ulie how it is I'm still here and got to be so tight with a white girl.

"Well, that first night I was scared a her, and she was scared a me, too, I could tell. And mad? Lord have mercy! She say I was in her 'room,' or whatever, and she wanted me to go. She say she ain't never seen a Negro close up b'fo," I laugh, rememberin' that night. "Like maybe I was some exotic zoo animal or sumpthin'.

"Anyway, that night, I jus' listened to her go on and on, and when she all talked out, I tol' her I didn't have nowhere else to go. When I said that, she looked shocked. Her eyes, what I could see of 'em, 'cause it was almos' dark by then, got all big, like she couldn't imagine such a thing. And then you know what she done, Ulie?"

"What?"

"She give me some raisins she had in her pocket, say she come back with food."

"Wow."

"Truth be told, I didn't 'spect it. I didn't know if I wanted it, even. Some white girl bringin' food all the way up here for some down-on-her-luck colored girl who drank all her water and slept in her bed? Sounds like Goldilocks, don't it? I thought she'd starve me out. That would a been the bes' way to git rid a me. But the next day, sho 'nuff, she showed up with more water and plenty a food, too.

"Ever since then, all summer long, she been comin' up here mos' days. After not very long, we started likin' each other, and since then, we been havin' ourselves a righteous good time—mos' a the time. Don't git me wrong, we's had our battles, too. But the truth is I love bein' with Annie so much that sometimes I forgit to be worried 'bout where my mama at."

"So how'd Annie meet my folks?"

"She met your mama ridin' her bike past there every day on her way up here. We calls yo' mama Miz B. She tol' Annie all 'bout you, and Annie tol' me."

"Of course she did," he says. "Girl talk."

"It wasn't like that, Ulie. But anyhow, I'm here waitin' for my mama to come find me, and Annie and me bein' each other's bes' friend. But now she gittin nervous, thinks my mama ain't never gonna come. She tryin' to talk me into axin' Miz B for some help, 'cause school gonna start soon."

"What about you? Don't you have to go back to school, too?"

"Don't know. Don't know if I be able to go to school right now."

"Oh, c'mon. That's just wrong. Maybe you do need some help. Girls your age belong in school, getting your education."

"I know. My daddy wouldn't like it. But I don't like thinkin' 'bout it right now."

"Speaking of help," he say. "Time for you to help me now."

"Oh, yeah? What help you want?"

"Well, now that you've filled me in, you gotta help me decide what to do when Annie comes back: run, hide, run *and* hide. Maybe flap my wings, scare her off. Or should I just give her a hug and thank her for the food? What's your advice?"

I laugh. This boy downright funny when he ain't actin' crazy.

"Well, you want my opinion, I say thank her for the food, but if you's gonna give her a hug, you bes' do some washin' up over there first!"

"What? Are you saying I stink?" he say, raisin' his arms and smellin' his pits.

"Sumpthin' awful, Mister Ulie. Sumpthin' awful. They's some

211

clean clothes on the shelf in the cave you can try on if you want.

"But seriously, all I can tell you is this: I been here for weeks, and that girl ain't been nothin' but good to me. I ain't never been hongry, and she ain't never ratted me out to nobody, neither."

"Uh-huh," says Ulie, but I can tell he don't quite git the whole picture yet.

"She be a person a body can trust, tha's all I'm sayin'," hardly b'lievin' my own words after all I've put Annie through.

"Okay. That helps. By the way, I overheard Annie telling you this morning that Mrs. B bought the groceries. My mother?"

"Right."

"So is she the one providing the food for you?"

"Not all of it. Annie brings some from her house, too but Miz B started in helpin' out. Good thing, too, 'cause Annie's mama be givin' her a hard time 'bout takin' so much food out the house. Course her mama don't know nothin' 'bout me bein' here."

"But my mom? She knows where the food and clothes are going, right?"

"No. I tol' you. Annie ain't tol' her nothin'."

"And you're sure about that?"

"I am, yas. Annie wouldn't lie to me 'bout sumpthin' like that. But here's the thing. I'd say yo' mama prob'ly don't think Annie eatin' all a that food and wearin' these clothes herself."

"Probably not," he chuckles. "My mother's nobody's fool. In any case, I want to thank you for your hospitality. If I promise not to run Annie off, is it all right with you if I hang around here for a while?"

"I 'spose I wouldn't mind the company, long's we got a understandin'. Don't axe me to lie to Annie for you."

"Deal. This is my favorite place in the whole world. I can't tell you how much better I feel today."

He gits up and goes off the ledge on the other side of the lean-to to pee.

"My name Clydeen," I shout after him.

"Okay," he say, his shoulders shakin' with laughter.

Chapter 33
Annie

"Come in, child, come in!" says Mrs. B as she gives me a quick hug. "I'm so glad you're here. I've missed you."

Rocky is barking and running circles around us, and I stoop down and give him a good rub.

"How you doing, boy?" He smiles, showing his teeth and leaning into my legs, wanting more.

"Off, Rocky," commands Mrs. B.

He dashes out the doggy door, runs around the yard a few times, comes back in and flops down on the cool linoleum floor in the kitchen.

"Sit down at the table, and I'll fetch the cards, Annie."

I sit down and begin picking at a loose thread on my shorts, my sweaty hands refusing to be still.

Mrs. B returns with the cards, which she keeps wrapped in a black silk scarf with a brightly colored peacock on it. She unwraps the cards, takes them out of the box and sets the deck between us on the table.

"So ... do you have a question you want to ask, Annie? Something you are struggling with perhaps?"

"Uhhh ..."

I look helplessly at Eva, swallowing back what's really on my mind: Clydeen and the secrets I can't reveal.

"Never mind, Annie. We can do this one of two ways. I can do a reading without a specific question, or you can hold a question in your own mind. You don't have to tell me what it is."

"So if I do have a question, but I don't want to say it out loud, you can still do the reading?"

"That's right."

I breathe a sigh of relief. Maybe this is gonna work out after all.

"Just hold the cards between your hands and focus on your question for a couple of minutes. Breathe deeply and imagine pouring your question through the palms of your hands into the cards."

I have no idea what she's talking about, but I do the best I can to follow her instructions. In my mind's eye, I picture Clydeen and me standing outside the lean-to holding hands and looking at the sky, where ominous dark clouds are rolling in from the north. I conjure the first day of school, Clydeen's missing mother, and see everything we have created together this summer being swallowed by the approaching storm. The question is what to do about it.

I'm getting antsy making Mrs. B wait so long while I wade through my thoughts, but finally I settle on this: What do I need to do to make Clydeen understand that we have to find her mother before I go back to school? Isn't that the problem in a nutshell? I open my eyes and tell Mrs. B I'm ready.

"Good. Now go ahead and shuffle the cards like I showed you the other day. Do you remember?"

"Yeah, I think so," but when I try to do it, the cards fly all over the kitchen. "Oh, no! I'm so sorry, Mrs. B."

She laughs good naturedly, and says, "Well, that's as good a way as any to mix them up."

Mrs. B's laugher calms me, and the tension drains from my body as I scurry around the kitchen, scooping up the cards.

Mrs. B counts the cards to make sure none are missing, and when she's satisfied, she asks me if I'm ready to start.

"Can I write things down?"

"Well, you can, but it's hard to pay attention to a reading when you are also writing. I'll tell you what. I'll get out my old typewriter this evening and type it up for you."

"Thank you! That would be terrific."

"So let's begin."

I cut the cards, and Mrs. B shows me how to deal ten cards and lay them out in what she calls "a traditional Celtic cross pattern." She studies them for a long time before she says anything, while I hold my breath and wait.

"Right off the bat, I see something," she says finally.

"What?" I ask, leaning forward to peer at the cards as if the people in the pictures might start speaking to me and telling me what I need to know.

"Do you see all of these cards with swords on them? There are five of them altogether. That's somewhat unusual. Cards in that suit generally mean action, courage, ambition, and strife, and with so many of them showing up, it tells me there may be a conflict brewing that will require action and courage."

She looks at me, waiting for me to say something, but I just nod, and she goes on.

"It can also mean you are finding it necessary to take matters into your own hands, and right now, you're focusing a lot of energy on a situation you haven't figured out yet."

"That's true," I admit, still staring at the cards.

"So this first card, the one in the middle position, the first one you drew, is the Page of Swords. That card represents you and shows a picture of a young person, see?"

"Yeah, but it's a boy."

"Doesn't matter, Annie. The point is that this is a young person who is eager to take on whatever challenge he is facing. But he, or she, in your case, is immature and inexperienced, and that accounts for the storm clouds you see there in the distance."

Just like I pictured in my mind a few minutes ago, I think to myself.

"Meaning things might not be going as smoothly as you would like."

Bingo. I feel a surge of hope, and I can't help smiling.

"The second card, the one you laid crosswise over the first, represents the immediate challenge you are facing, and it is in opposition to the first card. In that position, we have the Five of Pentacles. This card shows a mature woman surrounded by the fruits of her labor. This woman is self-sufficient, disciplined, and patient. Perhaps your youthfulness is hindering you, and you need to reach out to someone who is more mature, someone who can lend a hand and help you bring your labors to fruition. Does any of that make sense, Annie?"

"Yeah, I think so. Could you say a little more?"

"I think the most likely interpretation is that you have resources available that you may not be using."

"So it's not bad, right?"

"It's not bad or good. None of the cards are. They show you what influences are at work in a particular situation, influences you may or may not be aware of. This card, for example, is simply pointing to a path that maybe hasn't occurred to you or you haven't chosen."

"Okay. I understand it better when you put it like that."

"Moving on, the card in the third position indicates something about the background of the challenge you are facing and how it came about, and here we have the Ten of Swords."

"Wow. That looks bad!" I say, studying the card.

It shows a man lying face down with ten long swords piercing his body.

"Is he dead?"

"This is not a death card, Annie, although it certainly looks like it, doesn't it? This card is about aggression, hatred, and feeling like a victim. Feeling powerless, perhaps having been betrayed by someone you trusted. Can you relate to that?"

Tears swim in my eyes as I recall being beaten by Stanley, which still sends waves of emotion through my body and makes me cry every time I think about it. What Mrs. B is saying makes the raw memory come rushing back, and I can't hide the tears. She gets up and hands me a Kleenex from the box by the refrigerator.

"This card is very powerful, Annie, and it suggests that the way your father treated you and your feeling that your mother didn't protect you has made you feel victimized and very much alone."

"Yup," I say softly, wiping tears away. "And I don't want anything to happen that's going to make me feel like that again."

"The reason this card is showing up here is because your relationship with those who betrayed you is a part of whatever is going on in your life right now."

"How?"

"I don't know, Annie. That's a question only you can answer, but maybe the rest of the cards will shed some light on it. The card in position number four here on the right tells us something about the immediate future, what might happen in the next few weeks or so."

Good, I think to myself. *Now we're getting down to what I need to know.*

"Here you have the Six of Wands. The picture shows a man riding a white horse through a cheering crowd. On his head, he is wearing a crown of victory. I don't know about the cheering crowd, but this card suggests that whatever challenge you are facing will most likely be resolved successfully in the next few weeks."

"Better'n the last one!"

"Yes, but remember, Annie, you have to take all of the cards together. When we finish, I'll be able to sum it all up for you."

"Okay. I'm ready for the next one."

"The card in position number five represents something that *may* happen in the future. As you can see, the card is The Sun. This is called a Major Arcana card and carries particular weight in a reading. But do you see anything different about this card?"

"It's turned upside down."

"Right. That's called reversed. The Sun reversed can mean that you are experiencing some setbacks, and you may be questioning your ability to handle the challenge you are facing. But the Sun is never a negative card, so it also means that you can overcome the obstacles in your path if you use the wisdom and resources you have at your disposal. You must be realistic about the situation, though, and not get too caught up in expecting it to turn out a certain way. Understand?"

"So you're saying I'm having a hard time on my own making what I think should happen happen? Is that what you're saying?"

"That's one way to look at it. Maybe it's hard for you to entertain the possibility that whatever the outcome of the situation, it might not go exactly as you want it to. You might have to let go of the reins a little bit, Annie, in order for new possibilities to emerge."

"Okay. Maybe so," I affirm.

Honestly? This possibility has not occurred to me before, and I'm not sure I like the idea of letting go of the reins. Won't that just lead to disaster?

"The sixth card delves deeper into forces you may not be aware of involving the foundation or background of the circumstance. Here we have the Nine of Swords. It shows a woman who is obviously in a great deal of distress. Nine swords hang on the wall behind her. She looks like she might have just awoken from a nightmare. This card is a caution against getting caught up in your own negative emotions, your own distress. It seems to be telling you that you need to give yourself a break and realize that not everything that's happening or will happen is within your ability to manage or control."

"Yeah, and that's exactly what I'm afraid of," I mumble.

Mrs. B waits for me to say more, but I don't.

"Okay, then. Let's move on. Card number seven is an advice card. It shows the fears you have about your present circumstances and points out ways to address what's challenging you."

"Okay. That's what I need, some advice."

Mrs. B looks at me curiously, and smiles.

"Well then, I hope you like this one, Annie. This card, The Lovers, is another one from the Major Arcana. It can mean a couple of things. Most likely it means someone you care about deeply is very much involved in the current situation, someone you're close to, someone you trust. It can also foreshadow the beginning of a romance, but that probably doesn't apply in your case."

"No," I laugh. "I'm too young for that! So what else?"

"Well, it seems to me that this is likely the heart of the matter. What this card, along with the others so far says to me is this: Someone you care about may be in a predicament of some kind, and you want to help. But the intensity of your concern, not only for this person, but also for yourself in relationship to this person, might be limiting you in some way.

"Okay. Maybe so."

"Are you ready to go on?"

"Yes. Go on."

"Okay. The eighth card is about what influences other people will have on the outcome of the situation. What do your friends and family think about it all?"

"What do you mean? What if they don't know anything about it?"

"Well then, what would they think if they did know? And just a word of caution, Annie. They might know more than you think they do."

"God, I hope not," I whisper to myself.

"Well, anyway, the card in this position is The Hierophant, another Major Arcana card, which means that the approval of people in your life may be more important than you think. This card represents the values we're taught by the society we live in, including religious values. You might be in a situation where you are at odds with the values you have been raised with, and you might be finding out that it can be pretty hard to go it alone. Does that make sense?"

"Uhh-huh," I say noncommittally.

"Almost done here. The card in position number nine represents your own hopes and fears, intertwined. In this position, the card is the King of Wands."

"It's upside down again."

"Yes. It's reversed, and because of that, this card can represent a severe, unyielding man, who is strict, intolerant, and prejudiced. Do you know anyone like that?"

I snicker but say nothing.

"I'm thinking this card represents characteristics of your father and your hopes and fears around your relationship with him. It could represent your fear that he might become involved in your current situation somehow, or maybe you hope he will. A third way to look at this card is that it may represent attributes of your father's personality that you share."

I scoff at that and stare out the window, thinking about my father. I never want to be like him. But what if I already am? Am I really more Ty the bully than I think? Am I trying to bully Clydeen into doing what I think she should do when she's not ready or doesn't want to? I sigh, bringing myself back into the room. I'll have to think more about this later.

"Anything else Mrs. B?"

"Well, yes," says Mrs. B, wrinkling her brow. "This card does indicate that there's the possibility of a quarrel in the making."

"Oh, that's just terrific," I say sarcastically. But then I smile at Mrs. B and pretend it's a joke.

"This card is a caution to you, Annie. As I mentioned, it indicates something about *your* tendencies. Once again, I would caution you not to have fixed ideas about how the challenge you are facing should end up. In other words, watch the ways in which you take after your dad and do not try to force your will on others the way he does, or it may backfire."

"Okay," I sigh.

"Here's the grand finale, card number ten," Mrs. B announces, picking up the card and waving it around. "What will the outcome be over the next few weeks? Well, here in the tenth position, we have the King of Swords, reversed."

"Upside down, right?"

"You're catching on, my dear. The King pictured in this card reversed is a very intelligent older man. He is manipulative and will use that strategy in furtherance of his own interests. He is controlling, a tyrant, and he can be a 'loose cannon.' You know what that means, right?"

"I do."

"This person worries you a great deal, and makes you lack confidence in yourself. He can make you feel defensive and angry, and you may find yourself in competition with him in order to be 'right.' You both have that need, but you won't win that contest. Instead, use your will and intelligence to find your own way. And one more thing. There's no sense stepping back from whatever it is you need to do, because there will be no avoiding his reaction anyway."

"Oh, brother. Those last two cards are bad news, right?"

"Not necessarily. Have you ever heard the expression, 'forewarned is forearmed?'"

"I don't think so, no. What does it mean?"

"It means when you are facing some obstacle, and you have been given a warning that the obstacle exists, you have the opportunity to change your behavior or your way of thinking in order to deal with it. Understand?"

"Hmmm, okay," I say thoughtfully.

My mind is racing. I am beginning to see that my desire to get Clydeen settled in with her mother (or someone) so that I can slip back into the school year with no one the wiser is looking more and more like pure fantasy. I'd better prepare myself for the likelihood it's not going to happen that way at all.

"Well, let me see if I can sum it up for you. This reading shows that you are dealing with a challenge that feels overwhelming right now. It involves your relationship with someone you care about very much. Unfortunately, this is all happening against a background of very strong emotions: sadness, betrayal, and a male figure who looms large and seems to represent your father. You may be headed for some trouble there, but it looks like trying to avoid it will get you nowhere. In addition, you need to be aware of any tendency within you to approach the situation as he would, because this will not serve you. Whatever situation you're dealing with, Annie, there are indications you will figure it out if you are able to identify and mobilize the resources you need for support. This will help you to loosen up and let go of rigid expectations you may have about the outcome that may be getting in your way.

"That's about it. Do you have any other questions for me?"

"Ummm ... not right now, but thank you so much for doing this, Mrs. B. It's interesting."

"Glad to do it. It's a lot of information. Give it some thought, Annie, and let me know if there's anything you want to talk over later. Remember, a reading like this is only a tool, nothing carved in stone."

"I should go now, Mrs. B," I say, glancing at the kitchen clock. "It's five o'clock."

"So it is. That took us a while, didn't it? Tell you what. I'll try to have the written interpretation ready for you tomorrow. Can you stop by then?"

"Sure."

"By the way, I am going to the grocery store in the morning. Anything you'd like?"

"Oh, let's see ... carrots, tuna fish. A couple cans of beans? Apples and bananas, maybe? Whatever's on sale."

"Sure thing. I'll have it for you tomorrow."

"Thank you, Mrs. B," I call out as I run to my bike and push off. Phrases from the reading are rattling around in my head, and I think back to my original question. Have I gotten any answers? I think I have.

First of all, I thought the reading was going to be about Clydeen and how I could make her ... but it wasn't. It was all about me. Second, Stanley, as usual, is very much in the picture, even though I'd like to pretend he's not. I see how much my dread of another confrontation with him is influencing me and causing me to push Clydeen into doing what I want the way I want it. I'm being driven by my fantasies of Stanley somehow getting involved in our situation, afraid that something terrible will happen if he does. It's worried me all summer long, but now it's really coming to a head. I vowed not to be a coward anymore. But here I am, acting on questionable motivations where Clydeen is concerned because of—cowardice, being afraid. What would Linda Brent do? Not what I'm doing, you can bet on that. No wonder what I've been urging Clydeen to let me do isn't working out!

Chapter 34
Annie

As soon as I got home from Mrs. B's yesterday, Vivian left with the boys to pick up Stanley at the airport, leaving me with Teresa, who was still sleeping. New products are hitting the grocery store shelves every day, and Vivian is determined to try them all while they're on sale, so the first thing I did was open the cupboard to see what was new.

"Tang," I read out loud, sniffing the orange powder inside the jar. "Hmmm. What is it?"

The label said it's some kind of dehydrated orange juice with a lot of vitamin C.

"That will be good for Clydeen," I muttered and put the jar into my black bag.

"What about this?"

I picked up a can with a plastic spout of some kind. Cheez Whiz, the label said.

"And it doesn't need refrigeration. Perfect."

I dropped the Cheez Whiz into my bag, along with a box of Ritz crackers and an assortment of as many other items as I dared.

While the stew I was cooking for dinner simmered on the stove, I hard boiled four eggs and fried six slices of bacon. I ran the fan at full speed and opened the windows to blow away the odor of bacon. Just in the nick of time, too, because ten minutes later I heard the crunch of car wheels on the gravel driveway. Just as the garage door rattled down, I ran downstairs and tucked my bag into my hiding place under the stairwell.

****

Vivian seemed pleased with the meal I served last night, so this morning I take advantage of her good graces and ask if I can leave early.

"Again?" she says, looking around to see what chores need to be done. Finding nothing pressing, she says, "Okay, Annie. I guess it's alright."

Off I go before she changes her mind. I stop by Mrs. B's, and true to her word, she hands me a long white envelope containing her summary of my reading and a paper bag containing more groceries. I'm hoping Mrs. B's formal typewritten review will be enough to impress Clydeen and make it possible for us to talk more honestly about what's coming. For my part, though, I'm going to make every effort to "loosen the reins" and see what happens.

When I arrive at the bottom of the wash, I whistle, but Clydeen doesn't come to help, which she has been doing of late. I wait a minute or two, and then start up the wash with my black bag slung over one shoulder. It's so full today, it makes my neck cramp.

"Clydeen," I call out.

No answer.

"Huh," I shrug as I head back down the wash to retrieve the water and the bag of food.

Just as I reach the top for the second time, I catch a glimpse of a tall, willowy figure with a big head of wild hair moving about on the far side of the lean-to. It's definitely not Clydeen. I nearly scream, but I'm able to stop myself, set the water bottles down carefully, and withdraw into the crevice. *How many times am I going to have to go through this anyway?* I'm breathing hard, just as frightened now as I was the last time I discovered an unexpected guest hanging around up here. This routine is getting a little old, if you ask me.

But where is Clydeen? The thought that she might be in trouble is enough to propel me into the open with nothing but my fury and clenched fists. I don't see anyone now, but I know I wasn't mistaken, either.

224

Just like I did those many weeks ago, I step out boldly and shout with as much bluster as I can summons, "Who's there?"

Silence. The tarp Clydeen hangs up at night rustles. It hasn't been taken down yet, which is unusual.

My legs begin to tremble.

I clear my throat to make my voice deeper and yell, "I mean it! I saw you. Show yourself!"

Barely breathing, I walk forward as quietly as possible on the crunchy surface of the ledge. Suddenly, the tarp gives a whoosh and out steps the figure I glimpsed before. A man. Young. Pretty messed up, too.

He stands facing me, with his arms akimbo.

"Hi, I'm Ulie," he says, extending his hand.

"What did you say?"

"I'm Ulie," he says again, louder this time. "You must be Annie."

"Where's Clydeen?" I demand.

"In there," he says, thumbing back over his shoulder.

"I want to see her right now!" I shout.

"Well, come on, then. Take a look for yourself."

"Do you have a weapon on you?"

He snorts. "Cleopatra's got the weapon! That baseball bat? She nearly cold cocked me with it yesterday—or maybe it was the day before."

"Yesterday? You were here yesterday?"

"Indeed I was, and by the way, thanks for the food."

"I hope you shared it with ... why are you calling her Cleopatra?" I ask, recalling the day I cut Clydeen's hair and told her she looked like an Egyptian princess.

"Well, she wouldn't tell me her name, so I said I would call her Cleopatra. It fits, don't you think?"

"It fits, alright."

I scuff the toe of my shoe in the dust and snicker in spite of myself.

"Go on now. Check on your friend," the stranger says.

Inside the cave, Clydeen is sitting up rubbing her eyes.

"Hi," she says, as if nothing the least bit out of the ordinary is happening right now.

"Are you okay, Clydeen? Who is that guy?" I whisper urgently, sitting down next to her on the edge of the cot.

"I'm fine, and that guy? He say he Ulie. I reckon he come back."

"So what's he doing here?"

"He scared, Annie. He think somebody might be after him."

"Huh ...?"

"But listen to me," she says, pulling me close and whispering in my ear. "He don't know his daddy passed, and I didn't tell him. I don't wanna be the one tells him that."

"Oh, boy. That's not good. Just so happens I brought plenty of food today, even though I didn't know we were having company. Why don't we all get something to eat, and then we'll do some serious talking and see what's what."

"Yas, okay," she says, putting her arm around my shoulder for a minute. "Lemme git myself goin' here."

I go out, but Ulie, if he really is Ulie, seems to be making himself scarce at the moment. "I brought food and water. Are you hungry?" I call out.

"Starving!" he says, popping up from the other side of the lean-to.

"Come sit. Clydeen's coming. I'll get the water. Help yourself. Where's Gary, Clydeen? I brought apples slices. He can eat some."

The three of us sit in a tight circle, with Gary in the middle. He chatters a lot now, something he didn't do when he was younger. For dessert, Ulie and Clydeen giggle over the can of Cheez-Whiz while they pass it back and forth, squirt it out and lick it off their fingers. When they finish eating, they carefully pack up what's left for later. Luckily, there's plenty to go around—at least until tomorrow.

"So," I say, addressing Ulie, "You got any identification on you?"

He laughs. "That's a good one! I left the country before you needed a passport, and I lost my school identification a long time ago, so, no, you're outta luck on that one. I'm *persona non grata*, as they say."

"What's that?"

"Well, in my case, it seems to mean I don't officially exist, and sometimes I wonder if I even exist unofficially."

"Yet here you are. How come?"

He thinks for a minute, and then begins to speak.

"Long story short? After the war, I was eventually rounded up and put in a displaced persons camp—DP camp they call it. I remember I went there with one of my buddies, but then he disappeared. Got sent stateside maybe? It's not clear in my mind, but I think I was moved several times to different camps while I waited for verification of my identity so I could be released.

"You'd think with a name like Ulysses Borsheim they could have found something. But no matter where I was, when I gave my name, they'd just look at me funny and accuse me of trying to pull a fast one. The next thing I know, I'd find myself in some other camp. Do I look like I don't exist to you guys?" he asks, looking from one of us to the other.

"Lemme pinch your arm."

He holds out a skinny arm, and I pinch it hard.

"Ow!" he yelps.

"Annie!" Clydeen protests.

"Guess that means you're real," I say, giving the two of them a smug, satisfied look.

"I guess so," he laughs.

"Anyway, maybe it was a mistake to run with no papers, I don't know. Maybe I should have been patient awhile longer. All I know is that now, being back here, it doesn't feel like I thought it would. I feel lost, like I don't know who I am anymore. Like I told Cleopatra, I built this place when I was a teenager. Used it for my studio, you could say, for the messy stuff I used to do back then. Camping out, too. So it's special to me, and I thought it would feel more like home, but so far, I feel ... untethered, I guess is the word."

"So what are you doing up here then? Go home! See your mother. She's done nothing but look for you ever since you dropped out of sight, and nothing would make her happier, don't you understand that?"

"Of course I understand. But I need to stay here until I figure out what's happening. Am I a fugitive? Am I about to be arrested? I'm not even sure how I got here, Annie. Everything seems unreal. I need some time."

"Okay. So what's your plan?"

"Stay here and keep an eye out. See what happens. You know my parents, right? Eva and Maury Borsheim?"

I hesitate before I answer, and when I do, I can't meet Ulie's eyes. "I know Eva, yes."

I'm glad Ulie has other things on his mind and doesn't pick up on what it is I haven't said.

"I don't want to bring any trouble to their door. Do you know if there have been any cops, FBI or anyone like that coming around talking to my folks?"

"Ulie, the only one I know of who is looking for you is your mother. She's been in contact with all kinds of people, including every kind of cop or anyone else she can think of who might be able to help find you. She's even written letters to President Truman. But whether anyone's been looking for you in bad way, I don't know about that."

Ulie's eyes fill with tears. "Boy, I must have put my parents through hell. I'm so anxious to see them, but I don't want them to get in trouble because of me, and frankly, I don't want to end up in jail myself, either."

"Have you done something you should be put in jail for, Ulie?"

"I don't know! That's what I'm trying to tell you." He's full on crying now. "I'm so confused. I feel like I saw my dad somewhere recently, but that can't be real, can it? It must have been a dream."

I hand him a napkin, and we wait.

"See what I mean?" he says, drying his tears and tossing the used napkin into the trash bag. "If you could help me, Annie, by doing me one little favor...."

"Depends on what it is."

"Could you try to find out if anyone's after me? In a bad way, like you said. I just can't quite remember ..."

He turns to Clydeen and studies her for a long moment, and then he fixes his gaze on me.

"My plan is to stay up here until I find out where I stand, and not just with the law, either. I kid you not when I say I don't know who I am anymore. I just want to stay where I'm safe and try to get back to who I was before I got caught up in that insane war. In the meantime, you two renegades seem like just the companions I need right now."

"Uhh-huh. That's *your* plan, but we get to vote on it. Were you in the army?" I ask him, still suspicious. I don't know about Clydeen, but I'm not ready to agree to anything yet.

"I was never a soldier. Not formally, anyway. Wouldn't take me when I tried to sign up in England. I wound up in France, joined the Resistance. After that, I was just a regular guy, along with many other men and women, trying to survive and do what we could to keep Hitler and his gang of thugs from winning the war. And now I'm finally back."

"Let me get this straight. You're not sure what's going on, so you want to stay up here with Clydeen while I try to find out what's happening without telling your mother you're here, is that right?"

"That's right. I just need to find out if I'm in any kind of trouble or not, 'cause my head's all messed up about stuff."

I groan.

"What about it, Clydeen? Do you feel safe, 'cause if you don't, that's an automatic no."

"Oh, you guys, c'mon. I'm not *that* guy."

"We don't know you," I say sharply. So what about it, Clydeen?"

"He been here a couple a days a'ready. He stay over yonder at night, not in the cave with me. He don't seem threatenin' to me, Annie."

"Two more days. Then we'll see. If you're behaving like a proper gentleman, we'll consider renewing your lease. That sound alright with you, Clydeen?"

"Sounds good to me."

"In the meantime, Ulie, I'll do what I can for you if an opportunity presents itself."

"And don't blow my cover, okay?"

"After this summer? I'm an expert at that, right Clydeen?" I say, rolling my eyes in her direction. "One more thing, though. It's gonna be tough for me to bring enough water and food for both of you, and I may not be able to do it for very long. Did Clydeen mention she's gonna have to leave here soon?"

"Yeah, she told me about that," says Ulie.

Clydeen scoffs and swivels away, turning her back on our little circle. "You sound like a broken record, Annie."

Before I can reply, Ulie leans over backwards so he can see her face and says, "So what's *your* plan, Clydeen?"

"Ain't got one yet," she mumbles down the front of her shirt where Gary's holed up.

"That's why I asked your mom to give me a reading with those cards of hers yesterday. We're hoping it will help us figure out what to do. I am, anyway."

"Oh, my Ma and her Tarot cards!" Ulie laughs wistfully. "My whole life she's been reading those cards! Bet she reads them all the time trying to find me, doesn't she?"

"She says they guide her, help her figure out what to do next."

"So how did she do a reading for you without knowing anything about Cleopatra here?"

"She said to hold a question in my mind. I didn't have to say it out loud. I've never said a word to her about Clydeen, but that doesn't mean she's not wondering what I'm up to. Food, water, your old clothes, all that stuff that's come from her. She's not stupid, and I'm sure she's figured out by now it's not for me."

"Right. Cleopatra told me the same thing."

"Your mother is such a good friend to me, Ulie. To us, really," I say looking at Clydeen, who's still pouting and won't meet my eyes. "Every so often, your mom asks me if I'm in any kind of trouble, but other than that, she never tries to force me to explain. That's what I love about her. She can be okay *not* knowing every little thing. Most adults aren't like that."

"Some friends ain't like that, neither," says Clydeen.

"The age of secrets, that's where you two are at. But my mom is top notch at reading those cards, and if she gives you information, in my opinion, you should pay attention. Ordinarily, she charges quite a bit of money for one of those readings. That's how good she is."

"Uhh-huh," says Clydeen in that drawn out sarcastic way she has.

I ignore her.

"What's your deal, Annie? How'd you come to be hanging out up here?" asks Ulie.

"I hang around up here 'cause I want to be with Clydeen. As to the rest of it, maybe I'll tell you sometime, but not right now."

"What about your parents? What do they know about this place and this here girl?"

"Are you kidding me? Nothing, and I plan to keep it that way.

My dad—Stanley—he works in town, and he's gone a lot. Vivian—my mom—well, let's just say we have an understanding. She feels guilty about something that happened right after we moved here, so she doesn't ask what I'm up to, and I don't tell her, either. We keep our arrangement between the two of us so Stanley doesn't go sniffing around, because that would not go well."

Ulie guffaws. "O-kay."

"But the truth is I've had a bad feeling lately. I'm afraid all of this will fall apart now that fall is coming," I say, extending my arm and sweeping it over our surroundings.

"So who will be the loser when that happens?" Ulie asks me.

"Who do you think?" I shoot back.

"Cleopatra. Clearly," says Ulie. "At least the way things stand right now."

"Bingo."

"What did the Wise One have to say about all of this?"

This seems to spark Clydeen's interest. She swivels around on her butt and rejoins us.

"I have it right here," I say, pulling the folded envelope from my bag and offering it to Clydeen. "Mrs. B wrote it all down. Do you want to read it?"

"Nah. I'll read it later. Can you jus' tell me?"

"Well, one thing that turned up is how much I care about you, Clydeen. I'm upset by our situation and what might happen when school starts. I have been trying to help you figure out what you should do, but I guess we're not on the same page. Mrs. B said there is someone—a mature person—who can help me, or you, or both of us, I'm not sure. Stanley is a threat, and I'm afraid of the trouble he'll cause if he finds out about us. No surprise there. Anyway, there's more. It's all in that envelope."

"Oh, c'mon, Annie. Ain't that what you been sayin' a'ready?"

"I don't know. Some of it, maybe."

"What about my mom?" Ulie interjects.

Clydeen and I look at each other. "*What about his mom?*" I ask Clydeen with my eyes.

"Well?" Ulie says, looking at Clydeen. "Isn't she exactly what you need? A mature person, a trustworthy person? After the years she's spent looking for me, she'll know how to search for your mother. C'mon, you two. It's a no-brainer," he says, his eyes shifting back and forth between us.

Ulie has no idea what he's stepping into. This is gonna get Clydeen all riled up, and if that happens, she'll probably never read what Mrs. B wrote. So I get up and tell the two of them I have to go.

"Let's talk about this tomorrow," I say as I begin to gather my stuff.

Ulie jumps to his feet to help me.

"Can you do what I asked, Annie?"

I turn to face him. "I'll do my best, Ulie. Because I love your mom, and she's gonna be so happy you've come back in one piece. The sooner she knows you're safe, the better. I'll see you tomorrow."

"Bye, Clydeen," I trill as I scurry down the wash. I am sick of secrets, but off I go with the worst one of all still under my hat, the one about Ulie's dad.

Chapter 35
Clydeen

Me'n Ulie sittin' up on the top a the mesa this evenin' at the spot where we can see Annie's house the best. She be right 'bout one thing. The days is shorter and the evenin's cooler. Tha's what make it real nice bein' up here, us watchin' the stars pop out one by one. It puts me in a mood to axe Ulie what he thinks I should do next.

"That's a really important question, Clydeen."

When he call me Clydeen 'stead a Cleopatra, I know we's 'bout to have a serious talk, and right now, tha's what I want.

"So before I give you my opinion, let me ask you something. If you could stop being so afraid of ending up in an orphanage or some other bad place, what's the first thing you would do?"

I search the skies for a shooting star. I don't see one, but I make a wish anyhow.

"I'd axe myself what Linda Brent would do."

"Who the heck is Linda Brent?"

I tell him all 'bout readin' *Incidents in the Life of a Slave Girl*, the true story of Linda Brent, whose real name was Harriet Jacobs. The sufferin' she endured. How she never let herself believe she was owned by anyone but her own self, and how, after many years, she managed to escape to the North.

"Well, that's some story," he say when I'm finished. "So tell me, then. What *would* Linda Brent do?"

"I can tell you one thing. She wouldn't be waitin' around sittin' on her thumbs like I'm doin'. It was okay for a while, but now, I got

233

to face what's real and what's not."

There it is. The truth I ain't let seep through the cracks b'fo, and it lands hard. I cry a little, and then I go on in a shaky voice.

"My mama ain't comin' up here to git me, but I been prayin' for it and sayin' it to myself for so long, I can't seem to let go of it. It's the only thing I got."

"Maybe, maybe not, Clydeen. So tell me this. If your mama isn't coming, what do you see when you look into your future?"

"Nothin'. I see a flock a sheep goin' over a cliff and me right along with 'em, and then—nothin'. If she don't come, tha's jus' the end a me, is all."

"Wow! That's a lot to carry, my friend. But is that really true, Clydeen? Smart girl like you, maybe you need to create a new vision for yourself."

I don't look at him. I'm pouting. I feel like he's tryin' to take sumpthin' away from me.

"Like what new vision?" I say with irritation.

"You said Linda Brent hid in a crawl space for seven years."

"That's right. In the top of a storeroom way up under the eves."

"So who helped her? She couldn't have done that on her own or she wouldn't have survived."

"Her uncle Phillip built that place for her. Him and her grandmother called Aunt Marthy was the only two people knowed she's up there. It was too dangerous for anyone else to know. Dr. Flint, her owner, he was a'ways hangin' around threatenin' everybody, tryin' to force them to tell him where she's at. But Aunt Marthy and Phillip—they never tol' Flint nothin'. The two a them took care a her all them years. Fed her, brought her blankets, did everything they could for her so she could stay hidden and none a them die at the hands a Dr. Flint."

"Does it feel like Annie is doing something similar for you perhaps?"

"I guess so. What of it?" I shout. "Now leave it be, please."

"Okay, I'll leave it be."

"Do we really have to do this?"

"No. Suit yourself." He gits up and starts back down the trail.

"Ulie, come back!"

He knows he's got me over a barrel. I axed for it, didn't I?

He comes back, sits next to me, looks me over, and says, "Okay. Let's shift gears. What else did Linda Brent's people do for her?"

"Well, let's see. Phillip was a'ways on the lookout for the chance to git her on a ship goin' North. It was him made them arrangements for her and got her on board. He and Aunt Marthy must have managed to pay for it somehow, too. Maybe tha's why it took so long to git her out."

"Do you feel like you are under some kind of threat, Clydeen, that's keeping you up here?"

"Oh, shit, Ulie. There you go agin. I don't know. What you gittin' at now?"

"I think you know. I don't need to spell it out for you, do I?"

I shake my head, start pickin' up rocks and makin' a spiral outta them.

"Is this too much, Clydeen?" Ulie asks, tryin' to look into my eyes.

I shake my head again, but I don't look at him.

"One more thing I want to ask you about Linda Brent's story: When she got to the North, wasn't there a whole squad of abolitionists waiting for her there?"

"I reckon there was, 'cause she didn't have nothin' ...."

"You know when I made up my mind to leave London and go to France to try to find my way into the Resistance, I was barely 18 years old, scared and all alone. Hell, I had no idea if I would even make it across the Channel. I didn't speak French, and I certainly had no clue how to find the Resistance once I got there. But the people who helped me? All of them were strangers I encountered along the way, and I had no reason to trust any of them.

"Those abolitionists that helped Linda? They were strangers, too, and some, if not all of them must have been white. Linda had every reason to be distrustful and afraid, but she kept her eye on the ball and took a chance anyway, didn't she?"

"Okay. But she didn't have a choice. Dr. Flint prob'ly gonna kill her."

"Maybe, but she still had a choice, Clydeen. And so do you. When I thought I was so alone, I wasn't alone at all. That's one of the most amazing things I learned on this journey of mine. Linda wasn't alone, and neither are you, my friend, although I get how scary it is when you can't see what's coming around the next corner. What if you stopped waiting for your mama and accepted the fact that your life is going to go on, with or without her. Because, you know what? It already is."

Holy shit, if that don't shut me up for a good long while! The notion a *my* life bein' separate and apart from Mama's? The idea that my life been on its own track all a this time, despite everything I been tryin' to do to stop it? No, I did not see that till now.

"So is it my responsibility to go out on my own and find Mama?"

"I don't know. Is it? Is that what you want, little sister? I'm just saying that if you decide to do that, in my experience—and in Linda Brent's experience, too—you will not be alone. I don't know if you will find your mama or not, but I can tell you almost for certain sure that the help you need will come to you when you need it, just like it has this summer."

"What I want is to go back home, but I can't think 'bout that till I find out what happened to Mama."

"Sounds right to me. So do you have a plan?"

"Can't you help me, Ulie? When you go home, that is?"

"I'd like to, but I don't think I can, Clydeen. I'm sorry," he says, and tears well up in his eyes.

"I don't know where to start," I sigh.

"I know. Let's try this. Close your eyes. See if your mind shows you a picture of someone who comes to help you."

"Like a prayer, you mean."

"I guess. Sure, like a prayer."

I close my eyes and wait. After a few minutes, I see a plump colored woman walkin' toward me. She's tall, smilin', full of energy. I start describin' her to Ulie.

"I see a woman, a grown-up, colored like me. I like her. She's friendly. She's reachin' out to me, and I'm not afraid."

I open my eyes and sigh.

"Dammit, Ulie. I know lots a people like that back home, my aunties, so many womens from my church, but I don't know anybody like that here in Colorado," I wail.

"Don't let that get in your way. Keep going. What else?"

I close my eyes again.

"She wears nice clothes, has her hair done up on top a her head and tied with a scarf in bright African colors. I don't know where she lives, but she shows me a telephone. Oh ... she has a car, too, and we're sittin' in it. It's warm inside the car."

"What if the person who came to help you turned out to be white? Would that be a deal breaker for you?"

I want to push this idea away. It's not what I want, but finally, I close my eyes and watch. No picture comes, and finally I give up and tell Ulie I don't see nothin' 'bout that one way or the other.

"But I'll tell you this, Ulie. If they's white, they would hafta to be somebody considerate and not all full a hate 'bout people like me."

"Absolutely."

"They wouldn't look down on Mama, neither, 'cause they don't know what she been through."

"Yes. All of that sounds very reasonable. Can you think of anybody like that?"

"Jus' Annie."

"Anybody else?"

"Uhhh ... not that I know of."

"Have you read what Annie gave you yet? Maybe there are some ideas for you to think about in it."

"I ain't read it yet, no."

"In the morning, maybe you'd like to read it together?"

"Let me sleep on it, okay? Let's go back now. If we stay much longer, it'll be really hard to make our way back down in the dark."

****

The next morning, my curiosity gets the better of me, and I decide I do want to read the notes from Mrs. B's. When Ulie comes 'round the bend from where he sleeps over on the far side of the lean-to someplace, I axe him to sit with me. We read through the several pages a couple of times, shuffling them back and forth between us.

"So what you think, Ulie?" I axe him.

"Well, the first thing I see is that this reading really is all about Annie, but she clearly had you in mind. This part right here where it says, 'there is someone in the picture you care about very deeply. You may be trying to protect this person, and your efforts may not be entirely welcome.' What do you think about that?"

"Okay. Yas. I have been really stubborn, but I didn't know—"

"—maybe how conflicted she is right now?"

"I guess I been makin' this all about me, when she's got some pretty big troubles a her own. Her daddy, for one, like these notes say. They is things that have happened to her that she's tol' me about, Ulie, so I git that part. It say she need the help a some 'mature person.' She said that yesta'day, remember?"

"I remember."

"She been tryin' to tell me that herself. I guess maybe it's true. Maybe she been tryin' tell me that as much as she would like to help me now, she can't do it, at least not by herself, and maybe not at all. I been thinkin' I was the only one feelin' alone and kinda helpless, but she's feelin' that way, too, ain't she?"

"I think that's spot on, Clydeen."

"She been puttin' pressure on me to let her talk to yo' mama 'bout us, but I been puttin' jus' as much pressure on her 'bout not lettin' her do it. Drivin' her crazy, prob'ly."

"So think, Clydeen. Besides Annie, is there anyone else you can call on?"

"You know the answer to that, Ulie. I ain't got nobody. Jus' Annie."

"After reading my mother's notes, do you think Annie knows what's best for you?"

"She thinks she do," I snort.

"But does she?"

"I think mostly she scared her daddy gonna find out 'bout us 'cause I'm colored, but she don't want to leave me behind, neither. She don't understand what it's like, not knowin' nothin' 'bout nothin' and not knowin' a soul in a big city I never had a chance to git used to. You axe me where me and Mama was livin' b'fo? I couldn't find my way back there if you paid me a hun'ert bucks."

"Do you want to hear what I think?"

"Sure. You's a 'mature person,' ain't you? Like the readin' say?"

"Well, that's dubious, but let's pretend it's true for the sake of argument."

Ulie be lyin' on his side on the ground, playin' with a twig and the ants. I can tell he thinkin' real hard 'bout what he gonna say next. I fidget and wait.

"I been all over this world, Clydeen, saw way more death and destruction than someone ought to at such a young age."

"Yeah. Me, too, Ulie. Seen too much. Too much bad stuff, I mean."

"I know you have, Clydeen. And that makes a body think there's nothing better coming. But from where I sit, I can tell you one thing. After all I've been through, all the misery I saw over in Europe, all the people I met, ones who had my back and ones who didn't, there's one person still at the top of my list of people I trust, and that's my mother."

"So what you sayin'? You wanna drag me to that white lady's house jus' like Annie? No, Ulie. I still ain't gonna do it. I jus' don't see it happenin' that a way."

"Think for a minute, Clydeen. Don't you realize my ma is already caring for you and supporting you? She just hasn't met you yet."

"Dammit, Ulie. That's true. But maybe she doin' it 'cause she ain't seen me yet. What you think she gonna do when she find out I'm colored?"

"Nothing she wouldn't do if you were white, Annie. You see, my mother has studied certain things most people have not. A long time ago, she got involved in studying what she calls 'esoteric spirituality,' and her perspective is much different than most white people in our society."

"I have no idea what you're talkin' 'bout."

"It's the study of otherworldly stuff, I guess I would say. Mysticism. That's another word for it. Anyway, she belonged to this study group for years, and there were many different kinds of people in that group. They used to meet at our house sometimes, people from India, immigrants from other countries in the Far East, Negros from the U.S., and white people of various backgrounds. It was a tight-knit group because most people would have called it blasphemy or worse. I never had an opinion about it one way or another myself, but I was too young to really get into it.

"Anyway, there was a splinter group of women, including my mother, who studied various decks of Tarot cards from all over the world. They became experts, gave readings and taught classes. Those ladies spent a lot of time at our house, and I remember a couple of them very well. One was a Negro woman named Belinda ... Belinda ... let's see, I can't recall her last name right now, but I liked her a lot. She was an English teacher at East High School in Denver, I do remember that. The one I knew best, though, was Imani Jackson, because she was my mom's best friend. She's also a Negro lady, and when I knew her, she was a social worker, married, two kids around my age, Mellie and Victor. I was such a drip when I was a kid, they were just about my only friends," he laughs. "Gee, I wonder where they are now?"

"Wait! Did you say Imani Jackson?"

"Uhhh ... yeah."

"I know her!"

"What do you mean you know her, Clydeen? How?"

"Well, I don't know-know her. But Annie met her one day at your mom's house. She told me about her, and I remember her name."

"Oh, my God, Clydeen. She's here?"

"I reckon so, Ulie."

"See? That's what I'm talking about! You *have* to meet her, Clydeen. Look, all I was trying to tell you before you so rudely interrupted me," he say, rollin' his eyes and laughin' a little "is that *my* mother is not your typical racist asshole."

"Language!" I shout and burst out laughing myself.

"Just trying get my point across."

"I git your point, Ulie, and I thank you for it. Remember a while ago when I said I was gonna axe myself what would Linda Brent do? I didn't tell you, did I?"

"No, you didn't. You only told me what she *wouldn't* do."

"Now I know what she would do. *What she did do.*"

"Okay. Tell me."

"Well, first of all, even though she was a slave, she figured out for herself what really mattered to her in her life. And she did that when she weren't no older'n I am right now, Ulie! That gave her the strength to stand strong, even when she was afraid and had to take life-or-death chances without knowin' how things was gonna work out. Some people betrayed her, yes, but many others didn't. Ain't that what you's tryin' to tell me, Ulie?"

"That's been my experience, yes."

"Tomorrow, I'mma tell Annie she don't need to worry 'bout it no mo', 'cause from now on, I'm carryin' Linda Brent with me, and I'mma follow in her footsteps. I know tha's sumpthin' Annie will understand, too, 'cause we a'ready been talkin' about it.

"But now, the time for talkin' is over. No more excuses. It's time for me to git down to the bidniss a figurin' out *my* life and what I got to do next."

"Amen, little sister!"

Chapter 36
Annie

When I stop by Mrs. B's to fill the water bottles, she reminds me our library books are due on Saturday.

"Has it been three weeks already?"

"Indeed it has, Annie. Do you want to go with me?"

"Definitely. I'll ask, okay?"

"Yes. Let me know."

I make a mental note to bring the books home from the Nest today so I'll be ready to go on Saturday. I'm already straddling my bicycle ready to take off, when Mrs. B lays a hand on my arm, and says, "Wait a minute. I'll be right back. I have some canned food and a few more clothes, if you want them."

Do I ever! We have no way of washing clothes up at our Nest, and there are no clean clothes left. If only I could tell her that the clothing she is offering will likely be worn by her own son. Soon, I hope.

"These were on sale yesterday," Mrs. B says as she moves stuff around to make room in my basket. She puts in two tall cans of baked beans, four cans of corn, carrots, bananas, and a paper bag of carefully folded garments.

"Hope those cans of beans aren't too big. As you know, Annie, I'm never one to pass up a bargain," she chuckles.

"Oh, no! They're fine, Mrs. B."

It's hard for me to look at her, because every time I do, the temptation to spill the beans (ha-ha) almost overwhelms me. I want to scream and shout and wave my arms and tell her Ulie has returned, and I know where he is! But I've promised Ulie I will keep his whereabouts a secret until I've figured out how to get information that will reassure him that it is safe to go home.

Up at the Nest, where we are now three, everything is different. With Ulie around, Clydeen no longer seems to be so fearful of someone discovering her presence. She's lost interest in many of the activities we've shared all summer. We no longer pray and sing. We don't play our favorite games or spend time in the shade of the boulder reading and talking, and we don't hike the trail on top of the mesa anymore.

So it's no surprise that when I get here today, Clydeen and Ulie are nowhere in sight. Ulie grew up around here. He knows everything about this place, and he and Clydeen have taken to going off exploring for long periods of time.

I sigh as I reach the ledge and find them gone—again.

"Where'd they go this time?" I grumble as I unload the food and head back down the wash for the water. There is a closeness between Clydeen and Ulie now that I don't share, and it hurts.

"Annie!" Clydeen calls when I reach the top of the wash for the second time.

"Hi, Clydeen. Where were you?"

"Oh, we's jus' down in those woods," she says, breathless with excitement. "Where our boulder is. Out yonder they's a pond. Did you know that?"

"I did not. We never went out that far out, I guess."

"Well, they is, and it's a great place to cool off."

"So where's Ulie?"

"He over there watchin' his mama's place right now."

"Could you ask him if he wants to eat?"

Ulie comes bounding up from somewhere on the other side of the lean-to. He seems transformed. His face is no longer gaunt, nor his body so thin he can barely keep his pants up. That, coupled with his reddish beard and dreads, as he calls them, makes him look like he belongs here. But for his oddly sallow complexion, which has not changed, he looks like a mountain man thriving in the wilds.

"Annie, hi!" he calls out.

"Hey, Ulie. How's it going? Come sit down and eat. Where's

Gary, Clydeen?"

"He be 'round here someplace. He come and go. Ulie say he got to learn to be on his own, now he almos' grown."

"Have I told you how much I appreciate your hospitality, Annie?" says Ulie, his mouth stuffed with a bite of tuna fish and pickle sandwich.

"Well, no. But you're welcome, Ulie."

He grins in that silly way he has, and then resumes wolfing down his sandwich, his eyes smiling at me all the while.

I'm thinking about Gary off on his own. I want the little guy to be right here perched on the orange crate sharing every meal with us like he used to, and I almost start to cry. Another change. Where will it end? My breath comes out in a huff, and my two companions stop chewing and study me.

"Nothing," I say. I swallow hard, clear my throat and ask them what they've been up to.

"Well, we went out to this pond I know about," says Ulie. "And I showed Clydeen what I think might be a dinosaur footprint. It's over on the other side of the mesa where there's another ledge kind of like this one. It's a long way around, but I could show you, too, Annie."

"Okay. That'd be fun."

"Do you have any news for me?" asks Ulie, looking up from scooping beans into his mouth.

Of course I know immediately what he means.

"No, not yet, Ulie. It's hard for me to talk to your mom right now. Because I know you're here, and I'm not able to tell her. It feels like I'm doing something wrong behind her back, you know what I mean?"

"I can understand that."

"I *am* going to do what you asked, though. I said I would. But I haven't figured a way to go about it yet. The good news is I haven't seen anything unusual, have you?"

"No. I am keeping my eye on my folks' place, but I haven't been doing a very good job of it these last couple of days," he laughs, shaking his head and looking at Clydeen, who meets his eyes and smiles. "It's really boring!" he adds. "I haven't seen anything suspicious. No police cars or men in dark suits and sunglasses driving shiny black cars. Maybe I'm way off base, you know?"

Clydeen and I exchange a look that says, *Yeah, maybe you are.*

"So Clydeen. I don't want to bug you, but have you had a chance to read Mrs. B's notes about the Tarot reading?"

"Yas. I have. Ulie read it, too."

"So what do you think?" I ask, keeping my voice low and even to stifle the urgency I can't help feeling.

I hold my breath and look from one to the other. Once again, they exchange a look, and my gut reminds me that now there's "them," and then there's "me." It's like the two of them are in the middle of a conversation I'm no longer a part of. But then I remember something from the Tarot reading, the part warning about me not thinking I am in charge of how everything goes. I relax a little and wait.

"We been talkin' 'bout it. I'm startin' to think you might be right, Annie, 'bout my mama. Maybe she ain't gonna find me longs I stay up here and don't find a way to start lookin' for her myself."

Thank God! I almost blurt out, but I don't. Instead, I clear my throat before squeaking out just one word. "Oh?"

It sounds so weird coming from me, I expect Clydeen to crack up, but she just gives me a solemn nod and grabs another handful of Fritos.

I want to dive right in, start making a plan, write stuff down, but once again, I stop myself. Using all my will power, I sit quietly, waiting for more.

"What would Linda Brent do? Tha's what I been axin' myself, Annie, and you know as well as I do what she would do, so from here on out, I'm takin' charge. I don't need you to fuss anymore 'bout what's gonna happen when you go back to school. I'mma handle it. When I make up my mind 'bout how it's gonna go, we'll talk, okay?"

Where is she going with this? Why is she shutting me out? Instead of being relieved as I was a moment ago, I'm frightened by this sudden turn of events.

"But Clydeen ..." I protest.

"Hush now, Annie. You heard what I said."

"Ulie? Have you been ...?"

He shrugs, a smug look on his face.

"What can I say? She wants to be her own person, Annie. She's using the Linda Brent playbook, is all."

Neither one of them says another word about it. I'm bubbling over with questions, but clearly, the subject is closed for now, so I keep my mouth shut and try to calm down. And then Ulie changes the subject.

"So let me ask you two something," Ulie says, talking with his mouth full again, baked bean juice trickling into his beard.

"What?" Clydeen and I say in unison.

"I been wondering ... that orange crate over there," he says, wiping his chin with the back of his hand. "The one you got covered with a baby blanket, what is that exactly?"

"You tell him, Annie."

"That's our altar. Those are special things we found. Things I brought from home, too, like the candles there. See those little carvings? Clydeen's been making those."

"What?! Do you mean that girl has a knife?" he says, falling over backwards. He springs up, grabs Clydeen by the shoulders and gives her a shake. She grins up at him.

"Okay, little sister. Tell me you didn't have a knife on you the night I came."

Clydeen and I look at each other. She's smiling all cockeyed, like she's the happiest goofball on earth.

"Well, yas," she tells him. "I reckon I did. I jus' didn't think of it, 'cause I uses it for carvin' or cuttin' up food. Never thought of it as somethin' to hurt a body with," she says, tilting her head and grinning, all flirty like.

Good grief! What's gotten into her?

"Holy crap!" Ulie shouts. "You mean I could of been cut to ribbons instead of just getting all bruised up with that baseball bat? I didn't realize how lucky I was."

I like Ulie. I can't help it. He's funny and playful and smart, too. He's easy to be around—for a boy, that is. I say "boy," because I don't really think of him as a grown man. There's something in his eyes that shows me that right now, he's more of the boy he once was, that lost part of himself he talks to us about trying to get back.

"Okay," he says, letting go of Clydeen. He flops down and props himself up on one elbow. "So why do you have an altar up here?"

"Because we've been praying for you, you jackass," I say laughing. "We light a candle, and we sing and pray."

"Oh, my. I never thought ... I'm overwhelmed with gratitude," he says, placing his right hand over his heart. "But you can't be doing all of that just for me."

"Well, no. Your mom told me all about the war and the camps, and you, naturally. I never knew about any of that stuff, and I guess I was kind of spooked by it all. I told Clydeen. I went on and on about it, until she got sick of it and started telling me about the slaves here in America. Turns out I didn't know much about that, either, so I got some books from the library for us to read. We started praying for all of the victims of the war, including the Japanese folks who were sent to camps right here in the United States, which your mom also told me about. We've been remembering the slaves. We've been praying for ourselves and our families, and you, Ulie. We didn't know what else we could do."

"Huh. Is that right?"

"What about you? Do you ever pray?" Clydeen asks him.

He scoffs. "Not me. That's my mom's department, her Tarot cards, her intuition and all of the other spiritual stuff she studies. I used to tease her about it. She'd say, 'Oh, Ulie, one day you're going to wake up and want to know about some of what I study.' I think she was right. I think I might have missed out.'

"My dad was born a Jew, but he was not religious, and he never taught me anything about it. Still, that was one reason I stayed overseas. Once I heard the rumors about what was going on with the Jewish people—ghettos, concentration camps and all—I had to find out for myself. Turned out those rumors were true, so I stayed. I don't pray, at least not the way I think you two mean. But I can't say I have never prayed. Have you ever heard this saying? 'There are no atheists in a foxhole'?"

"No. I don't understand that. Do you, Clydeen?"

"No."

"Well, in the First World War, before any of us were born, men dug deep trenches on the battlefields, and the two sides shot at each other from inside those trenches. Those trenches were called foxholes. Atheists, as I understand it, are people who don't believe in a higher power. 'There are no atheists in a foxhole' means that when the chips are down, everyone says a prayer of some kind, hoping there's something or someone out there greater than themselves to respond to their anguish. God, maybe? Jehovah? Jesus? Ganesha, my mother would probably say. I don't know what to call it, but when I was in France, there were plenty of times I said 'God help me!' Or 'God, don't let me be killed today.' Those are prayers, right?"

Clydeen and I consult one another with our eyes. "Yas. Those be prayers, Ulie," she says, her voice soft and tender.

I nod in agreement. We sit quietly for a few beats, and then I remember the books.

"Oh, Clydeen, I have to take our books home today. They're due on Saturday. Remind me, will you?"

"Clydeen told me about a book you read called *Incidents in the Life of a Slave Girl*. What else have you two been reading?" Ulie asks. "Nothing inappropriate for the likes of two innocent young girls, I hope." he teases.

I blush. So does Clydeen, I think, but the summer sun has turned her skin darker, so it's hard to tell. When he teases us, it undoes us, and we become captives in the warm glow of his attention.

"Unless you call two-year-olds being thrown in jail 'inappropriate'..." I fire back at him, that terrible image from *Incidents in the Life of a Slave Girl* still fresh in my mind.

"Well, yeah. I probably would. So c'mon now. What y'all been reading? I'm a big reader myself, you know."

"Well, the last thing we read was *The Adventures of Huckleberry Finn*. We were still discussing it when you showed up here."

"What? You two been reading that piece of racist crap? Tell me it ain't so!" he mugs and falls over backwards again.

I'm sitting there with my mouth gapping open. But Clydeen? She jumps up, raises her arms in the air and pumps her fists like she's just scored a home run with the bases loaded.

I glare at her and say to Ulie, "What do you know about it? The librarian told me for a fact that *Huckleberry Finn* is an anti-slavery book."

Again, I wonder if this is true or not. If not, why am I making it up? Maybe I just want to argue with him because I'm feeling left out these days.

"I'm trying to look at it historically," I add, feeling like an idiot.

"Historically," he hoots. "I suppose this librarian is a nice white lady?"

"Well, yeah. Very nice. Miss Clark's her name."

"Oh, Lord, is she still there after all these years? Let me tell you something, Annie. You gotta stop listening to nice white ladies. With the exception of my mom, that is. Most of them just repeat what they've been told by somebody else. But you, my friend, you've got spunk. You've got smarts. And you've got a future. You need to think for yourself, and don't you forget it. The same goes for you, Miss Clydeen over there. I want you two to listen to your Uncle Ulie now, because I been all over the place, and I've learned a thing or two.

"My advice? Exchange that book for *Uncle Tom's Cabin* and give that one a go. That book is so anti-slavery and anti-racist that when President Lincoln met the author, Harriet Beecher Stowe, he said to her: 'So this is the little lady that started this big war.' Or pick up something about Harriet Tubman and the underground railroad. She was a magnificent Negro woman who was a great crusader for abolition. A true American hero. In this country, you need as much pride and gumption as you can get, Clydeen, and believe me, you sure ain't gonna get it reading the likes of Mark Twain!"

"I keep thinkin' 'bout what my daddy tol' me one time."

"What's that?"

"He say, 'In the English language, nigger and trigger are a'ways gonna rhyme.'"

I'm shocked into speechlessness. Why would her father say something like that to her? Ulie is nonplussed and goes to her at once. He puts his arms around her, and says, "I will do my best always to keep you safe, little sister."

"What are you talking about, Ulie," I shout. "How could you possibly promise her something like that? Don't tell her things that aren't true!"

But Ulie just looks at me with his kind eyes and says, "'There are more things in heaven and earth, Horatio, than are dreamt of in your philosophy.'"

I get up and stomp off. They pick up their conversation about Mark Twain as if nothing of importance at all just went down. I feel like crying, but I don't want them to see me. Gary comes running after me, and I pick him up and hold him close while I choke back tears. When he squirms out of my arms and takes off, I follow him back to where Clydeen and Ulie are still sitting and talking like they didn't even notice I was gone.

"What about you, Annie?" Ulie asks.

"What about me?"

"You're not gonna give Mr. Mark Twain a pass, are you?"

I still have my head in the ozone, and before I can think of anything to say, Ulie charges on.

"Many people think Twain was a great humorist who was trying to use satire to make a point about the absurdity of Southern attitudes toward Negros and slavery so that society would see the errors of its ways and change. I bought into that myself after I read *Huckleberry Finn* for the first time when I was about your age, because that's what I was taught. But when I read it again as an adult, I saw very little humor in it. In my opinion, it doesn't work for a couple of reasons. The way Jim is portrayed as blandly accepting of his own powerless in the world of white people. The way he is so passive in the face of the cruelty he endures at the hands of Tom and Huck and various other characters—well, the stereotype is so overstated it goes from humorous to painful to read.

"Besides that, it seems to me that the lack of any path to redemption or model of transformation in the book shows us nothing that would cause a society to change its attitudes or behavior in any significant way. The whole enterprise lacks balance. Do you see what I mean? If Huck had actually been the great white hero some give him credit for, Jim's humanity and his thirst for freedom would have been a major focus, not just a loosely constructed fantasy easily dismissed. Huck would have made a real effort to see that Jim got to the free states ... but, of course, that's a different book altogether."

"Yas!" shouts Clydeen.

"Okay. I understand what you're saying Ulie," I say with a sigh. "The last few chapters ... and there were other parts, too ..."

"What about you?" he asks, turning to Clydeen.

"Like I tol' Annie a few days ago, in my opinion, mos' a that book be 'bout two hair-brained white boys and a few other ne'er-do-wells humiliatin' poor Jim. Jim thinks if he stick with Huck, he gonna help him get to a free state, but that never happens. How's that s'posed to change 'sivilization' as Huck calls it? Look to me like jus' the opposite. Didn't the book end up sayin' it be well and good for a couple a no-count white boys to abuse a colored man for they own entertainment? Anti-slavery? Anti-racist? My ass!"

"Right you are, my young friend. We are blind when it comes to race in this country. Do you know what guys from other countries used to ask me when I ended up in Germany after the war ended? They'd rib me about the segregation they saw in the American military stationed over there, Negros in their platoons, whites in theirs. 'How can you Americans talk about German racism against the Jews and claim to be the ones gonna teach them about democracy and all men created equal and all that shit?' I may be fuzzy on a lot of stuff these days, but that there is something I *do* remember clearly.

"Anyway, what could I say? I had no answer. I felt ashamed, because some of those dark-skinned American soldiers, mainly Cajuns from Louisiana who spoke French, risked their lives to channel money to the Resistance so we could go on fighting. You think any of us cared one wit about skin color when our lives were on the line? Time after time, those fellas risked their lives for us. It changed me to see that," he says, swiping hard at the tears that have filled his eyes.

"You okay, Annie?" Clydeen asks. "You look ...'"

"I'm okay. I love this. Sitting here in the sun with the two of you, talking about things that really matter. I wish this day would never end. Heck, I wish this summer would never end and we could go on having these conversations forever. It's very special, is all," I say, looking from Clydeen to Ulie. My heart is wide open with love and appreciation for both of them now, leaving no more space for the jealousy I've been feeling recently.

Chapter 37
Clydeen

"Wake up!" whispers Ulie. "Wake up!"

"What you want, Ulie?"

"Come see."

I'm right in the middle of my Friday afternoon nap when Ulie come 'round a-botherin' me. It be the middle a August now, and it's hot! It rained last night, and they's a damp, muggy feelin' in the air. That's why I'm so sleepy. But I groan and hoist myself up offa my cot and walk outside where the sun so bright, I can barely see.

"Ulie?" I call out. "Where you at?"

"Down here. Come take a look."

"What?" I say, comin' up behind him.

He be down at that spot where we do our watchin' a his mama's place. When I git up close to him, we both start slidin' and hafta grap a tree branch to keep from tumblin'. It ain't an ideal spot, but still, we hang out here as much can, 'cause this be the bes' place to watch his mama's house from.

"Look," he say, pointing. "There it is. A big black car at my folks' house."

"Well, I'll be.... They sho 'nuff is," says I.

"Didn't I tell you?"

"Yes, sir, you did. What you think it means?"

"Don't know. Looks official, though. And official means trouble!"

"Oh, Ulie, you don't know nothin' yet. Don't be jumpin' to no conclusions, makin' yo'self all crazy, you hear?"

"I hear you, Cleopatra. But ..."

"But nothin'. Let's jus' stay here awhile and see."

We do, but nothin' happens. We be real quiet, like we's almost scared a breathin'. But it ain't no use. Nobody gets in or out of the car or goes in or out of Miz B's house, neither.

"Wait! Wait!" Ulie say, leanin' forward and reachin' back to grab my arm so's he won't fall. "Is that Annie right there?"

We both bend ourselves over far as we dare to get a closer look.

"Yas. That be her comin' on her bike. What she doin'? She already come up here today, but it sure look like she headed this way agin. Maybe she forgot sumpthin'?"

"Oh, my God! Do you think she'll stop when she sees that car?"

"Don't know, Ulie. We gonna hafta see."

We watch as Annie pedals up the road alongside Miz B's house, and Ulie, he git even more excited.

"Stop! Stop! Stop! Oh, please stop, Annie!" he cries out, stompin' his feet and shakin' that tree branch he hangin' onto.

But Annie hurries on by and turns the corner where we can't see her no mo'.

"Dang it all!" says Ulie, turnin' away in disgust and climbin' back onto the ledge.

He say he goin' to git some water. I stay where I am and wait for him to come back, and then I see Annie agin—goin' back the other way.

"Ulie! Come see. She goin' back! She turned around!"

He races over to where I'm perched watchin'.

"Oh, boy! Oh, boy! Is she's goin' in?"

"I think maybe she is. She's gone 'round to the front a the house."

"This could be it, Clydeen."

"Okay. Let's jus' take it easy. You gonna have to wait till she come up here, see if she bring any news. Maybe they's nothin' a'tall for you to git all worked up about."

We watch for a few more minutes, but we don't see Annie or anyone else after that.

"C'mon," I say finally. "Ain't nothin' happenin' right now. Let's go git that water. I'm dyin' a thirst."

"You go. Bring it over here, would you please? And bring me some of those peanuts, too. I'm gonna hang out here and watch for a while."

We watch, both of us bored stiff, for I don't know how long. We git so tired a watchin', we move to sit on flat ground and start playin' hangman in the dirt. The next time we think to take a look, the black car is gone.

"Holy crap!" says Ulie, jumpin' up and bangin' his fists on his thighs. "I missed it! I should have been paying attention. What was I thinking?" he say, slappin' his forehead.

"Yeah, but Annie was there for a long time," I remind him. "I bet she'll have sumphin' to say next time she come."

Chapter 38
Annie

Stupid Vivian! She just told me we're going to Cheyenne tomorrow, Saturday, to visit the grandparents, and we will be staying until *Monday*.

"No way!" I yell as I race out the door, jump on my bike and take off. It's late afteroon, and Stanley will be home soon, but I don't care. I have to tell Clydeen and Ulie about this. I can't go away for three days and leave them, but how am I gonna to get out of it?

Unburdened by my usual load, I'm one hundred percent focused on getting to the Nest as fast as I can. I'm in such a rush, I sail right past Mrs. B's house and don't notice the car parked on her corner.

Shortly after I turn right onto the dead-end path that runs along the base of the mesa, it registers. Big, shiny, black car. It's the kind of car Ulie believes will bring trouble for him, and he's repeated that phrase so many times, it's burned into my brain.

"Well, I'll be ..."

I slam on my brakes and skid to a stop. A cloud of dust flies up around me and makes me sneeze. I pause for a moment, spit the grit out of my mouth and think about what to do next.

"What the hell? It's probably nothing. He's imagining things," I mutter to myself, but just as I'm about to continue on my way, my gut says, "But then again ... maybe he's not."

I turn around, and when I get back to Mrs. B's, I park my bike and take a good look at the car. Black, shiny as a mirror, four doors, tinted windows, two antennas. Its rounded top makes it look like a sinister black beetle. Maybe this is my chance to find out something that will help Ulie so he'll let me off the hook and go on home.

I knock gently on Mrs. B's front door, half hoping she won't answer. Whatever is going on inside is no doubt grown-up business where I don't belong, and I'd rather be someplace else. But the promise I've made to Ulie makes me bold, and so I stand tall, plant my feet and wait.

I'm about to leave when the door swings open. Mrs. B looks surprised to see me, because I generally come through the back.

"Oh, Annie, child," she says. "I'm glad you're here. Come on in."

There are two men dressed in suits sitting on either end of the white flower-patterned sofa. They're bent forward, with their hands folded and their elbows on their knees, looking ill at ease.

"Gentlemen, this is my young friend, Annie Cahill," says Mrs. B. "I would like her to stay, if that's all right with you."

"That'd be fine, ma'am," says one of the men. "It's up to you."

"Annie, this is Special Agent Sanders," she says, gesturing toward one end of the couch, "and this is Special Agent Richardson," she says, indicating the man at the other end.

"Hello," says Agent Sanders.

"Hi," I say shyly.

Neither of them stand, and they do not offer to shake my hand, which is fine with me. Proves I'm still a kid and I'm to be disregarded in the world of adult affairs. That's exactly how I want it right now. My purpose here is to spy.

"Come give me a hand, Annie. I'm making some coffee for these gentlemen," says Mrs. B.

We go to the kitchen where the coffee is percolating. It smells wonderful, but I'm not allowed to drink it yet. My parents say it will stunt my growth, but I doubt this is true.

Mrs. B's fancy silver coffee service is sitting on the table. The sugar bowl and creamer have already been filled, and delicate hand-painted china cups are lined up around the edge of the tray.

"Eva, who are those men?" I whisper. It's the first time I have called her by her first name, but I'm done with that ridiculous rule, and she doesn't seem to notice.

"I'm not sure yet," she whispers back. "They got here a little while ago, but then one of them made a lengthy phone call. I've been waiting, and all I know so far is that they're from the State Department."

"Do you think it might be about Ulie?"

"Oh, God, Annie. I hope so."

"Should I go?"

"No. Please stay. Frankly, I could use the moral support."

The percolator winds down, and Eva places it in the center of the silver tray.

"Can I get you something, Annie?"

"Water. I'll get it in a minute. Let me open the door for you."

She picks up the heavy coffee service, and I bring the spoons and napkins and hold the swinging door open so she can pass through.

"Here you are, gentlemen. Please help yourselves."

Her voice sounds strained, more high-pitched than usual.

"This is very kind of you, ma'am. We don't usually get a fresh cup of coffee on our official visits."

I come back into the room with my water and position myself in the wicker rocker on the side of the room opposite the two men so I can see and hear everything. I study them as they help themselves to coffee, one adding sugar and cream, the other cream only. Otherwise, they are like carbon copies of one another, dressed in dark suits, plain dark ties, freshly ironed white shirts and highly polished black shoes.

The tension builds, and all of a sudden, words pop out of my mouth.

"So have you come about Ulie?" I ask.

I blush. How could I be so rude? I pinch myself on the arm to remind myself that I need to sit here and keep my mouth shut.

I look at Eva, expecting her to shush me, but she doesn't seem to care that I have spoken out of turn. She's sitting on the edge of her seat, her body rigid with expectation, a weird half-smile on her face, waiting. I can sense how afraid she is of what these men have come to tell her, and waves of guilt wash over me. How can I sit here pretending to know nothing when I know exactly where her son is at this very moment?

"Well, yes. As a matter of fact, we have come about Ulie. Ulysses, right?" Special Agent Richardson says, ignoring me and turning to

Eva.

"That's right. Ulysses Borsheim. My son. Please tell me. Have you found him?"

"Unfortunately, after a thorough investigation, it has been confirmed that your son perished in France in the spring of 1943, ma'am. I am so sorry for your loss, and I wish there was some way to soften the blow of this terrible news."

Eva's face turns white, and she grips the arms of her chair, gulping air.

"No!" I say, half rising from my seat. "That can't be!"

I glare at the two men. How dare they!

"Do you have his body?" I ask.

"I'm sorry to say we do not. His remains were never recovered, and that's one reason it's taken so long for us to reach a conclusion. In response to your many inquiries over the years, ma'am, we have obtained multiple eye-witness accounts of what happened to Mr. Borsheim, which have now been verified by the governments of both France and the United States."

"Isn't it possible ...?"

"Well, no, young lady, actually it's not."

I feel slammed. I hit the back of my chair so hard, it almost tips over. Sweat pours down my spine. What the heck is he talking about? These guys are just wrong! I can't wait for these suits to get the hell out of here so I can set Eva straight.

Eva blows her nose and turns her attention back to the two individuals sitting on the sofa. "Is there anything else, gentlemen?" she asks.

"Ma'am, I'm so sorry we weren't able to bring you the news you were hoping for," says Special Agent Sanders. "But no. That's not all, and I hope what I am about to tell you will make you proud of your son and perhaps bring you a measure of comfort."

Eva looks up and nods, encouraging him to continue.

"Apparently, your son did some very heroic things during the war when he was part of the Resistance movement in France," Special Agent Sanders continues.

"French Resistance, you say. I thought that might be the case."

"Yes, ma'am. Mr. Borsheim was apparently one of their demolitions expert over there, did you know that?"

"Oh, for crying out loud!" Eva says, bursting into tears.

After giving her a few moments to recover, Special Agent Sanders continues telling the story.

"We have learned that the group your son worked with was particularly successful in sabotaging the Nazi war effort in many different ways and on many different occasions. But in one particular instance, Mr. Borsheim and his comrades, after several months of effort, were able to acquire enough explosives to blow up a critical railway bridge the Nazis used to bring supplies into France, including weapons and ammunition. After placing the explosives, they lay in wait for several hours waiting for the Nazi supply train to come along and make its way onto the bridge. They blew up the bridge and the train with it, closing off that supply line for the duration of the war. It also made it somewhat more difficult for the Nazis to transport Jews out of France to concentration camps in Germany and Poland.

"I said 'they' detonated the explosives, but it was really your son, ma'am, who gave his life to stay close enough to the site to detonate the explosives and blow up the bridge and the train at exactly the right moment. He did this after sending his comrades to safety away from the immediate area. When he stood to push the plunger to set off the explosives, he was gunned down by a German soldier guarding the back of the train. His body fell on the plunger, and the bridge and train were destroyed."

"Oh no, no, no!" cries Eva, covering her face with her damp handkerchief and weeping into it. "Not our boy. I promised Maury ..." she sobs.

My mouth drops open. I start to rise from my chair to protest again, but at the last second, I change my mind and sit back down. Thank God no one's paying any attention to me now. I rock furiously, trying to quiet the pounding of my heart. What the hell is going on here? Ulie is nearby, safe and sound not twenty minutes from here, but these bigwigs from the United States government are saying that's not true. I can't stand seeing Eva in so much pain, but getting into a pissing match with these agents is not a contest I'm likely to win. No matter how hard it is, I'll have to wait until they've gone to tell Eva the truth. I'm so busy in my own head, I almost miss the next revelation.

"There's more, Mrs. Borsheim, ma'am," Agent Richardson is saying when I tune in again. "For this and other acts of bravery and in recognition of his service to the Resistance, your son has been awarded a medal of honor, *Medalle de la Resistance* in French. It's a decoration bestowed by the French Committee of National Liberation on those who showed unusual courage and rendered significant assistance to the French cause during the war. It was commissioned by General Charles de Gaulle himself.

"I'll read this part, if you don't mind. The decoration is bestowed 'to recognize the remarkable acts of faith and courage that, in France, in the empire and abroad, have contributed to the resistance of the French people against the enemy and its accomplices since 18 June 1940.'"

Eva and I look at each other with disbelief, but not for the same reasons, I suspect.

"So let me be the first to offer my congratulations, as well as my condolences, ma'am," continues Special Agent Richardson. "Your son is a hero, and our own government is very grateful to him as well."

Special Agent Sanders nods, silently offering his assent.

Eva lifts her glasses and wipes her eyes again.

"Hero," she repeats softly. "Well," she says, "I never expected anything like that, but thank you."

My mind is whipping from pillar to post. My eyes grow wide thinking of the tattered young man, who is in hiding, so afraid of men like these he can't risk coming home to his mother. And now she thinks he's never coming home. What am I going to say to her?

What I have heard from these men has raised enough doubt in me that I'm no longer one hundred and ten percent certain that the Ulie I know is the same Ulie these men are talking about. If Ulie died in France, then who is the person Clydeen and I have been hanging out with up at the Nest for the last number of weeks, the one who has become like a wise older brother to the two of us? If the guy up on the mesa turns out not to be Ulie, I'm gonna personally wring his neck. But until I find out for sure, I can't tell Eva anything. I can't give her hope if there is none. All I can say is this: If the Ulie I know is an imposter, he's awfully good at it.

No, no, no. Wait a minute. Why would anyone go to the trouble of impersonating Ulie? It makes no sense. Besides, I find it hard to believe that the gentle, soul-weary young man I've come to know, with all of his fears, his nightmares, his confusion, *and* a story that closely matches the one these men have told us can be anyone other than Eva's son.

I have to get up there and get to the bottom of this, but I can't go now. It's too late. It's already past six, and I dare not be any later getting home than I already am.

"The French government has invited you to come to Paris to accept the award on behalf of your son, Mrs. Borsheim. This won't be for several months yet, but we will be in touch to make the appropriate arrangements."

"Paris," Eva repeats vaguely. "Paris," she says again.

The next thing I know, the two men are rising to leave. They hand Eva their business cards, and each of them offers Eva a hand to shake.

She recovers herself and gets to her feet. She looks clear-eyed and dignified as she faces the two of them and shows them to the door.

"Thank you, gentlemen, for coming all this way to bring me this news," she says.

She closes the door behind them, and bursts into tears again.

Chapter 39
Eva

"Oh, Annie," I wail, no longer holding myself back as I was trying to do when those two men were sitting in my living room. "I'm so glad you're here. I don't think I could bear this alone."

"You're in shock, Eva. So am I," Annie says, reaching out to steady me.

"If you can stay a little longer, I'm going to make us a cup of hot tea, and maybe we can talk about what just happened. I know it's late ...."

"No. Don't worry. I want to stay."

When we've settled ourselves in the breakfast nook, I begin pulling at the threads of what the two agents said and tossing them onto the table between Annie and me.

"They said Ulie died in 1943 in an explosion, right?"

"Not exactly. They said he was shot by a German soldier from the back of a train he was in the process of blowing up."

"Oh, that's right."

The tears come again. I get up, go to my bedroom and take a clean handkerchief from the dresser drawer.

When I return, Annie says, "But wait a minute, Eva. Remember? They don't have his body."

"Oh, my sweet girl. Thank you for saying that.... Well, maybe I should just tell you something."

"Tell me what? Did you already know?"

"Not exactly. Do you remember when I showed you my Tarot

cards the first time?"

"Sure."

"I told you how I use the cards to help me search for Ulie."

"Yes, I remember that."

"Well, I didn't tell you everything, Annie. There *is* a Death card in the Tarot deck. It's a Major Arcana card called—"

"—Death. Right?"

"Yes. That's right. It's been showing up with some regularity reversed in the tenth position in my own readings for some time now. When it's reversed, it's message can, under some circumstances, be a dire warning. I've only seen that card in the tenth position reversed twice in all the years I've been doing readings for others, and I've done hundreds of them. I never told those people that the card might foretell an imminent death. It's not a burden a reader should place on someone, because there are other more benign meanings, too. I always gave a softer interpretation, but sure enough, in both cases, a death had either already occurred unbeknownst to the client, or took place shortly after the reading.

"If I had been honest with myself, I would have recognized the strong possibility that Ulie had either died or was in mortal danger. But I always pushed that possibility away, despite the recurring appearance of the Death card. So yes, I'm shocked, because now it's real. But when I take a step back, I know the possibility that he did not survive has been lodged within my heart for quite a while now, and from that point of view, I'd have to say it's more like a confirmation than a total surprise."

"But even though the cards said he might have been killed, you didn't stop looking for him."

"Well, a strong possibility he might no longer be alive wasn't enough for me. It didn't change my love for him or my desire to keep looking. I didn't want to give up and miss a chance to find him, if there was one, and, of course, there was my promise to his father."

Annie smiles at me from across the table, nodding.

"What am I going to do now? Searching for him has been my sole purpose for years. I think I'm going to feel about as useless as an old purse forgotten in the back of the closet," I sigh.

We sit quietly, staring out the window as the sun slides down behind the mountain tops.

"May I make a suggestion?" Annie asks.

"Please do."

"I think you need someone to stay with you tonight."

I hadn't thought of this before, but now it seems like a good idea.

"I can call and ask ..."

"It's fine, Annie. I'll call Imani. Thank God she's back. She's exactly the friend I need right now."

I get up, go to the phone, and place the call.

"She'll be here as soon as she can. She's living about 40 minutes away, up in the mountains right now," I say as I hang up the phone. "Would you like a sandwich, Annie?"

"Sure."

I can see that Annie's nerves are getting the best of her. She paces around the kitchen while I make her a fried egg sandwich, but when I call her attention to how late it is and invite her to go on home, she refuses. The clock is now edging toward seven o'clock.

"I'll go when your friend gets here, okay? I'm sorry I'm so wound up. This is a lot. I've never known anyone who died before. Of course I didn't really *know* Ulie," she adds quickly.

I beckon her to me. "Come here. You are such a good friend to me, Annie."

"We'll see about that," she murmurs.

I'm about to ask her what in the world she means, but my train of thought is interrupted by Imani's arrival, and the next thing I know, Annie is gone.

Chapter 40
Annie

It was getting dark by the time Eva's friend arrived, way past the time I should have been home for dinner.

"You're grounded!" my father shouted as I pushed through the backdoor.

"Huh?" I said, having forgotten all about what would happen at home.

I barely paused to glance at him as I walked through the living room to my bedroom. "I am *so not grounded*," I snickered to myself as I kicked my shoes off and threw my dirty socks into the laundry basket and hit the sack, not bothering to undress further.

It's early morning now, and I've spent another sleepless night. Vivian bustles into the room and tosses a small duffel bag on my bed.

"Get packed, Annie. We're leaving at nine o'clock, and you know how crabby Dad will be if we don't get started on time."

"Mom, wait."

"What is it, Annie?"

"I'm not going. I'm staying here," I say in an offhanded way, but she just scoffs and hurries off.

I'm right on her heels.

"Listen to me! I don't want to go!"

She doesn't even bother to look at me as she pronounces the verdict.

"You're going. You're too young to stay home by yourself for that long."

I almost burst out laughing. Once Teresa started sleeping through the night, there were occasions when I unlocked the backdoor and slipped away to spend most of the night up at our Nest with Clydeen, the two of us cuddling and laughing ourselves silly. If she only knew, and for a nanosecond, I want to throw it in her face. But of course, I don't dare. Instead, I turn my pockets inside out looking for any other arguments I can find that might make her change her mind.

"Mom, you and Dad go out and leave me in charge of all of the other kids for hours on end, sometimes until two in the morning, and you've been doing that since I was ten. I'm 14. I'm in high school now. I can stay by myself for a couple of days. Pleeeese?" I beg. "I *really* don't want to go this time."

"No, Annie."

"But there's never anything to do at Grammy's and Grandpa's," I whine. "Dad and Grandpa drink whiskey and play pool. The rest of us just sit around all day. At night, you guys play poker and make so much noise it keeps us awake half the night. I hate the bed. It feels damp and smells funny. If Grandma and Granddad Mack were in town, it would be different. I could go down there ..."

"Well, you can have a nice visit with Grammy Cahill this time."

"I don't even *like* Grammy Cahill. And neither do you."

"Yes, I do," she says defensively, drawing back and placing a hand on her throat.

"Liar," I mumble under my breath.

"Annie, hush now. I'm not going to argue with you anymore. Get packed right now."

I march off and throw a few random things into the duffle bag, and EUREKA! I spy the library books lying on the top of the highboy. They are due today, and I need to take them to Eva. I whoop with glee.

"Mom, I have to take my library books over to Mrs. Borsheim so she can return them to the library today," I call out to Vivian.

"Be back here and ready to go no later than nine!" she shouts, leaning out the kitchen window as I speed off.

I have no intention of making the trip to Cheyenne cramped up in the back seat with my two brothers while Stanley and Vivian smoke us out. Makes me gag just thinking about it. But what's my Plan B?

When I get to Eva's, I find her out back taking care of the animals, just like any other morning.

"Eva, where's your friend?"

"Oh, Annie. You startled me. Imani had an appointment in town this morning. We didn't sleep much. She'll be back later with some groceries."

I get busy helping her with the chores, working silently while I worry over the details of Plan B. If it works out, I'll have plenty of time to sort things out with Ulie.

When we've finished the chores and all of the animals have been fed, we head into the house. I sit on the bench in the breakfast nook and watch while Eva puts on a pair of rubber gloves and attacks the dishes that have piled up in the sink overnight.

"Uhhh ... Eva, do you think I could stay here for a couple of days?"

She turns and looks at me like she's surprised to find me sitting there.

"What? Why, yes, Annie. What's up?"

"I am supposed to go to Cheyenne with my family today—until Monday. I can't go right now, Eva. There are things .... I look at her helplessly, because there are no words I can share about *what* things. She'll find out soon enough as soon as I get to Ulie and bring him home to her—or not.

"Anyway, never mind about that," I say, scooting forward and sitting up straight. "My mother says I'm too young to stay by myself, but I really don't want to go. That's the point."

"Well, okay. How about I call your mother and invite you to stay with me?"

"Eva, you are the best! Thank you!" I throw my arms around her and hug her from behind, the knot on her apron strings burrowing into my belly.

"Just give me a minute," she laughs, "and I'll call."

But as luck would have it, "just a minute" is a minute too long.

Chapter 41
Annie

There is an urgent pounding on the front door.

"Who in the world could that be? Imani won't be back for hours yet."

Eva strips off her gloves, dries her hands and hurries to the door, where Stanley is standing on the porch shifting impatiently from one foot to the other.

"Oh, no!" I say under my breath.

I glance at the clock on the mantle. It's now a quarter to nine.

Eva turns to me with a question in her eyes.

"Dad! What are you doing here?" As if I don't already know.

Eva steps up and offers Stanley her hand.

"It's very nice to meet you, Mr. Cahill. Won't you come in?"

Eva opens the door wide so he can pass, but he ignores her hand and her invitation in favor of glaring at me instead.

"Annie, you need to come with me right now. Everyone's in the car and ready to go."

"Dad, I don't want to go—just this one time."

"Didn't your mother make herself clear this morning? You are coming with us, so get in the goddamn car. Now!"

"Come in for moment, please," says Eva calmly, drawing back slightly in the face of his bluster.

Stanley steps inside but not far enough for Mrs. B to close the front door.

"We need to get on the road," he shouts at me.

"I want to stay here for the weekend, Dad."

"It's fine for Annie to stay with me, Mr. Cahill. In fact, I was just about to call Vivian to invite her."

"No! She's coming with us," and with that, he grabs my upper arm and pulls hard.

"Ouch! Let go of me! I'm not going."

When I try to jerk my arm away, he tightens his grip. Usually, I wouldn't resist him, but with all that's at stake today, I have absolutely no intention of going. But he can't let it go, can he? A burning anger spreads through my body and blazes its way to the top of my head. My ears ring, and my head buzzes. He hangs on, but so do I. I rock back on my heels and shoot lightning bolts out of my eyes at him, breathing so hard, I think I might faint.

"Just a minute, Mr. Cahill. That's not necessary," says Eva, stepping in and laying a hand on his arm in a soothing gesture.

He's having none of it and raises his arm so abruptly, he throws Eva off balance and nearly causes her to fall.

"Dad!" I shout, and he lets go of me.

"What in the world is going on here?"

It's Vivian, standing in the open doorway with Teresa in her arms.

Startled, Stanley spins on the balls of his feet. "This goddamn kid won't mind me and get in the car!" he says.

He sounds as whiny as Charlie and me when we fight and a higher authority arrives to break it up.

Vivian looks at Stanley and then at me but says nothing. We all stand there, like we're posing for a photograph we will look at years from now and say, "Remember that day when we ..."

Eva is the first to recover and step out of my imaginary picture frame.

"Vivian," she says, smiling and offering a welcoming hand.

Vivian hesitates, and Eva moves in next to her, gently puts her arm around Vivian's waist and leads her to the sofa.

"You, too, Mr. Cahill. Please sit down and let's see if we can figure this out."

Addressing Vivian, Eva says, "I was just telling your husband that Annie is more than welcome to stay here for the weekend. She seems to feel very strongly about not wanting to go out of town today."

My parents exchange a look. Stanley takes a seat—sort of. He perches on the edge of the sofa cushion and leans forward, scowling. If he were a dog, he'd be baring his teeth and growling right now. Neither of my parents look at me, and I feel as though I may have become invisible. But really it's just that we are all so unprepared to deal with my persistent act of disobedience.

"Can I get you anything?" offers Eva. "A glass of water, perhaps?"

"No, thank you," says Vivian, with an excess of polite. "We need to get on the road. The boys are waiting ..." she trails off, smiling faintly.

Eva settles herself in one of the rocking chairs, and I go and stand behind her where I feel protected. I gaze at my parents, who look so out of place in this room where only Eva and I have ever belonged. Once again, I have the sensation of everything coming to a standstill, as if we are all suspended in time with no way to move forward. What happens to me in this state over the next few seconds astounds me. I'm feeling dazed and a little light-headed. My parents look small and fragile, as if I am seeing them through the wrong end of a pair of binoculars. Teresa twists in Vivian's arms. Vivian clings to her and looks a little frantic. Perhaps she's afraid Teresa is going to cause a disturbance, too.

Stanley's eyes are downcast; he's studying the design in the carpet. Neither of them have any idea how or why they have ended up sitting like bookends on a sofa in the living room of this stranger, but they are bravely pretending otherwise and doing their best to come to grips with their confusion.

I feel a rush of sympathy for them. They have no more of an idea how to navigate this situation than I do. A softening comes over me, dipping underneath my anger. At the same time, I'm aware that any second now, Stanley is going to wake up and realize there is absolutely nothing keeping him here. He will force me to get in the car and off we'll go. Eva will not be able to stop him, nor will I.

I suck in air, and a shiver passes through my body, like I'm just waking up from a bad dream. This is a moment of reckoning. It's time for me to explain what's been going on all summer and tell them why I need to stay here this weekend. It's madness, I know. It may do nothing more than postpone the inevitable and get me in big trouble to boot. But there's a part of me that is so exhausted with the effort of keeping secrets, I just want to stop.

I think back to the reading the other day, the last card in particular, the one with the picture of the mean king. "There will be no avoiding his reaction," Eva told me.

Okay, then. Let's see what happens when I lay my cards on the table. What I have to say is going to come as a shock to more than one person in this room right now.

Chapter 42
Clydeen

It's late when I gits up offa my bed this fine Saturday mornin'. No clouds, but not too hot, neither. And the trees? Well, they smell like glory halleluiah to me, and I'm feelin' jus' fine.

Gary come runnin' up, and I'm so glad to see him, I scoop him up and axe him, "Where you been little guy?"

Course he don't say nothin', but I think he grin a little. He been gone for the past two days, learnin' to be a squirrel that lives in the wild, like Ulie say he got to do. But all the same, I'm happy he ain't forgot 'bout me jus' yet.

I pull the tarp off the lean-to boards and look around. No sign of Ulie yet. I play with Gary for a while, and when Ulie still don't show up, me and Gary go lookin' for him.

"Ulie!" I call, but he don't answer.

Maybe he decided to go on home after we saw that black car yesta'day. I shrug and pull a b'loney sandwich out of the lunch box and sit down in the shade to eat. No sooner do I git settled and sink my teeth into the soft white bread and taste the spicy mustard than I hear a loud crack from somewhere nearby, followed by a lot of rustlin' down below the ledge.

"What was that? A gunshot?" I say, scramblin' to my feet.

I turn this way and that, not sure were the noise come from. My heart thumps in my chest sumpthin' fierce, even after it's quiet again.

Gary, he's crawled up under my shirt, and I hold onto him as I

272

dash this way and that, tryin' to puzzle out what be goin' on, peerin' over the ledge first on one side of the lean-to, and then the other. I stand still and listen for voices, but I don't hear none. Where is Ulie?

"Ulie!" I shout, louder this time. I stand still and listen hard, and then I hears a whimperin'.

"Ulie?" I call agin. "That you, Ulie? Where you at?"

"Clydeen, please! Help me!"

"Where you at, Ulie?"

"Down here. Just follow my voice."

He keep right on talkin', and I follow his voice to the watchin' spot. But he ain't there, so I peer down the slope, and there he is, his body jammed up against the trunk of a tree. He be rollin' from side to side moanin', his face all screwed up with the hurtin.' One a our glass bottles a water is lyin' close by, and the water's slowly tricklin' out onto the ground.

"Ulie, what happened?"

"I woke up early, and I came down to watch. Trying to see if there's anything going on at my folk's house this morning, since I was so stupid that I missed seeing who was in that car last night. No cars there today, though," he say, grittin' his teeth.

"You leaned out too far and lost your balance, am I right? How many times that almos' happen?"

"I know! I know! I think my leg is broken," he say, layin' a hand on his left leg. "I grabbed a branch trying to break my fall, but it snapped, and I kept on rolling until this tree stopped me."

"Oh! That must a been the noise I heard sounded like a gunshot."

"Yeah. It made a loud crack when it broke."

From where I stand, I can see blood seepin' through his pant leg just below the knee. He tries to git up, but the slightest movement make him scream.

"Jus' lay still, Ulie. Take off that long-sleeved shirt and tie it real tight 'round where your leg's bleedin'. Can you do that?"

He rests for a few minutes, and then he does what I tell him. I keep on talkin' to him, sayin' we gonna figure this out. A few minutes after he tied the shirt on, I don't see no mo' blood comin' through, but I can't see so good from up here, so I axe him to take a look.

"Ahhhhh!" he yell as he raise hisself up. "There's no blood coming through the shirt, Clydeen."

"Good."

He pale, pantin' like a dog, too.

"Now see if you can git ahold a that water bottle, set it up so no more water drain out of it."

He stretches and screams, stretches and screams, but he finally gits the bottle and stands it up. Then he collapses and closes his eyes.

"Ulie? You okay?"

"Just resting," he say so soft I can barely hear.

I let him rest for a while, and then I axe him how much water lef' in the bottle.

"Uhhh ... about half."

He lies back down, closes his eyes again, and we wait. I watch him and wonder what we gonna do now.

Then all at once, that zany white boy start to laugh and roll his body from side to side screamin' "Ouch! Ouch! Ouch!" the whole time, he be laughin' his fool head off.

"Stop it, Ulie! Ain't nothin' funny. We gotta figure out how to git you outta there."

"That's a swell idea, Clydeen, but I have no clue, do you?" he hoots.

"Why you laughin' like that? You goin' off the deep end for real this time?"

"No! Not bonkers," he whoops.

"Uh-huh. Shoot, Ulie! Shut up and tell me what's the matter with you."

"Nothing! Everything!" he guffaws.

"You outta yo' mind, boy," I tell him.

"Look, Clydeen," he hoots. "I went through all that shit in England and France and who knows what other countries, and I never got seriously injured. Not once. No bullet ever found me. No explosion ever took me out. I didn't starve. Nobody gave me such a beating that a couple days of rest didn't take care of it. I ran and ran and never tripped or broke any bones, and I come back here to my own place, and in no time at all, I fall and break my bloody leg!"

"Ah, yas. I see."

"It hurts so bad to laugh, but I can't stop!"

"Ulie, please stop now. You gotta lie still. You don't look so good. You prob'ly in shock."

"Yeah, I'm in shock alright!" he roars.

I jus' stand there starin' down at him, hopin' he'll quiet hisself down and be still so's he don't hurt hisself some mo'. Finally, he settle, and I watch him real careful to make sure he still breathin'. After a time, a little color come back in his face, and he looks a little better.

"I'm goin' for help, Ulie," I call down to him. "Drink some water, but save some for later, okay?"

"No wait, Clydeen. YOU CAN'T DO THAT! There's something ..."

But before he can finish whatever he gonna say, I'm slip slidin' down the wash knowin' 'xactly what I got to do next.

Chapter 43
Annie

"Listen!" I say in a loud voice, sweeping my eyes around the room, taking in my parents, my baby sister, Eva. "Please, listen! I ... uhh. I ... uhh. I ... uhh ..." I have held the words in for so long, they refuse to come out, and I nearly burst into tears with frustration.

"Take a breath, Annie," says Eva, turning around in her chair to face me. She has no idea the blow I'm about to deliver, but I hope she'll thank me later.

And then, right on cue, Stanley gets to his feet.

"We need to get going. Let's go, Annie. No more argument."

At least he's calmed down.

"Dad, wait a minute. I have something to tell you."

"Not now, Annie. Get in the car."

Vivian rises, hoists Teresa over her shoulder and prepares to follow Stanley out the door.

I don't move. I wish I could grab my parents and sit them back down like dolls in a dollhouse to buy myself the time I need to gather my thoughts. I gulp air and let out a whoosh. Vivian motions for me to come, her face a warning scowl. All she wants in this world right now is for me to walk out of here and not cause any more trouble.

"Stop!" I yell, coming around from behind Eva's chair. "Don't leave yet!"

"We're leaving," says Vivian. "Now mind your father and get in the car."

"No! I am not going! I am staying here. Please, listen to me.

There's a reason."

My parents look at each other. Vivian rolls her eyes, but they do stop.

I swallow hard, my mouth dry, but before I can utter another word, the backdoor flies open, and there stands Clydeen, her eyes blazing as she takes in the scene that greets her.

"'Scuse me! 'Scuse me! Annie?" she yelps. "I got sump-thin'..."

Everyone stands stock still, their mouths gaping, staring at the skinny, nappy-headed Negro girl dressed in cut-off jeans, a stained yellow T-shirt, and dusty brown oxfords with no socks.

They look gobsmacked.

She looks terrified.

"Clydeen! What are you doing here?"

And just like that, thanks to Clydeen, everyone is frozen in place—at least for a few seconds until Stanley springs into action.

"Call the police!" he demands, looking at Mrs. B. "I'll take charge here."

If he had a gun, I suspect Clydeen would already be dead.

He starts to advance on her, but I'm quicker, and before he can get to her, I station myself between the two of them and reach behind my back for her hand.

"No, Dad. It's fine. This is Clydeen. She's my friend," I say, pulling her up next to me. "Uhhh ... Clydeen, this is my dad."

Vivian is watching with interest, a slight frown on her face.

Eva shakes her head and smiles but says nothing. She's a sharp lady, that one, and she's already put two and two together.

"What do you mean, she's your friend?" bellows Stanley, spittle flying out of his mouth, anger rising like a geyser.

"Call the police!" he orders for the second time.

"We'll see," says Eva, smiling broadly now.

She walks over to us, steps in front of Stanley, and just as I knew she would, she says, "Hello, Clydeen. I'm Eva. I've been waiting a long time to meet you. Won't you come in and join us?"

"But Ulie ..." Clydeen stammers, her eyes coal black, darting this way and that.

Eva's head jerks back in surprise.

"Ulie? Did you say Ulie?"

"Who's Ulie?" Stanley demands, but no one pays any attention.

"Ulie ... he hurt. Up on the mesa."

"My son? My son is up on the mesa? That's impossible!"

"No ma'am, it ain't. But I think he broke his leg, and he needin' some help."

"Oh, my God!" says Eva, covering her mouth with one hand. "Ulie. Here," she says with disbelief, turning to stare at me before removing a handkerchief from her apron pocket and collapsing into her rocking chair.

"Eva, are you okay? Would you like some water?" I ask.

Stupid question! Of course she's not okay. This is all way too weird.

"I'll be all right," she says. "I just need a minute ...."

I go in the kitchen and draw two glasses of water, one for Eva and another for Clydeen.

Stanley is now so thoroughly caught up in the drama unfolding in the room, he has apparently forgotten all about getting on the road.

"Annie, who is this nigger?" he asks, moving in way too close to me.

"Dad!" I say. "Don't call her that. I told you. She's my friend, and her name is Clydeen."

Clydeen hands me the empty glass. She still looks absolutely petrified as she absorbs the hostility emanating from Stanley.

Vivian has moved back to the comfort of the couch. She hasn't said a word since Clydeen's dramatic entry, but her eyes are now shining with curiosity. Teresa is watching, too. She's perched on Vivian's lap, sucking her thumb. The boys have come in at some point, and they are now sitting on the floor near Vivian.

"Well," says Eva, glaring at me. "Obviously, I need to go to my son."

She goes to her desk and takes the heavy black telephone into the hallway, trailing the twisted cord behind her. I can hear her dialing and then speaking to someone at the fire department. She gestures for Clydeen and me to join her.

"I need one of you to explain exactly where Ulie is and how to get to him."

"I'll do it," I say.

I give them Eva's address and explain Ulie's whereabouts from here.

"Someone will meet you at the dead end," I tell them before hanging up.

"Okay. Let's go," says Eva, grabbing her walking stick and heading out the front door.

Clydeen and I follow right on her heels.

"Wait!" Stanley says. "I'm going with you. I can help."

"That's okay, Dad. You can go ahead and go to Cheyenne. I'll be fine here."

"I said I'm coming," he says.

The last thing I want is for him to go poking around up at our Nest before I've had a chance to explain like I had intended to do. But it's too late now, and there's nothing I can do to stop him.

He turns to Vivian, tosses the car keys to her, and says, "Take the kids home. Call Dad, tell him we won't be coming. I'll meet you at home later."

Stanley is a rescuer. He loves situations like this. If a co-worker falls ill or someone he knows has a terrible accident, he morphs into a different person. During those brief intervals, I watch as he becomes the caring person I wish he were at home. But once the crisis is over, he reverts back to the same old Stanley, almost like he's two different people.

"Crap!" I mutter under my breath as the four of us take off walking.

Shouldn't I warn Clydeen about the possibility that the person we know as Ulie might not be Ulie at all? I'd like to, but with Stanley breathing down our necks ... Besides, in a short while Eva will get a look at the guy, and then we'll know for sure.

Eva looks grim. She marches forward, taking long steady strides as if getting there is a matter of life and death. Which maybe it is. At this point, how can anyone know?

When we are almost to the corner, she slows down and waits for Clydeen and me to pull alongside of her.

"He's up there where he and his dad built that lean-to years ago, isn't he."

"Yas," Clydeen says.

"He called it Xanadu. And that's where you go all the time, am I right, Annie?"

"Well, yeah, but ..."

"And you saw him up there? Both of you?"

"Yes," I say softly, hanging my head.

This is exactly what I was afraid would happen. By keeping a promise to one friend, I have betrayed another.

"You didn't think to tell me, Annie?"

"He wouldn't let me! I wanted to, but he made me promise. Please don't be mad at me, Eva. Besides, maybe it's not even Ulie."

She gives me a sharp look. "Maybe not. We'll see."

"When he first showed up, I accused him of being an imposter, but he seemed to know so much about you, about everything around here, I let it go."

Eva sighs and puts her arm around my shoulders.

"Okay. Let's just wait and see."

"Wait a minute. You think Ulie not Ulie now, Annie? Why?" Clydeen asks.

"Just wait until we get up there, Clydeen," I say, dipping my head toward Stanley, who, now that we've slowed down, is walking with us four abreast.

He's huffing and puffing from years of smoking, and I hope it will make him too short of breath to pay close attention to our conversation. A half an hour ago, I was ready to spill everything, but now, I've reconsidered. If I had my way, he would be on his way to a weekend boozing it up in Cheyenne right now and not hanging around here, sticking his nose in my business.

I glance at Clydeen, and when her eyes meet mine, I take her hand and squeeze it, trying to tell her without words that something really big is happening, and we need to be careful.

"I know my son," says Eva. "Yes, I do. He would come home straightaway. So why hasn't he? Does anybody have any ideas about that?"

I was right to shush Clydeen, because here's Stanley looking down the row of us, all ears, eagerly waiting for the answer.

"Okay," says Clydeen to Eva. "I been stayin' up there for a while waitin' ... well, that be another story. Ulie come, oh, maybe 'bout three weeks ago now, snuck up on me in the middle a the night and liked to scared me half to death. But when he said his name, I knowed who he was, 'cause Annie tol' me 'bout him. We got to talkin', and he say he need to stay up there for a while till he figure out is the po-lice or anybody like that after him."

"Why would he think that?" asks Mrs. B.

"Yeah, why would he?" Stanley croaks. "Is he a crook? Is he on the lam?"

Clydeen ignores him and goes on.

"To answer yo' question, Mrs. B, he say sumpthin' 'bout maybe not gettin' back in the country the right way? But he not real sure how he got back, and me'n Annie, we think he may be a little off base, you know?"

"Can you tell me more?"

"Ulie don't seem quite right," Clydeen says, tapping the side of her head with her finger. "Every little noise scare him and make him wanna hide. He have nightmares, too, real bad ones he say he almos' can't wake up from. Sometimes, he jus' stares off into space with a funny look on his face, like he don't quite git where he at or what's goin' on. Oh, and one more thing. He don't know nothin' 'bout his daddy."

"What about his dad?" Stanley wheezes.

Eva ignores him and continues speaking to Clydeen.

"About his father having died, you mean?"

"He don't know nothin' 'bout that, but he thinks he saw his daddy recently. Me'n Annie know tha's impossible, but we didn't want to tell him any diff'rent, right Annie?"

"Yeah. We thought it was best to give him some time to sort things out first."

"Well, that means he never got my telegram. No surprise there."

"We're almost there," I say, "but we have a climb ahead of us."

"So is this guy a crook, or not?" Stanley wants to know, fixated as usual, on one detail of a complicated scenario.

"No, Mr. Cahill, he's not," Eva answers.

"Let's keep what happened yesterday between you and me for now," she whispers to me.

We've turned the corner, and we're nearly to the bottom of the wash when a siren chirps behind us. We all turn in unison and watch as a firetruck and ambulance slowly make their way toward us.

Three firemen jump from the truck. The ambulance driver stays put "to maintain radio contact on the ground," he says. Clydeen gives the firemen the details; they grab heavy rope, pullies, a long basket, and other equipment, and the seven of us start up the wash. I hang back, waiting for Stanley, who moves at a snail's pace, his leather-soled shoes slipping and sliding on the loose rocky surface of the uphill grade.

When we reach the ledge, Stanley bends over, trying to catch his breath, while I take a look around. On the other side of the lean-to, the firemen are clustered in a tight circle with Clydeen in the center. It looks like she's crying. Mrs. B is standing outside the circle, her back against the sandstone wall, her eyes downcast. She has the deflated look of a ragdoll, her previous get-up-and-go all gone from her now.

"What's going on? Where's Ulie?" I yell as I run to the other side of the lean-to where they've gathered.

Clydeen reaches for me, but the men tighten their circle around her.

"Oh, no you don't," says one of the firemen to Clydeen.

"Where is he, Clydeen?" I ask, trying to peer around the closed circle of firemen.

"He ain't there, Annie. He gone!"

At that point, Stanley arrives and addresses one of the firemen, who explains that there is no sign of a young man with a broken leg anywhere about, "especially not down there where this nigger said he was when she went to get help."

Stanley laughs. "Well, if you take the word of a nigger, what do you expect?"

He's such a hopeless case, I don't even bother correcting him this time.

"That's true enough," agrees the fireman, whose name is Fred, according to the embroidery on his jacket. "No worries, though. The chief will be calling the authorities, and she'll be looking at some jail time for turning in a false alarm."

"The hell she will!"

Our mantra—Clydeen's and mine—what would Linda Brent do?—takes possession of me for a few seconds, and then I scream at the firemen, "He was here! He's been here for a few weeks now. I've been here with him, too. If Clydeen says he was hurt and he was down there, then you need to look for him and stop accusing her."

Eva looks surprised, but says nothing. Stanley looks at me with his mouth hanging open like he's never seen me before.

"Oh c'mon, girlie," says one of the firemen, whose name is Bill.

He gets right in my face and says, "Where would you have us look for someone with a unsplinted broken leg except right where she says he was? Huh? He couldn't have put any weight on a leg in that condition. So she's lyin'."

"His leg was broke! It was bleedin', too. I saw it!" shouts Clydeen, less intimidated now, I suspect because she thinks my white-girl testimony will help her story carry more weight.

"Look down there," she points. "See that bottle? That's the bottle a water I tol' him to stand up so's he'd have some water to drink whiles I went off to git him some help. He was in so much pain, he almos' couldn't pick that bottle up. Like Annie say, he down there someplace."

"Look in the lean-to. You'll find a big green rubbery rain poncho thing. That's his," I tell them.

"That doesn't prove anything," one of the firemen scoffs.

"What do you say, Chief?" Fred asks.

"Well, we're here now. We might as well take a look or risk being called back later, I suppose. Let's rig up those pullies and go down, see what we can find just in case."

"I'll help," says Stanley.

"Okay, you can help Fred steady the line up top."

Stanley is pleased and goes to shake Fred's hand. Fireman Bill skids down the slope, taking a heavy rope and pully with him, which he attaches to the very tree where Clydeen says Ulie was lying when she ran to get help. Once the rigging is in place, the chief himself goes down, steadied by the ropes held tight by Stanley and Fred, who are putting tension on them from up on the ledge.

"Do you see any blood? The nigger gal says his leg was bleeding through his clothes," Fred calls out.

"Not a drop," says the chief.

"What about the shirt she was talkin' about?"

"Nope. No sign of anything like that, either."

Using more ropes, they begin a tough sideways crabwalk, one man going off in each direction from the tree. They call Ulie's name and scramble around rocks and vegetation looking for any sign of him. They find nothing and receive no answer.

Eva, Clydeen, and I stand together at the edge of the ledge and watch.

"Tell her now, Eva," I whisper.

She does, filling Clydeen in on what the two men from the State Department told us yesterday.

"What does that mean?" whispers Clydeen. "They say Ulie dead? I been livin' up here with ghost a some kind? Is that what you's tellin' me? Lord have mercy! If that what you's sayin', I gotta get myself outta here!"

"Shhh, Clydeen. We don't know what this is yet."

"Well, I ain't lookin' to stay and find out!" she proclaims, a shiver of revulsion passing through her.

Good grief! All the time I spent worrying and trying to persuade her that it's time for her to leave this place, all the time she resisted, got angry, blamed me, said she was going to take care of it herself, and now suddenly she can't leave fast enough? Frickin' Ulie, I laugh softly to myself, remembering the attentive way he listened to Clydeen, the tender way he talked to her and teased her. All the time he was gently goading her into trusting him and at the same time, building up her self-confidence.

But where the hell is he now? Is he playing his Ace in the hole, pretending to disappear, because he knows nothing in the world will chase Clydeen out of here faster than for her to be convinced he's some kind of ghost? Or maybe it's Eva he's hiding from, because he *is* an imposter.

One of those two things. That's all that's happening here, I tell myself, a shiver going through me.

My certainty lasts only a second, and I'm off again with more questions. How could he have moved about with such a serious injury, no matter who he is? Because I believe every word Clydeen says about what his condition was when she left him. She has no reason whatsoever to lie. And now, just a short time later, he's hidden himself so well, even the firemen can't find him? Every time I think I've got this figured out, I bump up against a piece of the puzzle that doesn't fit, and I end up with more questions and no answers that make any sense.

A few minutes later, the chief clambers back onto the ledge.

"Nothin' down there," he says, scowling at Clydeen. "Either Fred's right and you're lyin', or that boy wasn't injured that bad and run off for some reason. Which is it?"

"Uhhh ..." Clydeen says, looking around like a trapped animal.

"Well, I'm gonna have to call the authorities and have you picked up for questioning. There's penalites for this sort of thing, turning in a false alarm and such, if that's what this is."

Clydeen's eyes grow wide. She reaches for my hand, and Eva moves in and puts her arm around her shoulders, murmuring softly to her. Shouldn't Eva be frantic right now? Why isn't she begging the firemen to continue searching? But she's neither frantic nor begging. In fact, the entire time the men were searching, Eva seemed remote and disinterested, as if what was going on had nothing to do with her. She's utterly calm now, and I'm dying to ask her what's happening. When I try to make eye contact, though, she avoids my gaze, letting me know now is not the time.

"Before we head out," says the chief, "can I do anything for you, Mrs. Borsheim? Anything you need that we can help you with?"

"No, thank you. I'll be fine. I appreciate you and your crew for coming, Chief, but I want you to know that if it comes down to it, I will not make any statement saying this girl lied or caused a false alarm to be sent, because I don't believe she did. My boy isn't here now, but I'm sure there's a good explanation. I will look into it and call you if he needs assistance. Clydeen's a minor, and I would guess it's unlikely she would receive any kind of detention, despite what Fred over there said, am I right?"

"Well ... yes, you are correct about that," he agrees with some reluctance.

Clydeen lets out a whoosh of air and a sob when she hears this.

"So what do you say we just chalk it up to Clydeen having misinterpreted what she saw and let it go at that for now?"

"I suppose it's not worth ..." he muses, thinking this proposition over for a minute. "Okay. I don't want to cause you any more grief, ma'am, so I'll let it go this one time," he says, scowling at Clydeen. "Good luck, folks," he says, giving us a little salute and turning to go.

Eva, Clydeen, and I look at one another and smile, relieved.

"Good work, Mrs. B!" I murmur softly.

Chapter 44
Annie

Within minutes, with Stanley's help, the firemen have gathered their equipment and disappeared over the lip of the wash. Clydeen, Eva, Stanley, and I do not follow, but remain where we are, as if dumbstruck, not knowing what to do with ourselves now that the excitement is over. When we hear the whine of engines as the emergency vehicles make their way to the main road, we come to life again.

"Well ..." says Eva.

We all smile, even Stanley, because that just about sums it up.

I go to the cave to get a bottle of water. The morning has left us all tired and thirsty. I hand the bottle to Eva first, then she passes it to Clydeen. Stanley watches with a look of horror and refuses to take it when Clydeen passes it his way. I take a drink and then offer it to him again.

"Here, Dad," I choke. "Have some water. That was a lot of effort."

He declines the offer again. To his credit, he's managed to do so twice without insulting anyone, at least not in so many words.

"Let's go then," I say.

"Wait a minute," says Stanley. "What is this place?"

"It's a place Ulie built when he was kid, Dad. It's his place," I say, nodding my head.

"Oh," he says.

"Easy peasy, thanks to Ulie," I whisper to myself.

"Clydeen, we'll come back later and look for Ulie again. Maybe all those people coming up here scared him, and he'll turn up when things quiet down."

"Okay," she says.

Eva says nothing.

None of us has much to say on the walk back to the farmhouse. Once again, Stanley is breathing heavily, and the rest of us slow our pace so he can keep up.

When we reach our destination, he throws up his arms and says, "Now what? I forgot I sent your mother off with the car."

"Come in. You can use my phone, Mr. Cahill," says Eva.

While he's inside calling Vivian, Clydeen, who hasn't spoken a word since we started down the wash, pulls me toward the side of the house, and whispers, "Annie, maybe I bes' be goin' back, wait for Ulie? I know he up there somewhere."

"No. Stay with me, Clydeen, please. Everyone knows about us now, so there's no need to hide. We'll look for Ulie later, okay?"

"But these people ..." she says, pleading with me. "These the people—"

"—that scare you, I know, Clydeen. Yes, they are scary, but it'll be okay."

She looks away and sighs.

"What would Linda Brent do, remember?" I whisper urgently, invoking Linda's persona, which has become our touchstone for finding the courage we need in moments like this. "So what would she do?"

"I reckon she'd take a chance and stay right here for now," she whispers back, "but I'm no Linda Brent!"

"But she's your ancestor, Clydeen."

It pleases her when I remind her of this, and she can't help but smile. Even though her eyes remain clouded with worry, she stays.

"I hope you knows what you's doin', is all."

"I hope so, too," I whisper.

My father and I sit on the white wicker chairs on Eva's front porch, waiting for Vivian. Clydeen sits on the bottom step as far away from us as possible. Eva has gone inside to lie down.

"We need to have a talk, young lady—" Stanley growls out of one side of his mouth like a gangster.

"I know."

"—about what you've been up to." He points at Clydeen. "What the hell have you been doing? You know these aren't the kind of people—"

"—allowed out here, according to you. I know."

"I have papers. It's legal."

"The house papers, you mean? I've seen them. I read them one day while I was babysitting, so I know exactly what they say, but that doesn't mean I think it's right."

"Oh, hell," he says. "You are an idiot. You have no idea what you're talking about."

At that moment, Vivian pulls up in front of the house.

"Hurry. I left Charlie at Larry's house and the other two are napping," she calls through the open passenger-side window.

"I'll drive," says Stanley.

"Come on, Clydeen," I say as Vivian gets out and crosses in front of the car.

Clydeen gets up and trails reluctantly behind me.

"Get in, Annie," Vivian says, ignoring Clydeen, who's standing right next to me.

What is wrong with these people, I wonder, not for the first time. *Has Clydeen suddenly become invisible now?*

"I'm bringing my friend," I announce, folding my arms over my chest and refusing to move.

"What did you say?" asks Stanley, dipping his head and peering at me from where he's now taken his rightful position as the driver.

"I said I'm bringing my friend."

He's totally unprepared for this. His face turns beet red as he zooms from zero to sixty on the rage scale, but I stick to my guns and stay right where I am, even though I'm trembling. *Linda Brent, Linda Brent, Linda Brent*, I say to myself over and over.

"Annie, you tell that *Negro* to get lost, and get in this car. Now!" he shouts.

"Nope. She's coming. We're both getting in the car."

"Let it go, Stanley," Vivian says, holding down the front seat so Clydeen and I can get in. "We'll figure it out at home."

"But if anyone sees ..."

"Oh, please. There's nobody around *to* see," Vivian scoffs.

Stanley glares at her but says nothing more. He's not used to being challenged by her, even on small matters like this. I take note, because I'm not used to seeing her do it, either.

When everyone is in, Stanley guns the engine and makes a sliding U-turn on the dirt road that nearly throws the car into a ditch. Clydeen and I fall into each other. Vivian screams and braces herself against the dashboard. When the car comes out of the skid, Stanley slams on the brakes and we all fall forward.

"Stanley!" Vivian squeals. "Stop! What the hell are you doing?"

"That kid!" he shouts, referring to me, of course. "I've had just about enough of her."

He guns the motor again, hunkers down low in his seat and drives like a maniac toward home. It's already past one o'clock, and he's usually into his third or fourth highball by this time of day on weekends. He's badly in need of a drink.

When we get home, he puts the car in neutral, yanks on the emergency brake and heads inside. He's going to get that drink, and in the state he's in now, I wager it'll need to be a double shot of straight bourbon.

Vivian turns around and regards the two of us for several minutes before making a move to get out of the car.

"I'm sure Willie and Teresa are still asleep, but I need to check. I'll meet you two around back."

Around back? Am I exiled from my own home now?

"Good thing we're used to sitting where there's nothing but dirt and rocks," I grumble to Clydeen as we head for the backyard, "'cause that's all that's back there."

A few minutes later, Vivian comes to find us. "They're both still asleep," she says.

We sit down in a tight circle, wiggling our bottoms around on the rocky hardpack, trying to find a comfortable position.

"Where's Dad?"

"He's ..." She gestures vaguely toward the house. "Why don't the three of us talk out here. I need to understand what's happening, Annie. But first, tell me about this morning. Dad said something about the fellow who was injured not being found?"

Clydeen and I both nod.

"That's true. When the firemen got there, they couldn't find him. He wasn't where Clydeen left him."

"Huh," she says. "That's odd."

"He probably hidin' someplace," Clydeen jumps in. "He jus'come back from where he was in the war. He not quite right in the head, so we's goin' back and find him later, see that he git to the hospital, ain't we Annie?"

"Sure."

"All a them people comin' up there prob'ly jus' scared him off."

I don't mention the other possibility, yesterday's report from the State Department. I haven't come to terms with it yet, and clearly Clydeen hasn't either. Maybe we *will* find Ulie when we go back later to search, although it's becoming harder and harder for me to imagine that will happen. Nothing is the same now as it was this time yesterday. In a few short hours, my entire summer has been brought to an abrupt and dramatic conclusion. All of this reshuffling of the deck and strange new possibilities to consider is making me feel like I'm losing my grip. Painful as it is, I focus on my body and make a conscious effort to feel myself firmly planted on the ground so I don't float away.

"Okay. So what about you two?" Vivian asks, her voice breaking into my thoughts.

"What?" I ask, struggling to clear my head.

"I asked, what about you two?"

"We're fine," I say, still fuzzy.

"Oh, Annie. You know that's not what I mean."

"I know."

"So tell me."

I'm relieved Stanley's not around. I take a deep breath and begin the tale of my secret summer. I describe finding the lean-to up on the mesa, Clydeen coming, and then Ulie. I don't go into great detail, but I don't lie or make excuses, either.

"Well, that sure explains some things," she says, shaking her head when I've finished the story. "It never occurred to me ..."

She doesn't seem angry, just bewildered.

"So you're telling me that the Nest, as you call it, this cave or whatever it is, that's where you've been going every day all summer, Annie? And you've been taking food and water for this girl? Have I got it right?"

"That's about it, Mom."

"But why so secretive?" she asks, looking from one of us to the other.

"Are you kidding me? Isn't it obvious?" I say, nodding at Clydeen. "Why are we sitting on hardpack in the backyard right now, Mom? But also because I was so mad at you after that Sunday when Dad ... well, you know what I'm talking about. You think I'd tell you anything after that?"

She sighs and looks off into the distance for a while.

"What about you?" she asks, turning her attention to Clydeen. "What's your story?"

Clydeen and I consult each other with our eyes while Vivian's question hangs in the air. Clydeen sucks in a breath and grabs for my hand. Vivian watches as I take her hand in mine but doesn't comment.

"Uhhh ..." Clydeen stammers. "Can you, Annie?"

"No, Clydeen. This is your story to tell—if you want to."

I think of Eva. How the Tarot reading has helped me recognize moments like this when I need to step back. I understand that the last thing Clydeen needs is for me to patronize her by telling her story for her.

"Well ... uhhh," Clydeen begins, swallowing hard. "So, my mama, she be missin'."

She raises her eyes and looks at Vivian like this is all there is, or maybe she's just waiting for a reaction.

"What do you mean she's missing?"

"Go ahead, Clydeen," I say, smiling at her to help give her the courage to continue.

"What happened was the po-lice got ahold a her awhile back, and I don't know what they done with her. When she didn't come back to where we's livin', this white man say he gonna call somebody to put me in a orphanage or someplace like that. So I ran away, got on a bus and stayed on till the driver put me off. Turns out I was way out here someplace.

"After a couple days and a lot a walkin', I ended up where Ulie built that lean-to Annie and me calls our Nest. Nobody there, but I didn't figure on stayin'. I was jus' lookin' for a place to rest, and Annie had a cot and a sleepin' bag, comic books, bottles a water, stuff like that up there. After I was there three, maybe four days, Annie come. I thought she's gonna make me go, but instead she say she gonna bring me some food and more water. Course I never in a million years thought some white girl do that for me," says Clydeen, smiling at me.

"You never told me that, Clydeen," I break in, feeling hurt.

"Well, that be what I thought, Annie," she says.

"But I was wrong," she continues, turning her attention back to Vivian. "Annie come back the very next day and the day after that, bringin' me what I need and mo'. That's how we got to knowin' each other."

She looks at me, smiles again, and squeezes my hand.

"I was 'spectin' my mama gonna come find me when she could. But I guess I was not thinkin' right 'bout that. It's been a long time now, and she ain't come, so I'mma hafta to git down to the bidniss a lookin' for her myself."

"Okay. I'm starting to get the picture now," Vivian says, shifting her eyes between the two of us. "So all this started after that dreadful Sunday with your dad, is that what you're telling me, Annie?"

"You thought it was dreadful, Mom? You never said a word to me about it."

"Oh, Annie. I've got four kids who are depending on me. That's always in the back of my mind when your father ... Well, you know how he can be. It keeps me from speaking up and saying things I know will cause trouble between us. But, yes, that day was dreadful."

"I thought you didn't care," I say tearing up.

"The truth is, I've agonized over what happened that day, Annie. But I've made up my mind. I won't let it happen again—not to you, and not to any of the other kids. And definitely not today."

I'm speechless, and my mouth drops open, I'm so surprised.

Vivian runs her hands through her hair like she does when she's a little bit excited or frazzled.

"We are going to have to deal with what you've told me at some point, though."

"You mean talk to Dad, right? Tell him about this?"

"Well, after today, there's not much left to tell, is there?" she laughs, glancing at Clydeen. "But yes."

"Crap."

She sighs. "This move has been much harder on your dad than he expected, Annie. He's gotten what he's wanted for such a long time, but the added responsibility of a big mortgage and a new baby is more burdensome than he anticipated. At the same time, you have the audacity to grow up right before his eyes, which makes him feel out of control. He's just so overwhelmed sometimes, he lets his temper get the best of him. Does that make sense?"

"I guess."

She studies the two of us.

"I turned you loose this summer, because things were getting out of hand between you and your dad, and I didn't know what else to do. But Lord, in my wildest imagination, I never would have ... Of course, you've always been ..."

She slaps her forehead and begins to laugh again. Clydeen and I join in. What a relief it is to laugh.

"Maybe you gave me just enough rope to hang myself," I say, turning my head to one side, sticking my tongue out to mimic hanging myself.

"Oh, Annie, stop it!" she says, laughing even harder.

I can't remember the last time I heard her laugh or even saw her smile. All summer long (when I've bothered to pay attention) she's looked sad and defeated. Exhausted. But this afternoon? Suddenly, she's clear-eyed, her body upright, shoulders squared, smiling and attentive. Different.

"Seriously though," she says to me now. "I don't see that you've done anything wrong, Annie, but convincing Dad to see it that way isn't going to be easy. The food you took, he's not going to like it, but don't worry, we can afford it.

"The bigger problem is you showing up with all of these new people in your life. It scares him. Mrs. Borsheim, a woman he doesn't know with a strange name. And now, even worse, a colored friend. Dad thinks he's moved us out here to keep us 'safe,' from such people—no offense, Clydeen. But what can I say? He's probably going to have a fit, unless I can ... Well, we'll see."

Turning to Clydeen, she says, "Please understand it's nothing personal, Clydeen. It's how he was raised. The truth is, it's how most of us were raised. But my father was a brakeman on the railroad out of Cheyenne, and he worked with more colored than white. So I don't feel threatened in the same way my husband does."

"Uhh-huh," says Clydeen.

I know she's not buying it, and I don't know what to think. Has Vivian forgotten what her father said about "nigger milk" all those years ago when he was supposedly so tight with the colored folk on the railroad? And by the way, why is she putting up such a stalwart defense of Stanley? I'm the one who's gonna need defending when this all comes to a head.

"Let me think a minute," Vivian says.

She stands up, turns her back and walks a short distance away from us.

Clydeen and I stand up, too, and I take her hand again, even though our palms are sweaty. We're like a pair of defendants waiting for the verdict at the end of a lengthy trial.

"Well," Vivian says as she rejoins us. "I have to go check on the little kids again. But here's what's *not* going to happen. We are not going to have another scene like we had in the spring, Annie. You will need to talk to your dad at some point, as I've said, but now is not the time."

"So where is he now?"

"He's ... resting."

Which is shorthand for catching up on his drinking.

"Can we go in the house and use the bathroom?"

"Sure. Go downstairs so you don't disturb Dad. But let me finish first. Here's what we're going to do. I'm going to take you back to Mrs. Borsheim's and ask if you can stay with her for the rest of the day. You, too, Clydeen—if that's where you want to go."

I look at Clydeen and shrug. I can't believe my ears, because all of a sudden, I'm not sure what to make of the person who looks like my mother but is making this outlandish proposal. I know what she's doing, though. She's putting distance between Stanley and me for a while, and I'd be crazy not to be grateful for that.

When we lived in north Denver, it was my neighborhood that enabled me to be happy and gave me ways to sidestep Stanley and his moods. Vivian was busy with Charlie, who was a sickly child, and after that, Willie and Teresa, who were born in quick succession. She had little time for me, but I never felt it as a lack.

It never occurred to me that the day would come when I would need her protection from Stanley. But these past few months, thrown together the way we are in this isolated suburban wilderness? It seems to have brought out the worst in him and left me with none of what I had relied on previously to keep me out of the line of fire.

That Sunday when Stanley went off his rocker, for the first time, I needed my mother's protection. I hated her when I didn't get it. I hated her as much as I hated him. But as I look at her now, I'm able to see how it was for her. She was as lost in unfamiliar territory as I was.

I stumble over the rocks, the hardpack, the cement chips, and for the first time in years, I cling to my mother and bawl my eyes out. She puts her arms around me and pulls me close. It's been so long since I've had any physical contact with her, her scent is no longer familiar to me.

"Thank you, Mom," I choke out.

"It's going to be okay, Annie. Give me a few minutes," she says, releasing me and heading to the house. "Go ahead and get ready to go. I'll drive you."

Clydeen and I look at each other again. There are tears in her eyes. She knows everything about me and understands exactly what kind of a moment this is for me. But maybe it's making her feel more alone, too. I sling my arm over her shoulder, pull her close, and lead her into the house.

Within minutes, we are off. Willie is sitting on my lap in the back seat next to Clydeen. Teresa is in a basket strapped to the passenger seat with an old sheet my mother uses for that purpose. Willie stares at Clydeen and drools down the front of his shirt.

"Willie, this is Clydeen," I tell him, kissing him on the top of his head. "Can you say hello?"

"Hi," he says, burying his face in my shoulder.

Pretty soon, he engages Clydeen by blowing wet raspberries in her direction and bouncing around on my lap to keep her attention. When she takes his arm and blows a raspberry on him, he throws his head back and laughs with delight.

****

"Oh, my! What have we here?" says Eva when she opens the door to our knock.

"Eva, I know you've had a terrible day," Vivian says.

Eva and I exchange a look. She doesn't know the half of it!

"Well, if there's something you need, Vivian ...."

"I know this is an imposition, but could Annie and Clydeen stay with you for a while? I need to ..."

She breaks off, turns and flaps a hand in the general direction of our neighborhood.

"Oh, sure," says Eva. "I have a friend here, so the more the merrier. If you wish, they can spend the night."

"Thank you," says Vivian with obvious relief.

She searches around in her purse and pulls out her wallet.

"Here's money," she says, handing me some bills. "Treat yourselves."

I stare at the money. Treat ourselves? Stanley keeps a tight hold on the family budget, and handing out bills for a treat is never an item on the agenda.

"Mom, can you afford—?"

"It's fine, Annie. Don't worry."

As my mother says her good-byes, she's grinning from ear to ear. I suspect she's relieved to have been handed the time she needs to deal with Stanley. At least I hope that's what's on her mind, because I am far from ready to face him on my own right now.

"I'll talk to your Dad, Annie," she calls through the open window as she drives off.

Chapter 45
Annie

The shades are drawn, and the house is cool inside. It takes a minute for my eyes to adjust to the dim light, and when they do, I see Imani Jackson sitting on the sofa across the room. She gets up and comes to greet us.

"Imani, you've met Annie a couple of times, I believe," says Eva.

"Yes, I have."

"This is her friend, Clydeen. I'm sorry, I don't know your last name, sweetheart."

"Hollifield," she says, staring at Imani and smiling broadly.

The moment is electric. I can see how utterly relieved Clydeen is to see someone who looks like her in the very room where earlier today she was confronted with such hostility. I touch her hand for a moment, and a chill runs up and down my spine.

"Clydeen Hollifield," says Imani, taking one of Clydeen's hand in both of her hers. "It's a pleasure to meet you, my dear."

"You, too, Miz Jackson," says Clydeen shyly.

"Is anyone hungry?" asks Eva. "Girls?"

I glance at the clock and note that it's way past lunchtime.

"Yas. I am!" says Clydeen.

"Me, too. I'm starving!" I chip in.

"Well, that makes at least three of us," says Eva, turning to Imani.

"I haven't had lunch yet, either," says Imani.

"That makes it unanimous. Could I interest you all in some

297

pizza?"

"Yeah!" Clydeen and I reply in unison.

"If I remember correctly, there is a pizza place over on Colfax close to the library. We can drop our books at the same time."

"You'll join us, won't you, Imani?"

"I absolutely will," she replies.

I've never had pizza before, and I suspect Clydeen hasn't either. The one and only time I ate at a restaurant was the day after Willie was born. It was a snowy day in mid-November. Vivian was in the hospital, and Stanley was taking Charlie and me to Cheyenne to stay with our grandparents. We headed out of town early to avoid the worst of the storm, and on the way, we stopped for breakfast at a café that smelled of fresh coffee and sweet cinnamon rolls. We sat in a red vinyl booth too big for the three of us. Charlie and I were so excited, we barely touched the eggs and pancakes the waitress brought, but that day is still one of my very best memories.

"Uhhh ... I think my mother gave me way too much money," I say, staring at the three five-dollar bills in my hand.

"Yes, looks like it," Eva laughs. "I would guess pizza and Coca-Colas will cost us no more than three or four dollars for the four of us."

We climb into Imani's car and head for town, bouncing along on the gravel roads. After we drop the books in the slot at the library, we walk around the corner, and Eva points across the street at the pizza parlor, which is called Joe's Pizza Heaven.

We cross the street and go in. A bell tinkles as we enter, and a white man wearing an apron stained with tomato sauce approaches us with menus in hand. He's the only one in the place at this odd hour. He looks us over and frowns, holding the menus close to his chest. He hesitates for so long, I think he's going to refuse to seat us in his hole-in-the-wall pizza parlor. His judgmental scrutiny is making me squirm; I can't imagine how Clydeen and Imani must be feeling. *Holy crap, is this what people like them deal with every day if they want to eat someplace where everybody's not colored?*

Eva clears her throat. "A table please?" she prompts.

At which point, the guy makes up his mind, looks around, and leads us to a table in the back as far as possible from the front entrance, which is flanked by two large windows where we could be noticed by passers-by.

"Well," says Imani once we have seated ourselves. "Nice to be wanted."

I look at Clydeen, who says nothing. *What is she thinking?* I wonder.

We order a large pizza with cheese and sausage to share, and I hand the man a five-dollar bill. He counts the change into my hand, nearly two dollars, which I stuff into my pocket with the rest of the money. While we wait, Imani tells us about herself.

"I can tell you one thing, girls," she says, her brown eyes dancing. "I am so happy to be back here closer to Eva and other dear friends again. I've missed everyone so much."

"Where were you living before?" I ask.

"Detroit, Chicago, that part of the country, for oh, let's see. Five years or so. My husband's business took us there, but he passed away over a year ago now. My daughter invited me to come back and live with her family. That's where I'm staying now, but I'm having second thoughts about being up there in the mountains where they are. It's been wonderful getting to know my new granddaughter, but I'm getting the feeling it's not the right place for me to settle down."

Her skin is caramel-colored, slightly lighter than Clydeen's, and she's wearing the same gold bracelet she had on the day we first met. She's a tall woman, a bit on the heavy side. Her voice is deep and musical, and her good-natured chuckle is so infectious, we can't help laughing every time it comes rolling out of her.

When the pizza comes, it's already sliced, bubbling with cheese and sprinkled with paprika. The pizza guy pops the tops of our Coca-Cola bottles using the opener mounted on the edge of the table. We unwrap our paper straws, and settle in to enjoy our meal. It feels like a celebration, just like that day years ago when Willie was born.

"Okay, girls," says Eva as Clydeen and I tie into the pizza.

We look up. *What?*

"Imani and I want to hear everything. About you two and about Ulie. The long version, every detail, if you don't mind."

"But shouldn't we head back soon's we can, see if he a'ight?" asks Clydeen.

"Ulie will be fine, Clydeen," replies Eva. "Like the firemen said, if he was badly injured, he wouldn't have been able to move. So we'll let him be for a while, and you and Annie can go check later."

Clydeen looks at Eva, and then at me, her forehead wrinkled with concern. She's flummoxed by Eva's change in demeanor, which she is noticing for the first time. Just a few hours ago, Eva was so frenzied, she couldn't get to Ulie fast enough. Now, she has lost all sense of urgency and seems unconcerned, even disinterested in the whole business of finding Ulie.

Because I trust Eva more than anyone else I know, I've been watching her closely for clues about what she thinks happened today, but I feel disinclined to ask her just yet. I have come to the conclusion that she knows something we don't, but she's not ready to share it. At the same time, a seed of knowing has begun to grow in me. By some miracle or some obscure twist of fate, I think Ulie may no longer be with us. Later today, yes, we will search for him up on the mesa, but I'm pretty sure we're not going to find him there.

I lean in and whisper to Clydeen. "It's okay. We have time to sit here and talk for a while, and then we'll go."

She sighs, nods, and takes a sip of her Coke, apparently reassured for the time being.

There is no longer any reason for secrecy, so we give the two women the embellished version of our story, this time sparing no details of our summer adventures. We tell them how Clydeen and I met, how we spent our time before Ulie arrived, and how things changed after he came. We tell them about Gary, the altar we made, singing our prayers and more. We tell them everything we can think of about Ulie, what he said, what he did, what he was like. We talk and laugh and spew crumbs of pizza crust all over the table. With thin paper napkins, we wipe up rings of sweat from our green-glass bottles of Coca Cola. We wipe away tears, too, because underneath the celebratory mood, we are still worried about Ulie. There are so many questions that remain unanswered.

When we finish the tale of our summer, we lean back and sit quietly for a while. The large tin pizza platter is now empty, and our Cokes are long gone. I go to the counter, hand the guy a dollar and ask him to bring us four more.

"Where do you think he is, Eva?" I ask as I sit back down. "Ulie."

"How about I tell you what I think when we get back to the house. Right now, I'd like to hear from you, Miss Clydeen, wouldn't you, Imani?"

"Indeed I would," says Imani.

For the second time in one day, Clydeen tells her story, this time with a great deal more confidence. Sitting across the table, Imani smiles and nods, making eye contact with Clydeen and giving her her full attention. It's exactly the encouragement Clydeen needs to speak freely.

"So when my mama didn't come back, tha's when I got on that bus with no idea where I was goin' and ended up way out here. And then I met Annie," she says, coming to the end of the beginning of our summer saga.

"Oh, my goodness, Clydeen. You, my dear, are a survivor," Imani tells her.

"That's an understatement!" Eva chips in.

"I guess," says Clydeen uncertainly.

"I want to ask you what *you* think has happened to your mother. Do you have any ideas?" asks Imani.

Clydeen hangs her head and turns away. "Don't know," she mumbles, and I can hear in her voice she's holding back tears.

"Clydeen," says Eva, reaching across the table and gently lifting her chin so she'll make eye contact. "There is no shame whatsoever in what you've been through, my dear, only heartbreak, so please tell us what do you think may have happened to your mother."

Clydeen sighs, and says, "I think maybe she in jail or a hospital— or else she run off and lef' me. Maybe she had to."

"Can you tell me more about that?" Imani asks.

"Well, for the last few weeks b'fo she got picked up that night at the bar, she's havin' a rough time."

"A rough time, you say."

"Nerves, I guess. Not sleepin'. Not bringin' in ironin' like she was b'fo. Pacin' around, angry, smokin' a lot. Talkin' to herself."

"Had you ever seen her like that before?"

"Yas. After my daddy got killed."

"Your father got killed?" says Eva, raising her eyes to Clydeen's with alarm.

Clydeen failed to include that part of the story; she doesn't like to talk about it.

"How did it happen?" Imani asks gently.

The awful truth comes tumbling out, accompanied by a well of grief Clydeen has never revealed before. By the time she's done with the telling, she's moved to the other side of table where Imani is holding her close in loving arms.

"Is there anything else you want to tell us," Eva asks when Clydeen quiets.

"Yas, they is. I been waitin' for my mama to come get me all summer long. I ain't minded bein' up at there at our Nest, 'cause the weather's good, and me'n Annie, we been doin' lots of interestin' and fun stuff together. And then Ulie come, and things was even better. He was—*is*—like our big brother, ain't that right, Annie?

"Absolutely."

"Kep' me from worryin' so much 'bout where Mama at. But I don't think I can wait up there much longer. Annie, she goin' back to school. I been talkin' to Ulie about it, tryin' to make a plan. But after today, after what y'all tol' me 'bout him gittin' killed in the war, when I jus' saw him this mornin' with my own two eyes? Well, I'mma be scared to stay up there, unless we find him."

"Of course you are," Imani and Eva say at the same time, which makes us all smile.

"Go on with what you were saying, Clydeen," Imani says.

"Well, the main thing, Miz Jackson, is I want to find out what's happened to my mama, and then I might want to go back home." She looks from one to the other of the two women. "Miz B, Ulie tol' me he been all over the place, met all kinds a people, and you still be the one person in the world he trusts. He tol' me you wouldn't hold it against me bein' colored, 'cause you ain't no racist asshole. Sorry," Clydeen says, lowering her eyes.

"Oh for heaven's sake," Eva sputters. "That's what he said?" and she bursts out laughing. Imani joins in, and they laugh so hard I think they're gonna bust a gut.

"Oh, my goodness," says Eva finally, wiping tears away. She looks at Imani, and they both start laughing again.

"That boy of yours, Eva," hoots Imani. "How I love that kid! Always have."

Clydeen and I look at each other. We can't help smiling at these two laughing-crying women who somehow remind us ... of us.

"Well, he was right," Eva chokes out finally. "The color of your skin is of no concern of mine. I just hope you're proud of who you are, sweetheart. I'd be honored to help in any way I can, but my friend here may be a better choice. She worked for many years for Children's Services in Denver, and she really knows the ropes. You do still know the ropes, don't you, Imani?"

"Girl, it's like riding a bicycle," Imani chuckles. "I been away for a while, but I still have a few contacts in high places, and it just so happens I'm between gigs, too. Clydeen, maybe you and I could spend some time getting acquainted. I can explain to you what I know and how I might be able to help. Since you are a minor, there may be some legalities involved, but if no missing person's report has been filed, what say we keep it on the downlow for now."

"You mean you ain't gonna report me?" Clydeen screeches.

The white man at counter stops what he's doing and stares at us. *Guess colored folks aren't allowed to raise their voices.*

Imani glances at the man, then turns her attention back to Clydeen. "Isn't that what you are most afraid of? Somebody in a position of authority finding out about you?"

"Well, yas ..."

"Okay then, it'll be strictly on the downlow, unless coming forward is the only thing we can do to get the information we need to find your mother."

Clydeen, overcome with emotion, can barely speak. "I thank you, Miz Jackson," she says finally.

"No worries. You'll be doing me a favor," says Imani. "There don't seem to be any other Black people up there in the mountains where my family lives. They like it just fine, but I don't care for it. For one thing, I don't want to be stuck up there when winter comes and the roads get so bad I can't get down to church on Sundays. For another, it's becoming quite clear to me I'm not good at being retired.

"I've already been looking at places to live, and there's one or two that will work out just fine. You, Clydeen, are giving me the push I need to get myself in gear, move back to town and get back in the game, just not officially quite yet.

Clydeen smiles and nods through her tears.

Without Imani, would any of this be happening?

All this talk. All this laughter. All these tears. Maybe we *have* been making quite a scene. A few people have come and gone, taking their pizzas with them, but the tables around us have remained largely unoccupied. Now, closer to dinnertime a few other customers are beginning to drift in and take seats.

"Why don't you, Eva, and I have a conversation tomorrow, Clydeen? If you think you might want our help, we can talk about the details. If we decide to go forward, it will be a team effort, and it will be best if you're nearby ready to do your part. Hopefully, it won't be that difficult. We'll just follow the breadcrumbs of official records, and if everything is in order, we will get answers, and when we do, we'll reevaluate and see where things stand with you and your mother. What do you think, Eva?"

Eva turns to Clydeen and says, "Maybe you would consider staying with me while we sort this out?"

Clydeen hesitates. She's mopping away a flood of tears with a whole fistful of napkins now.

"What about Ulie?" she croaks, making no promises just yet.

"We'll see, Clydeen," says Eva, her face drooping under a heavy wave of sadness that only I can see from across the table where I am now sitting by myself.

"But we's gonna look for him, ain't we, Annie?"

"Absolutely."

Chapter 46
Eva

As soon as we get back to the house, Clydeen and Annie head up to the mesa to look for Ulie. When they return two hours later, it's almost dark. They report having found no trace of him, other than his poncho and his worn-out clothes, despite having searched all of the places he showed them in the weeks he was there. Of course, I'm not surprised.

"I'm going to make us some tea, and then we'll talk about Ulie," I say.

"I'll get the tea, Eva," says Imani, and the girls follow her into the kitchen like puppies and watch while she makes a pot of my favorite tea made from dried peach leaves, lemon peel and a bit of dried mint.

"Let's sit in a circle, shall we?" Imani suggests.

"Yes. I'll get a candle."

I bring the lighted candle and set it in the center of our circle.

"I would like for us to start this conversation with one of our favorite Sanskrit mantras, if that's alright with you, Eva," says Imani.

"Perfect. I would love that."

Annie and Clydeen consult each other silently and smile before settling in to listen. From what they've told me about life on the mesa, this will be a ritual not that unfamiliar to them.

"The words are *asato ma sadgamaya*. It means 'lead me to truth' in the ancient Sanskrit language. You may close your eyes if you wish."

Imani and I recite the chant, repeating it three times, followed by *'Om, shanti, shanti, shanti,'* after which we remain silent for a couple of minutes. I'm glad for the silence. It gives me a few moments to decide how to begin this most difficult of conversations.

"I had a dream last night," I say, meeting the eyes of everyone in our tiny circle.

The girls smile and nod their heads, their bright, attentive eyes urging me to go on.

"I dreamt about Ulie. I knew it was him, even though he was all grown up. He had a beard, reddish in color, scraggly hair, skinny, taller than he was when he left. There appeared to be some kind of frayed rope tied around his waist to hold his pants up, perhaps? To me he looked every bit like one of the Desert Fathers of long ago."

"Yup. That was him, a'ight. Tha's jus' how he was—uhhh—*is*."

"He held his hands out to me, and he said, 'Ma, I have come back, but I can't stay.' There was a hazy figure standing next to him. A girl perhaps from what I could make out. Her face was in deep shadow. The sun was behind her, shining through her hair in a way that made it look like she was wearing a crown of light."

"Oh! That's Clydeen," shouts Annie. "I've seen that dozens of times climbing up to our Nest. When she stands at the top to meet me, and the sun shines through her hair in that certain way, it looks like she has a halo. That's her!"

"Hmmm. Maybe so. In my dream, Ulie turned to her and smiled, and she disappeared. Then he handed me a note on a folded piece of paper. He waited while I read it. 'My life is complete, Ma. STOP. Papa is coming for me now, and I'm ready to go with him. STOP. Don't worry; we will be fine. STOP.' A typical war-time telegram, the one I'd waited for but never received.

"I woke up trembling. It was one of those dreams that was so vivid, I know I'll never forget it."

"Like that dream I had the night after Stanley ... the one where I dreamed about Sophia."

"Exactly, Annie. Thinking about the dream this morning, I remembered a quote from a wise man named Carl Jung. He said, 'We have forgotten the age-old wisdom that God speaks chiefly through dreams and visions.'

"Obviously, in my dream, Ulie was saying good-bye. What did the other figure have to do with it? I can't say. I don't want to speculate too much about that part of it. But when I woke up, even though I was shaking all over, I could still see his big happy smile and feel the warmth of his love as he handed me that note."

"So that's why you didn't ask the firemen to keep on looking for him today."

"Yes, Annie. Between the visit from the State Department yesterday, my readings and my dream, I guess you could say I had been prepared. I wanted desperately to find him up there this morning, but I was not surprised he was gone, either."

"Here's the thing," I go on after taking a few breaths to compose myself. "Imani and I have been readers of the Tarot cards for many years, right Imani?" I say, turning to my friend.

"Don't you know it, girl."

"We studied Tarot decks from many different traditions. Through that work, we were drawn into the study of other esoteric teachings, including Jewish mysticism, Christian mysticism, and the teachings of the masters of the Far East."

"Esoteric teaching. What's that again?" Clydeen asks. "Ulie told us, but I forgot."

"It means secret or hidden knowledge. Knowledge that appears to come from mysterious, otherworldly sources rather than through our five physical senses. It's not of much interest to people here in the Western world, because it's outside the realm of what most folks consider to be our 'reality.' Even our husbands pretty much thought we were nuts, didn't they, Imani?"

"Oh, honey, you got that right," she laughs. "They didn't get what we were up to *at all.*"

Clydeen and Annie look at each another. *This is creepy*, their eyes seem to say.

"It's nothing to be afraid of, girls," says Imani, catching the drift of their silent exchange. "Go on, Eva."

"We studied for a time with a group called the Theosophical Society. It took me months to learn how to pronounce it," I laugh.

"Here's something that will interest you, Annie. Theo comes from the Greek word, *theos*, which means 'God' or 'divine,' and the second part of the name comes from the Greek word, *sophia*, which means 'wisdom'.'"

"Wow! So in my dream, Sophia came to bring me wisdom? Is that what you're saying?"

"Does that make sense to you?"

"Well, I don't know about wisdom, but things sure started happening after that, that's for sure," she says, gazing at Clydeen with affection.

"Anyway, we began to study the theosophical teachings after we went to see a teacher whose name is Jiddu Krishna-murti. To make a long story short, the study of various spiritual teachings became a passion Imani and I shared. Like I said, we were particularly interested in teachings that had begun to trickle into the Western world from the Far East. We also learned about the rich history of spiritualism in our own culture. We became curious about those teachings and practices, as well. Maybe Imani will tell you more about that a little later."

I get up and go to my bookshelf and gesture to the top row. "This is where I keep my many books on spirituality and spiritualism, Madame Balvatsky's book, *The Key to Theosophy*, and the King James version of the Bible among them," I tell the girls.

When I rejoin the circle, Annie asks, "So what is spiritualism exactly?"

"Well, many people believe, and most religions teach, that human beings possess some sort of essence beyond the physical body. You've probably heard it called the soul or the spirit. Spiritualism is the practice of communicating with souls who are no longer living among us, such as deceased ancestors and the like."

"Ghosts," says Clydeen.

"Are you talking about ghosts, Eva?"

"I will say this. Reports of encounters with disembodied spirits—ghosts—if you wish, go back thousands of years, at least to the ancient Egyptians and no doubt long before recorded history. When people use the word 'ghost,' they are usually talking about departed spirits who reveal their presence in ways some humans can perceive with one or more of our five senses. Spirts may manifest in a variety of ways—by speaking through a living being who is in a trance state, or by less dramatic means, such as moving objects around, turning lights on and off, opening and closing doors and other such shenanigans. Spirits sometimes appear in physical form to those with the ability to perceive such phenomena. It is quite common for deceased loved ones to appear as they were in life to those who are themselves in the process of dying but have not yet crossed over into the afterlife."

"Are you tellin' us you think Ulie one a them ghosts?" asks Clydeen, her eyes wide.

"It's complicated, Clydeen, and I'll try to explain it as clearly as I can. My studies have led me to believe it *is* possible for beings from the unseen world to clothe themselves in human form and become visible. I think Imani would agree with that."

"Absolutely. Some come to be of service—to an individual, a group of individuals, or all of humanity. One well-known example of the latter was the appearance of an apparition of the Virgin Mary as Our Lady of Guadalupe in Mexico in 1531, and there are many others."

I go to the bookshelf again, and pull down a volume with a picture of Our Lady on the cover and pass it to them.

"According to the theosophists, another example was the appearance of the Ascended Master Saint Germain here in United States in the 1930s. A man named Guy Ballard encountered this being while hiking on Mount Shasta, a sacred mountain in northern California. Saint Germain (meaning Holy Brother), was identified as having been Count Saint Germain, a philosopher and alchemist who lived in France in the 1700s. Ballard had many encounters with the master, who transmitted volumes of spiritual teachings to him. In 1934, Ballard began publishing the material he had received. He came under heavy criticism and even outright harassment from people, who did not believe his claims and called him a fraud. The harassment was so unrelenting, Ballard felt it necessary to publish his books under a pseudonym, Godfre Ray King."

I pull a copy of *Unveiled Mysteries* by Godfre Ray King from the shelf and hand it to them. I search the shelf again, and take down another book, *Autobiography of a Yogi.* I hold it up for them to see. The orange cover shows a picture of an East Indian man with long, flowing, black locks, not smiling, but looking alert and serene.

"This book was published just four years ago in 1946. The author, Paramahansa Yogananda, is an Indian yogi (or saint) who now lives and works here in the United States. He describes meeting a being known as Mahavatar Babaji, a saint who some believe was born with the birth name Nagarajan in the year 203 CE (roughly two hundred years after the birth of Jesus). Yogananda's teacher, Lahiri Mahasaya, had many encounters with Babaji as a physical presence between the years 1861 and 1935, as did other spiritual masters and gurus from the Far East. Babaji has reportedly lived for centuries in the Himalayan mountains of India. He has appeared infrequently in human form, but often enough for there to be an accumulation of stories and teachings told by people who have at one time or another been graced by his presence.

"Then we have mediums like Alice Bailey, an English woman who wrote over twenty books dictated to her by a Tibetan spirit named Djwal Khul. Others claim to bring individual messages from deceased loved ones to grieving family members, although many of these so-called mediums have been exposed as frauds. Imani, do you have anything to add?"

"Yes. I have read in some of the spiritualist literature that when someone dies very suddenly and unexpectedly, the individual may not know their life has ended, or they may have an attachment to some unfinished business that is so compelling, it holds them close to the earth plane for a while, clothed in what is called the astral body, a replica of their physical form when they were alive."

"Jus' so's I understand, when you guys say spirit, you talkin' 'bout dead people, right?"

"People whose bodies have died, yes. To follow up on what Imani just said, I suspect there are many people who have had direct encounters with beings in spirit, but they didn't recognize them as such, because there was nothing so unusual about them that they stood out in some way. Ulie seemed a little peculiar to you, but not so much that it alarmed you, right?"

Clydeen snorts. "He looked like any other dirty, half-starved white dude, near as I could tell. But wait a minute! I wanna git this right. You's sayin' Ulie weren't real? He some ghost?"

"He was 'real,' Clydeen, but not in the way we ordinarily think of as what is 'real.' That's what I'm saying. In the course of our everyday lives, we are not aware that the veil between the world of the living and 'other side,' is much thinner than most of us would like to think it is. We don't give it much thought one way or the other, of course, but if we were to be confronted with evidence, it would be very frightening to most of us, so we avoid it if at all possible."

The girls look at one another again. Who knows what they're making of all this?

"Before I go on, I want to tell you up front that I do believe my son died in 1943 as confirmed by the State Department. I also do not think the fellow you knew as Ulie was an imposter or someone impersonating him. If both of those things are true, then what we're left with is a mystery, pure and simple. What Imani and I have been telling you from our experience is meant to give you a context for coming to terms with Ulie's appearance and now disappearance, if you chose."

"Oh, no, no, no, no. He alive. He real, and I'm gonna see him agin!" shouts Clydeen, bursting into tears.

She gets up and runs to the bathroom, and the candle in the middle of the circle flickers wildly in her wake.

"She loves Ulie," Annie tells Imani and me while we wait for her to come back, which she does about ten minutes later.

"Okay," Clydeen says with a sniffle, resuming her place in the circle. "I been thinkin' back to when he first showed up. It wasn't jus' scary, it was downright weird the way he come outta nowhere in the middle a one a the darkest nights we had all summer, and the next day, say he had no idea how he got there. He didn't have nothin' with him, neither. Not a thing 'cept that poncho he's wearin'. All along, his mind be in a muddle over some things and not others, but we thought ... You know what I'm sayin'?"

"She's right," says Annie. "So much of what Ulie told us was made perfect sense, especially what he said about the time he spent in the Resistance. But what happened to him after that? Well, he wasn't so sure about that. Said he was shell-shocked, is all."

"You two are going to think I've gone completely off the reservation when you hear what I'm going to say next," I say, addressing Annie and Clydeen. "Imani, I have no idea what you're going to make of it, either. But for me, it's the thread that ties all this together, so please hear me out, okay?"

"Okay," says Clydeen.

"Yes," says Annie. "Tell us."

"As I have indicated in some of what I said earlier, there is considerable evidence to suggest that we may return to this plane of existence multiple times and live many and varied lives."

"Oh, c'mon," Clydeen scoffs. "At the Redeemer Baptist Church back home, they say we live, we die, we go to heaven or the other place, and tha's it."

"Hold on a minute," says Annie. "I remember in my dream, Sophia said something about 'this time around,' and having been with me 'for eons.' I had no idea what she was talking about, but maybe ..."

"Sophia was talking about what's called reincarnation, Annie. It's a prevalent belief in many cultures around the world. In the spiritual circles Imani and I frequent, it is assumed to be true, supported by evidence gathered over the ages."

"And to your point, Clydeen, to the early Christians, birth-death-rebirth was a given until a bunch of men got together in Rome a few centuries after the death of Jesus and removed it from the biblical teachings."

"You don't say," Clydeen responds thoughtfully.

"We could say a lot more about that, but for purposes of our discussion, I am going to ask you to assume that reincarnation is a fact, that our souls do live on after death, and do come back to earth to live again and again. Let's also consider the possibility that each of us is a part of a collective of souls with whom we engage repeatedly over many lifetimes. Before our souls reincarnate, that is, take physical form as human beings, we make agreements with other souls in order to define the roles we will play in one another's lives 'this time around,' as Sophia said," I say, nodding to Annie.

"But once we incarnate and find ourselves in a human body, we have crossed what I will call the River of Forgetfulness. Thereafter, we're flying blind, because we no longer remember the soul agreements we made before we were born as human beings."

"Sometimes, though," says Imani, "we do subconsciously retain memories of soul companions or happenings from previous lifetimes and may experience what is known as *déjà vu*. For example, we may have overwhelming feelings of familiarity when we meet someone who, as far as we know, is a complete stranger.

Or we might find ourselves in a particular situation in which we have the feeling that we have been there before, even to the point of being able to predict exactly what's going to happen next. These phenomena can occur both while we are awake and while we sleep."

"Wow. Okay," says Clydeen. "That's sumpthin'."

"Going back for a minute to what you were saying before, Eva," Annie jumps in, "are you suggesting that Clydeen and Ulie and I had soul agreements with one another? Is that it?"

"No one can be sure, of course, but yes, that's what I'm suggesting. I'm also wondering whether your Nest, or Xanadu as Ulie called it, is an energetic anchoring point for the three of you and might also have something to do with how this mystery unfolded. I find the importance you placed on that old washtub particularly interesting, because after having been there today, I have to tell you, the bottom of that wash is not at all hidden. I saw it clearly without any help from an 'optical illusion' and would have had no trouble finding my way to your encampment. It's curious to me that in all of the weeks you were there, no one else ever did."

"Very interesting, indeed," says Imani.

Clydeen and Annie consult each wordlessly again. *Creepier and creepier*, their eyes say.

I turn to my friend.

"This is the part you might find wanting, Imani, but we'll see. Here's my theory," I say, turning back to the girls. "Think of yourselves as a three-legged stool. Annie, Clydeen, and Ulie. Maybe Ulie's death at such a young age left agreements among you unfulfilled. He left the stool in this life with only two legs, so to speak. Perhaps you two could still sit on the stool, and maybe it wouldn't tip over if you were on level ground, didn't put too much weight on it, and didn't make any sudden movements. But when things got shaky, and by that I mean when you began to worry that your summer together and possibly your friendship could end badly, the stool threatened to collapse. Without the third leg, it couldn't take the 'weight' of all of the fear and confusion the two of you were needing it to bear.

"Annie, you were determined to deal with your concern about Clydeen's well-being by trying to forge a relationship between the two of us. Were you trying to prop up the stool by replacing the missing leg with *me* perhaps?"

I pat myself on the head and everyone laughs. This moment of humor lifts the mood in the room and gives me time to gather my thoughts before continuing with what may be nothing more than my own wild imaginings.

"Anyway, what Annie was proposing was a nonstarter for you, right, Clydeen? You weren't buying it."

"Well ... no, ma'am, I wasn't. It was 'cause I thought you would ..."

"Yes, I know, sweetheart, and I don't blame you one bit. But the two of you were at an impasse and didn't know where to turn."

"Yas. I reckon so," says Clydeen.

"As I understand it, that's where things stood when Ulie came along."

"Tha's right. 'Bout the same time as you gave Annie that readin', Miz B."

"Oh, my goodness. Isn't that an amazing coincidence?"

The girls look at me blankly, and then they turn eyes on each other, consulting again in their silent language.

"What do you mean?" Annie asks.

"Looks to me like Ulie and I were double-teaming you. He knew it, I didn't. I was too busy searching the world for him," I hoot, unable to contain the raucous laughter that rises from deep within. "Oh, my lucky stars! Isn't the Universe amazing Imani?"

"Oh, yes, Eva. Just chock full of surprises," says Imani rolling her eyes.

I wipe my eyes with my handkerchief and give myself a moment to calm down.

"Anyway, who knows what circumstances might have brought the three of you together had Ulie not died so young. My mystical leanings allow me to imagine Ulie being called forth from the astral plane, not only by the strength of the SOS signals your distressed psyches were throwing out, but also by his own awareness of having abandoned a sacred obligation he had to the two of you when he was taken from the Earth prematurely. Maybe his unfinished business with you was compelling enough to have kept him from moving on in his afterlife journey, as Imani suggested a while ago. It's conceivable that he needed your help to free himself just as much as you needed his help to loosen the grip of emotions that were holding you back.

"Here it is in one sentence: It was just a matter of cosmically balancing that pesky three-legged stool!"

With that, we all laugh. We get up and mill around for a few minutes, taking a welcome break from the intensity of our conversation.

"So here we are," I say when we are back in the circle again, "gathered together in my living room, and you, Annie and Clydeen, have done what seemed so impossible to you. You have left the mesa together. Your friendship is intact without either of you having been endangered, betrayed or abandoned by the other—or anyone else, for that matter. That's true so far, at least, and I expect it to continue if Imani and I to have anything to say about it."

"It's on account a Ulie, Miz B. He tol' me some stuff ... made me think 'bout what I want. Helped me git my head on straight and stop assumin' everybody gonna be against me," says Clydeen.

"It's terrific he was able to do that for you, Clydeen," says Imani, gently touching Clydeen's arm. "But I also want to acknowledge that you had good reason to feel threatened."

"I know. But thank you for sayin' that, Miz Jackson."

I smile inwardly, pleased to witness the rapport that's developing between Clydeen and Imani.

"I've gone on way too long, my friends, but there is one more piece of this I'd like to speak about."

"Please," says Imani.

Studying the two beautiful young girls whose faces are bathed in soft candle light, I begin to shift the conversation to what happened today.

"So, girls, after a few weeks of being a threesome—and let me remind you that you, Annie, and you, Clydeen *were the only two people ever to lay eyes on Ulie*—he somehow 'injures' himself."

"Tha's right, Miz B."

"But the most astounding thing is what happened next."

"What are you talking about specifically?" Annie asks.

"Well, from my point of view, the two of you took off like a couple of rockets. Almost simultaneously, you brushed aside all of your troubling thoughts and fears and sprang into action, neither of you having any idea how things would work out and what might happen to you as a result. It's like a spell had been broken."

"So you believe in magic spells, too, Miz B?" Clydeen teases, giggling a little.

"Could be, child. Could be," I say, giving her a salute and a pat on the back.

"So brave, though." says Imani. "I bow to your courage, both of you."

The two girls look at each other with surprise. *Don't give us too much credit,* say the two pair of eyes sparkling in the light of the candle flame. *We had no idea we were gonna open this can of worms.*

The expression on their faces makes Imani laugh.

"Let's back up a minute. What I was getting at, what I was congratulating you for, is that as a Black woman, I recognize the magnitude of the conflicts your newly opened eyes have thrust upon you. Our society grants no permission for you to honestly expose and act in accordance with the deep regard you have come to feel for one another. Quite the contrary. Haven't we dealt with that a time or two ourselves, Eva?"

"Absolutely, and not without considerable discomfort for both of us, either."

"You all saw what it was like today at fricking Joe's Pizza Heaven. But let's don't dwell on that. You've managed to engage in a profoundly transformative experience together and come out on the other side without having broken each other's hearts when there are so many reasons that could have happened. At your tender age? Why, that is a miracle. You two girls have managed to do what so many never do, and that is to set yourselves on the path of your true education: discovering who you are and who you want to be in this chaotic world of ours. I'll tell you right now, I can't wait to meet the women you will become in a few years."

They are both weeping quietly and don't say a word.

"Too much?"

They both shake their heads, but I'm not so sure.

After a few minutes, Clydeen sniffles and says, "I wanna go back to sumpthin' Miz Jackson said earlier 'bout *déjà vu.*"

"What is it, Clydeen?" asks Imani.

"Well, it reminded of that night when Ulie come. Like I said, he scared me real bad. He didn't mean to; he didn't know I was there. But from the moment he tol' me his name—Ulysses, and then Ulie, he said it was—it was like puttin' a key in a lock and openin' a door. From that moment on, I was never afraid of him again. I trusted him way more'n seemed right. I kep' havin' to remind myself that I didn't really *know* him at all, it jus' felt like I did. It could be downright spooky the way he'd look so deep into my eyes he could see all the way through me, right down to the very bottom a me. See me in the places I didn't even know I had, and I'll tell you what. It almos' did me in more'n once.

"I thought I might be goin' a little crazy," she says, turning to Eva. "I gotta say, Miz B. Me! Feelin' so close to some random white boy, after bein' 'round him for jus' a couple days? Heck! Me feelin' close to some white boy a'tall, 'specially a grown man, which Ulie was ... It didn't make no sense, but I never said nothin' 'bout it 'cause it was too embarrassin'!"

"You didn't need to say anything, Clydeen," Annie snickers.

"Really?"

"Yeah, girl, really."

"Whew! I miss him," Annie chokes out tearfully, grabbing a tissue. "We had these wonderful conversations that brought us close in a way I've never experienced in my life. Like we're doing right now in this circle. Those time just filled me up with so much love, and I remember telling Clydeen and Ulie one day that I wished the three of us could stay like that forever."

"Maybe it was in a moment like that when Ulie decided everything was in good order. He had done what he came to do, and it was time to go. And then a fall. A broken leg. Blood and pain. Was it 'meant to happen,' or did it 'just happen'? Did it 'really happen' at all?" I ask the circle, making air quotes with my fingers. "Whatever the truth of it is, there was something that triggered his depature. Maybe a sense of closure, or maybe that visit from the State Department. Whatever it was, his apparent injury and need to be rescued propelled you forward at warp speed, didn't it, Clydeen?"

"You think?" she says, smiling broadly.

"Without a second thought, you dropped any remaining concerns you may have had about your own safety, because you cared enough about him to go for help no matter what it cost you.

Bless you for that, child."

"All the way down to yo' house, Miz B, I never thought once 'bout what I was doin'. I jus' knew it was right, and I wasn't afraid a nothin', neither. When I got here and saw all a them peoples, well tha's a diff'rent story," she says, her eyes growing wide.

"When you burst through my back door this morning with all of Annie's family right there, Clydeen, all of the secrets, all of the fear and worry about what might happen had been tossed aside, and there was no more need to hold onto any of it."

"Yeah. It didn't take long for me to realize that I'd blown things way out of proportion," says Annie. "For Pete's sake, I literally thought Stanley would kill me on the spot if he ever found out about Clydeen and me, and I'm not exaggerating. I know how he hates ... what he expects. But then he did find out, and Vivian, too, and now, I don't know what's going to happen when I finally talk to him about it, but I feel like he can't touch me."

"Why is that?"

"Because I know what's true, Eva. People can say and do all kinds of things, but they can't change what you've learned. And they can't change how you feel about somebody unless you let them," she says, casting an affectionate gaze on Clydeen. "Like it or not, Clydeen, you are the best friend I've ever had, and it's gonna stay that way unless you kick me to the curb someday."

"Oh, Annie, I ain't gonna do that!" Clydeen protests.

"What do you say, Imani?" I ask.

"I say amen. The Lord works in mysterious ways, Eva, but I do love the way you can weave the mystical teachings into a tale with such finesse."

"Thank you, my friend," I say bowing to Imani. "Girls, I don't know if any of what I've said is the way it happened or not. Unfortunately—or fortunately—I don't really know for sure, it is a story about things we mortals are not meant to know with any degree of certainty. But still, it's one I can live with. How about you?"

"I guess we can, too, can't we, Clydeen?"

"I reckon so," she answers with a sigh.

The four of us put our arms around each other and sit together in silence for a while. It's a moonless night, and it's pitch dark outside now. The only light comes from the candle that glows in the center of our circle. My whole body, our surroundings, everything seems to be vibrating with energy, and just as I am wondering if the others are feeling it, too, Clydeen whispers, "You feel that?"

"What?" whispers Annie.

"That hummin'. I used to feel it at night up at our Nest. I used to feel it other times, too, when things was real quiet like this. What is it?"

"The Hindus call it shakti, Clydeen," says Imani. "It's the life force that animates everything and courses through every atom of creation, and yes, sometimes, like right now, because we have created this powerfully energetic moment together, we get to feel its presence."

We bow our heads reverently and remain quiet for a time. But a few minutes later, Clydeen gets up and starts pacing, her arms folded protectively over her chest, her eyes fixed on the floor as she walks about.

"So ... not exactly a ghost? But sort of a ghost, is that what you womens is sayin'?"

"Oh, honey, I guess that's as good a way to put it as any," I laugh.

"But what I want to know, is Ulie gone now? No sense to go lookin' for him up there agin?"

"I think he came, took care of business, and now he's moved on, Clydeen."

"Wait'll I tell Mama 'bout this!"

"Heaven only knows what I'm going to tell the people who witnessed what happened up there on the mesa today. I'll have to think of something. But I want to thank you both for giving me a glimpse of my son through your eyes this afternoon while we were eating. It was wonderful."

"Sojourner Truth. Tha's her name!" Clydeen blurts out suddenly. "Weren't she one a them spiritualists?"

"Indeed she was. So you know of her, Clydeen?" says Imani.

"I saw a picture of her once. I think my mama showed it to me, and I think she used that word, 'spiritualist,' now I think about it."

"You, Annie?"

"No, I don't know anything about her."

"Well, some of the most respected spiritualists in the nineteenth century were Negro women, such as Sojourner Truth. After the Civil War, she went north to Michigan, where there was a community of spiritualists. In public, she spoke the truths of the ancestors as they came through her while she was in a trance state. She had quite a following, too, mostly white folks, many of them Quakers, who were known for their anti-slavery, anti-racist views. You can read more about that in a book from the same period called *Uncle Tom's Cabin* by Harriet Beecher Stowe if you like."

"Ulie tol' us to read that book," Clydeen says, beaming now, sitting close to Imani on the sofa, engrossed in what she is saying.

"There was another Negro spiritualist from that era who comes to mind," offers Imani. Harriet Jacobs was her name. She was also a former slave, who had the ability to channel the ancestral beings."

The girls share a startled look of recognition.

"Did you say Harriet Jacobs?"

"Yes. That's right. Why?"

"Ain't that the name a the slave wrote that book we read, Annie?"

"Yes! Harriet Jacobs. She published under a pseudonym, Linda Brent, but her real name was Harriet Jacobs."

"You actually read her book?" asks Imani with amazement.

"Yes. Both of us," Annie says, gesturing between herself and Clydeen. "It's called *Incidents in the Life of a Slave Girl.* The librarian gave it to me the day Eva took me to the library. She said they found it in a sack of books somebody donated."

"That's unbelievable! In an article I read somewhere, the author called that book 'one of the most interesting cases of escape from slavery ever seen.'"

"Shoot!" Annie says, jumping to her feet. "We dropped it in the slot at the library just this afternoon!"

"Truth is me'n Annie admired Linda Brent so much, we kinda fell in love with her. When sumpthin' scary come up, we been axin' ourselves, 'what would Linda Brent do?' Guess we must a done it 'bout a dozen times today, right Annie?" she giggles.

"At least a dozen."

"Oh, my goodness, how wonderful." I say.

It's getting late, and the candle is burning low. Imani yawns, reminding me of how tired I am and how tired our two young friends must be as well.

"May I share just one more thing before we call it a night?" I ask.

"Please do," says Imani.

I get up, go to the bookshelf again, and take down the Holy Bible.

"I want to read you something that may or may not have much to do with what we've been saying about Ulie. I'll let you be the judge. It's very beautiful, though," I say, flipping through the Bible's thin, gold-edged pages. "Okay. Here's what I'm looking for. It's in the book of Hebrews chapter 13, verse 2, and this is what it says: 'Do not be forgetful of hospitality, for through this, some have entertained angels unawares.'"

Chapter 47
Annie

"Goodnight, girls. I'll see you in the morning," Eva says as she leaves us alone in the guestroom and closes the door behind her.

It's after midnight. Exhausted, Clydeen and I fall into bed and drop off to sleep almost immediately. Sometime later, though, I'm awakened by the sound of Clydeen quietly weeping.

"What's wrong?" I ask her. I reach out in the dark and run my hand over her teary face.

"Oh, Annie. We's not gonna be together no 'mo. I miss Ulie. And Gary, too," she wails.

"I know. We've really had ourselves a time this summer, haven't we?"

"Yas, we have," she sniffles.

"Then there was today—yesterday, I guess it is by now. That's got to be *the* most confusing and *the* most amazing day of my entire life."

"Girl, you got that right!" she snickers and hiccups at the same time.

"But I need to tell you something, Clydeen."

"What?"

"When your mama didn't come and I was getting all nervous about going back to school, a big part of it was because school was like a home run for me. After that, no one—especially Stanley— would ever find out about you and me. That's what I wanted more than anything."

"I know. B'cause I'm a Negro," she sighs. "Tha's why you didn't want him findin' out."

"I thought if my parents found out about you—about us being friends and all—it would be such a catastrophe, we might not live through it. That's how scary it seemed to me. It was partly because of what happened to me before. And *this* is so much bigger than a chipped sink."

"I git it, Annie. Now that I've had the pleasure a meetin' yo' daddy, I can see why you felt that way. Still, it hurts."

"I know, and I'm sorry, Clydeen. Stanley's a piece of work, but that's no excuse.

"Before Ulie came, I had already begun asking myself this question: If Clydeen were a white girl, would I be so tied up in knots about Stanley finding out about us? Of course, the answer was no, but still I couldn't find a way to picture things any differently. Then there were the books we were reading ... And then Ulie came, and—I don't know—things changed. The things he said, the way he was with us, especially the way he was with you; the Tarot card reading with Eva, too. It helped me settle down, stop twisting in the wind and start preparing myself for whatever was going to happen."

I look at her in the dark, but I can't see her face.

"Is it okay that I'm telling you all of this?"

"Well, it ain't easy to hear, but go ahead."

"I'm ashamed of myself for being a racist asshole, Clydeen. That's the bottom line.

She giggles and gently punches my shoulder.

"But there's more. When you burst through Eva's backdoor, I was horrified, but just for an instant. After that, I felt pure relief, like a thousand-pound weight had been lifted off of me. *It was over*. The catastrophe was happening, but at the same time—it wasn't happening."

"What you mean, Annie?"

"Lemme see if I can explain it. When you came through that door, and my whole family stood there watching, everything changed—but at the same time, nothing changed. *Inside me*, I mean. I felt the same about you as my friend—my sister—*after* you came through the door as I had *before. I was solid, on the inside.* Part of me was so surprised, you could have knocked me over with a feather. I don't know what I expected myself to do. Pretend I'd never seen you before? Let my stupid father call the police?

"No. Instead, I just felt so proud of you for what you had done, Clydeen. I know what it took for you to risk coming to Mrs. B's to get help for Ulie. It was amazing! I wanted nothing more than to stand with you and acknowledge you as my friend. An ease came over me then, because all of the conflict I had been struggling with about you being colored, me being white, what could happen, blah, blah, blah, crumbled away. Somehow, I had absorbed so much bullshit. But now I think it's all stuff people made up so they could take advantage of other people. In the end, there's no reality to it other than that!"

I kick my legs and laugh, remembering how good it felt to have freed myself. I was not beholden to Stanley, my mother, my grandparents, my 'sivilization,' none of it.

"I've been taught to see you as a human being of lesser value than me or any other white person. I want to apologize to you, Clydeen, because *nobody* should see you as anyone other than the smart, witty, loving, talented and beautiful girl you are. Especially me! I'm supposed to be your friend, your best friend, I hope. Yet— I'll admit it—I was trapped. I had embraced the racist beliefs of white society and my own family. I see that now. I worried about what they would think of *me* being friends with you, and I never wanted them to find out. In fact, I thought I would be punished severely if they did. Through that lens, you were diminished and unworthy to be in my life. It never once occurred to me that maybe it was *me* who was unworthy to be in *your* life.

"And the way those racist firemen treated you today ..."

I'm crying now, lying on my back, glad the room is so dark.

She snuggles close to me. I keep on talking.

"I wanted you to come down with us after the firemen left, because I knew you didn't want to stay up there, with all the bruhaha about Ulie. But you must have been just as afraid of what might happen if you did come with me."

"Tha's true."

"What the hell, Clydeen? Why should that be? Just think about it. If you were white and I said you were my friend, of course, you would come. You would be welcome, everyone would treat you with respect, and there'd be no reason at all for you to be afraid to hang out with my family. Even Stanley would behave himself around you."

"Okay. I see what you's sayin'. Same if I was take you to my neighborhood, if I had one, but maybe not quite as bad as yo' daddy. Doubt anybody be tryin' to call the po-lice on you."

"Oh, Clydeen, I'm so sorry about that. Stanley can be such an idiot. Anyway, that's my confession. Can you forgive me?"

"Course I can," she says, tickling my ribs. "We sisters, remember? But this thing between the races, white and colored, it ain't simple, Annie. It's been goin' on for hun'erts of years now."

"So I'm learning Clydeen. It's bigger than I ever could have imagined, and so wrong! Whatever happens, though, I hope we can stick together. Maybe it's up to our generation, regular people like you and me, to change things."

"Maybe so. My daddy say our peoples are tied together forever by the history a this country, and ain't none a us gonna be free till all of us is. So yas, we bes' be gittin' to it."

"Wow. This is huge, isn't it? I hope when we find your mama, she'll understand what we've been through together. I hope she doesn't take you away, because I would miss you *so* much, Clydeen. What do you think she'll do?"

"Guess we'll see, Annie.

"In the meantime, I hope we get the opportunity to spend more time with Mrs. Jackson. I'll bet she's got lots to say about all of this."

"I'll bet she does. I'm really lookin' forward to my meetin' with her and Miz B tomorrow—today, I guess."

I curl up close to her then, all talked out. She grabs my hand, and just before dawn, we fall into a deep, easy sleep.

Chapter 48
Annie

No one else is stirring in Eva's house when I get dressed and silently close the backdoor behind me. I retrieve my bicycle from the barn and head for home. Whatever I'm facing, I want to get it over with.

I'm relieved to find the backdoor unlocked and my mother in the kitchen giving Willie and Teresa breakfast at this early hour, just as she usually does.

"Hello, Annie," she says pleasantly.

"Uhhh ... hi, Mom?" I say like it's a question, looking around, but still seeing nothing out of the ordinary.

Willie is sitting at the table eating a bowl of cereal, and Teresa is in her highchair, gumming a piece of dry toast.

"Where's Dad?"

"Still asleep. Don't worry. Everything's under control now."

"Huh. Okay."

Whatever that means. I walk toward my bedroom, looking this way and that like I'm afraid of encountering the monster that lived under my bed when I was five. But the house remains quiet and serene. I'm as tired as I've ever been in my life, and I'm about to go into my bedroom to lie down when Charlie appears in the hallway and motions for me to come into the boys' room.

"What do you want, pipsqueak?" I hiss.

"Shut up, Annie. I have to tell you something. Mom and Dad had a big fight yesterday," he whispers.

"Oh, come on. They never fight."

326

I turn around, start to leave.

"No wait, Annie. It was a real fight. When Mom came home and told Dad she'd taken you and your nigger friend to Mrs. Borsheim's to spend the night, he flipped out."

"Charlie, please don't use that word. It's a bad word, okay?"

He smirks, but he doesn't argue about it.

"Anyway, Dad said he was gonna go right back over there and bring you home because you're grounded. Mom said no you aren't grounded, and that's when the fight started, 'cause she wouldn't tell him where the car keys were."

"Oh, my God," I laugh. "Are you making this up?"

"No, I'm not. Listen!"

"Okay. Then what happened?"

"Mom told him he wasn't getting the keys, 'cause he gets way too angry.

"'I'm the boss around here, now give me the damn keys and get out of my way,' Charlie says, imitating Stanley's deep voice. "But she told him no. She said if he went after you, she was gonna take us kids and go stay at Grandma and Granddad Mack's house."

"Wow. Really? Are they getting a divorce?"

It's a terrifying thought. Divorce is as rare hen's teeth in my world, so rare that I've never known anyone whose parents got divorced.

Charlie looks at me blankly, and I realize he doesn't know what that word means.

"Never mind, Charlie. What happened next?"

"Dad laughed at Mom, told her she couldn't leave, 'cause he wouldn't give her any money if she did."

"Yeah, well, he does have all the money. So I suppose that was the end of it?"

"Nah. She said she had a good job once, and she could get one again. He told her she was out of her mind. But then she went downstairs and started bringing up suitcases."

"Really? You saw her?"

"Yeah. Me'n Willie were standing in the hall, but then she sent us to our room. We could still hear 'em, though.

"When she came upstairs with those suitcases, Dad said, 'Wait. What are you doing?' I was really scared, Annie. So was Willie."

"I'll bet."

I can't believe this. Nothing like this has ever happened around here. Stanley calls the shots, and Vivian goes along. That's it. There's hardly ever so much as a discussion, let alone a rebellion.

"What did Dad do then?"

"Well, he got really upset and started begging her not to go."

I can't help it. I start to laugh and have to slap my hand over my mouth to quiet myself.

Charlie looks at me and frowns.

"Okay, okay, little buddy. I'm sorry. Go on."

"Mom said she was gonna go unless there were some new rules around here."

"Like what?"

"She said, 'Rule number one. You're not going to beat on her like you did a few months ago, Stanley. So if that's what you have on your mind, I won't allow it. It wasn't right, and you're not going to do anything like that to her or any of the other kids, either, not ever.'"

"Oh, boy. I'll bet he didn't like her talking to him like that."

"He said, 'Damn it Vivian, she deserved it, and you never said a word about it, either.' He was talking about that day he wanted us all to go to church, remember that?"

"How could I forget? Worst day of my life," I tell him, wiping away the tears that still come whenever I think about it. "But go ahead. Tell me the rest."

"She said she should have stopped him."

"Go, Mom!" I say, smiling through my tears at Charlie.

I see now how wrong I was, and it's such a relief. I thought my mother was indifferent to my predicament with Stanley, but now it seems as if she's found her inner mama bear after all.

"Okay, Charlie. Thanks," I say, and start to leave the room.

"Wait, Annie! Wait. This is the part you're really gonna wanna hear."

"What? There's more?"

"Yeah. Mom said she should never have let him take Pepper to the pound."

"Holy crap, Charlie. Are you sure that's what she said?"

"I'm sure, Annie. I want Pepper!" he wails, knuckling both eyes.

"I knew it!" I whisper-shout, pounding my fists on my thighs.

"You knew Dad took Pepper away?" he sobs.

"No, Charlie. I didn't know for sure. I just thought he might've. What else did Mom say about that?"

He sniffles and thinks for a moment.

"That's all she said about Pepper, I think. They went into the living room, and I couldn't hear what they were saying very well. I think she was telling him more of the new rules."

"Oh, my God! He must have flipped his lid. Nobody lays down the law to him."

"He wasn't yelling, though."

"Maybe things will be better now."

"I don't want them to fight anymore," he says, rubbing his eyes again. "I didn't like that."

"I know Charlie. But they might. Mom's just trying to protect us."

The top of his head smells like sweaty boy as I pull him to me and give him a hug.

"Thanks for telling me, and I'm sorry I called you a pipsqueak, pipsqueak," I tease, popping him gently on the shoulder.

"Okay," he says, his face brightening.

I'm so relieved by what I've just heard that I fall on Willie's bed like a wet noodle and stretch out beside him. He's sitting against the headboard trying to rewind a yoyo string. I bury my face in his belly, but he's not in the mood, so he pulls my hair.

"Ouch!" I say opening his fist and removing the strands of hair twisted around his sticky little fingers.

He grabs at me again, but I jump up, rub the top of his head with my knuckles and run out of the room.

Sure enough, when I pass by my parents' room, there's one large and two smaller suitcases stacked against the wall, waiting to be packed.

****

To my great relief, the rest of the day passes without incident. I tell my mother about Eva's friend, Imani Jackson, and how I think meeting her is going to change things for Clydeen. When Teresa goes down for her afternoon nap, I go with her for some much-needed rest.

Stanley avoids me for the rest of the day, but not in a bad way. He's not a glowing ember of hostility like I would expect. He's more like someone who's been left adrift, unsure of what comes next.

"Thank you for this delicious meal, Vivian," he says, smiling at my mother as he places his highball on the table and we all sit down to dinner that evening.

"You're welcome, Stanley," my mother says graciously, as if such an acknowledgement were an everyday occurrence, which believe me, it is not.

In fact, it surprises Charlie and me so much we raise our eyebrows and exchange a secret smile across the table. For my part, I take this as a hopeful sign that perhaps Stanley has yielded to my mother's ultimatum, at least for now.

That night in bed, I think about guardian angels. Sophia who "opened the door." Eva, whose presence has steadied and supported me since the day I first met her. And now, my own mother, perhaps. I think about the courage it took for her to threaten to leave with four kids.

In my mind's eye, I picture my friend, Clydeen, who is at the center of everything I have experienced this summer. I consider the praying and singing we have done over these past weeks, and I wonder if it played a part in drawing Ulie to us when we needed him to be there.

I reflect on the monumental changes beginning to take shape in just these past couple of days. It comforts me to think perhaps this is how prayers, spoken and unspoken, are answered and make it possible for people to change.

I take my two hands and run them gently over my entire body. I curl my hands over the top of my head and hold them there for a while. They grow hot and make me sweat. Life has taken me a long way in a very short time. *I'm somewhere different now.* That's all I really know for sure. For this one moment, and I hope for many more to come, all is well.

Chapter 49
Eva

In my dream, the sun has set, and there's a campfire blazing in the backyard. Bits of conversation and laughter drift through the open window in the breakfast nook where I am sitting so I can watch the three young people play.

I gaze at my son, who looks so different now. He's sitting on an old chaise lounge with his left leg elevated on two pillows like the doctor ordered. The plaster cast is so white it glows in the firelight. His crutches lie close beside him on one side, and Rocky lies on the other. Every so often, the old dog raises his head and gazes at Ulie, as if he's checking to make sure he's still there.

The girls' voices are soft and lilting, teasing Ulie about something. I can't make out the words, but Ulie laughs, and says in an unfamiliar, booming voice, "Hey, you two. I'm in pain here. Give a guy a break!"

They have taken Ulie's old radio outside with them. Even in my dream state, I know this is ridiculous, because there's no source of electricity on the porch railing where the radio is sitting. Nevertheless, a song is playing, and Ulie shouts, "Turn it up! Turn it up. I love this song! The Weavers, right? We used to sing this around our campfires at night, if we thought we were deep enough into the forest so some Nazi jerks wouldn't hear us."

Clydeen reaches for the dial and turns up the volume, and they all start to sing along at the top of their lungs.

> *Irene, goodnight*
> *Irene, goodnight*
> *Goodnight, Irene*
> *Goodnight, Irene*
> *I'll see you in my dreams.*

Annie holds her hands out to Clydeen, and they begin to dance and sway, paying no attention to the dust that flies up around their bare feet. Ulie is chair dancing along with them, waving his hands and bouncing in time to the music.

They haven't a care in the world. Even though I know Ulie is a grown man now, in my dream, he seems both older and younger, as if the youth he left behind never caught up with the man he became.

"Oh, Maury," I say, invoking my dead husband as I often do in my dream time.

I speak to him as if he's sitting right here with me in the breakfast nook he built for me.

"It wasn't until the firemen brought him up from where he had fallen that I got a good look at him, and I'm ashamed to admit I would not have recognized him with his tangled beard, wild hair and layers of dirt," I tell Maury. "But while they were getting ready to load him into the ambulance, he gave me one of those lopsided grins of his and motioned for me to come to him.

"'Ma,' he breathed into my shoulder, hugging me so tight I almost couldn't take a breath. That's when I knew for sure it was really him."

"'I could have tried to come back sooner if I had known,' he said, squeezing my hand.

"Known what, my love?"

"'About Papa.'"

Out in the backyard, the volume on the radio is lower now, but loud enough for me to hear Bing Crosby crooning in the background. *Brother Can You Spare a Dime,* one of my favorites back in the day. "Remember, Maury?" I say to him in my dream, and I start to hum along.

When I look outside again, Clydeen is handing Ulie a stick with a toasted marshmallow dangling from the end of it, and Annie is offering him a cup of hot chocolate, which he raises just in time to catch the marshmallow as it falls. They all burst out laughing, and so do I.

The connection with Maury breaks, and in my dream, I feel him float away.

"Maury," I call out to him, reaching, reaching, reaching as if I myself might drift up and out of my kitchen. "Please don't go too far," I beg. "Now that Ulie is back, I'm afraid you'll leave me forever."

In the backyard, the *Tennessee Waltz,* another favorite of mine begins to play on the radio. I want to join the party now. I want to feel the heat of the fire and eat one of those toasted marshmallows before they're all gone. I slip on my yard shoes, pull my shawl around my shoulders, and skip down the back stairs, which I'm surprised to see are covered with pink and white rose petals. Three smiling faces, golden firelight dancing in their eyes, turn in my direction and welcome me into their circle.

Acknowledgements

Many thanks to the team at Atmosphere Press for the amazing opportunity to send *Somewhere Different Now* out into the wider world. It's been an absolute pleasure to work those I have met—Nick Courtwright, Erin Larson, Evan Courtwright and Cameron Finch—and those behind the scenes that I have not. To my editors, Alexis Kale and Tod Hunter (avenueliteraryservices.com), I thank you for challenging me to go deeper. Closer to home, I extend my appreciation to the core members of my writers' group in Grass Valley, California—Kimberly Clouse, Marianne Barisonek, and Lisa Schlift. For the past four years, we have provided not only a structure and disciplinary framework for one another's creativity, but also advice, support, feedback, and most importantly, friendship. Last but not least, for the unique journeys that inform the lives of each human being and give rise to the stories that nurture our curiosity and promote our understanding, I am deeply grateful.

About Atmosphere Press

Atmosphere Press is an independent, full-service publisher for excellent books in all genres and for all audiences. Learn more about what we do at atmospherepress.com.

We encourage you to check out some of Atmosphere's latest releases, which are available at Amazon.com and via order from your local bookstore:

The Embers of Tradition, a novel by Chukwudum Okeke

Saints and Martyrs: A Novel, by Aaron Roe

When I Am Ashes, a novel by Amber Rose

Melancholy Vision: A Revolution Series Novel, by L.C. Ham-ilton

The Recoleta Stories, by Bryon Esmond Butler

Voodoo Hideaway, a novel by Vance Cariaga

Hart Street and Main, a novel by Tabitha Sprunger

The Weed Lady, a novel by Shea R. Embry

A Book of Life, a novel by David Ellis

It Was Called a Home, a novel by Brian Nisun

Grace, a novel by Nancy Allen

Shifted, a novel by KristaLyn A. Vetovich

Because the Sky is a Thousand Soft Hurts, stories by Elizabeth Kirschner

About the Author

Donna's creative writing journey began late in life, but has somehow miraculously produced her first novel, Somewhere Different Now. Donna is the mother of three grown children, all girls. A life-long learner and spiritual seeker, she enjoys meditation, deep conversations, various outdoor activities, drumming, and playing the Native American-style flute.

She was born in Cheyenne, Wyoming and spent many magnificent summers with her grandparents at a remote one-room cabin in the Medicine Bow National Forest. She lived the remainder of the year with her family in the Denver area.

She received a Bachelor of Science degree in nursing from the University of Colorado. In the 1960s, career paths considered suitable for women were few, and eventually, she realized how temperamentally unsuited she was to her chosen profession. She became an entrepreneur and owned a small business for many years. In 1983, she entered law school and graduated from the University of California, Berkeley in 1986 with a law degree, a state bar card and a job. During the course of her career, she did a great deal of both legal and technical writing, none of which, it turned out, was of much help in writing a novel.

Now retired, she lives with her dog, Toby, in the beautiful Sierra foothills of northern California. She is a certified end-of-life doula and volunteers in that capacity in her community and elsewhere.

She welcomes your comments, observations and questions at DonnaPeizer.com, where you will also find additional free content posted from time to time.

CPSIA information can be obtained
at www.ICGtesting.com
Printed in the USA
BVHW091046160822
644711BV00013B/989